MW01006752

westland publications ltd

The Rise of Sivagami

Anand Neelakantan is the bestselling author of *Asura: Tale of the Vanquished,* which told the story of the Ramayana from Ravana's unique perspective. He followed it up with the hugely successful Ajaya series. Ajaya Book I: *Roll of the Dice* and Ajaya Book II: *Rise of Kali* narrated the Mahabharata from Duryodhana's point of view. Both *Asura: Tale of the Vanquished* and Ajaya Book I: *Roll of the Dice* have been nominated for the Crossword Popular Choice Awards in 2013 and 2014 respectively.

Anand has also written the screenplays for various popular TV shows, including Star TV's mega series *Siya Ke Ram*, Sony TV's *Mahabali Hanuman* and Colours TV's *Chakravartin Samrat Ashoka*. He has also written for major newspapers such as *The Hindu, The Times of India* and *The Indian Express.* Besides English, he also writes in Malayalam and has published stories as well as cartoons in various Malayalam magazines.

He lives in Mumbai with his wife Aparna, daughter Ananya, son Abhinav, and pet dog Jackie the Blackie.

Anand Neelakantan can be reached at:

website: www.anandneelakantan.com

email: mail@asura.co.in

Facebook, Twitter, and Instagram: @itsanandneel

Also by Anand Neelakantan

Asura: The Tale of the Vanquished

Ajaya: Roll of the Dice

Ajaya: Rise of Kali

Bāhubali: Before the Beginning

The Rise of Sivagami

Book I

Anand Neelakantan

westland publications ltd
61, II Floor, Silverline Building, Alapakkam Main Road,
Maduravoyal, Chennai 600095
93, I Floor, Sham Lal Road, Daryaganj, New Delhi 110002

First published in English by westland publications ltd 2017

10 9 8 7 6 5

ISBN: 978-93-86224-44-6

Typeset in Bembo Std by R. Ajith Kumar, New Delhi
Printed at Manipal Technologies Ltd, Manipal

To my sister, Chandrika and
brother-in-law, S. D. Parameswaran,
for making me what I am.

Foreword

The story hunter—How we thought of going before the beginning.

S. S. Rajamouli

When we created *Bāhubali* we were in a dilemma. The story-world of Mahishmathi kept growing as we worked on the theme. There were so many stories to be told. The stories of Mahishmathi could not be contained within the two-and-a-half hours of a film, even with two parts. We did not want to let go of the fascinating story world that was emerging. There were characters lurking in the shadows, waiting for their stories to be told. There were secrets that had to be unveiled, there were whispered conspiracies that could thrill and terrify. We knew if we went back further in time, a series of interesting stories would emerge. We needed someone to go hunting into Mahismathi's past, for more stories.

In my younger days reading was something of a favourite pastime. I wouldn't just read books but, consume them. Thrillers, mysteries, dramas—the category didn't matter. However, as I grew older and got busier with other pursuits, reading faded from my life. It's true that one reason for this was the paucity of time but the main cause of my turning away from my beloved childhood habit, was that the books I read stopped moving me. I would still buy books, hundreds of them in fact, and try to rekindle my love for reading but to no avail. A few chapters in and I would lose interest. And then, one day I got my hands on *Asura: The Tale of the Vanquished*.

Not only did I finish this book but it left me shaken. Certain scenes in the book were so powerful, indeed so moving, that I had to pause and reflect while I held back tears. Even today I believe that the writing in that book is comparable with the best in the world. After I finished *Asura*, I knew I had to meet its author. His writing had not only blown me away but had brought back the reader in me. Thus began the story of my association with Anand Neelakantan, the author of *Asura* and now *The Rise of Sivagami*. As we sat and discussed our individual creative processes, I decided that Anand should be our official story-hunter who could travel back into the forgotten annals of Mahishmathi's history and bring them back to light.

As he developed the story, Anand would send me ten chapters at a time to read. As soon as I was done with one lot, I would call him, mail and message him; I needed to read the rest! The wait for the next instalment was excruciating. I am certain that you, the reader, will understand my eagerness when you are through with this phenomenal book.

I am amazed at what Anand has created with the few inputs I shared with him at the conception of this book. As one of its first readers, I can vouch for the fact that the story contained in the pages of *The Rise of Sivagami* will not let go of you easily.

I may have brought Sivagami to life on screen but in *The Rise of Sivagami*, Anand Neelakantan has given her wings.

Dramatis personae

Sivagami
A fiery young woman she is extremely intelligent and is a trained warrior. She is the daughter of a nobleman of Mahishmathi kingdom, Devaraya, who was executed as a traitor by the king. The wounds of her childhood have scarred her.

Kattappa
A twenty-one-year-old slave, he is dedicated to his work and takes pride in serving the royal family of Mahishmathi. Kattappa is deeply honoured to have been chosen to serve Bijjaladeva, the elder prince of Mahishmathi. He is the son of Malayappa, the personal slave of Maharaja Somadeva.

Pattaraya
A rich and ambitious nobleman, he is a bhoomipathi, a title of great importance in the Mahismathi kingdom. He is known for his cunning and ruthlessness. He is a self-made man who rose from poverty to riches through his intelligence and hard work. He is dedicated to his family and loves his daughter Mekhala more than his life.

Shivappa
The eighteen-year-old younger brother of Kattappa, he resents being born a slave and dreams of freedom. He loves his

elder brother but is often at logger-heads with him. He wants to build a new world and dreams of joining the Vaithalikas, the rebel tribe that is fighting against Mahishmathi from the forests. He is deeply in love with Kamakshi, a friend of Sivagami.

Prince Bijjaladeva

The firstborn of Maharaja Somadeva, he is anxiously awaiting the day he will be declared crown prince. He demands respect and is slighted at the slightest show of irreverence by anyone. He is surrounded by a coterie of sycophants who back him for their own selfish reasons. He is contemptuous of his younger brother and resents his popularity with the masses.

Prince Mahadeva

A dreamer and an idealist, he treats everyone with compassion and love. He is conscious that he is not a great warrior. He looks up to his father and respects him but wilts under his domineering mother. He loves his elder brother but is afraid of him. He is a poet and a romantic.

Jeemotha

He considers himself a great trader but actually is a pirate. He is an expert sailor and sails often at the precipice of illegality. He is aware of his charm and the effect it has on any woman. He often uses his wit to get away from tricky situations but does not desist from violence if the situation demands it.

Keki

A thirty-year-old eunuch, she is the assistant of the famous Devadasi Kalika. Keki is a pimp who finds beautiful women for Kalika's trade. She has a sharp tongue and uses it like a whip. For now, she is in Bhoomipathi Pattaraya's camp.

Skandadasa

The deputy prime minister, or Upapradhana, of Mahishmathi, Skandadasa is a man of principles. Honest to the core, he carries deep insecurities within for his lowly origins. He belongs to an untouchable caste and is a misfit among the other high-caste nobles of the court. The common people admire him but the corrupt officials and nobles dislike him.

Thimma

The foster father of Sivagami, he used to be a close friend of Devaraya. A powerful Bhoomipathi, he is kind and soft-spoken and a doting father to his children.

Ally

Brought up by the elusive rebel queen Achi Nagamma, she is an elite warrior and spy in an all-women rebel army. She is not shy of using her sexuality and powers of seduction to get her work done.

Kamakshi

An innocent and lovely girl of seventeen, she is Sivagami's closest friend in the orphanage. Her only ambition in life is to live in peace with her lover Shivappa, far away from the cruel city of Mahishmathi.

Gundu Ramu

Sivagami's young friend in the orphanage. Son of a slain poet, the plump boy adores Sivagami, whom he calls Akka. He is witty and also a bit of a glutton.

Hidumba

The little man of Mahishmathi is quite dangerous. He is a khanipathi, a step below a bhoomipathi and he thinks he has been denied his promotion only because of his size. He is now in the Pattarya camp, but even Pattaraya is wary of this dwarf.

Devadasi Kalika

She is the head of Pushyachakra inn, more notoriously known as Kalika's den. She is a seductress and has half of Mahishmathi nobles under her feet. She is adept in the art of kama and supplies beautiful young ladies to even the harem of Maharaja to entertain state guests.

Maharaja Somadeva

The King of Mahishmathi. He is a distant figure, respected, admired and feared by his subjects.

Malayappa

The personal slave of Maharaja Somadeva, he is Kattappa and Shivappa's father. He is a proud man with a strong sense of duty.

Mahapradhana Parameswara

The seventy-five-year-old prime minister of Mahishmathi, he is trusted by the king who considers him his guru. He is kind-hearted but a suave politician. He is also Skandadasa's mentor.

Roopaka

The trusted aid of Mahapradhana Parameswara.

Maharani Hemavati

The haughty and proud queen of Mahishmathi.

Rajaguru Rudra Bhatta

The chief priest of Mahishmathi. He is a close friend of Bhoomipathi Pattaraya.

Dandanayaka Pratapa

The police chief of Mahishmathi, Pratapa is feared by the common people. He is a friend of Pattaraya.

Vaithalikas

The rebel tribe who want to wrench Gauriparvat back from the clutches of Mahishmathi.

Bhutaraya

The enigmatic and powerful leader of the Vaithalikas.

Guha

The Bhoomipathi of river people. An old man, cruel and cunning, he is revered by his people. He bows only before Maharaja Somadeva.

Akkunda

A powerful Bhoomipathi.

Achi Nagamma

The leader of an all-women vigilante army. She is fighting against the corrupt and evil people of Mahishmathi. Ally is a member of her army.

Devaraya

Sivagami's father who was executed as a traitor by the government.

Raghava

Thimma's son, who grew up with Sivagami. He is madly in love with her.

Akhila

Thimma's five-year-old daughter. She is Sivagami's favourite.

Mekhala

Bhoomipathi Pattaraya's daughter, who often does not agree with her father.

Brihannala

A eunuch, who is the head of the Royal Harem. She has her own secret.

Nala

A merchant and adopted brother of Brihannala. He often doubles up as Brihannala's messenger.

Nanjunda

A divine man, a crook, a drunkard, he is willing to do magic for a bottle of arrack. He is an assistant of Jeemotha.

Bhairava

A lunatic who lives near the river. He used to be Maharaja Somadeva's slave.

Revamma

The warden of Royal Orphanage.

Nagayya

An elite slave who escapes with a terrible state secret.

Thondaka

The head boy of the Royal Orphanage who hates Sivagami.

Uthanga

A boy in the orphanage.

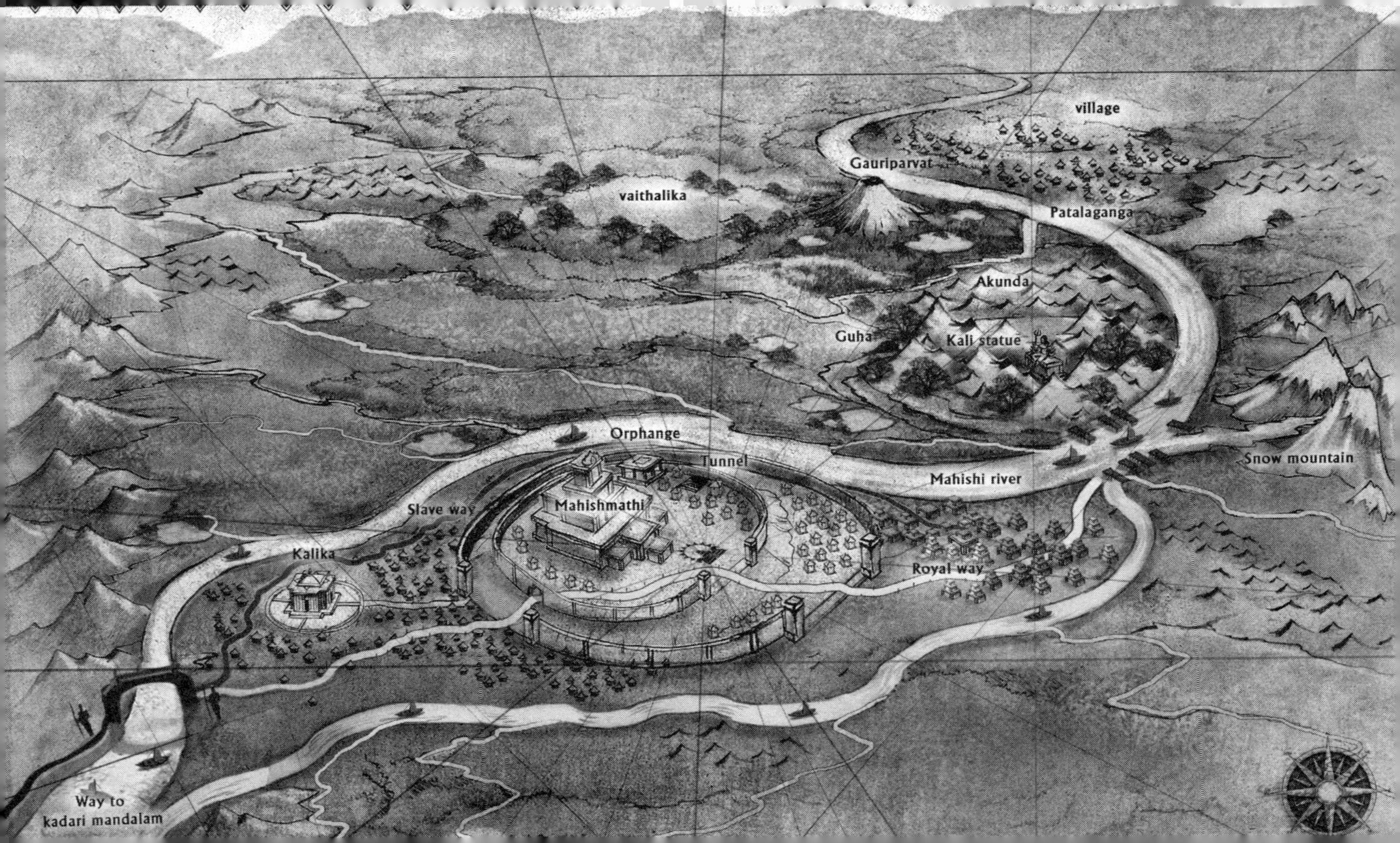
village
Gauriparvat
vaithalika
Patalaganga
Akunda
Guha
Kali statue
Orphange
Tunnel
Snow mountain
Mahishi river
Slave way
Mahishmathi
Kalika
Royal way
Way to
kadari mandalam

ONE

Sivagami

The night was dark, like death. It suited her. She did not want anyone to see them. A tiny lamp hung from the chariot, swaying wildly with each lurch that the cart made. She would have preferred to have it snuffed out, but the path was perilous. From either side, the jungle was reclaiming what originally belonged to it. Overhanging branches grazed her face as they sped through the winding hill path. She felt heavy with emotion. A thousand memories rushed from the dark recesses of her mind. They had broken free from where she had carefully buried them over the last twelve years and were howling in her ears. Like ghosts let free. She had never wanted to return to the place they were going to now. Not after what had happened to her family. Every tree that loomed in front of them reminded her of that gruesome scene she had been forced to witness at the tender age of five. Suddenly, the chariot stopped, making her lose her balance and hit her head on the side.

'A hare,' Raghava said from the cartman's seat. She could make out two eyes shining up at them from the ground and then the trembling silhouette of a hare. Their horse sniffed and the hare leapt and vanished into the bushes. It was typical of Raghava to be concerned about the life of even a small animal.

'Do you really want to go there at this hour?' he asked. Not for the first time that night. She did not reply. He nudged the horse with the end of his whip and the cart resumed its journey. Soon the thick jungle on either side gave way to patches of thorny bushes. Amidst them, huge boulders jutted out. They looked like crouching beasts waiting for their prey. Raghava hesitated at the beginning of the steep path that traced its sinuous way up to a fort looming in the distance.

'Can we go back?' Raghava asked.

She clucked her tongue in impatience. She could see him shake his head before prodding the horse to move. There used to be a garden here, she thought as the cart passed through a patch of land that sloped gently down the hill. It was overgrown with weeds. From here, it was going to be tough. The path clung perilously close to the edge of the cliff as they made their way up. The wheels of the cart caused a few pebbles to come loose, and they bounced down momentarily. The sound of flowing water became clearer as they continued to climb up.

The path ended abruptly at the edge of a precipice. Raghava pulled the reins and jumped down. He unhooked the lamp and came around to help her alight, but she ignored his extended hand and jumped to the ground. She moved to the edge and looked down. She could hear the frothing mountain stream many hundreds of feet below. There used to be a hanging bridge here, she remembered and as her eyes adjusted to the darkness, she could see it a few score feet to her left.

'It looks ominous. A ruin…' Raghava said, but she walked past him, climbing the crumbling steps to the bridge. She gripped the rope on either side and felt the wooden board with her toe.

'Are you going to cross the bridge?' Raghava's voice had an edge of fear. The ropes vanished into darkness after a few feet into the abyss. She took the lantern from Raghava's hands and stepped onto the bridge. A plank crumbled under her feet and spiralled down. Raghava gasped in fear. Despite the cold, her hands were sweaty.

She would not have made this trip had not she met old Lachmi—who had been her maid—after twelve years. The faithful servant was on her deathbed when she visited her. Among other things, Lachmi had mentioned a book that her father owned. A book that her father had told the maid to hand over to his child. A manuscript written in some strange tongue, which could perhaps solve the mystery of what killed him.

Her father, Devaraya, was a bhoomipathi, a noble lord in the kingdom of Mahishmathi. He was loved and respected until he was subjected to chitravadha—no, she did not want to think about that. Not now, not when she was crossing a bridge that swayed and creaked with each step.

'Watch out,' Raghava cried from behind. A yawning gap of seven feet lay in front of her. She handed the lamp to Raghava and took a few steps back.

'You are crazy,' she heard him say as she ran and gracefully leaped over the gap. She landed safely on the other side, though the bridge swayed wildly. She looked back and laughed, 'Throw the lamp to me and jump, you coward.'

Raghava looked down into the abyss. She clucked her tongue in impatience. Raghava mumbled a prayer to Amma Gauri and threw the lamp to her. It swung in the air, tracing an arc, and she caught it before it hit the ground. The flame went off, leaving the smell of burning wick in the air.

'Oh god,' she heard Raghava say. Except for the faint light from the stars, it was pitch dark.

'I can't see my own fingers how will I jump?'

'If you can't see anything, you will be less scared. It is just seven feet.'

'It is more like seven hundred feet all the way down. There are rocks down there.'

'Jump, you fool,' she cried. He landed near her a moment later, with a thud that sent shivers through the ramshackle bridge.

She heard him striking the flint many times. She stood tapping her feet, impatient at the delay. The flint flared up with a hiss and the lamp was lit again. They carefully threaded their way for the rest of the distance. Thankfully, all the planks were in place.

They got down from the bridge and walked to a huge wall that loomed in front of them. They stepped in front of an iron-spiked wooden gate that had a massive lock on it. It was sealed with lac.

'The maharaja's seal. We are not supposed to open this,' Raghava said, weighing the lock in his hand.

She took a stone and started breaking the lock open.

'What are you doing? Nanna will be held responsible. The fort is under his protection,' Raghava cried. She ignored him and continued hammering at the lock. Soon Raghava joined her and the lock gave way. They put their shoulders to the doors and, with a loud groan, it swung open.

She picked up the lamp from the floor and stepped in. A wave of emotions ran through her and she pressed her lips together. Everything was strange, yet familiar. The servant huts on either side had collapsed. The roof of the temple in which her father used to pray had toppled over. The wall around the courtyard well had crumbled. The mango tree where she used to have her swing had grown big and spread over the roof of her mansion. The two granite tigers that stood on either side of the steps to her veranda were still there. A broken toy horse lay half buried in the courtyard. Memories, sweet and bitter. Old Lachmi, running behind her, begging her to drink her milk. The pony her father had gifted her on her fifth birthday. The day they had taken him away in chains.

She stopped at the front door of her home. No, it was not her home anymore. She did not have a home. She was an orphan. She bit her lips. This time, Raghava did not wait for her. He broke the lock of the mansion and they stepped in. As the lamp illuminated the dusty interior, she sucked in her breath. For a moment, she wished she was still that five-year-old girl. Her father would come out of his chamber any moment with that smile that made him look so handsome. He would pick her up and swirl her in the air. Shower her with kisses. She longed for his smell, his touch, his affectionate way of ruffling her hair. For the past twelve years, every moment of her life she missed him. Uncle Thimma, Raghava's father, who had adopted her, was kind and affectionate, but no one could take her father's place.

'Is that you?' Raghava asked, pointing to a portrait on the opposite wall.

'My mother,' she whispered, emotion choking her voice. Her mother sat like Goddess Saraswati, a veena on her lap, serene and beautiful. She had never seen her alive. The portrait, and the image of her father looking longingly at it, were the only memories she had of her mother.

'She is as beautiful as you,' Raghava said.

She moved to the right towards her father's chambers, removing cobwebs with her hands. The window from that room faced the valley and the distant Mahishi River, which merged with the sky far away. She had spent countless hours sitting at the window ledge, watching the clouds swirl over the hills while her father sat at his table, immersed in his work.

Shutting her mind to the surging emotions, she stepped into her father's chambers. But for the cobwebs and dust, everything looked the same. On the day they had come for him, she was playing in the courtyard with the children of the servants. Only old Lachmi was there in his chambers, serving him his food. She still remembered her father being dragged away in chains through the streets. She had run behind the fast-vanishing chariot, crying her heart out before Lachmi had swooped her into her arms and run back to the mansion. But they were barred from entering by the maharaja's guards and her home had been sealed before her eyes. The servants were thrown out of their huts and the fort gate was shut. They had sat there until Uncle Thimma had come to take her to his home.

Old Lachmi had told her that her father was reading the strange book when they came for him. He had hurriedly handed it over to her and pointed out an opening in the floor where he had asked her to hide it. He wanted her to hand it to his daughter when she was old enough. A moment later, the soldiers had burst in. Lachmi had run behind her master as the soldiers dragged him away, and by the time she came back, they had sealed the mansion and thus the manuscript too.

She wished Lachmi were alive and with her to guide her to the place where the maid had hidden the book. It was only after some time that she was able to locate the secret opening in the floor and, with the help of Raghava, she broke it open. Inside was a manuscript.

'Paisachi,' Raghava exclaimed. 'That is the language of the first men of this country.'

'You know how to read it?' she asked.

Raghava was a scholar who spent most of his time reading. He shook his head. 'Not many are alive who could read this dead language. I wonder why your father chose to write in this strange tongue.'

'He did not write it. He got the book from someone,' she said, recollecting what Lachmi had said to her.

She ran her fingers down the spine of the manuscript and a thrill passed down her back. This had been held by her father.

'We have to hurry,' Raghava said. He was worried his father Thimma would have come back home and seen that they were missing.

She stood up, clutching the manuscript close to her heart. She looked around the chamber longingly. The image of her father stooped over his books flashed for a moment in her mind. She shook her head and, holding back her tears, walked out. Raghava quietly followed.

She paused in front of the dilapidated temple and closed her eyes in prayer. A wave of anger swept through her. They had destroyed her family. They had killed her father. She had seen him die, inch by inch. Chitravadha, they called it. The poetic name did not mask the cruelty of the punishment. She still remembered how they had locked him in an iron cage and hung it from a banyan tree in front of the arena. They had hung a wooden board from the cage, and it read: TRAITOR.

Devaraya, once a powerful bhoomipathi, later declared traitor, died the most painful death possible. She had heard it took about three weeks for him to die, eaten alive by sparrows and crows while jeering crowds from Mahishmathi picnicked under the tree and watched him die.

How she hated the king and the evil kingdom of Mahishmathi. Clutching the manuscript close to her heart, she whispered, 'Amma Gauri, I swear I will destroy this evil kingdom of Mahishmathi.'

When she turned, Raghava embraced her. The lamp fell from her hands and went off with a hiss. She was too shocked to react. Raghava kissed her passionately. 'Sivagami, Sivagami, together we will destroy them. Don't go away. Be with me…'

Sivagami pushed him away and slapped him across his face. 'How…how dare you, Raghava.'

She stood panting with anger and sadness. This was not what she had expected from her childhood companion, her friend. The passion with which he had kissed her left her with no doubt what was on his mind.

'I am sorry, Sivagami, I am sorry,' Raghava said, crying in anguish.

'I trusted you, Raghava. I always treated you as my elder brother,' Sivagami said, sadly.

He fell on his knees, covering his face. 'You can still trust me, Sivagami. There is no man who loves you more. But don't tell me I am your brother. I have loved you as no man can love a woman. But you are no sister to me.'

'No, Raghava, no, you are nothing more than a brother to me. I have considered Uncle Thimma as my own father. And his son cannot be anything more than a brother. Besides, I have only one aim in life,' she said, feeling pity for her childhood friend.

'No, don't speak such harsh words. Don't say anything. I don't want to hear it. I will help you, Sivagami. I will help you seek your revenge. No—don't speak…please…let me finish… Maharaja Somadeva is very powerful, but there are more powerful kings in the world. I will seek them out and bring them here. I will do it for you, Sivagami. I will travel to the ends of the world for you and beyond if required. I will leave before you are gone from our home. I don't know why Nanna is sending you away, but by tomorrow's dawn, I will leave Mahishmathi.'

'Raghava, please…'

'No, Sivagami, please don't speak. Just promise me that the day you destroy Mahishmathi, you will be mine. Promise me that you will be—'

'I do not want your help, Raghava. I want no one's help. I don't know how, I don't know when, but I will destroy Mahishmathi and its evil royals. I give no promise—'

Raghava closed her mouth with his palm, 'Sivagami, I will not speak about this anymore. But be kind to me for some more time. I am going away tomorrow. Please…if you do not want to make the promise, I will still go way with the hope that one day you will change your heart once I help you.'

Sivagami did not bother to answer. There was no point talking to Raghava now. Her emotional friend would come back to his senses soon, she hoped. They rode back home in silence.

Sivagami was so overwhelmed by old memories and her renewed anger about what the king had done to her father that she did not even think about Raghava or what he had said about Thimma sending her away.

TWO

Kattappa

The hunting party was speeding through the forest. A lean, dark young man ran alongside the elephant that carried the king of Mahishmathi. Ahead of him, his father rode a white horse that had a plume on its head. Behind him, amid the soldiers, rode the princes of Mahishmathi on their chestnut mares. A train of soldiers straggled behind them, weighed down by the carcasses of hunted deer and wild boars on their shoulders. Shadows of trees had started crawling towards the east. Mist was creeping up from the bushes. They had been hunting since morning, but for a party of three score people, the catch was pitiful. The drizzle that had started the previous night had made the forest damp and the earth squishy.

'Kattappa, run ahead and make arrangements for camping,' the man on the white horse turned and addressed his son. Kattappa selected a few slaves who could help him and left the procession. A group of bards was already waiting under the trees, busy twanging their tampuras and tuning their mrudangas when Kattappa reached the camping site. They stood up reluctantly. The black steel ring around his neck marked him a slave, but the way he carried himself made them show grudging respect.

Kattappa asked them to make space and they moved away, huddling together, whispering amongst each other as he got busy giving instructions to erect tents and lay down carpets. His thoughts turned to his younger brother, Shivappa. At seventeen, Shivappa was yet to graduate from the position of a palace slave, the one who did menial jobs for his masters, but he never saw the world outside the palace. He was not old enough to accompany the maharaja's hunting party, but had been adamant about joining them that morning. Only their father's scolding had made him retreat in sullen silence. But Shivappa was not one to give up so easily. Later, Kattappa had had to smuggle in his brother, who was now working at the rear end of the hunting party, helping soldiers carry their baskets and water pots. Their father, of course, was unaware. Kattappa worried that his impulsive brother may pick a quarrel with some servant or the other and blow his own cover. There would be a price to pay if their father came to know.

Kattappa shouted for everyone to work faster as he watched the first of the king's horses turn towards the camp. Servants were arranging bales of hay for the horses and filling huge copper vessels with water for the elephants to drink. Soon the air was filled with the sounds of whinnying and the tread of shoes as the hunting party approached. Kattappa ran his gaze all over the camp to ensure that it had been set up as per order. This was the first hunt where he had been given such a big responsibility and he did not want to botch it up. When he looked back at the contingent, the elephant carrying the king was already kneeling for his majesty to alight. Kattappa saw his father jumping down from his horse and hurrying towards the king. His father kneeled before the king and Maharaja Somadeva climbed down, stepping on Malayappa's shoulders.

'Hey, you, slave boy.'

Kattappa tensed. He knew there was nothing wrong with being called a slave boy; after all, that was what he was, but every time he heard it, it riled him. More than the word 'slave', it was being called a boy at the age of twenty-two by Bijjala, who was younger to him by a few months, that upset him more.

Hiding his distaste and putting on an expression of extreme servitude, he turned towards the voice. Prince Bijjala gestured for him to come near his horse. Kattappa walked over. He bowed, and the prince indicated that he should kneel down. People were watching him.

'Brother, stop. He is elder to you,' Prince Mahadeva said in a shrill voice. Bijjala snickered, 'Slaves don't have any age, or names, for that matter. They are bound to obey what we say.'

'But...'

Bijjala's arm shot out and slammed into Kattappa above his left ear. The world spun around the slave. He had not seen it coming.

'When I ask you to kneel, you have to kneel immediately,' Bijjala punctuated his order with another slap on Kattappa's cheek. Kattappa hurriedly knelt down. Bijjala stepped on his lean shoulders and got down from his horse. Kattappa swayed under the weight of Bijjala, lost his balance, and fell flat on the ground with the prince. There was silence and everyone looked at them. Prince Mahadeva laughed.

Bijjala stood up. His fine silk dhoti was smeared with mud. Kattappa was scared. He had made a big mistake. He saw Bijjala's anger growing on his face. He took a step back as Bijjala snarled and drew out his whip. Kattappa's throat went dry. Bijjala took a step forward and cracked the whip. It did not connect with Kattappa, but he was terrified. He closed his eyes, waiting for the lash to bite.

'No, Anna…' Kattappa could hear Mahadeva crying out. *Oh no, please, that will only anger him further,* Kattappa thought. Bijjala wound the lash around his arm and cracked it again. Kattapa took a step back in fear, stumbled and fell down on his back. Bijjala towered over him, his curly head blocking the sun. Kattappa could feel the dampness of the grass, and was acutely aware of the sharpness of the grass tips. He crawled on his back, pushing with his hands and legs to slide as far away from Bijjala as possible.

'Mercy, Your Highness, mercy,' he cried, as the lash arced above his head and cracked across his face. He gritted his teeth and tried unsuccessfully to stop the tears.

A tongue of fire burned across his cheeks, his shoulders, nose, stomach, thighs, as Kattappa pressed his lips tight, determined not to cry aloud. The lash cracked again and again.

This was his fate, the fate of his ancestors. He was nothing but a slave, a slave who was supposed to give his life to protect the royal family of Mahishmathi. Yet, somewhere deep inside his heart, it hurt. He was no better than a horse, or perhaps that was an overestimation. Horses had better food and had non-leaking roofs over their heads.

'Anna…' he heard Shivappa's voice at a distance. His eyes, blurred with tears and blood, could make out Shivappa running towards him. *No! Oh Ma Gauri, no, no,* he wanted to scream.

He saw Shivappa's wrathful face and closed his eyes. He opened them only when he heard Bijjala's agonized cry. The prince had covered his nose with his palm, but blood spurted through the gaps between his fingers. Kattappa saw a bloodied stone rolling away from his feet and Shivappa taking aim with another stone. Kattappa screamed at him to stop and run. Everything was happening so fast. Kattappa's heart sank as he saw their father rushing towards them with a whip in his hand.

The second stone that Shivappa hurled whizzed past them without hitting anything and bounced off the ground, splashing bobs of mud in its wake. Before he could pick up a third one, Malayappa's whip cracked and hit Shivappa across his face. The boy fell down screaming, and started rolling on the ground as his father continued to hit him mercilessly.

'You dare hurt the prince you are supposed to protect. You thankless dog!' Malayappa screamed as he cracked the whip. Kattappa tried to intervene but faced his father's wrath.

'Stay away! This is all your fault. How dare you disobey me?'

'Please stop. It was not Kattappa's fault,' Prince Mahadeva cried. Malayappa bowed deep when he heard the prince speak.

'I want him to die. He broke my nose. Kill him, kill him, kill him,' Prince Bijjala roared. The royal physician was applying medicines to his bleeding nose. Malayappa resumed beating his son.

Prince Mahadeva ran to Maharaja Somadeva. 'Father, do something. Please ask him to stop please, father, please.'

Kattappa saw his father stop, for a moment and await the king's response. Maharaja Somadeva's face was cast in stone and he was deaf to the cries of Prince Mahadeva.

Malayappa gave the whip to Kattappa and said, 'You will punish him now.'

'Father?'

'You brought him where he did not belong and he did what he was not supposed to do. It is your punishment too. Now, do it.'

Kattappa took the whip with trembling hands. Shivappa was already bleeding from wherever the whip had licked him. Kattappa looked at his brother's face, expecting the boy to plead for mercy, but Shivappa had a calm expression. He wished that his brother would at least cry out. But the twenty-one lashes that Kattappa dealt out could not even extract a whimper from him, though each shredded Kattappa's heart. Shivappa just stared into his brother's eyes as the whip arced around him before ripping his skin. It was at that moment that Kattappa started hating his life.

It was already past midnight when Kattappa went to his little brother. By that time, the bards had got too drunk to continue their praises about the illustrious ancestors of the Mahishmathi royal clan and their brave deeds. The dancing girls had gone with their suitors, and from the bushes around the tents, Kattappa could hear their hushed laughter. The king had retired to his royal tent and so had the other important dignitaries. His father, in all probability, was tending to the king. Kattappa was burning with guilt for how he had been forced to treat his brother.

Shivappa lay under a tree with gnarled roots and crooked branches. Kattappa walked carefully, trying not to break even a dry twig on his way. The smell of herb paste that the physician had applied on his brother's body intensified as he neared the tree. Shivappa was whimpering. A dull moon hung from the sky. As Kattappa neared his brother, something scampered away into the bushes.

'I am sorry,' Kattappa's voice choked up. 'Does it hurt?'

Shivappa did not respond. His eyes were closed. Kattappa's hand trembled as he reached out to touch the gashes the whip had made on his brother's skin. He withdrew at the last moment, and his eyes misted up.

'Kamakshi,' Shivappa was mumbling in a daze, 'you are right. I am just a slave.'

Kattappa recoiled. His brother was still seeing that girl. Despite his father's warning, despite his best advice. Who would drive sense into his thick head?

'Shivappa,' Kattappa shook him and his brother opened his eyes. 'You have no right to see her again. You want her to get killed?'

'Why are we slaves?' Shivappa asked, stunning Kattappa by the abruptness of his question.

Kattappa did not have an answer. This was something he often asked himself. He was vaguely aware of some vow taken by his ancestors many generations ago. His mother, when she was alive, would smile whenever he asked her that question, ruffle his curly hair, and say that it was their destiny. It was written. Some unknown god, sitting in some place had willed that some people should be masters and others slaves.

Kattappa could see the light from the dying embers near the king's tent. His father crouched in front of it. He could see part of his father's face, lit up by the golden hue of the fire. His father might be the closest aide of the maharaja of Mahishmathi, but it still left a bad taste to think that he was merely a slave. Kattappa knew that he, too, would live, serve and die for his master, unacknowledged and unlamented, just like any other slave.

Thankfully, his brother had closed his eyes, the question forgotten for the moment. He was moaning in pain.

'Are you feverish? Your skin is burning,' Kattappa asked, as he touched his forehead. But Shivappa only coiled into a foetal position and mumbled his lover's name. Kattappa stood watching him helplessly. Mist weaved itself through the tree leaves. The only sound was the drone of the crickets and the laboured breathing of his brother. There was a sudden rustle of dry leaves and Kattappa turned.

'Oh, so this is what the slaves do when the masters are not looking.'

Kattappa had never expected Prince Bijjala to come where the slaves slept. He bowed with alacrity, unsure of what to do next. From the corner of his eye, he saw Prince Mahadeva running towards them from the camp, calling his brother.

'You dared to throw a stone at your prince and you think you can get away with some casual whipping by your elder brother?' Prince Bijjala stood with a whip in his hand, glaring at them. He cracked the whip in the air and then wound it around his forearm. 'Clever, wasn't he, your blasted father! He thought quickly for a slave and my naive father fell for it.'

Kattappa fell at Prince Bijjala's feet, and clasped them as if his very life depended on it. 'Swami, mercy, mercy.'

Prince Mahadeva, who had arrived on the scene, tried to drag his brother away, but Bijjala shoved him. The older prince waved his index finger at his brother and said, 'Stay away, you coward. I will teach you how to treat slaves. This bastard thinks he can get away so easily after hurting the crown prince of Mahishmathi?'

Mahadeva cried, 'Shivappa, run, run to His Majesty and seek protection. Or else my brother will kill you.'

Shivappa hesitated a moment. Bijjala lunged towards him, snapping the whip. Shivappa moved to the side to avoid the blow and then began running towards the camp. Bijjala kicked Kattappa away and, screaming abuse, chased Shivappa, ordering him to stop.

Kattappa ran behind Bijjala, pleading for mercy. He saw Shivappa falling down as Bijjala closed in on him. His brother rolled away as Bijjala lashed the whip at him. Shivappa got up and continued to run towards the camp. He swerved to the left, where the king's elephant was standing.

A chill passed down Kattappa's spine. In a flash, he understood what his brother was trying to do. Shivappa fed the elephant, Gireesha, and the beast was quite attached to his brother. There could be no gentler creature on earth than Gireesha, and it was one reason why the maharaja had chosen to ride on this moving mountain. But Kattappa knew the elephant obeyed his brother's command and Shivappa was leading the prince to the beast.

'No, Shivappa, no,' Kattappa cried, but his voice was drowned out in the screams of Bijjala. Men who were dancing and singing around the campfire stopped to watch the unfolding scene.

Shivappa reached the elephant and stood panting near the legs of the beast. The elephant stood still, munching palm leaves. The mahout was asleep on the ground, near the beast, perhaps drunk. Bijjala swung his whip. It was as if Shivappa was expecting the move. He ducked and the whip caught the elephant under its eyes. It trumpeted in pain. The mahout woke up with alacrity, but when he saw the angry prince, he moved away. Bijjala was too furious to notice. He cracked his whip again at Shivappa. This time it cut Shivappa's face. He fell down, crying, begging for mercy. Kattappa knew it was a ruse. He saw his brother unchaining the elephant in a swift move. The next lash of the whip caught the elephant's legs. Shivappa rolled away to the other side of the beast and started pleading for mercy. Cursing, Bijjala walked around the beast to reach the slave.

Kattappa was a few feet away when he tripped on a stone and fell on his face. When he had steadied himself and stood up, his blood froze. He yelled, 'Move away, Your Highness—'

Before he could complete his sentence, the elephant had caught Bijjala with its trunk and lifted him up. The whip fell from Bijjala's hand as he flailed his limbs, screaming in abject terror. A moment later, the beast slammed Bijjala to the ground. The prince twitched for a moment and went still. The beast lifted its leg to crush Bijjala's head.

Time stood still. Kattappa shouted at the beast, 'Gireesha, no!' The elephant hesitated, holding its leg in mid-air for a moment. Kattappa dove and yanked Bijjala away as the heavy foot of the beast came down. It missed Bijjala's head by a whisker. Kattappa lifted Bijjala on his shoulder and started running. He could hear the beast trumpeting behind him. He ran for his life, but he knew it was difficult to outrun a charging elephant. With Bijjala on his shoulder, it was impossible. Then he saw Prince Mahadeva, who had been running towards them, stop in his tracks, stunned.

'Run, Prince, move out of the way,' Kattappa screamed, but Mahadeva stood transfixed by terror. Kattappa knew everything was lost. One, perhaps both, the princes were going to die. He would die with them, but his death would be in vain. He placed the unconscious Bijjala on the ground and turned towards the approaching beast. Behind him, Prince Mahadeva cowered with fear.

The elephant charged down at them with thundering speed. Kattappa tried to remember what his father had told him about marma vidya, the ancient martial art of stunning an opponent by striking at the nerve centre in the head. But he was not sure whether it applied to elephants.

The elephant charged at him and caught his midriff with its trunk. It lifted Kattappa up in the air. As it brought its trunk down to slam him to the ground, he pounded both his fists on the elephant's head with all the power he could muster. It was of no use. He was thrown violently to the ground. He had a glimpse of the gigantic leg of the beast coming down and he closed his eyes shut. A moment later, the earth shook as the elephant collapsed on its knees, trumpeting wildly. Everything went blank for Kattappa.

He woke up when cold water pricked his eyes. His head was throbbing and his surroundings still seemed hazy. The only sensation was the sharp smell of burning oils from the torches and the coldness of the rain. He blinked and slowly his father's face came into focus. Near him stood Maharaja Somadeva. Kattappa tried to get up, but the king gently pushed him back. The agitated cries of the birds in the forest canopy had died down, but the cold fear in Kattappa's heart was yet to thaw. His mind raced with different possibilities. Had Bijjala died? Had he failed to protect him?

Then he saw soldiers carry away a limp Bijjala. He saw Prince Mahadeva was tending to the fallen elephant. He was relieved that the elephant had not died. The effect of the stunning blow would fade away in one or two yamams. 'Your boy has grown up, Malayappa,' Maharaja Somadeva said. 'He saved my sons. No reward could be sufficient other than to give him the highest honour possible. I know he is young, but his deeds show him to be braver than any of the slaves or soldiers. Let him be the sevaka of Prince Bijjala.'

The soldiers around cheered and applauded and Malayappa was in tears. He fell at the king's feet. 'Prabhu, a great honour, a very great honour for a humble slave. I do not know how to thank your generosity.' He beckoned to Kattappa, and the slave boy slowly stood up. His knees were stiff and his back still hurt, but he fell at the king's feet alongside his father.

'Arise,' Maharaja Somadeva commanded, and father and son stood up, hurriedly covering their mouth with their palms and going as low as possible.

'For many generations, Kattappa, your family has lived and died for the sake of Mahishmathi, and I hope your sons too shall follow the glorious tradition of your ancestors,' the king said.

Mahadeva, who was tending to the fallen elephant along with the rajavaidya, stood up and walked to them. He took Kattappa's hands in his and said with a smile, 'I have no words to thank you, Kattappa. As long as I am alive I will be indebted to you for saving my life and my brother's.'

Kattappa bowed, his face flushing with embarrassment. He touched Mahadeva's feet and, unable to control the happiness and emotion sweeping over him, he started weeping.

Mahadeva picked him up and hugged the slave briefly. Then he was gone with the king's entourage.

No slave had the privilege to be touched by a royal unless it was during a war or in the line of duty. Unless it was to save his life, a slave was allowed to touch only the feet of his master. A prince touching him, thanking for merely doing his duty—such things were unheard of. Even the king had touched him. Words choked in Kattappa's throat and he stood dazzled by his fortune.

The bards had already started making songs about how the brave Prince Bijjala and Mahadeva had fought hand-in-hand with a slave to tame a charging elephant. Kattappa felt proud. For generations they would sing of the bravery of the prince of Mahishmathi, but a small part of the glory would be his. His name may not be taken, but it did not matter. He had made his father proud. He felt grateful to the king and the princes. He was fortunate to be born in Mahishmathi. For a slave, it was a great honour to be elevated to the post of sevaka of the eldest prince. His father had achieved that honour at the age of twenty-five, when he became a member of the personal guard of Maharaja Somadeva. Kattappa was barely twenty-two.

The king was no doubt a great man, but a thought kept nagging Kattappa. Why had the king not uttered a single word when he was forced to punish his brother at the whim of the prince? Perhaps he was too small to understand the wisdom of the king. His lot was not to think, but to serve. And he had served well.

He snapped out of his thoughts as he heard his father asking him to carry his brother. Shivappa was sitting near the tree where the elephant was tied earlier. He appeared too tired to lift himself up. For a moment, a wave of anger swept through Kattappa as he eyed his younger brother. No one else might have noticed it, but he had clearly seen what his brother did. It was unpardonable.

Shivappa's dark eyes burned like embers when Kattappa stooped to lift him up on his shoulders. It was drizzling again and the frogs started abusing each other from the bushes. A dark cloud had drawn a veil over the moon.

They were almost at the camp. There was a fire crackling in the middle and soldiers were preparing to sleep. Some were passing around pots of palm toddy. The singers were humming a ditty and raucous laughter broke through the night from one of the whores' tents. Dancing girls were practising their steps. Someone poured oil in the fire and it flared up, sending glowing fire ash into air. A soldier started barbecuing a piglet and the breeze carried the woody smell of charred meat mixed with the sweet smell of toddy. A bawdy joke was followed by howls of laughter.

'What you did was ignoble. You are trying to bite the hands that feed us,' Kattappa said as he placed his brother down.

'Would you have preferred that I died at his hands?' Shivappa's eyes flared.

There was no use talking to him now. His brother was hot-tempered and reckless. He would have to make him understand later. He had to teach him the virtue of duty and dharma. But this was not the time.

'Sleep well,' Kattappa said, gently. The sky was clear now, and silver-grey moonlight lit the tips of the grass, making them shine like diamonds.

'Where are you going, Anna?'

After a moment's silence, Kattappa said, 'From tonight onwards, I have to sleep outside Prince Bijjala's chamber.'

Shivappa did not reply. It would be the first time they would be sleeping separately since he could remember. A bat flapped its webbed wings over their heads and settled, upside down, on a branch above them.

'Anna,' Shivappa asked in a soft voice. 'Are you happy?'

Kattappa wished he knew the answer. He hugged his brother and said, 'It is my duty to be near him and protect him.' Kattappa could feel Shivappa tense up. Then his brother smiled. Kattappa looked into his eyes. The reflection of the campfire in them made them appear to be aflame. 'I am proud of you, Anna,' Shivappa said. Was there a trace of mockery in his brother's compliment? Kattappa tried to push the thought away.

Kattappa pointed to the extension of the silk carpet that jutted out of Bijjala's tent like the tongue of a monster. 'I will be sleeping there but I will have my eyes on you.'

'On the carpet?' Shivappa asked. Kattappa did not reply. Behind them, the singer's rustic voice rose high and there was a smattering of applause. Two nautch girls came running, their anklets tinkling, and started whirling around the fire. Catcalls, whistles and raunchy comments filled the air. A song started about the princess of Kampilya who lived a thousand years ago and who wanted to bed a hundred kings in as many days. The beats of thakil drums picked up in frenzy and a nadasawara started following the singer tune to tune.

'Good place it is,' Shivappa said, struggling to be heard against the din of music and whistles. Kattappa felt guilty that he would be sleeping on a carpet while his brother slept on the ground. Dew had started forming on the grass, and he could feel its soft cold between his fingers. For the first time in his life he would be sleeping not on the naked floor but on a carpet. He had earned it. His first achievement in life. He felt sorry that he could not take his brother along and make him feel the softness of the carpet.

Kattappa's thoughts drifted to the carpet. He was eager to find out how soft it would be. The one with intricate designs on it, woven from the wool of the unborn kid, extracted from the womb of sheep. That had to be soft. He had heard about it a hundred times from his father. Though he had never felt it, he knew how one's feet would sink into its softness. It would have a fragrance, as the feet of the royals had treaded on it many times. Just like how he could sometimes smell the silk dresses of the princes when they came near. He tucked his coarse lungi tight across his waist. Maybe, one day, he would even be able to touch the silk dresses of the princes. Perhaps that was too ambitious. He was an untouchable. No one would allow him to touch those dresses. But what was the harm in dreaming? The music had paused and the singers were readying for the next song.

'Good place for a dog,' Shivappa said.

It took a moment for the comment to register. Kattappa felt anger rising from his toes. Shivappa had already turned to the other side.

Kattappa did not bother to comment. He walked briskly past the soldiers' campfire and reached Bijjala's tent. Two sentries stood with crossed spears. As he approached, they moved their spears without asking any questions. That felt good. Kattappa peered in and saw Prince Bijjala snoring. There was a little space on the carpet. He patted it a few times and curled up on it. He was a privileged slave and he closed his eyes to thank the all-merciful god before sleeping, just like his mother had taught him. *Good place for a dog.* Shivappa's comment kept coming up like undigested food. He tried to push it away, trying to think about his mother's words about being contented with his blessings. There were so many who did not have even this in the world—who did not have anything to eat, who had nothing to sleep on. He was blessed. He was a lucky man. It would be a long time before sleep sneaked into his eyes. Until then, he could watch the million stars in the sky.

The words that Shivappa had said a few weeks back came rushing to his mind, unbidden and unwished for. On a dark, clear night like this, sometime back, they had been lying side by side. The sky was a diamond-studded blanket over their heads. Breaking Kattappa's blissful reverie, his brother had asked, 'Anna, I wonder whether a cruel god is boiling the stars in a black broth for fun, just like he does to the lives of thousands like us.'

Kattappa turned to the other side. Except for the smell of grass and the faint smell of footwear, the carpet was as good as he had imagined. He sighed and his brother's voice whispered in his mind:

'A good place for a dog.'

THREE

Parameswara

Mahapradhana Parameswara was panting by the time he had negotiated the winding steps down to the workshop under the armoury. He stood leaning on the shoulders of his assistant, Roopaka, to catch his breath.

An acrid metallic smell hung in the air. Though it was early morning and the dew had not yet evaporated from the leaves outside, inside the cellar it was hot and dry. Fire from the blazing furnaces and the din of hammer striking anvil made it appear like hell.

'I would have handled this, swami,' Roopaka said to the old man. Parameswara wiped the sweat from his forehead with the tail of his turban and smiled. 'I know you would have, son, but there are certain duties that cannot be left to assistants, however smart they may be.'

As the two stepped into the chamber, the din died away and the blacksmiths scrambled up to bow to the prime minister of Mahishmathi. A wizened old man came forward to bow low to the mahapradhana.

'How is the job going, Dhamaka?' Parameswara asked the head blacksmith. He then bent down to scoop a handful of pebbles from a casket on the floor. When he turned them over in his hand, the dull stones caught the light from the fire and sparkled an iridescent blue.

'We are running short of Gaurikanta. The swords will turn brittle if we do not use Gauridhooli, and the stones to make them are running low,' Dhamaka said uneasily, shifting his weight from one leg to the other. Parameswara dropped the stones back into the casket.

'What did Senapathi Hiranya say?' Roopaka asked, reading his superior's thoughts.

'He was...he was not pleased. He wanted us to hurry, but we are short of...' The head blacksmith hesitated.

'Gaurikanta stones. Yes, I know. Wait till Mahamakam,' the mahapradhana said while scooping up some of the lustrous powder in his palm and feeling it with his fingers.

'No, it is not only the stones we are short of...' Dhamaka did not complete his sentence.

'All twenty-one of you are comfortable?' the mahapradhana asked, peering into the head blacksmith's eyes. Fire crackled in the furnace behind them. The heat was unbearable and the locksmith's bare body glistened with sweat. He looked at the mahapradhana and his assistant and gave a reluctant nod.

'Yes...yes, swami.'

'Sir, there is a leak here and water seeps in often. One day we are going to drown in this hell, but no one seems to care,' a young voice cried from behind.

Dhamaka cried, 'Hush, scoundrel, do you realize who you are talking to?'

The young man glared at Dhamaka and looked up at the roof. A drop of water splattered on his forehead. An iron bucket kept on the floor was collecting water that dripped down.

The mahapradhana turned laboriously towards a huge circular iron door in the roof. He stared at the leak, his forehead knitted into a frown.

'We don't have enough hands and…' Dhamaka's words were cut off by the mahapradhana's raised palm.

'See to it that the senapathi's requirements are met. It is a matter of national security,' the mahapradhana said and gestured to Roopaka that their visit was over. He started climbing up the stairs.

'Sir, how about the leak?' the young blacksmith cried. Parameswara did not reply. As he walked away, he heard hammer striking metal with full force. The young man was taking out his anger and frustration on his work. Soon sounds of two score hammers hitting metal added to the din.

As he was climbing up towards the streaming light from the top of the stairs, he whispered to Roopaka, 'Tell them to seal the leak before they resume work. We do not want three years' work washed away in the river.'

Roopaka nodded.

'Sir, can I ask you something?' he hurriedly said before the prime minister could stop him. 'When speaking to Dhamaka, you mentioned twenty-one men, but I counted only twenty.'

The mahapradhana took a deep breath, drinking in the fresh air of the garden. It was a beautiful day.

'Sir?'

'Roopaka, that precisely is my worry too. One of the men is missing. Where could someone working on such an important task vanish?'

'Swami, this is a catastrophe. I hope no stones have gone missing,' Roopaka said in a horrified voice.

'Six are missing. The best quality of them,' Parameswara said quietly.

'But how? This place has the highest level of security,' Roopaka cried.

'He used the escape hatch in the roof.'

'But that opens into the bottom of the river, sir. And it can be opened only if keys are used simultaneously from outside and inside. After all it was meant to flood the workshop to destroy it in the unlikely event of an enemy taking over Mahishmathi.'

'It used to open to the bottom of the river when the place was built three hundred years ago, Roopaka. The river has changed its course. Now this place gets flooded only when there is high tide. It's clear that someone opened the door from outside for him, and he had keys made to open the door from the inside.'

'Such breach of security, swami. I should have taken sufficient care to prevent this catastrophe,' Roopaka said with his head bowed.

'We are a race that gains wisdom only after disaster strikes us. For us, security is an inconvenience. I am as much to blame as you. To think that this happened at the fag end of my career. But for Maharaja's request, I would have retired long ago and have been enjoying life playing with my grandchildren,' Mahapradhana Parameswara sighed.

'Does Maharaja know?' Roopaka asked.

'Not yet. If we find the missing blacksmith and the stones, then we can report to him. I do not want him to panic,' Parameswara said.

'Half a dozen Gaurikanta stones are missing, and one of the twenty-one blacksmiths who knows just what to do with them is gone. Sir, I am getting scared.'

'So am I, son. But my people are working on it,' the mahapradhana said, but his voice lacked confidence.

He turned to Gauriparvat and folded his hands in obeisance. 'Ma Gauri, preserve Mahishmathi,' he mumbled in prayer.

FOUR

Pattaraya

Bhoomipathi Pattaraya was irritated. He was getting late for the durbar and would not have stopped at the temple but for the frantic message from Rajaguru Rudra Bhatta. Dandanayaka Pratapa, the head of the dandakaras, who policed the city of Mahishmathi, was already waiting for him in the antechamber of the chief priest when he reached.

Pattaraya fished out Rudra Bhatta's message from the folds of his waist-band and read it aloud, 'Please come fast. The slave is being unreasonable. We are not able to handle him. He has attempted to escape twice. I cannot hide him here anymore. There are spies all around.' He slammed the palm leaf on the table and glared at Rudra Bhatta.

'Swami, you are a learned man, a scholar who knows the Puranas by heart, and is an expert in the Vedas. Why the hell do you lack common sense? How can you write such an explicit letter? 'I cannot hide him anymore, spies everywhere, blah, blah.' Do you want to get all of us hanged?' Pattaraya hissed.

'Pattaraya, swami was scared,' Dandanayaka Pratapa tried to placate the angry Bhoomipathi. 'The slave Nagayya has been throwing tantrums. He is saying he wants safe passage to Kadarimandalam for his wife and son too. He won't go alone.'

'Can't you make him understand that Jeemotha's ships are not able to enter the port? Can't you tell the fool that none other than Upapradhana Skandadasa is supervising the operation against pirate ships? He will have to be patient. And it is impossible to take his family. We are paying him handsomely. Let him get a new wife in Kadarimandalam with the money.'

'Try telling him that,' Rudra Bhatta said. 'He spat on my face when I suggested it to him.' The Brahmin shuddered at the thought of a slave spitting on his face. He wiped the imaginary spittle from his cheeks with the back of his hands.

Pattaraya pushed away the table and walked to the far corner of the chamber where a slave was sitting on his haunches. Beside him, a bundle of blacksmith's tools lay on the floor.

'Son,' Pattaraya said as he leaned towards him and lifted his chin with his index finger. 'What bothers you, son? Have we not promised you a new life? Freedom?'

'Have we not allowed you, an untouchable slave, inside the temple?' Rudra Bhatta said, but when he saw Pattaraya gritting his teeth, he withdrew.

Pattaraya turned back to Nagayya. He observed that the slave lacked his left ear. Not an easy person to smuggle out of the country. People would easily remember him. *Could not their spy have found a better person for the job than this scum*, wondered Pattaraya. He subtly covered his nose to keep away the stink emanating from the slave.

'I want my wife and son to come with me,' Nagayya said without looking up.

'Let us think about it. If we are pleased with your work, maybe we will agree to your terms. Won't we?' Pattaraya asked his companions.

'But how can we—' Rudra Bhatta was not allowed to complete his sentence as Pratapa prodded him.

'Of course we will,' Pratapa said.

'Nagayya, son,' Pattaraya kept his hand on the slave's shoulders, 'you have your tools. Why don't you get to work?'

The slave did not reply. His face remained in the shadows.

'Until my family is here with me, I will not start work,' he finally said in a determined voice.

Pattaraya stood up with a sigh and signalled to Pratapa. The police chief rushed towards the slave and kicked him squarely on his face. Nagayya was thrown back by the impact and his head hit the wall. He collapsed like a ragdoll.

'Ayyo, you have killed him,' Rudra Bhatta cried in anguish.

'Hush, brahmin,' Pattaraya said. 'Get me the lamp.'

Pattaraya looked at Nagayya's face in the light of the lamp. He saw that his nose had been crushed and blood was oozing out of the hole where his left ear should have been. He put his fingers near the slave's nostrils and frowned.

'Dead?' Rudra Bhatta's voice betrayed fear.

'Where are the stones?' Pattaraya asked, ignoring the rajaguru. Pratapa started scavenging the slave's bundle. When he could not find anything, he emptied the bundle on the floor. Hammers, chisels and files tumbled down, but no stones emerged.

'Oh, no. Did the idiot come without stones? Ayyo, ayyayyo,' the rajaguru cried.

'Shhh,' Pattaraya hissed. He fumbled around the folds of Nagayya's dhoti, and with a tug he removed it. He found what he was looking for in a cloth bag tied to the string that held the slave's loincloth in place. He untied the cords of the bag and emptied the stones in his palm. When the light fell on them, they sparkled blue, drenching the room in an eerie light. He looked at the ghoulishly blue faces of his friends and smiled.

'A fortune,' Pratapa said, sucking in a quick breath.

'Only if we can get someone to convert them into Gauridhooli,' said Pattaraya, stretching his blue lips to a grin.

When the hammer struck hard on his foot, it was so unexpected that Pratapa screamed at the top of his voice. Startled, Pattaraya dropped the lamp. It rolled on the floor and extinguished with a hiss. In one swoop, Nagayya snatched the stones from Pattaraya's hands.

Pattaraya and Rudra Bhatta jumped back as the slave swung the hammer like a man possessed. The hammer missed Rudra Bhatta's head by a whisker and cracked open the wall, showering them with mortar. Pratapa was still howling in pain. Pattaraya kept himself pressed to the wall, careful to stay away from Nagayya. The priest was not so lucky. The hammer connected to his ample stomach and the priest fell down, howling in pain. Nagayya jumped over the priest and ran out before Pattaraya could react.

Pratapa yelled for his men, but Pattaraya stopped him. He lit the lamp with a flint. A stone sparkling from a crack in the floor caught his eye. Before anyone could notice, he picked it up with alacrity and tucked it into his waist-band. His friends were still busy howling in pain. With the stone safe in his custody Pattaraya feigned concern and sent for a vaidya to tend to their injuries.

'I will murder that bastard. I will send the entire dandakara force under my disposal to hunt him down. I will flay him alive,' Pratapa said through gritted teeth.

Pattaraya said, 'Never send dandakaras. Not in their uniforms at least. Give instructions to your men to cut him down wherever they find him. If he spills any of what we have been doing,' Pattaraya moved his index finger across his neck.

Pratapa clapped his hands and two policemen came and bowed low. He gave them some instructions and they hurried away. Soon six men with the tails of their turbans partially covering their faces galloped out of the temple premises.

'What should we do now?' asked Rudra Bhatta.

'Pray that the bastard is eliminated soon,' Pattaraya said as he climbed into his chariot. 'And once the vaidya has finished applying medicines to bring down your swelling, and you two have stopped whining like children, try coming to the durbar. We do not want to attract anyone's attention because of our absence.'

Pattaraya whipped the horses and the chariot rumbled towards the palace.

FIVE

Sivagami

'Child.' Sivagami heard Thimma's broken voice from the seat ahead of her. They were in his chariot. She crossed her arms and sat looking out, facing away from him. A few days ago, her only friend, Raghava, had gone away. She still missed him, but it did not matter anymore. She was going to miss them all. She was leaving Thimma's house forever. Ever since Thimma had taken her there in his chariot, it had been her home. His wife, Bhama, had been the mother she never had. Akhila, Thimma's youngest daughter, had been her sister. Not anymore. They did not want her.

Near her, little Akhila sat sniffling. Akhila had made many unsuccessful attempts to start a conversation with Sivagami, but she had not even bothered to look at her. The eight-year-old sat sulking near her, playing with sea shells. Akhila had insisted she would come with Sivagami to see her off. The chariot swayed as it hit a crack on the paved road. Thimma cracked his whip.

'Child, you have every right to hate us, but one day you will understand that we are doing this for your own good. Devaraya was more like a brother than a close friend. I would not do anything that could harm his daughter. I am trying to put you in the royal orphanage because…'

'It doesn't matter,' she said, looking away. A teardrop had sprung up in her eyes and she hated herself for it. She would not let him see it.

'You will have lots of friends there,' he said.

'Fine,' she said, wishing the teardrop away. She did not want to wipe it and let him know that she was crying. She was Devaraya's daughter.

'Child, I have taught you whatever I know. Now you can use arms well, you can defend yourself, and you can read and write well too. I am no scholar, but I have done my best. All that I could possibly do, I have done for you. Believe me, I have your interests at heart. One day, you will thank this old man for what I am doing now,' Thimma went on.

'Thank you for all that you have done,' she said.

He did not reply but she knew her words had hurt him. She felt bad, but steeled her heart. He deserved it. If he did not want her, why had he brought her to his home? Why did he act—yes, 'act' was the right word—like he was her father? She was the daughter of Bhoomipathi Devaraya. This was god's punishment for forgetting her father and his words. An uneasy silence descended between her and Thimma. The clop of horse hooves on the cobbled streets only served to accentuate the silence.

She clutched the small bundle tight. It had all her worldly possessions in it. She ran her fingers over the cloth bundle and stopped when she touched the spine of an old manuscript. It brought back memories of her father and, annoyingly, the embarrassing behaviour of Raghava on that night.

She debated whether she should tell Thimma about the book. *It belongs to my father and, by right, it is mine,* a voice in her head insisted. She had no obligation to tell anyone else about it. She sat clutching that excuse while the chariot rumbled past the rest house for travellers.

'Akka, can I come and stay with you?' Akhila asked. Sivagami did not reply.

'It will be fun to have lots of friends. Even Raghava Anna has gone away for studies to some faraway land. Please, please, can I stay with you?' Akhila shook Sivagami's shoulders. She shrugged the child away and sat gazing at the passing scenery. The city streets were hazy and blurred. She realized her eyes had welled up despite her best efforts.

'I hate Nanna. Why should he send you away?' Akhila pouted.

Sivagami wished she knew the answer. She also wished Akhila would keep quiet.

'Akka, Akka, look at these three green stones I found yesterday. Now I have one thousand three hundred and eighty-four stones and four hundred shells. See this, see this, Akka.' The eight-year-old-girl waved the small cloth pouch in which she kept her myriad-coloured collection. She loved to collect colourful pebbles, shells and beads, and always carried a cloth pouch in which she deposited any fascinating thing she found. Once the pouch filled up, she transferred them to a wooden box kept under her cot.

'Would you please keep quiet,' Sivagami snapped. She was in no mood to indulge the girl and her prattle. Akhila moved to the other end of the seat and sat pouting. She started counting the pebbles and arranging them according to their colour.

The streets of Mahishmathi bustled with activity. Traders from all parts of the world could be seen in their exotic garments. Craftsmen from villages mongered their wares at the top of their voices. Cloth merchants with bundles of clothes in front of them haggled with their customers. A few men and women of the Kurava tribe passed Sivagami's chariot with their children dragging their dancing bears and monkeys behind them. Men were leading their horses and weaving their paths through the milling crowds. A few elephants, carrying haughty noblemen, ambled by like large ships struggling in a crowded harbour. Carts laden with pumpkins, mangoes, jackfruits and watermelons created knots in traffic which magically loosened after a few hot words were exchanged in various tongues and slangs. But none of this could distract Sivagami, who carried with her a sinking feeling.

Raghava, I will miss you, I am sorry, she said to herself. She should not have hit him, but then, he should not have done what he did that night. All through her life, she had considered him her brother and it still riled her that he had hidden such a passion for her.

The chariot had turned onto a narrow road, barely wide enough for it to pass, with overflowing drains that oozed dark, stinking water. At the corner of the road, there was a temple that fed the poor, and a line of emaciated men and women stood patiently waiting for the food. The smell of boiled rice and steaming rasam mixed with the stink of the drains wafted around. The chariot went past the crowd.

'Eat, amma.' It was Aunt Bhama's voice. Sivagami started and looked around. She shook her head, trying to shake away

the memory. She pressed her lips together, trying to suppress a sob that threatened to overwhelm her. She had probably eaten her last meal cooked by Aunt Bhama today. The reality sank in slowly, but that did not make it less painful. They did not want her. She was an outsider and did not belong to this family. She had no one.

'But...why?' Words choked in her throat. Why were they getting rid of her?

The chariot moved at a rapid speed and, as they progressed, the streets became narrower. Sivagami wondered where her uncle was taking her. When she thought the streets could not get any worse, the chariot took a sharp left turn and started rumbling down a dirty road, swaying as it ran over puddles and uneven surfaces. A few naked urchins standing in front of their thatched homes watched as the chariot creaked past them. Hens clucked and scattered away from its path. The stench of fish being fried mixed with that of overflowing drains assaulted their noses. 'It is a shortcut,' Thimma said as the chariot grazed a lamp post leaning from the pavement.

When a patch of sky was visible once in a while, she could see the roof of the arena rising at a distance. With a growing fear she realized that their chariot would be passing by that cursed place. The vision of her father swaying from the cage as sparrows and crows ate him alive came back to her as it did every night. She gripped the seat tight and squeezed her eyes shut. The chariot took another turn to the right and dilapidated buildings leaned from either side of the narrow street. She understood why Thimma was taking this route. He was trying to avoid taking her by the arena where her father had been hanged. Yet, there was no escaping the hurtful memories.

The chariot stopped abruptly and she opened her eyes. A couple of cows were sitting in the middle of the road, blocking their way. Thimma cursed and jumped down to shove them away. The street ahead wound uphill through an array of closely built houses.

This was her chance. Sivagami slipped down from the chariot and bolted. It took a moment for Thimma to realize that the girl had run away. Cursing his arthritis-affected legs and calling out Sivagami's name, the old man left the chariot and started hobbling after her.

Sivagami could hear Akhila running behind her. The street was littered and slippery with cow dung that had been run over by the wheels of passing carts. She heard Akhila slipping and falling down. For a moment, she wanted to turn back and lift the child up, but saw that Akhila had managed to stand up and was following her again. Sivagami continued running.

Akhila pursued Sivagami as she turned at the end of the street and entered a dark alley. The ground was slushy from the overflowing drain, the walls had stains of urine and the smell around was pungent. Suddenly from a side alley, a dark figure burst out and collided with Akhila. The little girl was knocked down and the other person slipped and fell on her. Hearing the collision, Sivagami stopped and turned. She let out a scream and ran towards Akhila. As she approached, Sivagami saw that Akhila's pouch had burst open and her pebbles were strewn all around. The man was fighting with the child for the pebbles.

Sivagami pushed him away from the girl. He was a thin man with hollow eyes and bad teeth dressed only in a loincloth. He cursed and tried to get up, slipped and fell again.

The man lunged at the little girl with an animal cry, but Akhila held the stones behind her and said, 'No, mine, these are mine. I am not going to give them away.'

Was this man insane to fight with an eight-year-old girl for pebbles? Sivagami was about to give him a piece of her mind when she saw the man's eyes grow big in terror. He seemed to be staring at something behind her. As she looked back to see what had so frightened the man, he took off.

A moment later, he collided with a lamp post and collapsed from the impact. Sivagami ran towards him, but before she could reach him, the street echoed with the sound of horse hooves. The man gave a frightened yelp and, clutching his head, got up and ran. Sivagami saw a man in a black turban galloping towards them on a horse, a spear pointed at them. She dove and caught Akhila by her wrist, rolling away from the path of the pounding horse hooves with the child in her arms. When the horse had thundered past them, she stood up, panting in relief. Akhila was trembling with fear, but she clutched her torn pouch as if her life depended on it. When she turned to look, Sivagami saw that the spear had pierced the fleeing man through his chest. The man continued to run for a few feet before falling down on his face.

The pursuer dismounted from his horse and walked towards the dead man. He pulled the spear out of the man's body and wiped away the blood on it with his thumb. He turned the dead man on his back and started searching him.

Sivagami, thinking it was best to slip away unnoticed, tugged at Akhila. The pebbles fell from the little girl's hands and she started to cry and fight Sivagami. She wanted her pebbles back. Sivagami tried to hush her, but the girl managed to wriggle away from her grip. She bent down and started picking up the pebbles.

The man stopped what he was doing and stood up. He clucked his tongue and started walking towards them. He tapped the blunt edge of the spear on the street with every alternate step. Sivagami could hear her heart pounding within her ribcage. She tried to prod Akhila, but the girl would not budge until she had retrieved all her precious collectables.

By the time the man reached them, Akhila had collected the pebbles and put them in her torn pouch. The man snapped his fingers and extended his palm. He gestured to the little girl that she hand over her pouch. Akhila shook her head and ran to hide behind Sivagami. The man moved to grab her, but Sivagami extended her leg, tripping him. He fell on his face. Sivagami grabbed Akhila's hand and ran. She could hear him getting up and knew he would soon give them chase.

'Child, where have you gone? Sivagami, child!' Thimma's voice came from the other side of the alley.

'Nanna,' Akhila cried. Thimma appeared at the far end of the street and froze. Akhila ran to Thimma and clutched his legs. Sivagami turned around, shielding Thimma, prepared to fight her opponent. The turbaned man was walking towards them. Though his face was covered, Sivagami felt that the man was laughing at her and her attempt to protect a frail-looking old man leaning on his cane and a little girl. Sivagami was not sure whether she could take on such a huge man alone. She wished she had her sword. But there was no time to think.

The turbaned man shifted his spear from one hand to the other, licked his dry lips, and stood a few feet away. She thought the best plan would be to attack him before he could make a move, but Thimma's hand on her shoulder stopped her. He stepped in front and signalled for her to move away. Reluctantly she stepped a few feet to the right with Akhila.

The man stood with his legs apart, ready to strike. He gestured at Akhila's pouch, but Thimma shook his head and said, tapping his walking stick on the road, 'Sir, surrender. You have broken the law. And you are facing Bhoomipathi Thimma.'

In answer the man threw his spear at Thimma. It whooshed towards the old man, but Thimma did not bat an eyelid. It missed him by a whisker and got buried into the wall behind him. Everything had happened so fast that Sivagami was not sure whether the assailant had missed him or Thimma had moved out of the way of harm.

Cursing, the man took out his sword from his scabbard and rushed towards Thimma. Both the girls screamed in terror. Sivagami saw Thimma twisting his body to reach the spear lodged in the wall. She knew it was futile. Old Thimma stood no chance against such a savage warrior.

The next thing Sivagami saw was the assaulter being lifted and slammed against the side wall. Pinned upside down to the wall, his head dangled six feet from ground. The blunt end of the spear protruded from his belly. He was speared to the brick wall and hung like a pig on a stake. His sword fell down with a clang as he flailed his limbs, coughed up and spat blood, and died.

Sivagami watched, her mouth agape. Never in her dreams had she imagined her old Uncle Thimma to possess such agility and strength. Akhila was jumping up and down in joy and ran to her father. Thimma hugged her and came up to Sivagami. His limp and slow gait was back. Sivagami stood before him awkwardly. She had a hundred questions, but she was too overwhelmed to ask them.

'Child, even an old father like me will find strength to do anything if he has to save his children,' he said with a smile. Sivagami's eyes filled with tears. She rushed into his arms and buried her head in his chest. He ran his fingers through her hair and said, 'These are bad streets, child. And these are bad times. Let what you saw here remain with you.'

Together they walked to the chariot. As they were climbing in, old Thimma squeezed Sivagami's shoulders and said, 'You are as much my daughter as you are Devaraya's. Sivagami, never, ever, run away from what you need to face. Always remember that, whatever I do, I keep your good in mind.'

Sivagami nodded and he kissed her forehead. The chariot started on its way. Akhila prattled on beside her, jingling her stones. Sivagami did not hear what the little girl was saying. Thimma was driving the chariot. So far, he had held the reins of her life. She was grown up now. She wished she could have remained a little girl like Akhila. A feeling of immense sadness for what she was leaving behind, and immeasurable love for Thimma, made her blurry-eyed with tears. She hugged Akhila close and shut her eyes tight, struggling to keep the tears from running down her cheeks, savouring the pain of memories, every moment of it.

A new life was about to begin for Sivagami.

SIX

Kattappa

'The next time you think of doing something stupid, remember this,' Malayappa said as he slapped Shivappa across his face. Kattappa stood motionless, staring at the shadow around his toes. The sun was a blazing hot ball over their heads.

'But *he* challenged me.' Kattappa winced at the shrillness of his brother's voice. Shivappa was right, but he was wrong too. He was more wrong than right. Father knew better.

'You forgot your position,' Malayappa said.

'He should not have challenged a slave boy to fence with the prince,' Shivappa said, angry tears streaming from his eyes.

'You are supposed to lose, idiot.' His father slapped him again.

'General Hiranya thought I would lose, but I didn't.'

Another stinging slap.

'You cannot hit me for winning,' Shivappa cried with indignation. There was a moment of tense silence. When Kattappa raised his head, he was horrified by what he saw.

His younger brother had caught hold of his father's hand and they stood like a tableau, father and son, glaring at each other. When Shivappa's eyes met those of Kattappa, he let go of his grip. Their father stormed away with heavy steps, looking ahead. Kattappa saw his eyes were smoking with rage.

'Nanna,' Kattappa called, but his father passed him by without bothering to look at him.

'Anna, I…' Shivappa's voice cracked. Kattappa raised his hand to stop his brother. He stood with his eyes closed. The tension between his father and brother was increasing every day and he was often caught in the middle. It worried Kattappa that his brother denied having purposely let loose the elephant on the princes that day. His brother's increasingly strange behaviour was making him nervous.

'Anna, it was General Hiranya who asked me to duel with Prince Mahadeva. Is it my fault that I won?'

Kattappa turned towards his brother and took a deep breath. 'That does not mean you have to play so hard. You know about Prince Mahadeva, that he—'

'Is a coward,' Shivappa laughed. 'They all are. They are cowards who act brave because we allow them to. They act important because we, in our minds, think we are inferior. Just because the colour of our skin is black and they are a shade fairer.'

'Shut up,' Kattappa said. He knew where this was leading. He was scared that if he listened to Shivappa, he would soon start thinking like him. Maybe his father was afraid of the same thing too. He heaved the bundle of short-swords and whip-swords onto his shoulders and started downhill. Shivappa ran to keep up with him.

'How long will we be slaves? There are free men in other countries. You pay a share of the produce and the king leaves you to lead your life. Or there are free men and women in the forest who bow to no king.'

'But die young in the gallows or get trampled under the king's elephant,' Kattappa said between breaths.

'As if no one has been killed on the maharaja's orders here. Every bhoomipathi is a law unto himself. Like weeds after the rains, noble men are sprouting in every village. Anyone with a horse and a kitchen knife is calling himself "Mahavira". The king is selling posts for some money and a song. And among small folk, no maiden is safe and no man is free. Dogs lead a better life.'

'Keep talking like this and soon you will find yourself headless. No wonder Nanna is worried about you.'

'He should be worried about his own head. How many of our forefathers have died in their own beds,' Shivappa spat.

Kattappa had no answer. He had grown up on tales of his forefathers dying for the kings of Mahishmathi. The tales were as old as those of the first king, three hundred years ago. He had heard tales that when his people, eighteen generations before him, were free men, they called themselves the sons of Gauriparvat.

'Why don't you help me with this load?' Kattappa asked.

'Anna, for you, I will do it. I do not relish carrying other people's burdens,' Shivappa said as he lifted a bundle onto his head.

As they walked on, Shivappa asked yet again, 'Anna, why are we slaves?'

'That is our fate,' Kattappa mumbled.

'Why can't we change our fate?'

'Shivappa, I am getting scared of these thoughts. You will break Nanna's heart. He thinks you have a bright future.' Kattappa eyed his brother. He did not like the derisive smile on his brother's lips.

'Future? Do slaves have a future, Anna? Carrying some prince's chamber pot is called future? Standing mute when they rape some farmer's daughter and handing over a towel to wipe their seed is called future? Burying their sins is called future? Dying a cattle's death is called future? No, thank you. I will create my own future.'

Kattappa was afraid. A few other slaves had been whispering that his brother had strange companions. Shivappa was too young to talk like this. When Kattappa had been his age, he had never even dared to think beyond what his father told him. A slave is not supposed to think, his father used to say. A slave is supposed to serve. And die for his master, if need be.

They had reached the back door of the armoury. Kattappa had to hurry to Bijjala's chamber after they had deposited the cache of weapons.

'Anna, just hold this,' Shivappa said, and without waiting for Kattappa to take the bundle, dropped it. The swords clanged loudly as the bundle hit the ground and the sound woke up the sleeping clerk who accounted the armoury inventory. He yawned and gave the slave boys a bored look.

'I will take your leave now,' said Shivappa.

Before Kattappa could react, he had vanished.

Kattappa looked around frantically. At some distance, he could see a young girl sweeping the floor. Blood rushed to his face. Their father had warned Shivappa many times not to talk to that girl. The next time his father whipped his brother, Kattappa vowed to himself, he would remain quiet. No one deserved whipping more than his devilish brother.

'Heard your brother punched the younger prince's nose?' the clerk asked as he counted the swords and made an entry on a palm leaf.

'It...it was an accident,' Kattappa stuttered. He was distracted by what was transpiring in the courtyard between his brother and that girl. The clerk's gaze followed Kattappa's and he chuckled.

'That brother of yours is a smart one. In fact, too smart for his own good,' said the old clerk, poking his ear with his little finger.

'Does he come here often, swami?' Kattappa asked, clenching his fist. He was itching to go and drag his brother home.

'They are often seen together. Everyone is gossiping—a slave boy and a girl of noble blood.' The clerk opened the bundle on the floor and started taking out the swords to hang them on the wall.

'She is a bastard child, swami,' Kattappa said, covering his mouth with his palm lest his breath pollute the clerk.

'Ah, but whose bastard? Bhoomipathi Pattaraya's brother's bastard. Krishna, Krishna, I can't imagine how the bhoomipathi would react when he finds out about this,' the clerk said, hanging the last sword on the wall and washing his hands. He had to do it ritualistically, as he had touched the same sword as Kattappa. *The clerk would also go home and take a bath for the same sin before starting to beat his wife,* Kattappa thought. Hell, Shivappa's words had already infected his thoughts.

'Swami, if the bhoomipathi had cared, she would not have been living in the orphanage and sweeping floors,' Kattappa said. His brother was holding the girl's hand and, even from such a distance, he could see the girl blush.

'Boy, blood is blood. Money has nothing to do with it. With the girl's father dead, Bhoomipathi Pattaraya might have thought the royal orphanage to be a better place for her to grow up. But when it comes to blood…hmm…but who could fault your brother. Have you seen the girl's breasts? Like budding mangoes!' The old man leered at the girl, young enough to be his granddaughter.

'Do you know her name, slave boy? Ah! Kamakshi, the lusty-eyed! Seventeen years of age and, every inch of her body oozes…Rama, Rama, why should I talk about all this in my old age. Now, your brother is one smart guy for a slave boy, but God has given him such a short life.'

Kattappa's fist curled in fury. He wanted to bang the clerk's head on the wall for talking ill of his brother. His father's disapproving face swam before his eyes. He was not intelligent like Shivappa, but he prided himself on being obedient and disciplined. He kept his cool, bowed low to the clerk and came out of the armoury compound. His brother was still standing with his lover, taking his time to say goodbye.

Kattappa was getting late and was thus nervous. But he had to give a piece of his mind to his brother before he left. He waited by the gate, clasping and unclasping his hands behind his back and pacing across the breadth of the narrow path. From the pathashala across the street, Brahmin boys were chanting the Vedas in a sing-song voice, and he tried to make sense of their words. Something to keep his fury in check. Finally, by the time Shivappa emerged, the shadows had started growing longer and the western breeze had picked up strength. Shivappa looked smug and happy and his mouth fell open when he spotted Kattappa waiting for him.

'Anna, don't you have work? Like massaging the feet of that drunkard prince?' Shivappa asked with a half-smile. Kattappa ignored the insult. Shivappa nervously glanced back to see whether Kamakshi had gone.

'Nanna has warned you before,' Kattappa said.

Shivappa looked down and whispered, 'I love her.'

Kattappa had heard this many times.

'And what is that going to achieve?'

'I am going to marry her soon,' Shivappa said, and the tone of defiance sent a chill down Kattappa's heart. The boy meant it.

'Wake up, Shivappa! You can't,' he said, shaking Shivappa's shoulders.

'Why not?' Shivappa pushed away his hand and took a few steps back.

'Because…because the king decides who we marry and when and if…'

'No king is going to decide my life. I am going to marry her.'

'You are too young to marry.'

'I am old enough to give her a child. That is enough.'

Kattappa slapped him across his face. Shivappa's face betrayed more shock than pain. He had never seen his brother get angry.

'The next time you talk about a woman with disrespect, I will not hesitate to pluck your tongue out.' Kattappa trembled with rage.

His brother turned his face away. He said, 'I…I didn't mean anything. It was just…' For a moment, Kattappa saw a trace of guilt flashing across his brother's face, but soon his usual belligerence took over.

'Why can't you understand that I love her? Why are you acting so high and mighty? This is the first time I have known love. All I heard before this was discipline, duty, rules…I am fed up. You cannot control me anymore. You do not decide what I do and what I don't. Why should I remain a slave always?'

Kattappa started walking away without bothering to answer, but Shivappa caught his wrist. 'You cannot go away without answering me.'

'I have no answers. Nor do I allow dangerous questions to trouble my mind. Get lost. I don't care what you do,' Kattappa said, raising his voice. The brothers glared at each other.

The evening breeze changed direction and dry leaves showered down on them. Kattappa heard the creak of the armoury gate being shut and soon the clerk was on his way out. When the old man saw Shivappa, he clucked his tongue and passed a lewd comment. Shivappa's eyes flashed with anger. Kattappa glared at him and his brother's shoulders eased.

They waited till the old clerk had gone on his way, humming a bawdy song about some whore who bedded an elephant, a horse, a bull and twenty men together.

Kattappa turned on his heel and started walking. His palm still stung and he was sorry he had hit his younger brother so hard.

'I am sorry, Anna,' Kattappa heard Shivappa's soft voice from behind and he stopped. His brother hugged him. He felt his brother's tears on his shoulder.

'Everything we own, the sword we hold, the cloth we wear, even our lives, belong to our masters. We have nothing other than our honour, Shiva. Would you spoil it by such acts, brother?' Kattappa's voice was hoarse.

'But even noblemen talk about women in that way,' his brother said between his sobs. Kattappa smiled. His brother sounded like a child. Was this the same boy who was prepared to marry a noble girl?

'All the more reason to not talk like that, Shiva. How would you feel if someone talks ill of our mother?' Kattappa said softly.

'Our mother is dead,' his brother said and Kattappa stiffened. His eyes misted up and he bit his lips. He should not have brought up their mother. His brother was yet to get over the shock, as was Kattappa.

A bullock cart jingled past them, swaying from side to side. The bulls were running at a fair speed, yet the cart driver kept cracking his whip on their backs.

'You see those bulls, brother? We are like that. We will pull the carts of our masters until our legs give way,' Kattappa said. The jingle of the cart faded away.

'And when our legs fail, they will butcher us.' The rage was back in Shivappa's voice, making his brother uneasy.

'Yes, even in death we should be useful. As food, as hide for the master's shoes, as scabbard for the master's swords. How meaningful is the draught bull's life,' Kattappa said.

His brother moved away from him.

'I am not ready to be anyone's cattle,' Shivappa said. Before Kattappa could react, his brother had jumped into the paddy field. He was standing ankle-deep in mud, almost hidden by paddy plants. Kattappa leaned forward to lend him a hand to climb back onto the road.

'Shivappa, brother…'

'No, enough. You will spoil me too. I am leaving,' Shivappa said. In the blink of an eye, he had vanished behind the plants.

'Where are you going? You can't just walk away, Shiva. Oh, what will I say to father?' Kattappa cried, stepping into the field. There was not a trace of his brother. Shivappa knew his way around. He must have planned it all. Kattappa found his anger rising again. His brother had made a fool of him.

'Shiva, stop. There are cobras in the field,' Kattappa called out.

'None as poisonous as some humans,' came his brother's reply.

'Where are you going?' Kattappa screamed, trying to assess his brother's path from the movement of paddy plants.

'To freedom.' His brother's voice fell like a heavy hammer on his head.

Kattappa cursed. The sun was setting and the field was like the sea, with waves upon waves of golden harvest. There was no trace of his brother.

Kattappa did not know what he would say to his father. How was he going to tell him that Shivappa had deserted? He knew what they did to a slave who ran away. Soon the ferocious dogs of General Hiranya would be hunting him. Dandakaras would be roaming around with the maharaja's orders to hang the deserter from the nearest tree. There would be a ransom on his head, and soon entire villages would be hunting for his brother. Kattappa's legs felt weak. He stumbled as he climbed up to the road. He started running towards the palace. The sun was a ball of fire in the western horizon, and night was creeping up from the east. He had to meet his father and somehow they had to bring his brother back.

Before it was too late.

SEVEN

Sivagami

Mahapradhana Parameswara stood before the king of Mahishmathi with a bowed head. Roopaka stood behind him like a shadow.

'This is serious, Mahapradhana. For a week you were unable to trace the slave who ran away with the stones, and now you report to me that he has been found dead along with another man. And you have no clue where the stones have gone. We are disappointed.'

Parameswara wished this conversation was happening in private, not in front of his deputy, and definitely not in front of the slave Malayappa who stood behind the king. He trusted Roopaka, but Malayappa was a slave after all. Though he and his forefathers had lived and died for Mahishmathi kings for many generations, Parameswara could never trust a slave. He always assumed slaves had to be seething inside, waiting for a chance to get back at their masters at the first opportune moment.

'The borders have been sealed, Your Majesty. All trade vessels, ships, boats, carts and caravans are being checked. The stones have not left Mahishmathi,' Parameswara said, not lifting his eyes to look at the maharaja.

'How is the supply? Will we last till Mahamakam?' Maharaja Somadeva asked.

'Six months to go for the festival. It will be difficult, but we will manage, provided we get the stones by that time. I hope Bhoomipathi Thimma is up to the task,' Parameswara said.

'Bhoomipathi Thimma may be old and frail, but he is loyal and trustworthy.'

'I have my doubts,' Roopaka spoke from behind.

'Really? And why is that?' Somadeva snapped.

It was Parameswara who answered. 'He has come with an appeal to admit Devaraya's daughter to the royal orphanage. Why should he do that unless he wants to flee the country? I doubt whether he will be able to bring himself to do the distasteful task at Gauriparvat once the Mahamakam is over. He was so close to Devaraya.'

Maharaja stared at a flickering lamp for some time. The only sound was that of the fan being whisked over his head by a slave.

'We too wish it to be stopped, but we have no choice. Ma Gauri is not being kind. She is hiding the stones deeper in her belly,' Somadeva said. His words hung heavily in the room, accentuating the silence that followed.

'It is all for the progress of Mahishmathi,' Parameswara said, dismayed at the lack of conviction in his voice. Could Devaraya have been right after all?

'Keep a watch on Thimma,' the maharaja said.

'He is outside, Your Majesty. He wants an audience,' Parameswara said.

Maharaja Somadeva sighed. 'Send him in, Mahapradhana. We can spare a few nimishas for an old official.'

Sivagami was waiting outside the royal chamber. Akhila sat on the floor, playing with her pebbles. Thimma impatiently paced the corridor right outside the royal chamber. Suddenly, a young, dark slave came running and stood panting near the entrance. The guards outside asked him to move away and he said something to them. They pointed to the far end of the corridor and he walked away, dejected. Sivagami watched the slave—there was something arresting about him.

The door to the royal chamber opened suddenly and they were ushered in. Akhila was asked to wait outside. Parameswara, who was on his way out, bowed to Thimma as he walked towards his office. Roopaka came out and enquired about Thimma's health, touching the older man's feet in respect before making his way out.

Sivagami stepped into a luxurious room with a high ceiling. The king sat on a dewan. A slave stood behind him. The king had grown old since she had seen him on that eventful night. Memories assaulted her and heat rushed through her body. Her nostrils flared. This man had ordered her father's execution and here she was before him with a begging bowl. Destiny was playing cruel tricks on her.

'Prabhu, Prabhu.'

Uncle Thimma's servile stance in front of the king disgusted her. The old man was bent over, his angavastra tied at his waist, as he stood with his head bowed and hands folded in supplication.

'Yes, Thimma,' Maharaja Somadeva smiled as he stood up. He was getting ready to retire for the day. They were not going to get much time. The king's smile did not do much to conceal his impatience.

'Your Majesty, may goddess Gauri shower her blessings on you and Mahishmathi empire always. I have a humble appeal to make.'

'Proceed.'

Thimma gestured to Sivagami to approach them. With heavy steps, the girl walked towards the man who had ordered her father's execution.

Thimma whispered to her to bow, and Sivagami made a half-hearted show of touching the king's feet. If the king noticed her reluctance, he did not show it.

'Your Majesty, this is Devaraya's daughter, Sivagami.'

The king placed his huge palm over her head in blessing, and Sivagami felt a wave of repulsion passing through her. No, she did not want him to touch her, this evil man.

'Your Majesty, it is about her that I wish to speak,' Thimma said. The king had started walking now and Thimma hurried behind him. 'In your infinite kindness, please allow her to stay in the royal orphanage. The girl is bright.'

'No doubt. She would have inherited her father's qualities.' The king stared at her and Thimma faltered.

'She is yet a child. She can be moulded, Your Majesty.'

The king laughed. 'Of course, my old Thimma thinks if we feed her royal milk, Takshaka's daughter will turn out to be an apsara instead of a snake.'

'Your Majesty, some stale kanji and a roof over her head is the only thing I ask. She will be one among the thousands of servants that Your Majesty feeds. My wife does not like her. I tried to keep her at my home. She is a good girl. And she is too young for—'

'She is almost a woman, Thimma. What is the guarantee that she will not turn into another Devaraya?'

'Swami, Devaraya's family served Mahishmathi for generations.'

'Are you trying to say that we have been ungrateful, Thimma? Have we not spared her life?'

'Your kindness knows no bounds, it is as vast as the Ksheersagara, Your Majesty.'

'Spare your breath, Thimma.'

'A little space…just until she is eighteen. A few more months…that is all I ask for.'

'Thimma. When an old faithful like you asks for something, it is difficult for us to refuse, even though we know we may regret this later.' He turned to his slave and extended his hands. Malayappa handed him a palm leaf and a stencil. The king scribbled something and pressed his royal insignia to it.

'Here, take this to Roopaka. He will take care of the rest. Remember, only till she is eighteen. If she misbehaves or shows any of her father's traits, she will follow her father.'

'You are an ocean of kindness, Maharaja.' Thimma prostrated on the floor. The king dismissed them with a wave of his hand. The slave started arranging the king's ornaments.

When they emerged outside, Akhila ran to Sivagami and hugged her. She was going to miss this little darling the most, Sivagami thought. Thimma stood staring at the fountain, clutching the official order from the king in his hands.

The announcer declared that the king was retiring to his Antapura. The guards became alert. The massive doors creaked open and Somadeva stepped out. Thimma bowed, but Sivagami stood with her head held high. The king's eyes flashed when he saw her standing upright. Reluctantly she bowed and he looked ahead.

A well-built man with shoulders like an ox came towards the king and bowed stiffly before him. Behind him, a handsome young man, perhaps of her age, cowered.

'Yes, Senapathi Hiranya?' the king asked as the man rose from his knees.

The man said, 'Your Majesty, Prince Mahadeva's progress is not very satisfactory. He was beaten by the slave's son. He is not improving in his training.'

The prince kept looking at his toes. The king said, 'Mahadeva?'

'I am sorry, Father,' the prince mumbled. The king stared at the boy for a moment and then made to move ahead.

The senapathi bowed and asked, 'Your Majesty, what is to be done?'

'Train him better,' the king said as he patted the boy's shoulders and walked away. Senapathi Hiranya stood speechless, watching the cortege move away.

Sivagami saw the prince's face lighting up with a smile. She noticed how handsome he was, but reminded herself that he was the son of the enemy. Unexpectedly he raised his head and their eyes met. Sivagami was surprised to see him blush. She turned her head quickly, ashamed that she too had blushed.

She heard Thimma call her and hurried away. When she looked back, the prince was still standing there, staring at her.

EIGHT

Kattappa

Kattappa had rushed to the palace as fast as his legs could carry him. He wanted to tell his father about Shivappa running away but it was impossible with the maharaja present. The guards would not even allow him to meet his father. He waited in the garden to see whether he would get a chance to speak to his father before it was too late.

Kattappa wondered how he would break the news to his father. He knew his father loved Shivappa more than him. There was a time when he had been jealous of that. But at twenty-two, Kattappa had grown used to the fact that his was not a lovable face. Nor did he have any special quality. He had already started balding and, before long, he would have to shave his head clean like his father.

But his brother…his brother had a dazzling smile.

The thought of Shivappa brought him back to the present. He had to find a way to get the boy back into the fold. He tried to catch his father's eye, but his father glowered back from the king's entourage and even from a distance his expression said it all. Kattappa was not to linger and waste his time. His place was with his master. With a heavy heart and heavier steps, he walked to Bijjala's chambers.

Kattappa was worried whether Bijjala would even want him now. Bijjala had asked him not to show his face after Prince Mahadeva was injured by Shivappa. His father always said that words of masters spoken in anger were not to be taken seriously. If the master commanded that the slave not show his face, the slave had no right to go away. He dare not come in front of the master, but had to stay at a distance where he could present himself the moment the master changed his mind.

When he reached the chamber of Bijjala, he saw that the door was closed and stood outside. He was not supposed to knock, or make his presence felt in any way. Outside the fort, he could hear the crowd dispersing after the day's durbar. For a moment, he wondered what would happen if his brother's dream of a world without slaves came true. Perhaps he would be one amongst those free folk, waiting for the king's justice outside the durbar. Or he would be a farmer by the valley of Gauriparvat, with a wife and children. He tried to imagine the face of his wife. Would she be as beautiful as Kamakshi, his brother's lover?

The thought was pleasurable, and made him strangely uneasy. He felt wicked and guilty. Not for him such thoughts, he chided himself. *Amma Gauri, let my thoughts not wander*, he prayed, and again worry about his brother rushed in. Was it better to think wicked thoughts, thoughts of freedom? *It was better not to think at all*, his father's voice said. He took a deep breath, drew back his shoulders and straightened his spine. Delicious aromas wafted through the crack of Bijjala's door, and he felt hungry. He stood like a statue, his dreams frozen, his taste buds numb, and his sense of smell plugged.

'Hey ugly, where is your handsome brother?'

Kattappa knew that voice; it belonged to the last person he wanted to see. What was this eunuch doing here? She was one among many that Kalika had employed, but other than Brihannala, he had rarely seen other eunuchs inside the Mahishmathi palace.

He stood straight, looking far ahead, acting as if Keki did not exist. He could hear the sound of her anklets jingling as she walked. She was coming towards him. There was a rhythm to her walk. When the jingling stopped, Kattappa drew his breath. She was so near him that he could smell her. He winced when a hand with colourful bangles rested on his shoulder. Fingers traced a path to his chin and moved towards his ears. Kattappa tried his best to remain impassive.

'Oh, my lover is angry with me,' Keki coyly fluttered her eyelashes and smiled. She had lovely eyes, with thick curved lashes, a permanent blush on her soft cheeks, and pouty lips. At first sight, she looked like a lovely woman. Only her gruff voice gave away that she was a eunuch. Kattappa's heartbeat increased. The smell of her perfume was sickening. She caressed his face and her bangles jingled. Kattappa stood with his hands crossed behind his back, not looking at her face, not even acknowledging her presence, but blocking her way to the chamber of Bijjala.

'Shall I...hmmm...pleasure you, Manmatha? Oh, you look so delicious, just like the god of love,' she said in a husky voice, as her fingers played with the knot of his dhoti. Kattappa tried to push her hands away, but she caught his hand and kissed it. He pulled back in alarm. She whispered in his ears and blood rushed to Kattappa's face, making it darker. He cursed the effect Keki was having on him.

'My lover boy, you'll have to wait. I have to meet the prince. Be a sweetheart, Kamadeva, and let this Rati in to meet your prince,' she said, trying to dodge past him. Kattappa's arms shot out to block her path. His hand brushed against her breast and she let out a dramatic sigh. She pouted her lips, fluttered her eyelashes and said, 'Handsome, why are you standing in my way?'

Kattappa tried to pull back his hand but she wouldn't let go. He felt his skin was burning where it had made contact with her breasts. She was as tall as him and as strong. Kattappa managed to free his hand at last and saw that her nails had made white marks on his dark skin.

'Shall I give you a present?' she huskily whispered. Her hand disappeared inside her breast-band. Kattappa was scared that someone would see them. This could become a scandal and he would become the laughing stock amongst other slaves. Whatever he did, he was doomed. All of a sudden, the door opened and Kattappa hurried to kneel before the prince. His face burned with shame. He did not want to look at Bijjala.

He winced when he heard Keki say, 'Your slave has an unfortunate face but a body of forged steel, Prince. Why don't you send him to my place? He looks so delicious.' Keki ran her tongue over her lips.

Bijjala laughed, adding to Kattappa's discomfort. Keki squeezed Kattappa's shoulder, and as she moved away, she ran the end of her silk shawl over Kattappa's face.

'You look handsome,' Keki said, admiring Bijjala, who blushed red. Keki adjusted the pearl necklace on his neck.

'Everyone is waiting for you, Prince,' Keki said as she turned and started walking, her hips swaying sensuously. As she passed, she leaned to brush her lips on Kattappa's cheeks. Before the slave could react she had moved away.

Bijjala hurried to catch up with her. 'We have to rush,' the prince said excitedly. Kattappa did not know whether to follow them or not. His duty was to be with the prince. After a moment's hesitation, Kattappa walked with his hand on his sword's hilt, following them with soft steps, looking straight ahead.

Prince Bijjala was dressed in his finest clothes. A sharp smell of perfume lingered in the air as he walked, chatting animatedly with Keki. Kattappa kept a respectable distance. When they were going down the spiral staircase, they came face-to-face with Prince Mahadeva.

'Where are you off to, Bijjala?' Mahadeva asked in surprise.

'None of your business,' Bijjala pushed him away and continued walking.

'But Mother is looking for you.'

'Get lost.'

Bijjala and Keki turned the corner. Mahadeva caught Kattappa's wrist and the slave turned around in shock. Fortunately, no one was there to see it. He was not supposed to touch a prince, unless it was to save their life. 'Will you tell me where they are going?' Mahadeva asked.

Kattappa continued to look at the invisible point far ahead. Mahadeva impatiently huffed, left him and ran up the wooden stairs. His heavy steps faded away and Kattappa resumed his pursuit of his master. Bijjala and Keki had reached the farthest end of the pillared corridor. Kattappa hurried to catch up with them. On either side of him huge stone dragons with their tails in their mouths rose twenty feet above him. Their eyes seemed to watch the slave as he ran on the chequered floors.

'Does this monkey have to come with us, my lord?' Keki asked with some displeasure.

'Who cares if a dog follows? We can keep him at the gate to bark when required,' Bijjala laughed.

'We have to be careful about Skandadasa's moles, my lord. If the maharaja got a whiff of where I am taking you…' Keki trailed off.

'As if my father was always an old man. Even at this age, he has no qualms being pleasured by Kalika's devadasis. Have I not heard enough bawdy songs about my father's exploits,' Bijjala laughed. 'I only hope my mother does not find out.'

'And if the maharani does?'

'I will say you compelled me to go,' Bijjala replied. Keki's face went white, but she recovered quickly. 'Of course, my lord, of course. The blame can always be put on this beautiful woman's shoulders. Anything for you, my prince.' Keki ran her fingers over Bijjala's shoulders.

'Keep your hands away from me,' Bijjala snapped, 'and take me to where you had promised.'

'We have to be quick and should return before we are missed,' Keki said and opened a door that led to the western garden near the palace. 'This way, my lord.'

They circled the harem of the maharaja and reached its rear door. By this time, Bijjala was sweating. 'Don't worry, my lord. The maharaja will be leaving soon with Senapathi Hiranya to Kuntala Rajya and will be back only in a fortnight,' Keki said.

'I know that. But why are we here?' Bijjala asked.

In answer, Keki scratched the door with her nails. Someone opened it and they entered. A woman was dancing in front of a man reclining on a dewan.

'Ah, Brihannala, is everything ready?' Keki asked. The woman turned with a dazzling smile. *Yet another eunuch*, Kattappa winced. Bijjala's face flushed red with anger.

'This is the head of Antapura and not the apsaras. Why have you brought me here, bloody eunuch?' Bijjala bristled with rage.

Before Keki could answer, Brihannala stepped forward and bowed gracefully. 'Your Grace, my friend Keki has told me about your need. This Brihannala is always at your service. The arrangements have been made.' She clapped her hands and the man who had been reclining on the dewan went inside. After a few moments of tense silence, a maid returned with a huge plate on which a merchant's dress was neatly folded. 'You will look dashing in this, my prince,' said Keki, smoothing invisible creases on the garment.

'This is what stinking merchants wear. I am the prince of Mahishmathi, and you expect me to wear this?' Bijjala roared.

'Necessary for discretion, my prince, or do you want everyone to be gossiping about you secret visit?' Brihannala said, keeping her hands over her chest and bowing deep.

'Or perhaps you want to do this once you're twenty-one? Wait a few more months? No one can question you then, not even the queen,' Keki laughed.

For a moment, it seemed to Kattappa that Bijjala would throw this creature out and rush back to his chamber in a rage. He would have preferred nothing better. However, Bijjala snatched the clothes and went behind a pillar. Keki smiled. 'Embarrassed to show us your handsome body, my prince? You are tempting me.'

Bijjala answered with an expletive and Keki laughed. 'That is too colourful for a prince. Princes should only use Devabhasha and not the language of poor people like us. But in case you are interested, we can pick up a few more colourful ones at Keki's place.'

Bijjala emerged, awkward in the merchant's clothes. He took off his pearl necklace and gold bangles and was about to hand them over to Kattappa, when Keki snatched them. 'Oh thank you, my lord. You are so generous.'

She quickly whistled and four men came with a palanquin. She gestured them to get in.

'Am I an old maid to get into this, you miserable eunuch?' Bijjala demanded.

'You want to parade through the streets on an elephant? How about riding along with a drummer to announce your arrival at Kalika's den? That would be very discreet, wouldn't it?'

Bijjala glared at her and then reluctantly got in.

'My lord, your sword will be too conspicuous. My men will hold it.'

'Forget about it. No one is going to see me. I am travelling like my grandmother. A sari is the only thing I lack now,' Bijjala muttered.

'You would have looked gorgeous in a sari and I swear that would have made a better camouflage. Next time, I will arrange that. Your sword please, or we can do this after two years.'

'You will pay for your tongue, eunuch,' Bijjala said, handing over his sword.

'I make a living with my tongue, my lord. There are many I have pleasured with it in this city, including names you don't want to hear. Spare the tongue and spoil the finger, is what we say in Kalika's den. You didn't get the joke? Maybe after a few months? Now move a bit so that your slave can get in.'

'How dare you! No way is an untouchable slave sitting with me.'

'Putting a big board on the palanquin saying this carries Bijjala, the first prince of Mahishmathi, on his way to whoring, would be a better idea than your slave walking along beside it,' Keki said wryly. Kattappa wondered how this eunuch could be so audacious with the prince.

Brihannala intervened. 'My lord, we must stay true to your disguise. You are a merchant on his way out of the harem after selling his wares to the women. We must not invite attention,' she said soothingly.

'But won't they check at the gates? That bloody Skandadasa's men shadow me everywhere.'

'Skandadasa is worried about your safety, my lord. After the incident with the elephant, the maharaja has ordered that you should be guarded at all times. Skandadasa is just doing his duty. But don't worry. Even he won't get a whiff of this,' Brihannala said. Keki rolled her eyes.

'But they will find out at the gates. They check everyone going in and out,' Bijjala stressed.

'You are right, my prince. They will check the palanquin at the gate,' Brihannala said. 'But we have a way to beat them. You are simply to play your part in the plan and all shall be smooth. Your Highness has to kindly allow your slave to sit with you. He will be too conspicuous otherwise.' Brihannala's soft words were reassuring.

Bijjala stared at Kattappa with distaste. Brihannala folded her hands, pleading. Bijjala nodded and looked away.

'Your Highness is too kind,' Brihannala bowed.

'Now, get into the palanquin, my groom,' Keki said, caressing Kattappa's cheek.

Kattappa was horrified that he had to sit in the same palanquin as his prince. What would his father say? He hesitated, holding the hilt of his sword firm in his hands.

Keki pouted. 'Is my heart of hearts angry with me? Can I make up with a kiss on your dark lips, yes? No? Oh you break my heart. If you don't get in before I count to three, I am going to kiss you full on your lips. And your master will be jealous that I am kissing his slave instead of him. Do you want to make your master angry, darling?'

Kattappa did not wait to hear anymore. He tried getting in, but his sword was in his way. Keki extended her hand for his sword.

Kattappa addressed the prince in panic. 'My lord, this sword is holy, handed over by the maharaja himself. I am not supposed to part with it until my death.'

'Let us leave this black monkey here. Let him sit here and chew his sword.' Keki spat a stream of betel juice and tried to get into the palanquin. Kattappa blocked her way in and Keki snarled, 'Move out of my way.'

'The prince is not going anywhere without me,' Kattappa said.

'Says who?' Bijjala cried from inside.

'Apologies, my lord, but that is the order of Maharaja Somadeva.'

'You see the pond there in the garden? Why don't you jump into it? Prince, why do you care about what a slave has to say?' Keki asked.

'Because he will go and tell my father. He is a mill around my neck.' Gritting his teeth, Bijjala snapped at Kattappa, 'Why can't you hand over your bloody sword and get in without wasting time, you son of a bitch.'

'I am sorry, my lord. I will only part with this sword when I die.'

Keki sighed. 'Let him keep his sword. Move a bit, unless you want his black ass resting on your lap.'

'Not near me. Keki, you sit between us.'

'And let the world see a slave travelling in a palanquin. That would be a great sight. All the urchins of the city and their uncles would crowd to see that.' Keki caught Kattappa's wrist and said, 'Get in.'

Kattappa waited for Bijjala's order but the prince looked away. Kattappa said a silent prayer. He was breaking all rules. He squeezed himself in, taking care not to touch the prince's body. He placed his sword between them.

Keki got in last and leaned over to draw the curtain on Bijjala's side. Her breasts brushed against Kattappa's face and when he winced, she winked and blew him a kiss. Kattappa recoiled in distaste. The palanquin rose with a jerk, swaying as the carriers adjusted the weight and started moving. They cried, 'Ho-ho, ho-ho-ho,' with each step and the front pair jingled a bell to make people give way.

They were stopped at the fort gate of the palace and Keki jumped down from the palanquin to deal with the guards. Kattappa could hear her say that she was taking the merchant to Kalika's den. He prayed that the guards would not bother to check the inside of the palanquin. Bijjala was sweating near him.

Kattappa saw Keki joking with the guards. He saw money changing hands and wondered how easy it was to smuggle someone out of the palace. If it was easy to smuggle someone out of the fort, it would be equally easy to smuggle an enemy in. Corruption was corroding the safety of his city too. He decided he would speak to his father and somehow bring this to the notice of the maharaja.

Keki jumped back in and the palanquin soon crossed the fort gate and moved fast through the streets. It was stuffy and humid inside. The body odour of the eunuch mixed with the perfume of Bijjala nauseated Kattappa. The eunuch's shoulders brushed against his but there was nothing he could do. He had a gnawing feeling in his mind that this journey would lead to great peril. He closed his eyes in prayer and gripped his sword tight.

NINE

Brihannala

Brihannala waited until the palanquin carrying Prince Bijjala had left the fort gate. It had grown dark. There was dampness in the air. Lightning split the eastern sky. A breeze played with her sari and lustrous hair. *It would be perfect,* she thought. She smiled at the benevolence of the gods. She went back to the Antapura.

Servants were lighting lamps inside. Her disciples had started singing. The sound of anklets came from the top floor. Soon the Antapura would reverberate with melodious songs. Flautists and veena players had started arriving. Since the maharaja was away, the concerts and performances would not be elaborate. Still, there were state guests, important traders and diplomats who had to be entertained.

Brihannala bustled in and shouted instructions in all directions. Some of her girls called out to her from the top floor. They asked her to come up and dance with them. She told them she would change into her evening finery and join them.

She entered her private chamber. A man sat there in his undergarments. He stood up when she came inside. Brihannala locked the door.

She removed her blouse and skirt and stood before the mirror naked except for a loincloth. She was no longer a eunuch but a man.

'How long will this go on, Dhananjaya?' the man asked.

'As long as it takes to achieve our dream, Nala,' Brihannala said, and added, leaning towards the merchant, 'I had warned you before, too, brother. That you should not call me anything other than Brihannala.'

'Sorry.'

Brihannala flexed his muscles and removed a sword that was hanging on the wall. He started practising his moves with it, as dexterously as a trained warrior. Gone was the feminine charm, and in its place was the grit of a fighter who was sure of his feet and sword.

'Nala, this was a promise I gave my mother twenty-five years ago. I will be a man again'—he sliced the topmost melon kept on the table into two clean halves with a swing of his sword, without even disturbing the pile—'only after we destroy the heartless state of Mahishmathi.'

'Mother has told me about—' Nala began.

'You are adopted by her, Nala. What she told you would not be even half of what she actually suffered. I lived through the hell. Acting as a eunuch is nothing compared to the difficulties our mother has gone through.'

Nala nodded gravely. 'Be careful, brother.'

Brihannala laughed. 'You be careful. And don't forget, our mother is Achi Nagamma, and we will achieve what we aim for, brother. Now go along with the musicians. Take this mrudanga with you.' He pointed to the drum kept in a corner. 'Make sure that they are ready. Let them wait for the prince on the way back from Kalika's inn. But tell them to be wary of that slave.'

Nala said, 'There will be twenty this time. If required, we will kill the slave.'

Brihannala smiled. 'Godspeed, brother.'

Nala, now dressed in a musician's garb, hugged his brother and went out with the mrudanga. As he opened the door, music from the top floor wafted in and died down when the door was shut again.

Brihannala started wearing her make-up and soon transformed into a dazzling woman. She caressed the edge of the sword before hanging it back. She tied jasmine in her hair and fixed anklets on her feet. She jingled them and smiled.

'*Da tha dhinta*,' she said as she practised her steps and laughed.

She ran upstairs and was greeted by a huge roar of applause. She spread her arms wide and started twirling. Her skirt ballooned around her and swirled. Her girls ran to join her and started spiralling round and round. The sheer energy of the performance inspired the musicians and drummers. Viewers threw money and garlands and the dance gathered momentum.

Today, she was giving her best performance.

TEN

Sivagami

'You are saved,' Thimma told her, clutching the royal palm leaf in his hand. He took her hand and hurried down the corridors, past the milling soldiers, past the guards sitting on the floor playing chaturanga drawn on the granite floor, past kitchens that carried the smell of roasted meat and frying fish. Sivagami could feel the gaze of many eyes on them. Akhila wanted to stop and look at everything, but Thimma hurried them. The stone steps that wound past flowery bushes had started cooling down. The light from the torches lit up the bushes. Sivagami noticed that the palace was huge, with intricate paths and various wings.

They stopped near an old building that had towering mango trees. Moonlight seeped through the canopy and formed chequered patches in the courtyard. There were people standing under these, a few squatting on their haunches near the steps.

Thimma gave the palm leaf to the scribe at the door, who squinted at it and pointed to the next scribe who was squatting on the floor and busily scribbling. Thimma stood before him for some time before he took the palm leaf, read it, and said his supervisor had gone out. The old man and the girl waited. A few of the scribes were putting their stencils and ink pots into the drawers of their slanted writing tables or packing their cloth bags.

Sivagami stood watching the bats that flapped their huge wings and squeaked among the trees. Akhila tried imitating their call and was chided by her father. Thimma was visibly worried and kept enquiring about Roopaka, the deputy of the mahapradhana.

The street lights were being lit by the nagarapalakas when a servant ushered them to the chamber of Roopaka. He sat cross-legged on a reed mat with a massive writing table before him. Oil lamps flickered, giving a golden hue to his plump face. Thimma gave him the royal palm leaf and Roopaka leaned forward to read it. He asked them to wait and went inside a huge hall. Sivagami could hear whispers from within. A moth flew in through an air hole in the thick wall and started circling a torch. It went around the flame in tight circles and Sivagami was sure it was going to dive into the fire soon. Before she could confirm it, they were ushered inside.

Mahapradhana Parameswara reclined on a dewan. His frail frame was propped up with many cushions. A servant was lighting a lamp that was twice as tall as Sivagami. When the seventh wick was lit, Parameswara folded his hands and mumbled a prayer. Thimma followed suit. Sivagami stood, awkward in the cavernous room, eyeing the glass of milk and dry fruits kept on the table.

'Roopaka, read me the royal decree,' Parameswara said in a soft voice, and Roopaka complied.

Parameswara said, looking at Sivagami, 'I doubt if she'd like it there. It is not a happy place to be.'

Thimma did not reply. Parameswara sighed. 'I know there is no other way. I wish I could have done better for her father. He was a good man. But what choice did His Highness have?'

Sivagami's ears bristled. They were talking about her father again. In riddles. Since childhood she had been asking everyone about her father. Apart from the statement that he was a traitor who was hanged, no one cared to say anything else. No one would answer her questions. She knew now that she would have to seek them on her own.

'Can I live with Akka?' Akhila asked suddenly.

Thimma shushed her, but Parameswara called her near him.

'Hmm...What is your name?'

'Akhila,' the girl shyly replied.

'Your youngest one, Thimma?' Parameswara asked as he lifted little Akhila to his lap. Thimma nodded. Parameswara asked the girl, 'Why would you want to do that? Is your father very strict?'

Akhila looked at Thimma and shook her head. She said, 'I just want to be with Akka.' She smiled at Sivagami. Sivagami felt a lump in her throat.

'Would you live without creating trouble?' Parameswara asked her with a kind smile.

'I have never created any trouble, Grandpa,' Akhila blurted out.

'Ssh! Your Grace...address him as Your Grace,' Thimma admonished her, but Parameswara chuckled.

'For her, I am more like a great-great-grandpa. Come here. Would you like some almonds?'

Akhila hesitated. Her eyes seemed to ask whether the old man would be offended if she refused. She looked at Thimma. He gently shook his head and she said, 'No, Your…Your Grace. Thank you.'

Parameswara gestured to his deputy who bowed and went out.

'What do you have in that pouch?' Parameswara asked the little girl.

'Oh, these are my treasures,' gushed Akhila 'Do you want to see them, Grandpa?' she asked, and started unknotting the string with which she had somehow held the torn pouch together.

'Akhila, enough. Do not bother His Grace,' Thimma's voice was stern. I beg your forgiveness, Your Grace. The girl keeps collecting stones, pebbles, crystals, and trinkets. All worthless things,' he apologized to Parameswara.

'Worthless for us, Thimma. But for her, they are the most precious things. Is it not true of all of us? We collect so many things when we are young, and when we reach a certain age, we understand most of them were worthless.'

Akhila was still struggling to untie the strings of the pouch. Parameswara said kindly, 'Some other day, child. Now tell me, do you know how to read?'

'Akka has taught me to read,' Akhila said proudly. Thimma looked at Sivagami in surprise.

'Oh, is it? Let me see what your Akka has taught you. Read this for me, will you?' Parameswara gave her a palm leaf. There were letters that hung from lines. She wracked her brains, but could not make head or tail of it.

Parameswara laughed aloud and took the manuscript from her hand. 'Unsuccessful?'

Akhila looked down in shame. 'Don't worry. That is in a script that not many can read. It is the devabasha Sanskrit, the language of the gods. How much ever you know, there will always be many things you won't know.'

Akhila looked at the palm leaf in wonder. The Mahapradhana saw her eyes move to the walls of his chamber, which were lined with manuscripts.

'I have read most of them, I read till my eyesight failed. Still, I get them read by Roopaka whenever he has time to entertain this old man.'

Sivagami, who had been silently observing this scene, felt a growing admiration for this man who had read so many books. Her father had a library, but his entire collection would not even fill half a shelf of what this old man had.

Parameswara observed Sivagami staring at the books in wonder and chuckled. 'Those go back thousands of years, and are mostly in languages known to man. They were collected by mahapradhanas before me, better men, wiser men, and stronger men.'

'Never a woman?' Sivagami asked.

Parameswara stared at her for a long moment and Thimma audibly sucked air in. At last the prime minister of Mahishmathi laughed, 'Well, there was one extraordinary woman thousands of years ago—during the early days of the first kingdom—Mahishi, the devil. Some say she was a witch, some say she was a cursed apsara, whatever she was, she enjoyed killing people. Maybe that was a lie spun by people who despised her, or maybe there was some truth to it. Who knows? But after her, no woman in known history has ever been the mahapradhana.'

'But the kingdom of Mahishmathi is barely three centuries old and you speak about the first kingdom?' Sivagami asked.

'Kings have changed, dynasties have waxed and waned, but the institution of the mahapradhana has never changed. We are the custodians of knowledge. We serve whoever sits on the throne of Mahishmathi.'

'But why then has a woman never again been the mahapradhana of Mahishmathi?' Sivagami repeated.

Mahapradhana laughed, but before he could answer, Roopaka came in, accompanied by a corpulent woman.

'Ah, here comes my able deputy with the mukhya of the royal orphanage. Revamma, here is your new ward. Daughter, tell her your name and take her blessings.'

Sivagami bowed to the enormously fat woman who carelessly extended her hand in blessing while talking to the mahapradhana.

'Swami, you don't understand our plight. The place is already overcrowded. I have been crying for more funds for the last two years. They eat like devils, those hungry brats. And now you are burdening me with another?'

'Roopaka, has Devi Revamma submitted her accounts?' the mahapradhana asked his deputy.

Roopaka hesitated to reply.

'Yes, I have, but not even last year's expenses have been approved yet, forget about new funds. And if I reduce the sweetness in the payasam by one notch, these brats go and complain to the maharani and then I am left giving explanations. It's funds I need, not another ward, swami.'

'Skandadasa is evaluating the claims. He has found many inflated expenses. Besides, he says the country cannot subsidise the warden's husband's gambling habits,' Roopaka intervened.

'That is an unnecessary allegation. What am I supposed to do with my husband, the good-for-nothing fellow? And who runs the gambling den where most males of this accursed city including my husband stay like dogs? Is it not devadasi Kalika, who pays the highest tax in the country? Kalika, who heads the royal harem? No one talks about that. They are after a poor woman like me just because I am no longer as pretty or young as I used to be,' Revamma ranted.

'Oh, and when was that? Eight decades back?' Roopaka asked.

'Swami, I do not want to talk when this impudent rascal is in this room.'

'Roopaka, pack my things and get my chariot ready,' Parameswara ordered, gently placing Akhila down from his lap.

'Swami,' Revamma continued, 'you are taking from one hand and giving to another. I cannot run the show like this. I do not want to do this anymore. I have a farm by the river, far to the east. I will resign and retire there. Enough of spoiling my life fighting for each copper.'

'She has been saying that for the past decade,' Roopaka said as he packed the mahapradhana's things.

'Enough, Roopaka,' Parameswara grunted and his deputy muttered an apology.

'I would've left years ago, but you know my native village is infested by the Kalabhairava tribe. Sometimes it is the Vaithalikas. They raid when they please and take away children or livestock. The famed Mahishmathi army has done nothing,' Revamma panted in anger.

Mahapradhana took a deep breath and said, 'I will talk to Skandadasa, Revamma. I will also ask Hiranya to look into the matter of Kalabhairava raids or Vaithalika attacks in the forest villages. I call you for something and you take this opportunity to pile up more problems on me. Sometimes I wonder how crazy I am that I stick to this thankless post. A quiet life among books is all that I wanted.'

'He too has been saying that for the past one decade,' Revamma said to Roopaka, and Akhila giggled. When everyone stared at her, she put her hands over her mouth and tried to stifle her laugh. Seeing her, Sivagami smiled.

'Seems like more trouble for me, swami,' Revamma said.

'She is a well-behaved girl,' Thimma said, and Revamma turned to him.

'Bhoomipathi Thimma! Hmm…' Revamma's eyes widened in wonder and then realization. 'That means this girl is…'

'Yes, you guessed correctly, Revamma,' Parameswara stood up with Roopaka's support. 'Even today I am late. The old woman will be sulking, like she has been doing for the last sixty-five years. You are wedded to your job, she used to say as a demure bride. Now she does not bother. There are enough grandchildren and great grandchildren to keep her busy. Ah, my knees. Wish I had summoned the rajavaidya. The pain in my knees…'

'Swami, I cannot do this,' Revamma said. Sivagami knew what was coming. She did not fancy going with this fat woman. She wanted to go home. She wanted to play with Akhila, be coaxed to eat more by her aunt Bhama, or fight with Raghava.

The mahapradhana had already reached the door. Revamma ran and stood in front of him. With folded hands, she pleaded, 'I have looked after all the sons and daughters of the martyrs of Mahishmathi. Do not spoil my reputation by giving me a traitor's daughter. Please, swami, I beg of you. Please do not make me give milk to a snake.'

Sivagami wanted to break free from Thimma's hands and run away. No one wanted her. Not even the warden of an orphanage.

'You are wasting your breath here, Revamma. Try your luck with the maharaja. It is his order,' the mahapradhana said as his chariot rumbled up to the porch. As Roopaka helped the old mahapradhana climb up his chariot, Sivagami ran to him.

'I want to know what my father did for all of you to hate me like this,' she cried.

Parameswara did not answer her. He gestured to the driver, and with a jerk the chariot lurched forward, crushing the gravel in the driveway. Sivagami stood watching the chariot winding away, past the ghostly trees and soon past the arched gate. In a few moments, even the swaying light from its lantern had dissolved into the mist and the jingle from its bells had faded away.

She turned, hearing Thimma crying. Akhila was sobbing nearby, clutching her father's dhoti. Behind them, Roopaka and Revamma were arguing about something. Thimma held Sivagami tight and said, 'I am sorry it came to this. You should have grown up like the bhoomipathi's daughter you are. I am sorry I am leaving you like this. May...may the goddess Gauriparvat be with you always.'

The old man sobbed. Sivagami did not have any words. She felt numb. She had no idea what an orphanage looked like. Maybe she would find new friends there. Maybe she would forget about her past and would find a new home. It was just a matter of a few months anyway. Once eighteen, she might have to start working as a servant in some nobleman's home. Maybe…

'Sivagami,' Thimma took her aside.

Thimma's voice was grave, 'Forgive me, child, but there is a reason why I am sending you away. One day, you will understand. There are terrible secrets which you need not know now. But know that your father was a great man. He was no traitor. Anyone with an iota of humanity would have done what he did. Now the yoke of duty has fallen on my shoulders. I understand my friend better now. I wish he had succeeded in what he attempted, but fate had other plans. I am trying to fulfil what he set out to do. There are some clues in a book that may offer a solution. Your father mentioned it to me a few weeks before his… I am sorry. I did not want to mention it to you before and make you feel worse. The maharaja had sealed your mansion and it would have required his permission to break it open. I—' Thimma looked around to see whether Roopaka and Revamma could overhear them but they were busy arguing with each other.

Thimma lowered his voice and said, 'I even climbed the fort wall and entered your mansion in search of the book. This was more than ten years back…I was younger then. I could not find it and it was too risky to try again. I secretly questioned some of your father's servants, but one could never tell who was trustworthy and who was not. Mahamakam was a decade away and, slowly, I fooled myself by thinking that a solution would present itself. Now that it is nearing, I am scared, my child. I did not tell you all this before, for you are too curious and would have pestered me for answers. And I am still in search of the book. Maybe your father did not keep it in his home but somewhere else… Anyhow, I do not want to go to my friend's mansion again. Too many painful memories. Though it is under my charge, I have never gone back after that attempt to find the manuscript. I do not know what it holds, child, but your father was confident about arriving at a solution with it. If I succeed, it will solve everything. If I do not, I will act as my heart says.'

Doubts and questions arose in Sivagami's head. For a moment, she was tempted to show him the book, but held herself back. She opened her mouth to ask him about her father, but he stopped her. 'Knowing more will endanger your life too.'

He hugged her awkwardly and walked towards his chariot without looking back. Akhila tugged at Sivagami's dress. Sivagami knelt down to face her.

Akhila said, 'Nanna says I cannot come with you. Will you speak to him please?'

Sivagami held her shoulders and, peering into her eyes, she said, 'Precious, you have to be with your parents. I will come to visit you soon or maybe you will come to visit me during Navarathri or Sankranti. Akka will have a great present ready for you.'

Akhila's eyes flashed with joy, 'Really? Promise?'

Sivagami hugged her close. 'I promise, my sweetheart.'

Akhila ran towards her father, waving goodbye. Thimma's chariot soon vanished, leaving Sivagami behind to her new life.

'I do not have the whole night to spend listening to your argument, swami,' Revamma said to Roopaka and turned to Sivagami. 'Walk,' she said gruffly.

'Easy on the girl,' Roopaka said.

'*Thup*!' Revamma spat. 'I know how to treat a traitor's daughter. No one teaches old Revamma.'

Roopaka shrugged and walked away, leaving the old woman and her ward.

'Walk,' Revamma repeated as she shoved her. Sivagami started walking, with the fat woman panting behind her. She looked straight ahead and walked with steady steps, holding her bundle, feeling her father's book inside it with her fingers. A thought stopped her cold. Was this the book Uncle Thimma was referring to? No, it could not be, she reassured herself, but the thought kept haunting her. She wished she had confessed to Thimma about the book. He could have told her the entire truth, but he was hiding something. She had no obligation to tell him about her secrets. *It was her father's book, it belonged to her,* she repeated in her mind again and again. But the bad taste of guilt refused to go.

The soldiers at the gate made some lewd comment about Revamma and the woman paused to spit and abuse them.

As Revamma traded insults with the soldiers, Sivagami saw the silhouette of a palanquin and a few men waiting beside it by the river. What were they doing at this time of the night? Revamma spotted them then, and she hesitated to go further. A tall figure stepped out of the palanquin. Sivagami squinted, trying to make out whether it was a man or a woman—the person seemed too tall for a woman, but the gait was feminine. As the figure approached them, she heard Revamma gasp. The moonlight caught the diamond stud in the figure's nose and Sivagami felt Revamma's grip tightening around her wrist.

'Is this the girl?' the woman asked in a surprisingly gruff voice.

ELEVEN

Mahadeva

Prince Mahadeva was in Queen Hemavati's chamber. More than his father, he feared his mother. He was scared the guilt and lie were written all over his face. He did not want to face her.

'Look up when I am speaking to you.' His mother stood up from her dewan and walked towards him. He reluctantly raised his head.

'Now look into my eyes and tell me where your brother has gone.'

Mahadeva was in a fix. He knew quite well where his brother had gone. But how could he tell his mother? Everyone knew who Keki was and where she worked. Their mother would definitely fly into a rage.

Queen Hemavati had always stressed that she did not want her sons to be typical spoilt princes. She belonged to the land of snow, far away in the north, where rishis went on spiritual quests. She had very strict ideas on how to bring up her sons, on which she was often in disagreement with the king. Maharaja Somadeva, though, never had too much of a problem with this. He had a harem where he would watch the most beautiful girls dance, semi-naked, if the rumours were to be believed. And his mother would sit inside the puja room in meditation.

Mahadeva often felt caught between the two worlds. His mother talked about noble things and his father about practical things whenever he could spare some time. When he asked his gurus, they often told him to follow his heart. As if he knew what he wanted. Sometimes, his heart was with his mother's prayers, and sometimes with the pleasures that his brother kept fantasizing about. Mahadeva had to agree that, despite his abusive and bullying nature, it was fun to be with his brother. He was always adventurous, full of life and vigour, and had interesting friends. He never bothered about his mother's advice and did whatever he pleased. Mahadeva was the exact opposite.

'Have you swallowed something? I asked you a question.' His mother's voice was ice-edged.

'He…he has gone out,' Mahadeva fumbled.

'Oh, I never knew that. I thought he had the boon of being invisible and was standing beside you now,' the queen's lips curved in scorn. 'Can't you understand even a simple question and give me a straight answer? Look here and not at the floor. And stop twiddling your thumbs. That is better. Now, answer me. Where did you last see your brother?'

'In the corridor,' Mahadeva looked down again.

'One son is a rogue and the other a coward. I heard that slave boy beat you in practice duel today.'

'I hate duels,' Mahadeva said without looking up. He heard his mother sucking in her breath.

'I will get that slave boy whipped. How dare he insult you in front of everyone?'

'He played fair and won. And there was no one there other than a few soldiers and Malayappa Mama.'

'I will pluck out your tongue. Mama! Calling a slave uncle! The soldiers must be laughing about the cowardly prince of Mahishmathi. How did I give birth to a wimp like you?'

Mahadeva had grown numb to his mother's taunts. It had ceased to hurt long ago.

'Oh Mahadeva,' the queen said, gritting her teeth and Mahadeva looked up.'

I did not call you, I was calling Lord Mahadeva. Shambho Mahadeva. I don't know what sins I committed in my previous life to be punished thus with unworthy children. Tell me, where has my rogue son gone?'

Mahadeva looked down again. He wondered how his father coped with his mother. Was this why he was always in the harem? What if he, too, had such a dominating wife when he grew up? For no reason, the pretty girl who was in the corridor when he was talking to his father flashed in his mind. The way the wind played with her curly hair…

'Answer me, Mahadeva!' His mother's raised voice shook him out of his reverie.

'I thought you were asking Lord Mahadeva,' he said, and immediately regretted it. He did not know where he had got the courage to talk back.

'Good, you are showing some spirit. I like it when you do so—but to others,' she lifted his chin and stared into his eyes, 'not to me.'

Mahadeva nodded.

'Were you thinking of some girl?' Hemavati asked suddenly, and Mahadeva flushed red. He shook his head.

'Like father, like son! One Kamadeva is enough for this palace. I don't want my boys to grow without ethics, morals, and values. You are my sons and the blood of Trayambaka flows through your veins. My forefathers were rulers during the Mahabharata war. We are not some mercenaries who suddenly rose to a royal status after murdering their masters. Unlike the house of Mahishmathi, our house dates back thousands of years. I want my sons to be like my father, not like some...'

Mahadeva had heard these words a hundred times. He wanted to escape from the chamber. If he could go to the open courtyard by the fountain, he could lie down in the grass and stare at the countless stars in the sky. He could perhaps dream about that girl.

'Mahadeva, I had asked you to keep an eye on your brother and report his actions to me. For the hundredth time, where has Bijjala gone?'

He knew Keki had taken him to the notorious den, though Bijjala had avoided his question. Mahadeva finally decided against telling his mother about Keki.

'He...he was called by Skandadasa,' he managed to say. 'He wanted Bijjala to know about tax collections.'

Mahadeva thanked his stars for being able to come up with a plausible lie. At this time of the evening, the only person who worked would be Skandadasa. Others would have gone home or to some tavern or devadasi's inn. His mother frowned.

'I would never have imagined Bijjala to show this much interest in his studies. And that too about tax! Are you sure you are not lying to me?'

'That...that is what he said,' Mahadeva spluttered, his heartbeat increasing manifold.

'He has made a fool of you, as usual,' the queen said disdainfully. 'Find him and bring him to me. If he is in Skandadasa's place, learning about the taxation laws, I am ready to sweep the streets from tomorrow.'

Mahadeva hurried out of his mother's chamber, relieved that he had escaped relatively unscathed. From the Antapura, a song floated out. He wondered how he would find Bijjala. He did not know the way to Kalika's inn, and it was not something the prince of Mahishmathi could openly ask about. He walked aimlessly. The song from the Antapura became louder. The roll of the mrudanga and the twang of the veena kept pace with the anklets of some dancer. He tried to imagine the face of the dancer. And, surprising him, the face of the girl he had seen in the evening came up again. He tried to shake off her image. Such a pretty girl was sure to have a lover. Mahadeva checked himself—what nonsense was he thinking. He shook his head and smiled.

The night was young and fresh. Moonlight glistened on the dark green leaves of the jasmine plant. The smell of nishagandhi lingered in the air. And again that girl was dancing somewhere in the corridor. He was going mad, he thought. Was he in love? He wished he could confide in someone, even Bijjala would do. Could that girl sing? He did not know, but in his imagination, she could. And her song was coming from the fountain.

Water cascaded like molten silver in the moonlight. And he saw her there. Sitting by the side of the fountain, her feet immersed up to her ankles, wearing a jasmine garland. He remembered the words of Kalidasa about Shakuntala.

The only thing that was missing was the mandatory deer. He smiled at the thought and ran towards her. He could hear her song, he could hear her anklets.

But when he looked again, she had vanished. No wonder his brother chided him—he had a poet's heart. But girls did not fall in love with poets or writers, except in the stories they made up. The thought depressed him. He was being stupid to fall in love with a girl who did not even know that he existed. She looked so confident, like a lioness. Mahadeva was never confident. His knees went weak and his throat dried up even when his father asked him to recite the mantras in the temple once in a while. People praised him whenever he finished, but he knew they were just being polite to the prince of Mahishmathi.

Truth be told, he never felt like a prince. Princes in the stories he read and heard were brave men. They confronted danger and were victorious. They slayed rakshasas and demons, and saved beautiful princesses. He could never imagine doing any of those things. Mahadeva knew he was not brave. He could wield the sword and his master said he was even quick with it, but what he lacked was the will to inflict injury. He was scared of blood too. Though not many knew his secret, he was afraid his father did.

He sighed as he walked past the fountain towards the gate. No girl with any sense would find it worthwhile to love him. Even if he managed to win her heart, his mother would never agree to let him marry an ordinary girl. There was no point in even thinking about that girl—he was never going to see her again. And yet, he couldn't get her out of his mind.

He drifted towards the southern gate of the fort and was walking out of it when he was stopped by the soldiers stationed there. They had instructions from Skandadasa not to allow him outside the fort without his security guards. Mahadeva resented the curbs on his freedom, but did not say anything. His way was to work around a problem, not confront it. He loved to sit by the river and dream. No restriction was going to stop him from what he wanted to do.

He knew what he had to do. In his countless wanderings since he was a little boy in the sprawling palace complex, he had discovered many things. There were corners where no one came, stairs that went nowhere or wound back and forth in endless circles, secret pathways and tunnels built to confound enemies. He knew a way out to the river. He had discovered it accidentally.

Many years ago, he had wandered near Parameswara's office and had slipped and fallen into an abandoned well. There was hardly any water but his fall had been cushioned by the soft sand in the bottom. He had shouted and screamed but there was no one who could've heard him. He had tried to climb up and stepped on a loose stone that had led to a trapdoor falling open in the well. Curious, he had entered it and found himself in a secret tunnel. He had been scared to go further, but decided that he must return later. He had somehow scrambled his way out of the well that day.

Later, he had started exploring the tunnel alone which, he discovered, was actually an elaborate labyrinth. Most times, he ended up in a dead end and had to walk back, but it was like a puzzle that challenged his intelligence. He loved to solve puzzles, and, finally, he had managed to find a way out which, to his delight, led to the riverbank. Since then, Mahadeva had spent many yamams staring at the river, composing poetry in his mind. Sometimes, the old ferry man, Bhairava, would keep him company. They talked about everything under the sun. Bhairava never treated him like a prince and Mahadeva liked him more for it.

Today, he decided to use the same path. He skirted around Parameswara's office. The old man had left for the day. He reached the well and started climbing down.

When he came out of the tunnel by the river, he felt like a free bird. The song he had heard wafting out of his father's Antapura burst through his lips. A short distance away the granite mandapa was bathed in moonlight. He started walking towards it, enjoying the coolness of the river breeze on his face. River Mahishmathi was to his left, flowing ink blue. Shards of moonlight glistened on the crest of waves. Frogs croaked from the bushes and from afar. From across the river, the faint rhythms of village drums could be heard.

Far away, Mount Gauriparvat rested in a quilt of mist. The faint roar of the Patalaganga falls could be heard. It was a beautiful place where he had spent many evenings, swimming in the placid pools formed between the rocks. He closed his eyes and imagined he was there, floating in the pool, with the waterfall roaring a few feet away. It was so serene and soothing. A moist breeze caressed his body. He floated like a leaf, carried by the current. He twisted his body and started swimming with powerful strokes. He was all alone in this beautiful world.

That's when he saw her standing on a rock, with the waterfall cascading behind her. That girl…What was she doing here? She stood like a marble statue, her hair flying in the breeze, and her arms held high and wide. Had she seen him? He could not breathe. Heat rose to his cheeks. She opened her eyes and turned towards him. He sucked in his breath. She was so beautiful. She stepped down into the water. It is too cold, he wanted to warn her, but no words would come out of his mouth. He stood watching, thankful that water covered everything under his waist. Her wet clothes clung to her curves. She ducked into the water and Mahadeva's heart pounded in his ribcage.

She was swimming towards him. He stood without moving, tense that if she came nearer, she may discover the effect she was having on him. He was ashamed and excited at the same time. She rose from the water, her hair wet and dripping. His gaze travelled towards a rivulet of water that ran down her breasts. He had forgotten to breathe. She smiled at him. Moonlight lined the curve of her lips. He gulped, as he saw water snake its way down and rest on her navel.

'By what name shall I call you?' his voice trembled.

Mahadeva was shocked out of his fantasy by a loud shriek. He almost fell into the water. At some distance was a palanquin resting on the ground, and two women shouting at each other. A fat woman had spread her arms wide and seemed to be blocking a tall woman's way. Mahadeva debated whether to run inside the fort or call for help. He did not want to get involved in anyone else's fight. He was about to run towards the fort when the fat woman moved to reveal the person she had been shielding—that girl!

He ran towards them. He saw a man emerging from the palanquin but quickly duck back inside. The man looked familiar, but Mahadeva could not place him. And why was he inside a palanquin? The man did not appear old or enfeebled. Nor did he appear rich. In fact, in that quick glance, the man appeared to be a slave. But how could a slave travel in a palanquin? He dismissed the possibility and walked towards the scene.

The palanquin bearers tried to stop him as he approached. The tall woman grabbed the fat one and dragged her down to the ground. Then she lunged at the girl. The girl swiftly moved away and the tall woman landed on her face.

'What…wh…what is happening here?' Mahadeva demanded, doing his best to sound authoritative.

'Mind your own business,' the tall woman said as she scrambled up from the ground. Mahadeva was perplexed. Her voice sounded like that of a man's. The bearers shoved him back.

'Your Highness, Prince Mahadeva, help me,' the fat woman cried. The bearers who were pushing and shoving him stopped in their tracks. They looked at each other, confused and scared. The first man to recover fell on his knees, and with his head bowed, mumbled, 'Apologies, Your Highness. We did not know.' His companions followed him with readiness. The fat woman also bowed down.

Someone cursed from inside the palanquin. The voice sounded familiar. Mahadeva walked towards the palanquin when the tall woman ran towards him. Keki! He was scared she was going to knock him down and he braced for a punch on his face. Instead, the woman fell on all fours and grabbed his feet.

'Mercy, Your Highness, mercy,' she cried.

Mahadeva gathered his courage and, in his best stern voice, asked, 'What brings you here, Keki? And why were you fighting with an old woman?'

'They owe me money, Your Highness. Her husband does. He comes to my place and gambles.'

Mahadeva did not know what to make of this. He knew gambling was banned in Mahishmathi, but it happened everywhere, even inside the palace between guards or sometimes between ministers.

'You are not supposed to gamble,' he managed to say.

'Oh, in the gamble of life, I have drawn the card of pleasure, Your Highness,' Keki smiled.

In the business of pleasure! He was embarrassed. He saw the girl staring at him and beads of sweat started forming on his forehead.

'I manage Kalika's Pushyachakra inn. And we do entertain princes. In fact, that is going to be our next big thing. We are specialising in the art of entertaining princes. If you care to come with me, I can show you a different world.'

'I. No...no...' Mahadeva stuttered. He coughed to hide his embarrassment. He desperately wondered how to effectively deal with her.

'Oh, Prince, so many beautiful moments await you. Why don't you join us tonight? We have a special guest today and you will make that two.'

Mahadeva knew she was referring to Bijjala. And the familiar figure he had seen ducking in as he came could only be Bijjala's slave Kattappa. He was confounded that his brother had allowed a slave to travel with him inside a palanquin. Lust made people do strange things, he thought. He realized that he would have to protect his brother's secret. If the fat woman found out that it was Bijjala inside the palanquin, going to Kalika's den, it would spread like wildfire in the city. And the slave would get punished for daring to travel with his master in a palanquin. Besides, what would the girl think about a Mahishmathi prince who frequented Kalika's den? Wouldn't she judge him too?

'I am letting you go without punishment only because...' Mahadeva searched for a reason.

'Because?' Keki smiled, nodding her head, taunting him.

'Because...' Mahadeva struggled. Nothing would come to his mind.

'Because Your Highness is too kind,' Keki filled in for him, and Mahadeva heaved a sigh of relief. That would have sounded stupid had he said it himself, but Keki made it sound not half as bad.

Keki made a face at the fat woman, bowed low, and got into the palanquin. This time Mahadeva glimpsed Bijjala sitting with his face covered with his turban and Kattappa sitting with his head buried in his knees. Keki held up the curtain a tad longer than necessary, giving Mahadeva enough time to be sure. The eunuch blew a kiss at him as she drew the curtains. The bearers lifted up the palanquin and started moving. Their voices crying, 'Ho-ho,' dissolved in the air and the torchlight became a dot on the horizon.

'Your Highness, may we plead your leave? It's a long way to the orphanage,' the old woman said.

'Devi,' Mahadeva said, 'I will come with you so that you are not troubled anymore. Times are bad.'

'Your Highness is too kind. If it is not too much trouble,' the old woman replied.

'Not at all,' Mahadeva said. He extended his hands to take the bundle from Sivagami and said, 'Devi, allow me.' She moved away, leaving him stung. 'I can help carry the bundle, devi,' he said, hoping his desperation would not show in his voice.

She had started walking without even bothering to look back. He ran behind her. She did not say anything when he took the bundle from her. He felt hurt that she did not thank him. Neither did she bow to him as a commoner should before a prince. The old woman chided her for allowing the prince to take her bundle, but she did not reply. She kept walking, with the old woman puffing and panting beside her. But the old woman had used the girl's name—Sivagami—and for that, Mahadeva was grateful.

The moon had painted the earth in ethereal silver and everything was bathed in its light. The river flowed quiet beside him. A nightingale sung from the groves. The drone of crickets sounded musical to his ears. Each blade of grass shone diamond-edged. Far away, Gauriparvat loomed, half in mist, half dissolved in the dark sky, aloof and divine.

Sivagami, my Sivagami, he wanted to repeat her name. She was so near, that if he extended his hands he could touch her hair. The breeze that caressed her cheeks caressed his too. What more did he want? The bundle he held now had rested in her hands. She had pressed it close to her breast. It would have heard her heartbeat. The bundle carried her smell. He would hold it for her till the end of the world, he told himself, and felt silly. And happy.

TWELVE

Pattaraya

Bhoomipathi Pattaraya's chariot turned the last curve, on its way towards his home. *Idiots!* Pattaraya could not control his anger. He was surrounded by nincompoops and fools. He smacked his chariot driver's head. 'Why can't they light the courtyard properly?' Not that the poor driver was responsible for his guards not lighting the courtyard. Still, it felt good to vent his anger on someone. Every one of them was a shirker, everyone was after his money.

He had been shocked to learn that the stones were still missing. Who had killed the dandakara that Pratapa had sent behind the slave Nagayya? The person had killed both and got away with the stones. His stones! Pattaraya gritted his teeth. He patted his waist-band. The one stone he had picked up when Nagayya was running away was still there. He would surprise his daughter Mekhala with that. She would be impressed.

Pattaraya knew that it was a dangerous game he was playing. It could change the history of Mahishmathi. Pratapa and Rudra Bhatta would be here soon. They had to find a way out.

He was puffing and panting as he entered his home. He kicked open the door, screaming, 'Mekhala.'

'Mekhala, Father is home,' Pattaraya cried out as he untied a bunch of keys from the chain at his waist. There was no response from his daughter. Not that he expected it. She had outgrown the age of running to greet him on his arrival almost a decade back. He could hear her practising dance on the first floor.

'Get a lamp, fast,' he said when he heard the footsteps of his daughter finally coming down. He inserted a key into the decorated lock in a door. The door creaked open, revealing another trap door to the left.

His daughter ran and fetched a lamp from the puja room. He opened the secret door that was cleverly concealed in the wall and took out a massive key to open a trap door under the carpet.

'Father, do you need to do all this? We have enough and, in fact, more than enough,' Mekhala said as she helped her father open the door.

'I am doing everything for you, Mekhala,' Pattaraya said with affection.

'I don't want you to do anything wrong, Father,' Mekhala said as they stepped in. A flight of steps led into a damp basement under his living room.

'Nothing is right or wrong, my daughter. It is all about how you view life,' Pattaraya said as they climbed down.

His daughter walked beside him with the lamp. Light scattered on the steps, illuminating its uneven edges.

His footsteps echoed in the dark passageway. A spider ran across his path. The musty smell of the room assaulted his senses. 'This place stinks,' he heard Mekhala say.

Pattaraya was puffing and panting by the time he reached the basement. As he walked, he kept observing the floor. Except for the fading footprints, made by him during his last visit, the floor was covered with a finger-deep layer of dust. Every time he was careful to take a different path inside the chamber so that the footprints would mark each visit they had made. Once a year, he would clean the floor with his own hands—not a job a vaishya would do usually, but it was a part of his elaborate security arrangement. He did not want to trust any servant with even the sight of the place where he kept his treasures. Once he counted the treasure and closed the safe, he would again spread sawdust on the floor. There were cobwebs all over the uneven roof and a few dangled over the huge iron safe. He never allowed anyone to clean it. There was dust over the handle and the padlock. It gave him some satisfaction that no one had touched it after his last visit.

He inserted the foot-long key inside the keyhole and used both his hands to turn it. The safe fought back for some time but finally gave in. With a loud noise, the door snapped open.

'Oh my god,' Mekhala exclaimed as the light from the torch reflected on the pile of gold ornaments, rubies, diamonds, pearl necklaces and gold bracelets inside the iron safe. Edges of gold coins shone through the calico sacks stacked inside. A huge golden peacock fixed atop the crown of a five-foot lamp stared back at them with its ruby eyes. For a moment, Pattaraya forgot about all his troubles. His chest swelled with pride. When he had started the business, he had inherited a few measly copper coins lodged in the dark corners of the safe.

He was a lad of fourteen at that time, with a sick mother to look after. They lived in a crumbling old mansion built by his great grandfather. It had been a struggle of three-and-a-half decades to reach where he was now. He had achieved a lot.

'Nanna, I am getting scared, this is too much, much too much,' Mekhala said, bringing him back to the mouldy dampness of his basement.

Pattaraya took out a stone from his waist-band and held it before Mekhala. He waited for her reaction.

'What?' she asked.

'Look at this stone. Have you seen anything like this before?' he gloated.

'Of course I have. Plenty of them too. In summer, when the river dries out, the riverbed is full of such stones,' Mekhala said with a smile.

'Oh, just a river stone, eh?' Pattaraya smiled and took the lamp from his daughter's hand. He held it near the stone. Slowly it started throbbing with a pale blue colour. Pattaraya stood, watching the amazed reaction of his beloved daughter. Her face turned blue as the stone started glowing. Soon the entire room was sparkling blue. He dropped it onto Mekhala's palm and watched his pretty daughter's face in the ethereal colour.

'Impressive,' a voice said. Mekhala looked behind Pattaraya and screamed. The stone fell from her hands and rolled on the ground. In the flickering blue light, a ghoulish face grinned at Pattaraya. Startled, he stepped back.

You…you here?' Pattaraya stuttered. His hands trembled and the lamp he was holding shook, casting shadows that danced around the room.

'Impressive,' the ghoul said as it entered the safe. The diamonds and pearls inside caught the blue hue of the Gaurikanta and sparkled.

The ghoul weighed a necklace in his hand and turned to Mekhala. 'Don't stare at me like that, young woman. I feel shy. I am no ghoul, but a poor dwarf, devi,' the dwarf grinned and bowed.

Mekhala looked at the dwarf in amazement as he scooped up some pearls from the floor of the safe and let them slip through his stubby fingers. They tinkled around the iron floor.

'Congratulations on your ill-gotten wealth, fat man. You are an inspiration.' The dwarf's voice echoed in the basement.

Pattaraya stood wavering on his feet.

'How the hell did you get here?' he demanded of the dwarf who was eyeing his daughter.

'You have not only amassed great wealth, you have made a beautiful daughter too, fat man. She looks like a sculpture in the temple. With a narrow waist, rounded breasts, wide hips…'

Mekhala blushed blue and Pattaraya gritted his teeth in anger.

'Shut up, you bastard,' Pattaraya screamed. He gestured for Mekhala to move away. The Gaurikanta was returning to its dull slate-grey colour.

'Oh Pattaraya, you are using filthy language before your daughter. Is this the way you are bringing her up? Apologies, devi, for making your father angry and inciting him to use swear words. Your lovely ears should not hear such language, even if it is from your father. *Especially* if it is from your father. He has one filthy tongue. Oh, we have not been introduced. I do not think your father will do that, since he seems very angry with me. So let me introduce myself,' the dwarf said. 'I am Khanipathi Hidumba. Your father's nephew, a bit distant and all that, but never mind that. A minor bhoomipathi, half a man and half a noble. My stature may be small, but my heart is big.' The dwarf bowed low again and smiled. His golden canine tooth glittered in the lamp light.

Pattaraya pushed his daughter out of the way and approached the dwarf who was now weighing a gold necklace in his hand.

'Why have you come here? You were supposed to have gone to—' he paused.

'Directly to Kalika's den. And wait for you there in that house of sin,' the dwarf said with a smile. Pattaraya eyed his daughter. He should have been more careful.

'How the hell did you get inside?' Pattaraya asked, quickly changing the topic.

'I am surprised. I thought you knew…' the dwarf looked at his misshapen legs. 'There is a new technique called walking. You put one step in front of another and you find that it can take you a long way.'

'Not any more, Chandala. You are done with your walking days.' Pattaraya slammed the door of the safe shut. He struggled with the door knob. The key fell down. He could hear the dwarf banging from inside.

'Mekhala,' he said, as he fumbled with the keys, 'the dwarf is lying. Don't believe him. Do you think I could ever…'

'Nanna, this is not something a daughter should have to hear about her father,' Mekhala's voice trembled.

Pattaraya stood wiping beads of sweat from his forehead with his palm. *Bloody dwarf*, he cursed silently as he bent down to pick the Gaurikanta from the floor.

'He was lying, Mekhala. And he is not going to get away with it. Let him be locked down here and feel the terror for at least a week.' Pattarya turned to the safe and started putting a double safety lock on it.

'Nanna,' Mekhala called, her voice betraying her terror.

Pattaraya finished locking the dwarf inside the safe. When he heard Hidumba banging the door from inside, he kicked the iron door and said, 'Serves you right, dwarf. In a few days, I shall serve what is left of you to my dogs. Be quiet till then.'

'Nanna…' Mekhala called again.

'I am not going to show any mercy, daughter. He dared enter my house and slander me. He says I go to whorehouses. I, the best of all men. He has to pay the price.'

'Nannaaa…' his daughter screamed. When Pattaraya turned, the key fell from his hand. There were two men inside the chamber. Similar-looking, each had a dagger at his daughter's neck.

Pattaraya rushed towards them, but one of the giants brandished a knife at him. He pointed at the door of the safe. Pattaraya fumbled around, looking for the key. Beads of sweat appeared on his forehead. Remembering that he had dropped the key, he went down on all fours, trying to find it. His daughter was screaming. When he looked at Mekhala, he saw a trickle of blood oozing from her fair neck.

'Please…please…' he pleaded as he struggled to find the key. Finally he spotted it and hurriedly opened the door and let the dwarf out.

'Well, well,' said Hidumba as he waddled out of the safe. 'Great welcome at your home, fat man. Wish I had had your daughter with me inside. Next year we could have celebrated the jatakarma of your grandson. You missed a golden opportunity.'

His thugs laughed at his crude joke. Pattaraya saw the dwarf had stuffed his waist-pouch with rubies and diamonds. The dwarf laughed, looking at the impotent rage in Pattaraya's eyes.

'You were in a hurry to open the safe, Uncle. You did not give me enough time to take whatever I wanted. Never mind. Oh, by the balls of the holy bull, my boys have been rude to your daughter.'

The two giants let go of Mekhala and grinned.

'Apologize to the lady, rogues,' Hidumba said. One of the giants fell on his knees, took Mekhala's hand and said, 'Sorry.' Mekhala stared at her father and he wilted under her accusatory stare.

'Charming, aren't they? The one with a scar on his left cheek is Ranga. His twin, who keeps grinning as if his father has just died, is Thunga. They are twins, if you hadn't observed. They are a bit dumb, but they have their uses. I like to surround myself with big men for obvious reasons,' Hidumba said, as he started climbing the steps.

Pattaraya followed him, with Mekhala's help.

When he reached his living room and shut the entrance of the underground chamber, he was enraged to find the dwarf sitting in his favourite chair. Pattaraya swallowed his anger and led his daughter to her bedroom. She appeared terrified and it was important to ensure her safety first. He mumbled some words to pacify her and hurried out of the room.

Pattaraya reached the hall to find Hidumba admiring the beauty of a ruby he had taken from the safe. He pulled a chair and sat facing the dwarf. 'You were called for a purpose and this is how you behave? How dare you barge into my home, unannounced?'

'Coming unannounced has its own advantages,' Hidumba said, squinting at the lemon-sized ruby and turning it towards the light.

Pattaraya slammed his fist on the table nearby, knocking over the lota of buttermilk.

Hidumba smiled. 'Easy, Uncle. A few rubies and some pearls for a poor nephew are not going to ruin you. No need to get angry.'

'You force your way into my home, steal my treasures, and ogle at my daughter. Am I supposed to feel ecstatic for the privilege?'

Hidumba adjusted himself to sit at the edge of the cushion and leaned towards Pattaraya. 'You think I missed what you showed your delightful daughter? I was standing inside the chamber, watching you.' The dwarf's eyes flashed in anger.

Colour drained from Pattaraya's face. 'I…I…'

'I did not take such a big risk for you to swindle it.' Hidumba slammed his fist on the table.

'It…it was only one stone. I will pay for it.'

'Ah, one stone. Pay for it you will. But what happened to the other stones?'

'What do you mean?' Pattaraya stood up, wringing his hands.

'The two dozen I procured. The rajaguru has a lot to answer for. You and that stupid Dandanayaka Pratapa will have to answer too. Pah! Why was that slave Nagayya killed? Everyone's neck is on the block now,' the dwarf said.

'No one wanted to kill him. But he ran away with the stones,' Pattaraya felt angry that he had to explain himself to this dwarf who came only up to his knee.

'What an elaborate arrangement. Impressive. Except for the fact that now we have neither the stones nor the blacksmith who could've worked on the Gaurikanta,' Hidumba snarled.

'Maybe they got washed away in the storm-water drain where the dead body of the slave was found. They could still be there or could have been washed into the river.' His argument did not sound convincing even to his own ears.

'While you are busy speculating, why don't you also think about how we are going to repay Chitraveni? We were supposed to deliver the Gaurikanta stones and a slave who knew the process of extracting Gauridhooli. An expert who could set up a workshop in her country and train her people. The bastard princess of Kadarimandalam is not going to buy the excuse that the slave we identified has run away with the stones and got himself killed. If she blows the secret, you know what will happen,' Hidumba said, wagging his index finger at Pattaraya.

Pattaraya said, 'I have a plan to repay the bastard princess. Just trust me.'

'Trust you after all this? Ha! Boys,' the dwarf called out, and Ranga appeared and helped him stand up. Hidumba adjusted his turban. 'Let us go to Kalika's mansion and have some fun. When we die and reach hell, Yama should not ask me what I did with my most important organ. I am doomed because of these fools and I want to go to the gallows singing and dancing.'

'Wait,' Pattaraya stopped the dwarf. 'Hold on, you fool. Leave such things to me.'

'Like hell I will. I took the greatest risk amongst all of you. You have covered your fat ass. I assure you, Uncle Pattaraya, if I hang, you will hang with me. I am not in this until you recover all the Gaurikanta stones.'

'What am I supposed to do, Hidumba? I am trying my best. If you have a better plan, please tell me…'

'Do you have a well in your kitchen courtyard?' Hidumba asked.

'A well? Yes…'

'And a millstone to grind? The one you use to make dosa batter?'

'Are you mocking me?' Pattaraya's eyes flashed in anger.

'Just offering some good advice, Uncle. You were wondering what the best course of action would be. I suggest you tie that millstone around your neck and jump into the well. Your daughter might have to go without dosa for some time, but I think she will survive.'

'How dare you!' Pattaraya rushed to slap Hidumba. Ranga and Thunga caught him and forced him to sit. Pattaraya panted in anger. He calmed himself, thinking fast. He had to pacify this dwarf. He had to take him to Kalika's den.

'Only you can save us, Hidumba. You play a big part in my plan,' Pattaraya said, adopting a defeated stance.

Without waiting for the dwarf's reply, he walked out and sat in his chariot. Puzzled by the change in his attitude, the dwarf and his two bodyguards joined him, and the chariot rolled towards Kalika's inn. During the ride, Pattaraya met every taunt, insult and barb from the dwarf with a smile and a calm answer that he would explain everything once Pratapa and Rudra Bhatta joined them. Soon Hidumba retreated into a sullen silence until the chariot stopped at the turn by the river to wait for their friends to come.

Ranga and Thunga helped Hidumba out of the chariot and gently placed him on the ground. They stood by the chariot with their swords drawn. Pattaraya paced up and down, glancing into the darkness and shaking his head, folding his hands and unfolding them, while Hidumba stood with an amused smile, chewing a blade of grass. Behind them, the outer fort of Mahishmathi city loomed high. This was a quiet spot, with the narrow path winding around the fort and the river. Not many frequented this path in the dark, as people preferred to go through the royal highway that ran through the fort, which was well lit and had sentries patrolling it often. This path was meant for the untouchables and the slaves, who rarely moved around after dark.

'Here they come,' Hidumba said, spitting out the chewed grass. Pattaraya rushed forward to welcome Pratapa and Rudra Bhatta. The rajaguru halted when he saw Hidumba.

'Welcome Rudra Bhatta, the great strategist,' Hidumba mocked. Even in the faded moonlight, Pattaraya could see Rudra Bhatta's lips drawing into a tight line in suppressed anger. The dwarf had a knack for getting on people's nerves.

'Hidumba, let us all agree that a mistake happened. Why do you need to rub it in?' Dandanayaka Pratapa tried to ease the situation.

'A mistake?' Hidumba threw up his crooked hands. 'What an easy word, what a sorry excuse. It is my head on the block. I established contact, I found Nagayya, I told you about the secret door and the tide. And you guys have lost everything. Everything!'

Pratapa and Rudra Bhatta looked shamefaced. Pattaraya said, 'Hidumba, I had told you that we have another plan and that is why we are now going to Kalika's inn to execute it.'

Hidumba kept pacing, his head bent in thought. Pratapa and Rudra Bhatta stood nervously. Pattaraya eyed the dwarf, his mind racing with plans. The dwarf was dangerous, but nothing that he could not handle.

'We have to find out more about who killed your man, Pratapa,' Hidumba said.

'We will. I believe he was Skandadasa's spy,' Pratapa said.

'Do you people even understand what a big mess you have created? We have taken a fortune from Chitraveni. And now what answer do we give her? Pattaraya claims he has a plan. We all know how the last plan ended up,' Hidumba ranted.

Pattaraya ignored the insult. 'Trust me, I have a plan to keep her pacified. We will pay her with something better.'

'Are you offering to marry her?' Hidumba said, and his two thugs sniggered. Pattaraya ignored him.

'We will pay her with the Gauridhooli itself, the finished powder that gives the weapons of Mahishmathi their great power. Until we can smuggle another slave with the expertise to set up a workshop, we will continue to supply her the Gauridhooli. She, of course, will have to give us sufficient compensation, in fact more than sufficient compensation,' Pattaraya laughed.

There was a shocked silence. Pattaraya waited for them to recover. Rudra Bhatta was clearly worried. Pratapa was deep in thought. Pattaraya looked at Hidumba.

Hidumba said, 'Oh, I believe you have a substantial stock of it. We all know it is available in the vegetable market; two copper coins a handful, right? Huh!'

Pattaraya smiled, 'No, not at all. I will take it from its source.'

'How?' Pratapa asked. 'The access to the workshop is only for the royals and the mahapradhana. The slaves do not even see sunlight. It is a state secret and heavily guarded. How the hell are you going to get the Gauridhooli out of there?'

'If only royals can access it, we will ask the royals to get it for us.'

'Of course, why didn't we think of it before,' Hidumba mocked. 'The great Pattaraya will go to the maharaja and say, "Your Highness, I have taken a bribe from a bastard princess of a vassal kingdom who is plotting your downfall. She needs some Gauridhooli. Would you be so kind as to deliver it yourself or should I arrange for the carts?" And the maharaja will open the workshop and declare, 'Pattaraya, my bosom friend, everything is yours. Take whatever you want.' What an idea. I should bow to you, nay, I should touch your divine feet and become your disciple.'

Ranga and Thunga laughed aloud. The dwarf smiled smugly at his own wit. Rudra Bhatta and Pratapa stared at him with distaste.

Pattaraya kept his cool and said, 'There are easier methods than asking the king directly. For instance, asking the elder prince himself to hand it over to us.'

'How much wine have you had, Pattaraya?' Hidumba threw his hands up and shook his head. Pratapa and Rudra Bhatta appeared uneasy.

'Trust me, friends,' Pattarya said. 'This is the reason I have called you all to Kalika's inn. Especially my dear friend, Hidumba.'

Pattaraya explained his plan to them. A reluctant smile appeared on Hidumba's face.

'Can she be trusted?' Rudra Bhatta asked.

'There is no one more loyal than a whore,' Pattaraya said. Pratapa had already started walking to the chariot.

'It is a sin to go to a whorehouse. I am a Brahmin,' the priest pouted.

'Aha, treason is not a sin for this great Brahmin but whoring is,' the dwarf said as he walked to the chariot. Thunga lifted him up and placed him inside.

Pattaraya took the old priest by his hand and led him to the chariot and climbed in. He ordered his chariot driver to ride to Kalika's den.

The chariot started with a jerk and the men inside sat in the darkness, each buried in his own thoughts. As they turned the corner where the avarna's path crossed the royal highway, onto that road which led to Kalika's inn, he had a feeling that the road was under surveillance. He was not in his official chariot but a private one which he kept for such purposes, but he was worried. *Had they found out about the missing stones,* he wondered. At least it seemed they knew something was amiss. *Beware*, he told himself. Pratapa and Rudra Bhatta were silent in the rear seat. The dwarf was amusing himself with a Chaturanga board.

A few of the street lights had already died out and darkness pooled under their lamp posts on the deserted road. The chariot rattled down the smooth royal highway, and the rhythm of the bells and horse hooves on granite slabs was sleep-inducing. If someone saw them now, Pattaraya thought, they would see some noblemen on a visit to a devadasi's abode. Nothing extraordinary.

There were sure to be one or two spies following them. Kalika's den would also have spies, thought Pattaraya. He had played this game many times. Though the tension that their cover was on the verge of being blown was at the back of his mind, he was warming up to the game. He scanned the river as far as his eye could see. There were no silhouettes of ships with dark sails approaching the city. Jeemotha had his own people in the city and the sly pirate-merchant would have received information about Skandadasa's check on all incoming ships in the port. He had enough sense to stay away when the tide was unfavourable.

A moth kept whizzing around the lantern swaying near Pattaraya's shoulders. He swatted at it unsuccessfully each time the moth bothered him, breaking his chain of thought. He had to find out who killed the dandakara and who stole the stones. Or did the stones actually get washed away in the drain? He had to recover them fast. Time was running out for Pattaraya.

The chariot swayed as it left the royal highway and took a sharp turn and left the riverside. The bells jingled furiously and Pattaraya snapped at his charioteer to drive carefully. The moth landed on his cheek and in anger he slapped himself and felt the warmth of the moth. He wiped its squishiness from his cheeks. In the swaying light of the lantern he saw the moth, writhing in pain, its one wing squashed in his palm. Skandadasa was becoming a pain in the neck. He had to take some tough decisions. He crushed the moth, ending its struggle, and smiled.

THIRTEEN

Sivagami

When they reached the orphanage at the edge of the fort, Sivagami's heart sank. The only thing royal about the Royal Orphanage was its name. It was a decrepit building, the sight of which was depressing. A little lamp by the gate struggled to light the steps. The gate was rusty and fragile. A few tiles above the door were missing and an ambitious creeper had tried reaching the sky through the holes in the roof. A boy was sleeping on the steps, his head covered with a torn sack. Revamma kicked him awake and the boy spewed out a stream of cuss words. He was barely ten, but his language would have made a seasoned soldier blush.

'Hush, devil. Hold your nasty tongue. There is someone important with us,' Revamma hissed.

The boy stared at Sivagami for a moment and laughed. 'This hussy?' Sivagami was shocked at his language. Revamma boxed his ears. It was then that he saw Mahadeva.

'New boy?' The boy walked around Prince Mahadeva, appraising him. 'But he is dressed like a prince.'

'Shut your trap if you want to retain your head. It is the prince of Mahishmathi.' Revamma pushed him out of her way and opened the rickety door.

'Prince? Did the king die for the prince to be admitted into an orphanage?' the boy asked, scratching his head in confusion.

Sivagami, who had forgotten all about Mahadeva's existence, eyed him. He was blushing and seemed terribly embarrassed. Revamma ignored the boy and invited the prince in.

'If Your Highness could see our pitiful condition, your heart would melt. Please come and have a look.'

Sivagami could see that, though the prince did not want to come in, he was not a person who could refuse anyone. Mahadeva acquiesced and Revamma quickly excused herself to arrange for a quick welcome for the prince.

The boy asked Sivagami, 'Is he really a prince?' She ignored him. He then repeated his question to Mahadeva, who nodded reluctantly, as if embarrassed of the fact. 'Hypocrite,' Sivagami muttered to herself. The Mahishmathi royals hid poison behind their smiles. One day, she would murder them all. She would finish the Mahishmathi royal clan.

The boy stood for a few moments as if absorbing the news, and then ran screaming that Prince Mahadeva had come to visit. Heads popped out from the balconies of the two floors. Doors creaked open. There was a rumble of footsteps as many feet treaded wooden stairs. Someone fell down in the melee and cursed. Laughter followed along with excited howls and animated whispers. Soon the courtyard was filled with boys and girls and a few grown-up men and women.

Mahadeva stood, nervous, and Sivagami noticed that he was still holding her bundle. She took the bundle from his hands and mumbled her thanks. It did not go unnoticed among the inhabitants. She heard someone whispering that she was his sister, a princess of Mahishmathi. Sivagami was mortified and was about to correct the false notion, when she heard some girl say that she might be the lover of the prince. Sivagami felt a deep loathing rise in her. She wanted to scream that she hated the royal house of Mahishmathi, she wanted every one of them dead for what they had done to her father.

Revamma came back, shouting instructions to light the courtyard. Soon the smell of burning oil from the lamps filled the air. Sivagami could see faces more clearly. There were almost two hundred boys and girls; more girls than boys. Their ages ranged from six to eighteen.

Revamma walked up with a bowl of saffron and turmeric water, with a lamp floating in it, to give the prince a traditional welcome. Standing by the side of the prince, Sivagami was suddenly aware that the entire process appeared uncomfortably similar to the welcome given to a bride and groom when they first step into their house. She stepped back without anyone noticing it.

In a voice dripping with honey, Revamma invited the prince to take a tour of the orphanage. She led him in, followed by the large crowd of children. Sivagami continued to stand in the centre of the courtyard, holding all her worldly possessions in the cloth bundle pressed close to her heart.

'That old woman is Kalakuda; no, she is more poisonous than Kalakuda,' Sivagami was startled by the voice behind her. A young woman of her age stood smiling at her.

'I am Kamakshi,' said the girl with a smile. She had a complexion as smooth as that of polished granite. When she smiled, her slightly crooked canine teeth gave her a naughty, childlike appearance. Her eyes sparkled with vigour.

'Sivagami.'

'I heard your name from Revamma,' Kamakshi said. 'How did you manage to get the prince of Mahishmathi to carry your bundle?' she asked.

'Why should it concern you?' Sivagami asked, surprised at the audacity of a complete stranger to ask such an intimate question. But when Kamakshi's face fell, she realized her reply had been harsh. After all, the girl was only trying to be friendly.

'How many inhabitants does this orphanage have?' she quickly changed the topic.

'How does it matter? It's just the two of us now,' Kamakshi said, looking around the empty courtyard and then bursting into laughter. Sivagami remained stiff and wary.

'There are two hundred and thirty-two as of today evening. You may be wondering how I know the exact number. Well, you are looking at the mukhya of the girls in this orphanage. Naturally, every other girl hates me. Since you are new and do not know of my wickedness, I thought I would try to befriend you.' Kamakshi's eyes twinkled with mischief. Despite herself, Sivagami found she was smiling. They could hear the entourage going through the first floor with the prince. Revamma's voice rose over the hum from hundreds of mouths.

'Come, I'll show you your room,' Kamakshi said. 'There's a spare bed in my room now that my roommate's left. I think you can stay there until Revamma finds you another.'

Sivagami looked around the dilapidated structure and shuddered. Slowly, her reality was sinking in. She had to spend at least the next few months here, among these people, in this ramshackle structure that looked like it might collapse in the next rain. And there was nothing to look forward to except maybe the life of a servant girl in someone's house. She shook away the depressing thought. There would be time enough for that later.

She saw a boy sneaking into a dimly lit room. Kamakshi paused her chatter and followed her gaze.

'It's that devil, Uthanga,' she said. She tiptoed into the room with Sivagami close behind. Sivagami looked around. There was a row of stoves with ash piled inside them. Clumps of charcoal lay on the floor. Big copper vessels with charred bottoms were stacked in a corner. It was the kitchen of the orphanage. The boy was rummaging through the shelves when they surprised him. It was the same boy who had been sleeping at the gate when Sivagami had arrived.

'Thief!' Kamakshi caught him by his ears and the boy howled.

'You can't punish me, you whore,' he said. Kamakshi gave his ears another twist. The boy squealed.

'Next time you use filthy words, I will fill your dirty mouth with ash,' Kamakshi threatened.

'Ayyo, leave me, Akka. It hurts.'

Kamakshi gave another twist, 'Akka? Hmm, now you are getting reformed. I think this method works.'

'Ayyo, this is not for me. It is for Thondaka. They are planning to drink.'

'Drink! Let me tell Aunt Revamma,' Kamakshi caught Uthanga's other ear and twisted it too.

'Bitch, her husband is the one bringing the toddy for the party. Why are you punishing me? Ask Thondaka if you dare. You are not my mukhya, you are the girls' mukhya. I do what my mukhya tells me to,' Uthanga cried and tried to wriggle away from Kamakshi.

'I will report it to the prince,' Kamakshi said, leaving him.

'You do not know any prince,' Uthanga said, massaging his ears with both hands.

'No, but this Akka does,' she said pointing to Sivagami. 'Now come to my room and clean it. We have to make arrangements for Akka,' Kamakshi ordered, shoving the boy out of the kitchen. She took the broom from the corner and handed it to him. She took the bundle from Sivagami's hands and placed it over his head.

After taking a few steps, Uthanga turned around. 'If she is the lover of the prince, why is she staying in an orphanage?' Uthanga said, eyeing Sivagami suspiciously. Sivagami's face flushed. These people had no business spreading such rumours. She was no one's lover. She had to tell Kamakshi as soon as they were alone.

'Small people should not concern themselves with big things. Run, you devil, and do what I said or this Akka will get your hide whipped tonight.'

They followed him up the spiral staircase, which creaked with every step. They could see Revamma on the other side of the courtyard with a group of boys and girls. The prince has been mobbed, Sivagami thought. They entered Kamakshi's room. Uthanga had already piled up old rags and soiled clothes in a corner and moved a cot to one side. He was on his haunches, sweeping, and Sivagami's bundle was on the floor.

'Not exactly a chamber befitting the lover of the prince, but still...' Kamakshi said.

'Will you please stop calling me his lover? I am not anyone's lover. I just met him,' Sivagami said. From under the cot, Uthanga crawled out holding a squealing mouse by its tail. He started walking out of the room.

'Hey, where are you going?' exclaimed Kamakshi, grabbing the boy.

'She is not the prince's lover. I heard her say so. Leave me, bitch,' Uthanga said, trying to wriggle out of Kamakshi's grip.

'You will do as I say, you devil.' As soon as Kamakshi had said this the boy threw the mouse at her face. She screamed and jumped up on her cot. The boy attempted to make a dash for it but stumbled on the bundle and fell on his face. Sivagami rushed to help him up.

The boy got up, and Sivagami was petrified to see that he was holding her father's manuscript. For a moment the boy stared at it and Sivagami's face in turn. She tried to take it from his hand, but he moved away.

'Ooo, ooooo, what is this? Witchcraft?' he cried. Sivagami tried to grab the book, but the boy ran out of the room with the manuscript. He ran through the corridor and Sivagami pursued him. She lunged at him. The boy was at the edge of the spiral staircase and, in a bid to evade her, he lurched forward. He suddenly lost his footing, and Sivagami could only watch in helpless horror as he tumbled down the staircase, hitting his head many times. She screamed. The boy was sprawled on the floor. Blood was oozing from his head, and he was not moving. Her manuscript lay a few feet away. She could hear screams and cries from the other wing. They had heard the sound of the boy falling or perhaps her scream. She could hear people running from the other side.

The manuscript! Her heart was in her throat. With all other thoughts blocked out, she stumbled down the stairs, half-falling, half-jumping, and reached an eye-batting moment before the others had crowded around them. She snatched the manuscript and shoved it in the folds of her breast-cloth. By that time, everyone had reached.

'Ayyo, ayyo, the boy is dead,' Revamma beat her head with both her hands. There were angry murmurs.

'I saw her pushing him,' a gruff voice said, and Sivagami raised her head. Her eyes were bleary and she could barely make out his face.

'No, he fell down, and in fact she tried to save him,' Sivagami heard Kamakshi's voice from behind.

No, Kamakshi, I killed him, she wanted to scream. She bit her lips, trying not to cry, but the guilt overwhelmed her. 'Ma Gauri, what I have done, what I have done,' she mumbled, without expecting an answer.

An argument broke out between Kamakshi and the other boy, while the other residents too joined in with raised voices. Revamma was crying hysterically. Sivagami felt numb. How could she have done it, she asked herself again and again.

'He is not dead. He is breathing.' At first, she did not comprehend what she heard. She vaguely recognized Prince Mahadeva's voice. Through her tears, she saw the prince wiping the blood from the orphan's face with his silk angavastra. He put his head on the boy's chest and said, 'I hear heartbeats. If we take him to the rajavaidya, we could save him. Do you have a cart?'

Revamma hesitated. Her husband might have taken the official cart to some whorehouse.

Without a word, the prince lifted the boy onto his shoulders. Revamma cried, 'Your Highness, one of the boys will carry him. Don't soil your royal clothes. He is just an orphan.'

But Mahadeva ignored her and Sivagami watched as he left the orphanage gate carrying the limp body of the boy on his shoulders. At the gate, he turned back and caught Sivagami's gaze. It sent a shudder down her spine. Did he know she had done it? She sat on the floor, her knees no longer strong enough to support the heaviness she felt.

'Others might believe he fell but I know you pushed him. This Thondaka knows. You will pay for it, bitch.' Sivagami saw that it was the same boy who had first accused her. *Yes, it was me who did it*, she wanted to scream. *Punish me*, she wanted to cry, but Kamakshi's hands squeezed her shoulders.

'Don't spread lies, Thondaka,' Kamakshi yelled at him.

'He was my little friend, and if he dies, you better count your days,' Thondaka hissed in her ears and hurried to follow the prince. Sivagami sat without moving, her face buried in her hands.

'It was just an accident,' Kamakshi said. Sivagami shook her head in denial. She had killed the boy. How was she going to live with the guilt? 'Oh Amma Gauri, let the boy live, let him be all right,' Sivagami prayed, covering her face, bereft of any courage to face the world. The manuscript felt heavy in her breast, the guilt in her heart was heavier. The orphanage was eerily silent except for the heavy breathing of Kamakshi sitting next to her.

FOURTEEN

Kattappa

The palanquin followed the path by the river, but the terrain had become hillier near the shores. Shrubs looked like dark patches in the moonlight. Trees rose on either side, muffling the roar of the river. They were climbing up a hill. Kattappa sighed in relief. That had been a close shave with Prince Mahadeva. Keki turned and saw Bijjala bathed in sweat. She leaned, deliberately brushing her breasts against Kattappa's face, and patted the prince, 'Believe me, my lord, this trip is worth all perils. By tomorrow, you will be thanking this poor eunuch and showering her with pearls and diamonds.'

As she leaned back, she winked at Kattappa. 'Blackie,' she whispered in Kattappa's ears, licking his earlobe. 'What is the one thing you would want to do before you die?'

Kattappa snapped alert, and drew half his sword out of the scabbard.

'Easy, slave boy, easy,' Keki said. 'It was just a question. There are black girls too in our den. We are going to see how well your little one can perform.' Keki grabbed Kattappa's manhood and, reflexively, Kattappa's elbow jerked outwards, catching Keki's face, cracking open her lips. The palanquin shook and Bijjala hit his head on its roof.

'You bloody slave,' Bijjala cried.

Keki wiped the blood from her lips with the back of her hand and said, 'It was my mistake, Prince. This blackie is too handsome. Poor Keki lost control.'

Kattappa held on tight to the hilt of his sword and looked straight ahead. The palanquin swayed and creaked. The voices collectively singing 'Ho-ho-ho-ho' was the only sound other than the faint rush of River Mahishmathi. The prince was silent until Keki held out a horn. A sweet pungent smell filled the palanquin. Bijjala's eyes widened.

'Aswasakhti—the extract of the best grass from the Gomedaka hills,' Keki said. 'A swig of it and even the old fart Parameswara would become a virtuoso in the art of love. The drink of Kamadeva and Rati!'

With trembling hands Bijjala took it. 'For me?' he asked like a child who had just got his first toy. Keki smiled. Kattappa considered grabbing the horn and flinging it into the river. The prince smelled it and emptied the contents of the horn into his mouth. The blood-curdling scream that followed scared everything around, with squeaking birds flying away from the bushes on either side of the road. The palanquin jerked and stopped.

'You are trying to kill me,' Bijjala cried, his tongue hanging out. He fanned it with his hands.

Keki howled in laughter. 'You should take a sip at a time, my lord. But I admire you. A whole horn of gold water in a single swig! That would have knocked down an elephant.

Kalika's girls are in for a treat; they will be swooning over you and will have great stories to relate in the morning. A man who can take a swig of Aswasakhti in one swig is a man more powerful than a horse,' she said, and ran her tongue over her dark lips.

'I am stronger than a horse,' Bijjala said, slurring his words. 'I am sorry, *hic*. Two horses.' The prince laughed and held up three fingers in front of Keki's face. He grinned and counted aloud, 'One, two, and three. How many elephants did I say, Keki dear?'

'Only two, my lord. And you said horses, not elephants.'

'Oh did I? I hope you won't hold it against me, Keki. *Hic*.' Bijjala folded one finger. 'Now are you happy? The arithmetic is right? Have you got more of that stuff, Keki darling?' The prince reached and caressed Keki's smooth cheeks. Keki kissed Bijjala's hands and handed over another horn.

'Anything for my prince, but let me warn you, my lord, it is stronger than the previous one.'

Bijjala snatched it and emptied it before Kattappa could even blink. The prince was now howling with laughter and he slapped Kattappa's back in jest. 'You are such a sweet black dog. A stinking dog, but my dog,' Bijjala said, and howled in appreciation of his own joke.

Keki said, 'Wait till we reach Kalika's den. You can swim in gold water there.'

'Swim?'

'Yes, swim; that too with naked apsaras.'

'In gold water?'

'Yes, my lord.'

'With apsaras?'

'Indeed, my lord.'

'And they'd be naked?'

'Of course, my lord.'

'Oh, how sweet,' Bijjala slurred before he fell unconscious. The palanquin swayed on. They turned from the river path and were now climbing a hill, and the carriers were panting with the effort. Kattappa wiped the drool from Bijjala's mouth. Things were going awry and Kattappa wished he knew what he should do. Every nerve in his body was becoming taut, warning him of impending danger.

Far away, through the curtains, he could see a faint glow of lights on the hilltop. Strains and sounds of music and laughter filtered through the woods. Kattappa felt Keki staring at him. He could feel her breath on his neck. Kattappa turned his head suddenly and found Keki's face very near his own. Her pouting mouth opened to a wicked grin, sending a chill down his spine. Kattappa sat like a statue. Bijjala was snoring on his shoulders. To add to Kattappa's woes, he kept worrying about his brother. He had to go in search of him and bring him back.

Finally the palanquin stopped and Keki pulled back the curtains. She jumped out and stretched herself. Kattappa took some time to wake Bijjala up and help him out of the palanquin.

The prince grinned like a fool and put his hand around Kattappa's shoulders as if he were his bosom friend and not a slave. Kattappa prayed that no one would witness the travesty. He could get whipped for it in the morrow.

When they turned towards the street leading to Kalika's den, they found it congested with chariots and palanquins, haphazardly parked. Sounds of merriment—the cacophony of thakil drums and nagaswara mixed with mrudangam and ghatam, whistles and catcalls, shrieks and laughter—grew louder as they entered the street. Kattappa could see the tavern was guarded like the fort of a king. Even though it was more than a thousand feet away, he could spot at least a dozen sentries at the gate at the far end of the street. He noticed many more guards with spears stationed in the ramparts above the high wall. Shops selling herbs, scented oils, silk clothes and cheap brewed liquor lined either side of the road. The street was crowded with servants of noblemen, charioteers, cart men and palanquin men shopping for themselves or their masters. Buxom women with painted faces sat in the balconies while their pimps called out for patrons. They shouted out the expertise of their wards in the art of love from the entrance of the pleasure mansions.

Bijjala looked around with wonderstruck eyes. A toothless pimp came and caught the prince's hand. 'Come in, swami, come to the palace of Mohini. Lovely girls with breasts like mangoes and nipples like grapes await you.'

Another man grabbed Kattappa. 'Sir, come in. Women with black tresses and skin as smooth as a black buck's, eyes so lustful and lips so delicious—come to the home of Ragini.'

Keki and her men drove the pimps away, but more kept coming. Pimps ran to advertise their wares and sing about their girls' physical assets and how they could pleasure each part of their anatomy. A silk scarf fell on Kattappa and he looked up. A girl stood leaning on the balustrade of her balcony. Her breasts were exposed and she shook them at Kattappa. He shuddered at the sight and realized what he was holding was her breast-cloth. He heard a peal of laughter from above and, despite himself felt lustful. *It is a sin, it is a city of sin*, he kept telling himself.

Bijjala wanted to enter the first house on the street, but Keki grabbed his hand and pulled him into a mansion on the left.

'This is a secret way, Prince,' Keki said as they entered a mansion.

It was dark inside, but Bijjala could see many figures on the floor, or on creaking cots, entwined in various positions of intercourse, slithering, puffing and panting. An animal smell hung in the air. Primal sounds, love calls and grunts, punctuated by shrieks of laughter, all made the place dark as sin.

'This way, this way,' Keki said, never letting go of Bijjala's wrists. Kattappa followed, stumbling through the darkness down a narrow corridor. Lamps burned in rooms, and smoke snaked up to thicken and hang under the low ceiling. Each room had a couple in it, some had more than one. Kattappa walked, careful not to look, but there was no escaping the sounds. A girl came running out of a room, chased by a man. She collided with Kattappa and he recoiled when he realized that she was as naked as the day she was born. She giggled at him, but the man who came running behind her hugged her from behind. They fell before Kattappa, laughing and screaming. Before he could react, the man took the girl from behind like a dog. The couple had cut off Kattappa from Bijjala. Kattappa stood frozen, not knowing what to do. The corridor was too narrow to side-step the couple.

Keki and Bijjala were about to turn into one of the many corridors. Kattappa closed his eyes and stepped over the couple. The girl caught his legs. 'Come, I want you,' she cried, reaching for his dhoti. The man slapped her buttocks and she laughed and shrieked with pleasure.

Kattappa struggled to get out of the girl's grip. By the time he was free, Bijjala and Keki had vanished. He ran, stumbling down the corridor, ignoring the lewd comments of the girl about his manliness. He saw Keki and Bijjala vanishing into a hole in the wall. He ran and reached the door just before it closed completely. Kattappa forced his arm in to wedge open the door. He could see Keki taking Bijjala down a flight of steps. The door was crushing his arm. He could hear some pulleys being operated by slaves, in all probability hidden in some cavity in the wall. He knew if he gave up, he would be left outside Kalika's den, and the prince would totally be under Keki's control. He held on with all his strength, pushing the door back with both his hands and, slowly, he managed to get his shoulder into the gap. That gave him some more leverage to push open the door. He slipped in and rolled down the steps. The door shut behind him with a bang. He saw Keki look back and then hurry along. As he ran down the steps he thought he saw anger flash in the eunuch's eyes. He reached them just before a door was about to cut Keki and Bijjala off from him.

'You won't give up, will you? Bastard,' Keki hissed.

'My place is beside my master,' Kattappa's voice echoed in the empty, unlit corridor.

As the door creaked open, the soft sounds of a veena being played floated out. From the damp, dark corridor that smelt of rat piss, they stepped into dazzling brilliance. The fragrance of exotic perfumes hung in the air. It was a world different from what he had seen just moments ago. His feet sank into soft carpets. Intricately carved pillars soared high and vanished into darkness many feet above his head. Carved sculptures of couples in coitus, as per various positions described in the

Kamasutra, adorned the walls. Pillars had beautiful yakshis carved on them, slim waists, curvy buttocks and round breasts with pointed nipples, holding a lamp on their palms. All the lamps were lit, and in their golden lights, the yakshis looked surprisingly alive and gorgeous.

At the centre of the hall, there were high cushions arranged on the floor. Gold-plated hookahs were kept near pillows. The pillars around this space had ornate mirrors hanging from them, and the light from the gold-plated peacock lamps placed near them lit up the area, giving it an ethereal glow.

'Devasabha,' Bijjala swooned.

'Yes, my prince, and apsaras will be here soon,' Keki said, making him sit on one of the cushions and pushing a hookah near him. Kattappa stood behind Bijjala, drinking in the luxury of the place. Not even the durbar of Mahishmathi looked so glittery. Inlaid jewels in the walls sparkled as flames danced in the breeze that came through jalakas. A foot-tapping rhythm emerged from the mrudanga and Prince Bijjala's eyes widened in pleasure and surprise. The veena switched to a faster pace and the sound of flutes soared. Bijjala, still half-drunk, started tapping his feet. Kattappa stood impassive, both his hands on the hilt of his sword and his eyes fixed on a dancing flame.

'Where are the apsaras?' Bijjala asked, in a voice that betrayed impatience and excitement. Keki smiled and clapped her hands above her shoulders. The walls around them split into many panels. For a moment, in rooms behind the walls, there was a glimpse of women dressed in the finest clothes, standing in dancing positions, before the panels rejoined to reflect Keki and the two men again. With each clap of Keki's hands, panels swung open again, and each time the dancers were in a different pose. Bijjala squealed in pleasure.

He joined Keki in clapping their hands and soon the panels started spinning, gathering speed according to the rhythm of the mrudangam. The effect was startling. Bijjala could no longer sit on the beddings on the floor. He ran to one of the dancers, only to find that just before he could reach her, the wall had swung close and another on the opposite side had opened to reveal a different dancer in a more sensuous pose. Bijjala started laughing in excitement. Cussing and swearing, spewing lewd comments, he started running from one closing panel to the next open one. The teasing continued until Bijjala became furious and flung a hookah on a panel that had closed on his face.

As the hookah missed its mark, the prince was startled by laughter that sounded like the strumming of a rudraveena. When Bijjala turned back, he saw a dazzlingly beautiful woman lying on the bedding, gazing at him. The prince's mouth fell open and he made to lurch at the woman.

Kattappa continued to stare at the blank wall, though he was acutely aware of the beauty lying a few feet before him, leaning on the cushion and looking seductively at Bijjala. He could not help glancing at her. She looked as if she had been sculpted by a master. In the light reflected by the crystals and diamonds in the wall, her skin looked almost iridescent. She was scantily clad, with a silk band tied across her shapely breasts and a dhoti that was tied many fingers below her navel and barely covered her upper thighs. She stretched a slender arm and called Bijjala with the flip of her index finger.

'Come, my prince. How long will you make this Kalika wait?' Her voice was husky and dripped honey. Kattappa's grip on the hilt of his sword tightened. Much as he tried, her musky smell was stirring deep desires.

A tune rose from a flute behind the swaying curtains. It was a familiar romantic raga. He tried to identify it. Anything to keep himself from getting bewitched by the beauty of Kalika. Khamboji—that was the name the vidwans had given to this raga. As if knowing the names of ragas was going to be of any use to a slave. He closed his eyes and opened it hurriedly for, even in his mind's eye, all he saw was Kalika. He was scared to close his eyes again. His father was right. He was yet to control his senses, his vow of brahmacharya was imperfect, and he was still assaulted by such evil thoughts.

Kattappa knew the prince was trapped in the grip of this beautiful woman. He should have stopped Prince Bijjala from coming here. Kattappa stole a glance at the prince, who was standing as if he had grown roots to the floor.

Keki took Bijjala's arms and, seductively, her steps in rhythm with the soft beats of the mrudangam in the background, walked him to Kalika. The prince moved as if he was in a dream, his eyes fixed on the beautiful arching figure on the floor.

'She is all yours, Prince,' Keki bowed, and Bijjala removed his pearl necklace from his neck and threw it at the eunuch. She caught it deftly. 'A poor gift, my prince, but I won't complain. What are good friends for, if they start expecting great gifts every time?'

Delirious with happiness, Bijjala fell on his knees and leaned to touch Kalika with his trembling hands. Kalika stopped the prince by placing her right foot on his chest. Kattappa averted his eyes from her ivory thighs.

'Go on, kiss it, Your Highness,' Keki whispered in Bijjala's ears. Kattappa stiffened. He hoped the prince would not stoop to the extent of kissing a whore's feet.

Bijjala took Kalika's foot and sucked her toes. Kalika moaned, arching her sinuous body against the pillow.

'Further up, Your Grace,' Keki said. Bijjala started kissing Kalika's calf, then her knees, moving to her thighs. The music increased in tempo. Kattappa averted his eyes, but there was no escaping the mirrors that reflected and amplified what he did not want to see. When Bijjala reached her navel, Kalika gently pushed him away. She sat up and her arms went behind her back. Kattappa could hear Bijjala sucking in his breath. She was untying the knot of her breast-cloth. When Bijjala tried to help her, she lightly slapped away his hand. She looked into his eyes and laughed. Bijjala was trembling with excitement. Her fingers lingered, playing with the knots, testing his patience. He lunged towards her, hungry to grab her breasts with both his hands. Suddenly, she slipped away from under him and ran, laughing. Bijjala cursed and stood up, his dhoti in disarray. He grunted in frustration and anger.

Kalika stood a few feet away, striking an elegant pose, her enchanting figure reflected in hundreds of mirrors. When Bijjala reached her, she slipped away again, only to appear somewhere else. Bijjala ran from pillar to pillar, trying to grab her. Keki kept laughing and encouraging the prince. Kattappa stood like a statue, looking at some invisible point in the shifting walls. Once in a while, Kalika would allow Bijjala to catch her and he would shower her with kisses. Once she even let him put his hands under her breast-cloth, but then she slipped away again.

Bijjala started to get angry. The next time she appeared, he was prepared. His warrior instincts had taken over. Surprising her, he moved like a whip and caught her. His hands fumbled with the knot of her upper garment, but before he could untie it, Kalika kissed him full on his mouth. Bijjala closed his eyes, enjoying the taste of Kalika's luscious lips on his. When he opened his eyes again, he was holding the breast-cloth, but Kalika had vanished. The music stopped abruptly.

Bijjala roared in anger. He asked Keki where Kalika was. Keki laughed. Bijjala shook Kattappa by his shoulders and screamed at him, asking him whether he had seen Kalika. Kattappa had seen Kalika without her breast-cloth, and had been so ashamed that he had averted his gaze. He stood with his head hanging in shame as Bijjala cursed. Keki kept laughing until Bijjala drew Kattappa's sword and pressed its edge to her neck.

'Bring her now,' the prince shouted. Keki's eyes bulged in fear. For the first time that day, Kattappa felt relieved. He hoped Bijjala would press the sword a tad more and finish the wretched creature here and now.

'I am all yours, Prince.' Kalika's sweet voice startled them. The entire room had changed. The mirrored walls had folded to one side, to reveal a long hall. At the end, Kalika was sitting like a queen, wearing dazzling jewellery and elaborate headgear decorated with colourful plumes. She had a gown of string pearls that covered her from her neck down to her ankles. It was fastened with an elaborate knot near her left collarbone.

Bijjala pushed Keki away and ran towards Kalika. Kattappa hurried behind him. Keki, who was on the floor, caught Kattappa's legs.

'Whoa, where are you going, slave boy?' she cried and held on firmly to Kattappa's leg. The slave continued to walk, dragging her along, but she would not let go of his legs. Bijjala had reached Kalika with his drawn-out sword.

'Enough of your games, you bitch. Come here,' Bijjala screamed. His voice was boyish and his face turned red when Kalika burst out laughing.

'Darling, my sweet prince, you look so adorable when you are angry,' she said as she stood up. Her fingers were playing with the knot of the string pearl gown and her lips pouted seductively.

'Come, come, my god of love, my Kamadeva,' she said and Bijjala took one tentative step. Her fingers yanked the knot and the gown disintegrated in a flurry of pearls flying in all directions.

Kalika stood gloriously naked, her left hand on her hip, her right hanging free, touching the top of her thigh, and her head thrown back. Exquisite pearls of all colours danced on the floor, bouncing, hitting the walls, pillars and steps, and rolled everywhere as if they were bashful of their mistress's nakedness. Bijjala stood transfixed, drinking in her beauty. Kattappa froze, unable to look away from the bewitching sight of the goddess. When the last of the bouncing pearls had rested, music rose again from the background—the veena drawing out an exquisite raga. Colourful smoke curled from the ceiling and filled the room with the scent of jasmine.

Kalika traced an invisible line from her lips to her navel and said in a husky voice, 'You have to earn me, Prince.'

'What should I do? Should I fight your enemies, should I bring you silk from Cheenadesa, attar from Arabia, clever dolls from the land of the barbarians? Tell me what I should…' Bijjala's excited words stopped midway when Kalika put a finger to her lips.

'My prince is so kind. All those are welcome, but I give myself only to those who can play games,' Kalika said, wetting her lips. Kattappa was alarmed. Something didn't seem right.

'What game do you want me to play? You want me to fight a raging bull with my bare hands? You want me to match my sword with the best of the warriors? What game?' Bijjala asked, and Kalika collapsed on her high seat, laughing.

She crossed her legs, hiding her charms, and said, 'I know those are too easy for my warrior.'

Kalika pushed a stool with a chaturanga board towards him. 'Let me see how well you play,' she said, opening a carved sandalwood box. 'Keki?'

Keki let go of Kattappa's legs and ran towards Kalika who handed the box over to her. The eunuch started arranging the coins on the board. Bijjala looked worried and glanced at Kattappa. The slave knew his prince was no good at chaturanga. He had never played it well. In fact, he was never good at anything that needed brains.

'Prince,' Kattappa bowed to Bijjala and said, 'it is time for us to go.'

Bijjala looked at Kalika, who sat smiling. He gulped as his eyes roved over her naked body. Kattappa knew he had lost when he saw the fire of lust in Bijjala's eyes. The prince said, 'I am ready to play. I can defeat a woman with my eyes closed.'

Bijjala climbed up onto the dais and sat on a chair, waiting for Kalika to get up and sit across him. Keki moved back after she had placed all the coins on the board. She handed over the dice to Kalika.

'I am impressed, my prince,' Kalika said, clicking the dice together. 'But I am not the one playing with you.'

Bijjala looked at her, confused and angry. Kattappa's fists curled in tension.

'Are you mocking me?' Bijjala asked. 'If you are not playing, who do you want me to play with? This disgusting eunuch or my stupid slave?'

'With me, Your Highness.'

Kattappa and Bijjala turned towards the voice. A dwarf came waddling from the side. 'Khanipathi Hidumba at your service, Your Highness. I will be playing against you.'

'A dwarf?' Bijjala started laughing. 'This dwarf is my opponent?' He slapped his thigh in merriment. Kalika threw the dice in the air and Bijjala caught them before they touched the ground. He clicked them together and cried, 'Ah, this is going to be fun.'

'Of course, Your Highness. Fun is what we all seek. Let there be a wager, let there be some witnesses. In fact, I have called the noblest men of Mahishmathi to witness our game,' the dwarf said. As if on cue, Bhoomipathi Pattaraya, Rajaguru Rudra Bhatta and Dandanayaka Pratapa walked in. Kalika rose to welcome them. She hugged Pattaraya and Pratapa, planting a kiss on their cheeks. Bijjala gritted his teeth. Rudra Bhatta was sweating and looking away from Kalika's glistening nudity. She touched his feet and sought his blessings, which he hurriedly gave, wiping his sweat with his angavastra.

Keki caught the priest regarding Kalika's naked behind and said, 'There is no sin in looking, Rajaguru, nor is there a charge. Look to your heart's content.' The priest's friends laughed and Rudra Bhatta looked down in shame.

'Shall we start? What is the wager?' Hidumba asked. In reply, Bijjala removed his diamond studded bracelet and slammed it on the table. Hidumba looked at his friends and with a scornful smile that made his face more hideous, did the same with his pearl necklace. Hidumba threw the dice, screaming, 'Pakida, pakida twelve.' An unseen percussionist in some hidden chamber rolled his fingers on his mrudangam as the dice spun on the table.

Kattappa knew, from the laughter of Hidumba's friends, that the game was lost before it had even begun.

FIFTEEN

Skandadasa

It was past midnight when Skandadasa returned to his chambers. Maharani Hemavati had summoned him. Both her sons were missing. The queen had been livid. She had screamed that if something happened to her sons, she would have his head rolling. She was justified in her anger too. Even when she insulted him and pointed to his lowly origins, Skandadasa had stood with his head bent. He was fortunate that the maharaja was not in the palace, else he would not have been given time till morning to find the princes.

Skandadasa had built up his reputation with hard work and dedication in a career spanning twenty-three years. At the age of forty-five, he remained a bachelor. He was married to his job. He always prided himself on his capability to do any job efficiently. When Prince Bijjala was almost killed by the elephant, he was the one in the durbar who was most vocal in criticizing the incompetence of Senapathi Hiranya and Dandanayaka Pratapa. He had given a speech before Maharaja Somadeva about how both the army and the police had failed to protect the prince. The king had patiently listened to him while Hiranya and Pratapa seethed and fretted. Once he sat down, Somadeva had consulted briefly with Parameswara and then ordered that, henceforth, Skandadasa would be responsible for the security of the princes and the fort.

Skandadasa had approached the job with his usual tenacity, but soon he found that it was no easy task. The citadel of Mahishmathi was built almost three hundred years ago and had grown bewilderingly complex over the years. Each king had added his own modifications. There were underground tunnels and confusing corridors, secret rooms and chambers. It would have been manageable had there been a plan of the fort. When Skandadasa had asked for it, certain that such a map must exist, Parameswara had stared at him in disbelief. He was told that it would be most stupid to have such a thing. An enemy would just have to get hold of it to gain entry. Keeping certain things committed to memory was the best way to assure safety, the old man had told him patronizingly. It still bristled when he thought about his superior's comment. Committing to memory was a crude method, he thought. What would happen if the only men who knew about certain aspects of the fort were killed in a war? He had not argued with Parameswara, but had started to map the entire complex in secret. Skandadasa was a man of method. It was a mammoth task and it would take many years, but he was not a person to give up easily. This would be his legacy, he kept telling himself.

He had also put strict restrictions on the movements of the young princes. It hurt his ego to know that both of them had fooled him and got out. Yet, that was what he hoped had happened. He was terrified to think someone might have kidnapped them.

He wanted to prove himself an able successor to Parameswara. He had neither legacy nor money. He belonged to a low caste and had come up through patient labour and determination. Becoming mahapradhana was something he desperately wanted to do. It would be the culmination of a journey, a promise he had made to himself when he came as a starving nobody to the city of Mahishmathi, thirty years ago.

Now, when people called him scrupulously honest and loyal like a dog, his chest swelled with pride. He was honest because that was his nature, he was loyal because he had been given one chance in his life, a chance he had grabbed with both hands. Mahapradhana Parameswara had given him that one chance. He had scrubbed floors in the taverns, washed dirty dishes in wayside toddy shops and studied whenever he could, standing outside schools and listening to the lessons. He was never allowed inside because of his caste, and even if anyone was ready to take him, he could not have afforded the fees.

If not for Parameswara, who had discovered and mentored him, he would have ended up as a server of palm toddy in some village tavern. Or he would have gone back to his village and taken up his caste profession of a bear dancer. That he became neither was a tribute to the kindness and foresight of the old mahapradhana.

Now the edifice he had built one brick at a time was threatening to crumble. He collapsed on his chair and massaged his head. After some time, he decided the only way to solve this was in his usual way. He would attack the problem methodically. He called for the records of all the gates and started checking who had entered and left the fort. There had been many carts and palanquins moving in and out, and the possibility of the prince hiding in one of them could not be ruled out.

After poring over the records for more than two yamams, Skandadasa found that the number of drummers who went out did not tally with the number that had entered. He did not know what that meant. He dismissed the thought of Prince Bijjala going out disguised as a drummer. He would have been recognized by the guards because of his sheer size. He decided to start his investigation by questioning the head of the harem.

Brihannala came in, in an awful mood. Skandadasa knew that the eunuch resented being summoned by him at this time of the night.

'Can I sit?' she asked gruffly.

'No,' Skandadasa said. Though he was above her in position, she was reputed to be close to the maharaja and was feared and respected by many officials. But Skandadasa had nothing to fear. He had come up through his own honest efforts. He needed no one's favour.

Brihannala stood tapping her fingers on the headrest of the chair. Impatient—Skandadasa noticed. He pushed the box containing the gate entry–exit records towards her.

'Check these palm leaves. An extra drummer has gone out of the fort. The records of the number of drummers gaining entry is one less than the number that went out,' he said, staring at her.

'So? My job is not to count how many drummers came, went, jumped from the tower and died or any such thing. I am the head of Antapura, not the watchman of the gate,' Brihannala said, with a derisive smile on her face.

Skandadasa was about to reply when the gate of his mansion opened and a group of people came running inside. A young man was carrying another boy on his shoulders. There were many excited soldiers accompanying them.

'Prince Mahadeva! What is all this, Your Highness? What has happened?' Skandadasa asked, when he recognized the boy.

'This boy needs the rajavaidya's attention, but for some reason the guards brought me here,' Mahadeva said.

Skandadasa had many questions to ask, but seeing the condition of the boy that the prince was carrying, he sent for the palace doctor at once. He helped Mahadeva lay down the boy on his table. The room was crowded with guards and people from the orphanage. Mahadeva fussed over the boy, opening his eyelids, checking his heartbeat and asking every moment why the doctor was taking so much time.

When Rajavaidya Madhavaru came, he paused for a moment on seeing the boy. His face became grave as he neared his patient. He checked his pulse and his eyelids. He kept his head on the boy's chest and frowned.

'I am sorry,' he said.

'Is the poor boy dead?' the prince cried in anguish.

Madhavaru shook his head, 'I wish he was, but his is a fate worse than death. He lives, but only barely. Even if he ever opens his eyes, which I doubt he will, he will never walk. In fact he has lost the use of his body. It would be better if he does not suffer like this and dies.'

'No, no, no,' the prince cried, holding the rajavaidya's hands. 'We cannot let him die. We will take care of him.'

The rajavaidya nodded grimly and dressed the wound in Uthanga's head. Skandadasa asked Revamma, 'How did the boy get injured?'

'He fell down the stairs,' Prince Mahadeva said before anyone could answer.

'He was pushed down,' a voice from the back cried out. There was a collective gasp.

'Pushed down? By whom?' Skandadasa snapped, and there was an uneasy silence.

'The new girl who has come today. The daughter of that traitor who was hanged,' cried the same voice from the rear.

'Says who? Come forward and talk without fear,' Skandadasa said, and Thondaka came out from the crowd.

'Swami, he is lying. It was just an accident,' Revamma hurried to say, and Prince Mahadeva supported her. The others were noncommittal. Skandadasa had to believe the prince's version, though he decided that he would enquire into the matter later.

'Can he be kept in the rajavaidya's home until he recovers?' Prince Mahadeva asked.

'That would be unwise. My home is already spilling over with patients and he needs constant care. Sir, if he is to be kept at my house, I need some boys from the orphanage to take care of him. He would need help for everything except breathing and I can't spare anyone for a hopeless case. As I already said, I think it would be kind to…'

'No, sir, I don't want anyone talking about killing the boy. You should be ashamed,' Prince Mahadeva's face was red with anger. 'You, a man sworn to save lives, is advising killing.'

'That is the only mercy we can show him now,' Rajavaidya Madhavaru said, unfazed by the prince's anger.

'Never mind your mercy. Revamma?' The prince turned to the caretaker of the orphanage. 'I want him to be taken care of at the royal orphanage.'

'Swami—'

'Even if it takes three decades for him to recover or die, we will take care of him.'

'But swami, it will be expensive.' Revamma stood scratching behind her ears.

'All expenses will be taken care of,' the prince said. There was a murmur amongst the crowd. Revamma appeared pleased. Soon the procession left for the orphanage with the injured Uthanga. The rajavaidya went with them to give instructions on the treatment of the injured boy. Skandadasa was about to return to his chamber, when he saw that the prince was still there.

'Your Highness, I have a few questions for you.' Skandadasa said. Prince Mahadeva stood with his arms crossed and his head bent, as if in deep thought.

'If you are going to ask me how I went out, I am not going to tell you, sir. I am fed up of living like a caged parrot. I know one day you will find out my secret escape route and close that option too, but until then I want to hold on to the little pleasures I can manage,' Mahadeva said.

'Your Highness, it is for your good and safety that I have put these restrictions. It was as per His Royal Majesty's orders,' Skandadasa said, bowing deep. He could understand the prince's frustration but he had to do his duty.

The prince stood deep in thought for some moments. Then he turned to Skandadasa and said, 'Sir, can I trust you?'

Skandadasa drew himself to his full height and said, 'Always, Your Highness. Your father will vouch for my trustworthiness.'

Skandadasa knew he had made a mistake the moment he uttered the words. His father's name seemed to have made the prince more withdrawn. From inside his chamber, Skandadasa could hear Brihannala humming a song. Mahadeva looked here and there, as if scared someone would overhear them. Skandadasa's patience was wearing thin.

'Your Highness...'

'My brother is in danger.'

The suddenness of the statement startled Skandadasa. The prince mistook his shocked silence for disbelief. He took Skandadasa's hands in his and told him what he had seen in the palanquin. He revealed that, by now, his brother was probably in Kalika's den and that he was scared for him.

Skandadasa allowed the prince to complete his frenzied appeal. Alarms were ringing in his head. He had heard reports that Keki was around and that she had visited Brihannala. His spies, who he had stationed near the port to watch out for Jeemotha's ships, had also informed him that Pattaraya's chariot had been seen on the path leading to Kalika's den. He had assumed Keki might have come to solicit Pattaraya and a few others for Kalika.

Though Skandadasa's morals were inflexible, he knew that such visits to the pleasure chambers were common. Neither the king nor Mahapradhana Parameswara cared too much about it. What people did with any part of their body was not the concern of the state, his superior was fond of reminding him. That was another resentment he had against Mahishmathi. No one valued his honesty, his kindness or his morals. No one bothered about his devotion to god. He had once tried to expose a few nobles enjoying their time with some whores, but was ridiculed by the entire court. His spies often reported drunken conversations in taverns about Skandadasa's continued bachelorhood. These conversations, the spies told him with a smirk, always ended with some tasteless comments about his possible impotency.

Skandadasa thought about the problem at hand. Prince Bijjala had foolishly gone to a dangerous place. Anything could happen there. He shuddered at the thought of someone kidnapping or killing Bijjala in Kalika's den, that too on his watch. God was offering him a chance to redeem himself. He had to go there and save the prince.

'Your Highness, I will immediately proceed to Kalika's den and see to it that the older prince does not come to any harm. However, I cannot let the people who compromised the security of the crown prince go unpunished. There will be a trial and the culprits will have to answer the court. But I will try to make it a private trial to avoid embarrassment.'

'Sir, sir, please…' Prince Mahadeva's eyes filled up.

These privileged kids wilt at the smallest of adversities, Skandadasa thought.

He threw his head back, spine erect, and drew himself to his full height, 'I am sorry, Your Highness. If you thought I wouldn't report such a big security breach to the maharaja, you came to the wrong person.'

Prince Mahadeva bowed, turned on his heels and left. Skandadasa felt bad as he watched the prince walk away, his shoulders stooped, his head hanging in worry.

He went inside and closed the door gently. When he turned, he froze. Brihannala was sitting in his chair, reading the records inscribed on the palm leaves.

When Brihannala saw him, she stood up with a smile. Her diamond-studded nose ring sparkled in the lamp-light when she turned her head, but her teeth had more brilliance.

'How dare you meddle with my official records?' Skandadasa asked, trying hard to control his temper.

'Ha, you only asked me to check these. It is tallied now. Would you care to check again?' Brihannala smiled

Skandadasa was sure she had destroyed the record of the extra drummer. Skandadasa had never liked Brihannala. Keki was devious, but Brihannala was the more cunning of the two.

'You...you...' Skandadasa was at a loss for words. His lips trembled with rage and he wagged a finger at Brihannala.

'Rage becomes you, swami,' the eunuch said, bowing low.

Her irreverence always got on his nerves. Had she not been a eunuch, he would have had her thrown out.

'Don't forget that you are talking to the upapradhana of the country,' Skandadasa's fists curled in anger.

'Swami, how can I forget that? The girls in Antapura say you look like a bear dancer, but I have always argued that you have a heart of gold. So what if you are not handsome? We all respect you, swami.' She bowed again with folded hands.

Skandadasa closed his eyes and took a deep breath. The 'bear dancer' was an allusion to his caste. And that was the least of the insults. But more than anything, her false humility was what irritated him the most.

It took all his self-control for Skandadasa to restrain himself from hitting her. He wished he had never sent for her. He had no clue how to deal with her. *You lack a sense of humour*, he could hear Parameswara's voice in his head.

'I have no time for your buffoonery, eunuch. I will meet you tomorrow. Get lost now.'

'Why are you breaking a poor eunuch's heart by being angry, swami? I beg your pardon if I have angered you.'

'Guards,' Skandadasa shouted.

'Easy, easy, swami. Ayyo, you get angry so quickly.'

'Guards!'

Brihannala prostrated herself on the floor and cried, 'Apologies, if I have offended you, Swami.'

Two guards came into the room and bowed. *Idiots*, he thought, *taking their own time to answer his summons.*

'Arrange a dozen armed guards and ready my horse,' Skandadasa said.

The guards bowed and left.

'Where are you going, swami?' Brihannala asked.

'To Kalika's den.'

'Aha, aha, I am fortunate to witness this dedication. You are not even waiting for dawn. The country's interest is supreme to you. What patriotism, what a sense of duty. You are the pride of Mahishmathi. You are going to save Prince Bijjala.'

Skandadasa stared at her. Brihannala realized her mistake a tad too late.

'How do you know that the prince is at Kalika's den?' he asked. Brihannala's face went white as a sheet.

'Your tongue has got you into trouble, isn't it?' Skandadasa smiled at her discomfiture.

'If my swami wants, I will stop speaking forever. You are such a great man. Mahishmathi needs more men like you. I am always your servant, swami. Jai Mahishmathi!' Brihannala said and tried to leave the chamber.

Skandadasa smiled at her. In a swift motion, he unsheathed his sword and pointed it at her throat. 'You are coming with me, my servant. I am impressed by your devotion. I know you were professionally trained at Kalika's inn by her mother. You know the place, in and out. Who better to accompany me on this mission? Let us serve our country together, patriot,' he said with a sly smile.

Who said he did not have a sense of humour, he thought and grinned at his own joke, enjoying the terrified look on Brihannala's face.

SIXTEEN

Sivagami

Uthanga was brought back to the orphanage and carried to the storeroom. Sacks containing dried chillies, pepper and ginger were moved to one side. Rice sacks were piled up in another corner. The plantain that had been hung to ripen was taken out and hung from the veranda roof. The floor was cleaned to make space. A few mice were bludgeoned to death and some spiders accompanied them to the abode of Yama. A cot with broken legs was quickly repaired and put in a corner of the storeroom.

The boy was carried there amid yelling and shouting, and placed on rough sacks spread over the cot. Someone brought some old rags, bundled it up, and made a pillow out of it. They placed the drooling head of Uthanga on it. His arms and legs were tucked in, and an old sari of Revamma's was torn into two and used to cover him.

Sivagami stood, making herself as invisible as possible behind a pillar, and watched everything. She kept biting her nails every time the crowd around the boy moved a little and she got a glimpse of him. *Oh, god what have I done, what have I done,* she kept repeating in her mind. She wanted to cry her heart out, but she could not.

'Thank god he is not dead.'

Sivagami started when she heard the whisper near her ears.

'Kamakshi,' she exclaimed, keeping her hand over her heart. Her eyes filled up and she turned away, leaning her head on a pillar. 'I want to die. What have I done!' she cried. Her friend hugged her to her bosom and Sivagami began sobbing. She felt numb, and neither Kamakshi's gentle words nor her soothing hands that patted her back helped Sivagami.

'I hope you are happy now, bitch,' a harsh voice broke in.

Thondaka was standing with his arms behind his back. There were three boys behind him. Their eyes were full of hatred.

'Thondaka, don't create a scene,' Kamakshi warned him. He pushed her away and lunged at Sivagami. In a flash a knife came slashing at her face. It would have sliced off her nose had she not turned away in the blink of an eye. Kamakshi was screaming murder, calling for Revamma, or anyone who could help.

Sivagami saw the other three boys rushing at her with sticks and iron pestles. She ducked the next swipe of the knife and pushed Thondaka away. It was a kitchen knife, she noticed. Not good for stabbing. He could only slash with it. While she was trying to assess the danger, one of the boys punched Kamakshi in her left eye and Sivagami saw her go down. That made her furious.

'I did not do anything, I did not, you bastards,' she screamed. When the knife came again, she grabbed it. She seemed oblivious to the pain as the sharp edge cut her fingers.

She was only barely aware of the warm blood that trickled down to her elbow.

A sharp pain shot up her right shoulder. A boy was aiming to hit her again with a stick. Her leg shot out and caught him between his legs. He collapsed on his knees, clutching his groin. A pestle blow was aimed at her head, but she felled the boy with a sharp kick on his kneecap. The pestle blasted the wall, showering her with lime plaster and brick chips. A fist slammed below her ribcage and took her breath away for a moment.

Space, space is what I need, she told herself, as she tried to breathe. A kick to her abdomen loosened her grip. She felt the knife slipping away, slashing her inner palm. Blood burst from the fresh cut. She saw the flash of the knife as Thondaka raised it. With a sudden burst of energy, she caught his wrist and flipped him over her shoulders. Thondaka collapsed on his friends. That gave her some time to escape from the corner. She somersaulted over them, yanked Kamakshi up from the floor and ran. She could hear them chasing her. She and Kamakshi ran through the crowded veranda with boys and girls yelling after them. They were baying for her blood. She could not have cared less. Thondaka was chasing them, thrashing wildly with his knife.

Do the unexpected, Uncle Thimma's words, which he had uttered many times during her training, came to her mind.

She slowed down so Thondaka could reach her. She stood holding a pillar, panting. Kamakshi trembled and screamed as Thondaka and his friends closed in. Sivagami stood as if she had not heard them approach. As expected, he came for her with his knife raised. She ducked at the last moment, turned and caught his midriff. She shoved him, using his own momentum, to fling him forward to the pillar.

Thondaka's face crashed on the stone pillar, breaking his row of protruding front teeth. His knife fell from his hand and clanged on the floor. He collapsed on all fours, and blood from his cut lips and broken nose pooled before him on the floor. He appeared dazed. Sivagami used her knee to smash his ribs and he toppled over to his side. The other boys hesitated. She picked up the knife from the floor and pointed it at them. They backtracked. She held Kamakshi's hand and walked straight to them. The boy she had kicked in the groin tried to aim a blow with his stick, but she did not have to even look at him before slashing her knife at him. He fell down, clutching his bleeding wrist while the other two took off.

She walked past the shocked rows of boys and girls. Revamma was screaming her head off, saying the daughter of the traitor had killed her boys. Sivagami walked by her without even bothering to glance at her.

'A rakshasi, a yakshi…or else how can she defeat me. Only god can save us from this witch,' she heard Thondaka crying. Soon the cries of 'yakshi' and 'rakshasi' rose like an angry chant. She turned on her heels and threw the knife at Thondaka. The knife grazed Thondaka's neck, went past the pillar and struck the wall. The sound of its hilt vibrating could be heard in the shocked silence that followed.

Sivagami went to the storeroom with Kamakshi close behind and shut the door. She collapsed on her knees and buried her face in her palms. Her skirt was wet with blood and her chest burned with every breath she took. The acidic smell of pepper and chillies from the sacks made it worse. Kamakshi fussed around to get something to stop the bleeding from her palm. Sivagami dragged herself to the cot where Uthanga was lying unconscious.

She looked at the immobile face of the boy without a word as Kamakshi dressed her palm with turmeric. Sivagami sat still like a statue, never taking her eyes off Uthanga's face. She did not respond even when Kamakshi untied her kaunchika and touched the sore point under her right breast. Blood had clotted in a lemon-sized bruise below her breast.

Kamakshi felt Sivagami's ribs and said, 'Does it hurt?' There was no response from Sivagami.

'Fortunately, nothing seems to be broken,' Kamakshi said while wiping blood from Sivagami's face, back and breasts. She applied turmeric on the wounds and retied Sivagami's kaunchika.

Sivagami leaned her head on the bed where Uthanga lay. Tears started flowing from her eyes and her body shook with sobs. 'Sorry, sorry,' she whispered.

'He will be all right. Let us not lose hope. You did not do it, Sivagami. No need to feel so guilty,' Kamakshi said, but that elicited no response from Sivagami. Kamakshi sighed and moved away to examine her eyes by the lamp. 'I look horrible,' Kamakshi said, touching her black eye. 'I am going to murder that boy.'

There was still no response from Sivagami. Kamakshi reached to squeeze her friend's shoulder and shook her head when she found her silently crying.

'I thought you were a strong girl,' she said. When Sivagami continued with her vow of silence, she began to make some space for her to lie down.

When Sivagami woke up, it was still dark. She did not know when she had fallen asleep. The only sound in the room was the breathing of Uthanga.

From a small crack in the roof, moonlight shimmered in. She heard some hushed whispers. Or was it the wind playing with the leaves? She listened closely. Someone was crying. 'Kamakshi?' she called out, but there was no response.

She stood up, biting her lips to suppress the pain. She limped to the door and pushed it. It creaked open to the emptiness of the central courtyard. She could see a sliver of the moon hanging precariously on a cloudless sky. Someone coughed and Sivagami froze. When nothing stirred, she moved towards the door, skirting in the shadows, through the veranda.

To her surprise, she found the main door ajar. She pulled it open and paused for someone to react to its mild creak. When nothing happened, she stepped out. A boy she did not recognize had taken Uthanga's place on the threshold. She gingerly stepped over his sleeping body and was outside the orphanage.

Sivagami glanced back at the building. In the shadows, with its edges accentuated by the faded moonlight, the orphanage looked gloomier than it did during the day. *How could he…He should not have done this to me. I considered him like my father.* She tried to suppress her rising hatred for Thimma. She debated running away somewhere. She could survive as a maid in some nobleman's home. She knew how to read and write, maybe she could tutor some children. Anything to get away from this hellhole. She could just find her bundle, make sure her father's manuscript was still there, and sneak away. It would be so easy and no one would know or care.

The unconscious face of Uthanga swam in front of her eyes and Sivagami had a sinking feeling. No, she could not leave him like that. She wiped her fast-filling eyes with the back of her hand.

Whispers again. Was that a man's voice? She became alert. There was not a soul in the street and the voices were coming from the side of the building. She tip-toed towards the sound. She was careful to keep herself in the shadows of the building. She saw them under a big fig tree—a man and woman in deep embrace. Behind them the abandoned stable of cart horses rose a few hundred feet away.

Sivagami edged towards them, close enough to hear their conversation. She hid behind a bush. She could only see their profiles in the dark. Up close, it appeared to be a young couple—around her age perhaps.

The boy was kissing the girl with a passion that made Sivagami blush. The girl was resisting, but from the eager way her hands dug into his back, it was evident that she was equally passionate. The girl succeeded in pushing him away and stood breathing deeply, leaning against a tree. She brushed away her hair from her face. Kamakshi! What was she doing here? And who was that boy?

'Please, Shiva, please listen to me,' Kamakshi pleaded.

'I am fed up of this life too, Kama. I will come for you soon and we will go away,' the boy responded.

Kamakshi turned her face away. 'Why can't we go now? I am scared to be here. That eunuch keeps coming, asking for me, and it is only Revamma's greed that has saved me so far.'

Eunuch? Sivagami stood wondering. And how had Revamma's greed kept Kamakshi safe?

'Now that a new girl has come, maybe Keki will set eyes on her instead. It is a matter of just a few days, my love,' the boy said.

'I don't want anything to happen to Sivagami. She is a dear friend, Shiva.'

'One has to be selfish when it is a matter of one's own safety, Kama. I would prefer that new girl to be in Keki's trap than you.'

'I don't want you talking like that.' Kamakshi turned away from him. He tried to cup her face in his palms.

What were they talking about? Keki? The eunuch who had stopped them on her way to the orphanage the previous evening? A cold realization crept up on her. There were no girls in the orphanage who were older than her except Kamakshi. Sivagami put two and two together. When she looked again, the boy was holding Kamakshi close to him. He looked down at her face. 'Kama, I am sorry. Just be patient for a few more days. We are planning something big. Nothing will be the same again—there will be no slaves, no orphans. The rule of kings and noblemen will be a thing of the past. Everyone will have equal rights. All of us will decide who will rule us.'

Kamakshi sighed. 'You keep talking about fanciful things. Nowhere in the world do such things happen. Is it not god's will that some have to be noble and some small folk and…'

'And some slaves like me, to be treated worse than animals, isn't it Kama?' The edge in the boy's voice alarmed Sivagami.

'I…I did not mean that, Shiva. Please, please look at me, please.'

Kamakshi threw her hands around his neck and started kissing him. He resisted and tried to push her away. She hugged him closer and when he tried to say something, she kissed him on his mouth. His fingers entwined with hers and he pressed her to the tree. Without moving his lips from hers, his hands fumbled with her kaunchika. He cupped her breasts and she turned her face away and moaned softly.

Sivagami's face turned hot and she felt embarrassed. She wanted to run back to her room, but despite her wish, her legs wouldn't move. Kamakshi's kaunchika was untied now, and her lover was sucking her left nipple. Her hands played with his unruly hair and she pulled him up to kiss his lips. He obliged but went lower again, kissing her all over. Her fingers tugged at the knot of his dhoti.

Suddenly, he freed himself and stepped away. Kamakshi opened her eyes. Sivagami was intrigued by the sudden change in Shiva's attitude.

'What happened, Shiva?' she heard Kamakshi say. He did not reply.

'Are you angry?' Kamakshi asked.

'No, my love. It's just that I want you to be pure always,' he said, tying Kamakshi's kaunchika back.

'I have always been yours and always will be.' There was a tremor in Kamakshi's voice.

'In case I don't return alive…'

She closed his mouth with her hand. 'Nothing will happen to you. The gods will take care of you.'

'Gods, ah,' he snorted as he ran his fingers through her hair. 'Just like they have taken care of our people always? The gods don't have time for us, Kama.'

'Shh, I don't want you to talk like that,' she said and kissed him again. This time he kissed her back tenderly. The two stood transfixed, lips locked, fingers entwined, and hearts keeping the same rhythm. A gentle breeze played with Kamakshi's hair. Moonlight coloured it silver. Sivagami's eyes filled up. It was the most beautiful sight she had seen in her life. It was so soothing, so divine, that for a moment she wished she was the girl in the lover's embrace. She smiled, trying to give a face to the lover, and stopped herself. No, not that person. Not the son of the king who had killed her father. Not that stupid, good-for-nothing, soft-spoken Mahadeva.

'If only my brother would join us,' Sivagami heard Shivappa say. He was standing with his hands on Kamakshi's shoulders. She was tracing figures on his chest with her fingers.

'He is the eldest, the scion of our tribe, the promised man. I am just a pale imitation. I cannot match his skills with arms, nor his intelligence. I have to take him to meet the leader. He can convince my brother. We need him.' Shivappa's words were fervent.

'Everything will be all right. You will win. All your dreams will come true. You are not doing this just for yourself. You are risking your life for others. The gods, too, love and favour those who act selflessly,' Kamakshi said, looking into his eyes.

'Kama, yours is the only love I want. It is what keeps me alive, keeps me going. I will come back, Kama, and by that time all men and all women will be free. There will be no king or queen, no noblemen, no upper or lower castes, no slaves. A free world, a great tomorrow.'

Kamakshi smiled at him. 'Don't tempt fate. You dream too much.'

Shivappa laughed, 'Make up your mind. Should I dream or stop dreaming?'

'Dream, but dream small dreams, little dreams.'

'A small hut by a river?'

'Hmm...'

'Cows in the shed?'

'Hmm...'

'A beautiful girl by my side...'

'Hmm...' Kamakshi said and turned her head away, bashful.

'To kiss whenever I feel like,' Shivappa planted a kiss on her cheeks, 'wherever I like...' He tried to turn her face to kiss her lips, but she resisted. He took her fingers and counted them, 'One, two, three...ten children to scream, howl and play.'

She pushed him away. 'Enough. This is not a small dream. You are being greedy.'

Sivagami almost laughed. She was thrilled that there were some rebels fighting against the king. She was tempted to reveal herself and join the boy who Kamakshi called Shiva. But Thimma's lessons about caution and patience kept her glued to where she was. She had to find out more.

'Time for me to leave, Kama,' Shiva said.

'Every breath, every moment, I will be praying for you,' Kamakshi said, and he hugged her one last time. Mist was curling through the bushes, dew dipped from leaves. As Sivagami watched, bleary-eyed, he drifted out of Kamakshi's arms and merged with the shadows of the abandoned stable. Kamakshi kept staring at the darkness where Shivappa had vanished and her shoulders heaved. She leaned on the tree for support and then collapsed. She started sobbing.

Sivagami walked up to her and sat down beside the crying girl. She pulled her friend close to her. Kamakshi was surprised to see Sivagami, but did not say a word. She buried her head in Sivagami's shoulder and wept.

Sivagami had known Kamakshi only for a day, but she felt as if she had known her forever. No words were spoken, none were required. Sivagami could feel her pain and her longing. Far away, only the tip of Gauriparvat could be seen, piercing the clouds. The morning star was smiling at them, the star on which one could make a wish. *Let all dreams, little or big, of my dear friend come true*, Sivagami wished. She wondered whether the star had winked at them.

SEVENTEEN

Pattaraya

Things were going as planned. Prince Bijjala had already lost more than two lakh gold sovereigns to Hidumba. He was also sufficiently drunk with gold water to not realize that he was sinking more and more into debt. Pattaraya smiled to himself. It was not for money that he was playing this game. It was for control. The prince would be in no position to share what transpired tonight with anyone. He would become a puppet in Pattaraya's hands. And Pattaraya would make good use of him to access the secret chamber where the Gauridhooli was being made.

He heard another cheer from Hidumba and an exclamation of dejection from Bijjala.

'You lose again, Your Highness. How sad,' Keki said.

'It is the apahara of Shani, Your Highness. You should feed the brahmins and give more offerings to the temple,' Rudra Bhatta, who sat with his back to the naked Kalika, said.

The slave stood as if he was another pillar in the room, motionless, and not even blinking. His bulky arm was flexed as his hand gripped the hilt of his sword.

'One more try, Your Highness, or are you ready to give up?' Hidumba asked, clicking the dice in his hand. Prince Bijjala grunted and took a sip of gold water. Across him, Kalika was applying scented oil to her neck. Her breasts glistened in the flickering light of the peacock lamp. Pattaraya saw Bijjala steal a glance at Kalika and the devadasi smile at him. The wench was driving the poor boy crazy, he thought. It was a masterstroke to involve Kalika in the plan. Risky, but rewarding. He was nearing his goal with every roll of the dice.

He had bribed other bhoomipathis to ensure support against Skandadasa. Not because he needed their support if his plans worked out, but that was what was expected of a politician who was aiming for the post of mahapradhana.

Despite the best plans, he knew that in politics things could change at any moment—loyalties flipped often, back-stabbing was the norm, and ethics were a matter of lip service. But Pattaraya didn't mind. That was what made the game exciting. This day would be a game changer, he had promised his partners in conspiracy.

His exhibition of raw ambition to become mahapradhana was a decoy. Even Chitraveni, the bastard princess of Kadarimandalam, had thought Pattaraya was a man who was greedy for money and position. When he had sent feelers to her, she might have thought she had a man inside Mahishmathi whom she could use. Little did she know that he was using her.

'Lo, His Highness has won this round, evil dwarf,' Keki said clapping her hands and cracking her knuckles on either side of her head.

'That is the power of Shani, Your Highness. You thought of feeding a hundred brahmins and the great lord has started rewarding you already. Think such noble thoughts and see how your luck turns,' Rudra Bhatta said.

Kalika walked from her seat, took Bijjala's hand, and kissed his fingers. 'For the prince of my heart,' she said. A tremor went through the young prince. She walked back, allowing Bijjala enough time to drink in her glory with his eyes. Rudra Bhatta hurriedly closed his eyes and opened them only after the musky fragrance had faded. The slave's eyes twitched.

'Your luck has really turned, Your Highness. What is the next wager?' Hidumba asked with a sad face.

'Fifty thousand gold sovereigns,' Bijjala said, looking at Kalika. She shook her head and continued to apply scented oil on her arms. Pattaraya could see that the smell of musk was driving Bijjala crazy with lust.

'Such a small prize for such an apsara, Your Highness,' Keki said. She walked towards Kalika and traced her curves with her fingers. 'Look how beautiful she is. How heavenly she smells.' She put her nose to Kalika's neck and took a deep whiff.

'One lakh sovereigns,' Bijjala squealed.

Does the fool even know how many zeroes there are in a lakh, thought Pattaraya. There was some protest and teasing and the game resumed. Another yamam of the game and he was sure the prince would be in no position to deny his demand. Once he had Gauridhooli in his hands, he had big plans. He had plans for the new sets of raw Gaurikanta stones too. He had a plan for everything that would take him to the throne of Mahishmathi.

'Again His Highness has won. Take that, you nasty dwarf,' Keki cooed. Bijjala clapped his hands and looked hopefully at Kalika. She smiled and stood up. Bijjala smiled foolishly at her.

She walked towards him, only a thin pearl chain around her hips. She lay down on her side a few feet away, facing him, her head resting on her palm. A hookah blocked Bijjala's view of her from her waist down to her knees. She winked at him. He started to get up, but Hidumba caught his arm.

'Not so soon, Your Highness. Only one among your four coins has homed. Another three to go. So what is the wager?'

Bijjala glared at the dwarf and looked at Kalika hopefully. She pressed her hand to her bosom and nodded her head, reassuring him. He snatched the dice and shook them in his closed fist. 'Two lakh gold sovereigns,' he cried.

'See, that is my brave prince. My lucky prince,' Keki kissed Bijjala on his ears and the prince blushed. He wiped the wetness of the eunuch's spittle with the back of his hand and cried, 'Pakida, pakida twelve.'

Pattarya felt sorry for the prince. How naive he was. Mahishmathi deserved a better ruler. Not this fool. A girl in a short dhoti and skimpy kaunchika served everyone gold water, but Pattaraya declined it. He had never had a drink in his life, and never felt the need for it. Nor had he ever been tempted by any of Kalika's girls. He had loved his wife when she was alive. Plump and plain his wife had been, but he was committed to her. She was the only woman he had ever had in his life. Now everything he was doing was for his daughter. When his wife had died, Mekhala was two years old. He was sad that he did not have a son, but that never stopped him from loving his daughter. He never thought of marrying again. A daughter is sometimes better than a son, he used to think.

The only disappointment was that his daughter had inherited her mother's traits and intelligence. She was too honest and straightforward. Pattaraya had learned the hard way that honesty never paid. Good people often lost out. To come up in life, one needed to be devious and cunning. Life was a struggle. When Mekhala was small, he used to take her to the forest. He would point out how each creature was using deception and cunning to hunt and to escape from being hunted. One had only two choices in life, he used to say to her, to hunt or be hunted. But she would counter him by saying that animals hunted for survival. There was no greed in them. Greed is necessary for survival, he would try and explain. Greed and cunning for a man are like two horns of a bull. Without those, a bull may be powerful but would never survive in the wild.

Ambition and strategy were like two wings of an eagle, a politician is a flightless bird without them, he would say. And she would argue that a politician was not an eagle but a vulture, feeding on the carrions after a war. Pattaraya would tell her that the only creature that survived after a war was the carrion-eating vulture. It was the only one who was unaffected by the outcome of war. For it, victory or loss in a war remained irrelevant, for its belly would be filled irrespective of whoever won. Their arguments and differences of opinion were endless, but Pattaraya would tell himself that his daughter would learn the ways of the world. She was yet young and inexperienced. She had led a sheltered life and had never faced any difficulties. She could afford to talk about honesty for she had never faced hunger and defeat.

In his youth, when his friends whored and gambled, he had struggled hard to work off the debt his father had accumulated. He worked till his hands were numb, travelled to many countries as a merchant and paid back every copper coin his father had owed, whether or not there were records of his debts with the creditors. That had won him many friends. But even those who were surprised to find their debts cleared could not call him honest.

'Lo, this time you lose, Your Highness,' Hidumba cried and Bijjala cursed.

'Swami, no new mantras for the prince? How about giving cows to brahmins? Do you people accept snakes as gifts? Or how about tigers? Will that change the prince's luck?' Hidumba sneered at Rudra Bhatta.

The rajaguru turned to curse the dwarf, saw Kalika's provocative pose, blushed red, and went back to mumbling his mantras. *The dwarf was good. He was a natural actor*, thought Pattaraya, *and a sly man too, a dangerous man.* Pattaraya knew he was playing with fire, but he needed such explosive people to trigger what he had planned.

He had his doubts about Princess Chitraveni. But with a sea port at their disposal, he needed the support of Kadarimandalam for his plan. He was dependent on Jeemotha and his ships for executing the remainder of his plans. None of the people he was dealing with were trustworthy. *But trustworthy people would not commit treason either,* he thought wryly. Whatever he did, he still had to reckon with the power of the Mahishmathi army and its able commander, Senapathi Hiranya. And he would be a fool to discount the cunning of Maharaja Somadeva or the old fox Parameswara. Other bhoomipathis were dangerous in their own way, and unpredictable too. Each coin on his chaturanga board was exciting and each move he had to make would become more and more dangerous as the game progressed. He had to knock off the coins one by one. Devaraya, he had knocked off easily in the first throw of dice itself. Straight trees are easier to cut. Next in line was Skandadasa.

'Lo, you win again, Your Highness! Dwarf, see how the gods have punished you for making fun of our holy man,' Keki said.

Pattaraya saw Kalika inching closer to Bijjala. The prince tried to touch her, but Kalika playfully slapped his fingers. 'My prince is so impatient. Win another three games and I am all yours,' she murmured.

'My pardons, Your Highness. I am a better player and I won't let you win,' the dwarf said with a rakish grin.

He caressed Kalika's thigh and the devadasi pushed away his hand. 'Don't you dare touch me until you win.'

'Here we go,' Hidumba slapped the dice together in his palm and mumbled some mantra.

'No, no, he is doing black magic,' Keki cried, and Bijjala got angry. He tried to snatch the dice from the dwarf's hands. The dwarf rolled the dice and laughed, 'Lo, I win.'

'You cheat,' Bijjala lunged to slap the dwarf, but Kalika threw her hand across the dwarf's face. Bijjala's palm connected with Kalika's flesh and she cried, 'You hurt me, my prince.'

Bijjala was on his knees. 'I am sorry, I am sorry,' he pleaded, as Kalika's eyes filled up. Pattaraya wanted to laugh, but managed to camouflage his mirth in a bout of coughing.

Bijjala said, 'Don't be angry with me. I will compensate.'

'How sweet,' Keki exclaimed.

Kalika smiled through her tears, 'My lord is so kind.'

Bijjala returned to the board and found that Hidumba had already moved the coins.

'The last throw was invalid,' Bijjala grunted.

'None of my throws are invalid,' the dwarf grinned.

'Let the dandanayaka judge,' Keki said, and everyone looked at Pratapa.

He thought for some time and said, 'His Highness is right, the last throw was invalid.'

'See, truth always wins,' Keki exulted and Hidumba sat with his shoulders stooped in defeat.

A grin spread across Bijjala's face. 'Twenty lakhs is my wager.'

Kalika exclaimed, 'Oh, that is too much, my lord. This poor woman is not worth that.'

Bijjala winked at her and, with excited hands, took the dice.

Keki slapped her thighs. 'That is royal blood right there. Take that, you ugly dwarf.'

'He will regret it,' Hidumba said.

'You are the one who is going to regret it, toad,' Keki said and turned to Bijjala. 'My prince, you need gods' grace. Take the benediction from our rajaguru.'

Pattaraya hoped that his messenger-owl had reached the shady merchant. Some called Jeemotha a pirate, but he held a licence from the king to trade. Ostensibly, he was just another businessman. *The lines often blurred between thugs, religious people and businessmen in this country,* Pattarya thought wryly.

Bijjala sat with folded hands and closed his eyes before the priest and promised him ten thousand gold coins. Hidumba looked on with a bored expression on his face. Rudra Bhatta kept his hands over the prince's head and started mumbling some mantras. The slave stood without batting an eyelid. Pattaraya saw Kalika stretching her legs towards the priest who was sitting with his back turned to her. As the priest was mumbling mantras, the devadasi ran her toe up and down the old man's spine. The tone of the mantra changed and the priest started sweating. Even the usually morose Pratapa grinned at the discomfort of the priest. Pattaraya pulled himself up to stretch his legs, smiling at the farce.

He walked towards the window that faced the streets. He threw it open and cold air rushed in, bringing with it the cacophony of music from various houses of pleasure. Three floors below, the streets were crowded even at this time of night. There was a streak of white in the sky. Drunk men were roaming around, some with women on their arms, some walking in groups and singing bawdy songs. A few drunkards were sprawled on the pavement. Street vendors were winding down their business.

Pattaraya stretched his back and yawned. It had been a long day. He was about to return to his seat, when he froze. What was it that he saw? He squinted to make sure he wasn't mistaken. He could feel his heart beating in his ribcage. Bastard! Son of a whore! Skandadasa was striding towards Kalika's den, with armed guards, and that Brihannala was leading them.

Pattaraya was furious. But he felt a grudging admiration too. How the hell did he know about the prince coming here? Someone must have bungled up. Maybe the big-mouthed Keki or perhaps the priest… He was about to warn Bijjala to get out when another thought struck him. The Gaurikanta stone! He was in possession of the biggest secret of Mahishmathi. Proof of a crime that could result in him losing his head.

He peered out to see how much time he had. Skandadasa and his gang had vanished. They were possibly using the secret route—Brihannala was leading them through the path that only a few knew. They would be here at any moment. Pattaraya felt breathless. He had to act fast but his mind was blank.

He could hear faint footsteps coming up. Or was it only his frenzied imagination? He rushed to the motley crew, still busy gambling.

He threw the pouch containing the Gaurikanta stone and said, 'Here is the biggest wager from my side. If His Highness wins, I pledge this stone to him.'

Bijjala snatched it from the ground and loosened the strings. He took the stone in his hand. 'A river pebble? Are you mocking me, Bhoomipathi?'

Pattaraya wished he could tell this idiot that this stone alone was worth half of Mahishmathi city. He ignored the incredulous and angry looks of his friends and pressed on, 'Your Highness, it is a humble present. Keep it with you until I ask for it. Hidumba will write off half of what you owe when you give it back to me.'

'Like hell I will. Are you drunk, Pattaraya? Lakhs of gold sovereigns are at stake,' Hidumba said. The footsteps were clearer now. Pattaraya snatched the dice from the dwarf's hand and threw it on the table. He held the dwarf's hands until the dice stopped spinning.

'You win, Prince, keep the stone. You will owe only half of what you had owed before when you return this to me,' Pattaraya stated.

The dwarf started protesting loudly, calling Pattaraya all sorts of names and Pattaraya felt like taking him by his misshapen legs and flinging him through the window. There was a knock at the door on the far end.

'Slave, take your master and run.'

'Why?' Bijjala asked. He had not taken the stone. It was lying on the table.

'Your Highness,' Pattaraya said, gritting his teeth, 'run if you don't want to be found out. Upapradhana Skandadasa will be here soon.'

'But what about my apsara, my Kalika…' Bijjala looked at Kalika who was now sitting up alert.

Pattaraya closed his eyes, prayed for self-control and said, 'You have not won her yet. Next time you…'

'Then I will play until I win,' Bijjala said, snatching the dice. 'What is the wager, dwarf?'

Pattaraya slammed his fist on the table, scattering the coins and breaking the chaturanga board into pieces. 'Slave, take your master away at once. Out, out this moment,' he said, pointing to the window.

Kattappa hesitated. The knock at the door had turned into a banging. Pattaraya said, 'I am sorry, Your Highness.' He slammed his fist into Bijjala's face, knocking him unconscious. He turned to Kattappa and roared, 'Out with this creature.'

Kattappa looked at the door at the far end that was being broken open. They could hear some fighting going on. Maybe Kalika's guards had come to stop them, but it would not buy them much time.

Kattappa heaved Bijjala over his shoulder. He rushed to the open window and peered down the streets. He heard Pattaraya call out his name and turned. The bhoomipathi threw a stone at him. Kattappa caught it in mid-air, and tucked it into his waistcloth. Whatever it was it would mitigate his master's debt by some amount. He took a deep breath and jumped out into the darkness with an unconscious Bijjala hanging on his shoulder.

The door crashed open with a bang and Skandadasa rushed in with his guards, holding Brihannala at sword point. He saw Pattaraya and Pratapa engrossed in a game of snakes and ladders. Khanipathi Hidumba was lying drunk on a pillow that was double his size. Keki was serving gold water to Kalika in a seashell vessel. To his disgust, Skandadasa saw that the devadasi was holding the head of the rajaguru between her legs with her left hand.

Pattaraya looked up from his game. 'Welcome Upapradhana Skandadasa. Have a seat,' he said, and returned to his game.

Skandadasa surveyed the room. There was no sign of Prince Bijjala but he would find him no matter where these rogues had hidden him.

Kalika took a sip of gold water and smiled at Skandadasa. 'Sweetheart, you seem to be in such a hurry. After all, you broke open my door. But alas, you are in queue. These gentlemen have been waiting since evening, but this priest just refuses to stop. Naughty old man.'

EIGHTEEN

Kattappa

Skandadasa walked out the front door of Kalika's den, seething with anger. The upapradhana with his entourage caused quite a stir in the streets. Keki came out with him, dancing and shouting to all who cared, 'See who has come to meet our mistress, the great Upapradhana Skandadasa.'

She kept taunting him and it took all his self-control not to hit her across her face. But more irritating than her was Brihannala. Every time Keki cracked a lewd joke, Brihannala would grasp his arm and whisper in his ears that he must ignore Keki as she was evil and only trust Brihannala.

Skandadasa hissed at her to stop, but Brihannala acted hurt and replied that she was supporting him and he should not get angry so fast. Keki continued clapping her hands and singing in a lewd manner. The crowd around erupted with laughter.

Keki cried, 'He went in and came out in no time. Friends, he is so fast. Our dear upapradhana is so fast. So fast, so fast.'

A few pimps tried to pull in Skandadasa by his arms. 'Swami, forget Kalika. We have better women. Please come to our place.'

A few whores came and took off their kaunchika to shake their melon-sized breasts at the upapradhana, adding to the merriment of the crowd. When Brihannala touched Skandadasa's arm yet again and whispered in his ears, he ordered his guards not to let her come near him. They promptly formed a circle around Skandadasa, pushing Brihannala out. Whores and pimps tried to break the circle, trying to touch Skandadasa. Some threw flowers at him. Skandadasa had never felt so helpless in his life.

He was worried about Prince Bijjala. He had checked Kalika's inn thoroughly, but could not find the prince. Was he hiding in one of the whorehouses? Skandadasa shuddered at the thought of raiding each house in this cramped street. He had not taken the permission of his superiors and had ended up making a laughing stock of himself. He did not know what answer he would give if the maharaja questioned him. There would be complaints about his behaviour the next day. More importantly, if he was unable to find Bijjala, or something happened to the prince, it would be the end of his career. He would be lucky if he lost only his job. The queen had threatened to cut off his head. Perhaps it was said in a moment of anxiety, but people had lost their heads in Mahishmathi for lesser reasons.

Suddenly, he thought he spotted someone jumping from a building next to Kalika's. He was carrying a limp figure on his shoulders. Though he could not make out the face clearly, he had a gut feeling that it was Bijjala's slave.

The street ahead exploded with shrieks as the man jumped and pushed his way through. Skandadasa tried to hasten towards the scene of action.

Suddenly Brihannala's voice announced, 'The exalted upapradhana will be distributing presents to all of you.'

A loud cheer went up among the people who were mobbing him. Scores of hands extended towards him, despite his bodyguards' best efforts.

Skandadasa helplessly watched the scene unfolding before him, mobbed by a group of pimps and prostitutes.

Kattappa landed hard on his feet. He had precariously hung on to a window sill when Skandadasa had come, and then quietly climbed up to the balcony of a nearby mansion. He had laid low, and when he was sure Skandadasa had left, he had jumped, with Bijjala on his shoulders. To his horror, he found that Skandadasa was amid a crowd of whores a few score feet away.

Praying that the upapradhana had not recognized him, Kattappa ran through the crowds. He waved his sword wildly to scatter people. Women screamed and men shouted angrily at him. He had no time to pause and look back to see whether he had hurt anyone. He had to save his master, and everything else was unimportant. Carts got toppled and horses whinnied in fear. He caught hold of the reins of a horse and stopped a passing chariot. He dropped Bijjala into the back seat. A devadasi who was in the chariot screamed in terror. Kattappa lifted her up and gently placed her on the street, mumbling apologies. The charioteer jumped into the passenger seat and lashed his whip at Kattappa. The first one caught him across his face, but when the whip came swirling again, he yanked it back. The charioteer toppled down. Kattappa whipped the horses and swerved the chariot in the opposite direction. The street was too narrow for the manoeuvre. A few shacks crashed and a pile of pots crumbled under the wheels of the chariot.

The chariot shot through the streets, swaying and rumbling. A crowd was running after it, shouting at the unconscious merchant and his slave who had destroyed their wares. Some threw stones, a few of which hit Kattappa. He winced, but continued whipping the horses for more speed. Across the street, he saw carts had been arranged to block his path. Guards of various devadasi houses stood with sticks and swords to block his path. He dashed through the blockade, toppling carts and cutting down sticks aimed at him. He shot forward, leaving a trail of destruction, and thundered down the hill towards the river.

When an owl hooted as he passed through the forest route, he ignored it. But soon when another owl hooted as he passed a huge fig tree and yet another when he turned towards the path parallel to the river, Kattappa's instinct warned him that this was no ordinary owl. He became alert and slowed down to look up at the tree. A huge net came tumbling down from it. Kattappa whipped his horses to make the chariot go faster so that he could escape the net, but the wheels of the chariot got entangled in it. Kattappa did not stop the cart. That was a mistake. The chariot skidded off the road and crashed against a rock. Bijjala was tossed a few feet away. Kattappa fell on his back, inches away from the horse that was thrashing wildly in its attempt to get up. Kattappa rolled over and was on his feet in a trice. He found himself surrounded by a dozen Vaithalikas. He crashed into the nearest Vaithalika, rolled over and reached where Bijjala lay. He stood holding his sword tight, ready to die for his master. Lightning cracked in the sky.

He quickly assessed that there were more than a dozen men with swords and spears. He was alone and his master was lying drunk and unconscious at his feet. It was dark and, confounding the matter further, it started to rain suddenly. When the attack came, the intensity of it took him by surprise. He was not scared of swords. He was quicker than anyone he knew. His father had taught him well. He proved it again by cutting down the first three who attacked him.

But the Vaithalikas changed tactics often. Six men attacked him together, four with swords and two with spears. Sword blows he blocked, but spears were a real problem. The Vaithalikas danced in, thrust it into his body and danced out of his reach. He cut down two more. Rain lashed in full strength. The ground became slushy and the sword slippery with blood and water. He had to protect his master from being pierced with a spear. Bijjala had woken up and was sitting, disoriented, in the middle of the fight. Kattappa was bleeding from everywhere, yet he fought on. For a fraction of a moment, he wished his master would lend him a hand. Bijjala was a good warrior if he was sober. Dead drunk, he was of no use. Kattappa dismissed the thought of getting Bijjala's help. It was the duty of the slave to protect his master. There was pride in dying in the service of one's master. Kattappa was sure he would die, but he promised himself that he would fight till the last drop of blood left his body.

As if mocking his false pride, a sharp pain shot up from his belly. He saw an arrow had pierced him. Kattappa felt his eyes going blank and his head spinning. It took every ounce of his strength to not scream in pain, yet he held on, blocking, parrying, thrusting and cutting with his sword. Many had fallen, he had no strength to count how many. Another arrow lodged in his shoulders, making it difficult to even lift the sword. 'Ma Gauri,' he cried, 'give me strength.' The heavens answered with a thunder that shook the forest. The gods were kind and were fulfilling his wish to die serving his master.

Skandadasa was forced to give away everything to the whores. He knew they would parade it the next day as a proof of his visit. They even took away his veerasrinkala, the chain of honour given by the maharaja for serving the country faithfully. They would possibly auction it on the streets and word would spread about the upapradhana who pawned the greatest honour the maharaja had bestowed on him at the feet of a whore. Skandadasa, the nitya brahmachari, the chronic bachelor who was wedded to his duty—what a fall, what a disgrace. He could almost hear the salacious rumours that would follow: *This is what you get when you make a bear dancer a high official.* All his years of work and dedication would be washed away with this one act of shame. He thought of fighting the whores. But a death by lynching at the hands of whores and pimps was a more bitter fate than what he was facing now.

Finally, when they found the upapradhana had nothing more to give, they left him. He walked unfazed, mentally cutting himself off from what had just happened to him.

When he reached his chariot and climbed up, the mob became quiet. He waited for his men to come. They came with their heads bent, ashamed that they had been unable to protect their master. Skandadasa patted their shoulders and said, 'You did well. Never mind what happened. Our duty is to the country. We need not prove anything to anyone.'

They looked at him with renewed respect. They climbed onto their horses and followed him. Brihannala came running behind and jumped into his chariot. Skandadasa thought of throwing her out but since he had brought her here, he felt duty-bound to take her back. He only prayed that she would refrain from her usual taunts. He felt his self-control had been tested enough. His world had crumbled, his honour had gone, and the last thing he wanted was a eunuch laughing at his misery.

Surprising him, Brihannala touched his feet. 'You are a great man, swami,' she said.

For a moment, Skandadasa's chest swelled with pride. Then anger came rushing in. He was not a fool to fall for this trick. Brihannala had too many things to answer for. He remembered that it was she who had declared he was distributing presents and incited the mob. Why did she do it? Did she want to delay him deliberately? He was not going to rest until he got to the bottom of this. *But he would not last till the next day if he was unable to find Bijjala*, he thought despondently.

His chariot was stopped by a group of armed men. Skandadasa's guards drew out their swords, but Skandadasa raised his palm to restrain them.

An old man came forward and cried, 'A merchant has destroyed our wares and shops. We want justice.'

Skandadasa's face brightened. 'Was a slave riding the chariot?' he asked with growing excitement.

The men murmured amongst each other and the old man said, 'Yes, a huge black slave. He injured many. We will tear him apart if we lay our hands on him.'

'Which way did he go?' Skandadasa asked.

'If we knew, why would we have waited here for you, swami?' the old man said with a scornful smile.

'Don't waste His Grace's time, you idiots, give way,' Brihannala cried, and this resulted in a huge uproar of protest from the men.

'Will you keep quiet,' Skandadasa hissed at the eunuch and turned to the agitated men.

'Split your men into two. One half will scout the highway up to the river. The other will come with me. We will search the jungle path. But no one shall touch the merchant or slave until they are brought to me. This is an order in the name of the maharaja of Mahishmathi.'

There were some angry murmurs but the old man said, 'We want justice. We want assurance that our loss will be compensated once we find the merchant.'

Skandadasa frowned. If his suspicion was right, it was no merchant but Prince Bijjala.

'No compensation will be given,' Brihannala screamed. 'You expect the king to compensate pimps and whores, you bastards?'

The men screamed in anger. Skandadasa glowered at Brihannala. She looked away.

'I will ensure you are compensated. No more time to waste. Scout the highway and the jungle,' Skandadasa said.

The group split into two and Skandadasa entered the jungle path with his guards and a group of men led by the old man.

He eyed Brihannala. Why did she look nervous?

Kattappa collapsed before the last two Vaithalikas had fallen. They approached him cautiously. One held a sword and another a bow. It was the arrows that had got Kattappa. He now lay on his back in a pool of blood, a few arrows jutting out of his body.

It was dawn and the rain had petered down to a drizzle. Kattappa was finding it difficult to breath. Each drop falling on his body felt like the piercing of an arrow. He eyed Bijjala. The prince was still sitting on his haunches. His lips and nose were smashed up, but he was largely unhurt. 'I failed you, my lord,' Kattappa mumbled. After they killed him, they would get to Bijjala. Kattappa closed his eyes and tears trickled down from them. He had failed his father, his family, his tradition. He was the first slave in his family who had failed to protect his master. 'Sorry father, sorry,' he whispered and waited for death to arrive.

The man with the sword approached him and placed his foot on Kattappa's chest. He raised his sword with both hands above his head. Kattappa waited for it to blast through his ribcage and pierce his heart. Instead, the man's legs slowly folded and he fell on Kattappa, his sword falling by the side. Kattappa saw Bijjala standing with a spear. The archer tried to notch his bow, but Bijjala turned to him and knocked away the bow with his spear. The archer took off on his heels as

Bijjala threw his spear at him. It missed the archer and he vanished into the bushes. Kattappa saw someone coming from the forest. The figure looked at the carnage and paused for a moment. When he saw Bijjala whose back was turned to him, the figure drew his sword. Kattappa raised his head and, to his shock, he found that the figure was none other than Shivappa.

At that moment, Skandadasa's chariot came crashing into the clearing, followed by many men bearing arms. Kattappa saw Shivappa disappear into the bushes.

Seeing Bijjala with the spear, the crowd that had followed Skandadasa looked at each other. Was this not the merchant who had destroyed their wares? They saw Skandadasa running to the prince and bowing low to him. They heard him calling him prince. The eldest man in the group whispered to his followers as Skandadasa was talking to Bijjala, 'Don't create a scene now. If it is indeed the prince, we can extract more money later. Kalika will know what to do.' There were some angry disagreements but the old man was able to prevail upon them.

He raised his clenched fist and shouted, 'Victory to Mahishmathi. Hail Rajakumara Bijjala.' Soon everyone was hailing the prince at the top of their voices. The prince, still half drunk with liquor, did not understand what was going on, but hearing his name being hailed, he picked up a spear from the ground and lifted it up in the air. The crowd became frenzied with enthusiasm.

When Skandadasa went up to the injured Kattappa, the slave said with folded hands, 'Prince Bijjala saved my life.'

NINETEEN

Sivagami

Three months later.

Sivagami tried to balance the bundle of firewood on her head. Sweat trickled down her cheeks and traced its path along her chin to drip down on her faded clothes. She panted as she struggled to climb the last few steps that led to the kitchen and then she dropped the bundle with a thud. A spider jumped out of it and hurried away.

Sivagami sat on her haunches to retie the bundle and heard a commotion from the central courtyard of the orphanage. She saw the cook, Bakula, also peering out into the courtyard. However, he too spotted her and immediately commanded her to go and draw water from the well. She could see Kamakshi slogging near the well. When her friend caught Sivagami's eye, she smiled at her.

It had been three months since she had come to the royal orphanage. After the incident with the knife, Thondaka and his gang had kept a respectable distance from them. Though they jeered at her often, they were careful to avoid any direct confrontation. Sivagami and Kamakshi had taken it up as a holy duty to take care of Uthanga. The boy's condition remained the same. They had to feed him gruel, which he swallowed with great difficulty. His eyes were glassy and he stared into the distance till one of the girls closed them at night. They changed his soiled clothes, wiped his body with a wet cloth once a week, and kept him free of bed sores.

They would even pour their hearts out to him. Kamakshi was the one who spoke to the unconscious boy more often. She lamented about the plight of her lover, and her own uncertain future. She laughed and cried and it was heartbreaking for Sivagami to witness her state.

Neither Revamma, nor any of the other residents, bothered to even peep into the storeroom. Prince Mahadeva, however, visited often to enquire about Uthanga. Sivagami felt most uncomfortable at these times. He was so helplessly in love with her that she found herself getting irritated. She continued to avoid him, finding some excuse or another whenever the prince came with the rajavaidya in tow. Revamma fawned over the prince and extracted whatever she could. Overall, the old woman found the presence of the unconscious boy, and the special interest the prince showed in him, quite profitable.

More than the prince's visits, what both the girls dreaded were the occasional visits of Keki to the orphanage. Revamma's husband sold girls from the orphanage to the Kalika's den. Often he took an advance as soon as a young girl was admitted into the orphanage. Revamma was a part of the racket too, and held on for as long as she could for the highest bidder. Corrupt officials, bribed by the duo, swore that girls volunteered for the jobs of devadasis. As it was rumoured that Kalika took care of her wards well, often pampering them with luxury, not many girls objected to this scheme, glad to flee the bleak orphanage.

Kamakshi was yet to be sold as Revamma was sure her beauty would fetch her a better price if she waited long enough. Keki kept coming for her, each time increasing the size of the offer from Kalika. Revamma, sensing a good opportunity, was driving a hard bargain. It would be a matter of time before the right bidder came along, and Kamakshi would be sucked into the dark folds of Kalika's den. It was also possible that she proved to be a fast learner in the art of love, in which case she would become one of the exalted dasis in Antapura, for the pleasure of visiting princes or kings. For Kamakshi, Shivappa was her only hope to escape the inevitable.

Today, there was going to be a puja which made both the girls tense. It was the day of amavasi—the day of Revamma's grand puja.

Sivagami hurried through the tasks at hand, but her mind was outside. From what she could gather from the loud jeers and snatches of conversation she caught, there was a newcomer in the orphanage. The boys seemed to be having fun at his expense. She could well empathize with the plight of whoever had had the misfortune to join this hellhole. Even after three months, the treatment they had given her when she had stepped into the orphanage for the first time riled her.

By the time she finished her work and hurried to the central courtyard, the shadows had grown long and night had already crept into the corners. The entire population of the orphanage was assembled there and the veranda was overflowing with howling boys and girls. She was unable to see what was happening, but she could discern the feeble cry of a boy. Though it was time to light the lamps, no one had bothered to do so. A bitter smell of sweat hung in the air.

'Now, fatso, show us how Hanuman jumped to Lanka!' Huge laughter followed. Sivagami could recognize the voice of Thondaka. Within a few months, he would be eighteen and would leave to join the army. Until then she and Kamakshi would have to be wary of him.

'See how his belly bounces?' Thondaka screamed in amusement, and the entire building shook with laughter.

'He looks like a monkey,' Malika's shrill voice added to the fun, and Sivagami could hear the boy whimpering.

'Maybe he was fathered by a monkey,' Thondaka slapped his thigh in merriment and was rewarded with another bout of laughter. 'Did your father come to your home or did your mother go to the forest to make you, fatso?' Thondaka screeched. There were howls and screams of glee.

Sivagami felt sorry for the boy. She walked towards the courtyard to see what was happening. She knew the pain of standing there, facing the hostility of all the residents.'

What is happening here?' Sivagami heard the swish of a cane as the boys and girls scattered. Revamma climbed up the steps. Within the blink of an eye, everyone except Sivagami and the fat boy had vanished.

'They were teasing me,' the fat boy said to the scowling woman.

'You are the new bride here, no?' Revamma said as she brought the cane on the boy's ample back with great force. He howled in pain. The old woman chased him as the boy tried to get away, and beat him till the cane broke. The boy lay whimpering on the floor, in foetal position. Revamma kicked him a couple of times before turning to Sivagami. 'What are you gaping at? Don't you have anything to do?' she yelled at her.

Sivagami knew it was better not to argue. She hurried to the kitchen. There was a mountain of soiled vessels to wash before dinner. She sat by the well and joined Kamakshi in scrubbing the pots and utensils with ash. They discussed the newcomer in hushed tones.

'Another one like us,' Kamakshi said as she scrubbed hard to remove the grease from the edges of the vessel. Sivagami did not reply. There was nobody who shared her fate. After a few days of teasing, they would accept him. He was not a traitor's son after all. Soon he would join the others in harassing her. She was a pariah, the daughter of a traitor amongst boys and girls who were the wards of martyrs. Every action of hers was suspected. They called Sivagami a witch behind her back. Thondaka had never lost a fight with any boy, but he had been forced to swallow dust against her. That had sealed her reputation as a witch.

She would always be the traitor's daughter in Mahishmathi, while the citizens prided themselves on being patriots. Sivagami hated the country that killed her father from the bottom of her heart.

Her thoughts travelled to his manuscript. She often wondered what was written in that book. Her reading skills were of no help, and Kamakshi could barely read. Raghava had told her that the book was in the old tongue of Paisachi. She did not know anyone who could read Paisachi other than her father.

Sivagami wondered why the book was in Paisachi. It was not a language many knew. Where had he got it from?

She was scared to even show the book to anyone and carried it on her person most of the time. It had a picture of a mountain etched on the leather cover. Many nights she would creep to the window and, by the moonlight, try to make sense of what was written in it. It was a risky thing to do. Already a few of the girls had asked her what she was hiding.

A girl was lighting a lamp before the idol of Kali, which stood in the centre of the courtyard. The wards were coming out one by one to say their prayers. Revamma had changed into a sari and was sitting cross-legged before the idol. The smoke from incense sticks clung over them like mist and spread a sickening fragrance. When Revamma tinkled her bell, everyone rushed to the courtyard. She started reciting shlokas in a voice that could have made a buffalo proud. Sivagami wiped her hands on her skirt and rushed out. Kamakshi followed her. When the aarti happened, everyone was supposed to be in the courtyard.

'Oh, what do we have here? Such precious, charming girls!' said a familiar voice.

They stopped at the threshold and Keki walked towards them, swaying her hips. She stopped in front of Kamakshi and turned to Revamma, 'Can I take this doll home?'

Kamakshi backtracked. Keki reached out and gave Kamakshi's breasts a squeeze. 'So firm, so…' Sivagami's hand shot out and grabbed Keki's neck. Kamakshi moved behind Sivagami, fearful. Keki laughed and slapped away Sivagami's hand. The next moment, a knife was being pointed inches away from her left eye. Keki froze.

'Move,' Sivagami said in a calm voice.

'Easy, easy. Can't you take a joke? We are all women, you know? What is wrong with one woman touching another?' Keki cried.

Sivagami grabbed Keki's head with one hand and held the knife close with another. This time the knife was almost touching the eunuch's eyeballs. Sivagami could sense Keki's fear, though the eunuch tried to laugh it off. Sivagami prayed she would not do anything foolish. She was not sure she could plunge the knife all the way into Keki's brain. She had never hurt anyone apart from Thondaka and his gang and that was self-defence. For the first time, she was the aggressor. It gave her a sense of power which frightened her.

'The witch is on the prowl again,' Sivagami heard Thondaka's voice. She could feel all eyes on her. Kamakshi was sobbing behind her. Sivagami pushed Keki away. The eunuch spun, bumped her head on a pillar, turned back and grinned.

'Revamma, I want this girl. You name the price and I shall get it. She is worth a fortune,' Keki said. Sivagami slashed out with her knife and it scratched Keki's nose. Clutching her bleeding nose, she cried, 'Oh god, you almost killed me. You killed me. Oh, how I love you. You are so sexy. Revamma, I want this girl. She's the one I want.' The eunuch danced around. She clapped her hands and hissed at Sivagami's face, 'Just watch how I get you now.' Sivagami stood coolly, though her heart was hammering against her chest. The eunuch danced away, loosening her hair and swirling her head round and round, spraying droplets of blood everywhere. She cried, 'Amma, amma,' and danced towards the Kali idol.

Sivagami walked Kamakshi to the storeroom which she shared with her friend and Uthanga and left her there.

When she came back, Bakula was jingling the bell while another boy lit camphor in front of the idol. Thondaka, now bathed and sporting a big tilak on his head, was throwing flowers at the idol. His eyes were closed in devotion and he was trying to outshout Revamma in singing the goddess's praises. Keki sat in the middle with her hair spread around her face, swirling her head like one possessed.

Sivagami said her prayers quickly. There was only one thing to pray for—death for people who had killed her father.

The prayers soon reached a crescendo and Revamma started shaking her huge body. It was to be one of those days when Kali possessed her. The cries of 'Amma, Kali' rose from everyone's throat. When she had seen it for the first time, Sivagami had been scared. Now she felt bored of the histrionics. She shifted her weight from her left leg to her right. Mosquitoes buzzed around and one landed at the tip of her nose. She tried to squat it and opened her left eye. It seemed to read her mind and, at the last moment, flew away.

She was about to close her eyes when suddenly she saw the new boy from earlier slipping away into the kitchen. She was horrified. Was he mad? She slowly crept away from the prayer area and ran to the kitchen. The stove was lit and she could hear water bubbling in the huge vessel kept over it. In the dim light, she saw him leaning over the table where the food was kept.

'Hey,' she cried and he almost jumped out of his skin. He knocked down the vessel, spilling its contents all over. Sivagami was scared someone would hear them. To her relief, the frenzied prayers of Revamma drowned out the noise. In the courtyard outside, each one was trying to outdo the other in a competitive show of piety.

'What the hell are you doing here?' she asked the boy, moving towards him. He shrank in fear, and his lips trembled.

'I...I...I was looking for something to eat,' he said.

'I can see that,' she said, crossing her arms over her chest. 'The question is why.'

He looked confused and searched for a way to escape. Sivagami was standing at the door, blocking his only way out. He looked at his toes.

'Why?' she repeated, a bit more stern now, tapping her feet impatiently.

'B...b...because...I was hungry,' he mumbled.

Sivagami burst out laughing. The boy's plaintive admission was the funniest thing she had heard after leaving Thimma's home. Days had been dreary, nights tiresome, and no one ever said a kind word to her in the orphanage except Kamakshi. But there was hardly any opportunity for humour. The boy's matter-of-fact words, coupled with the scene in the kitchen, made Sivagami laugh hard.

'You are funny,' she said, when she caught her breath. Shrieks of 'Ammaaa, Ammaaaa' came from the courtyard. Keki's shrill voice accompanied the braying of Revamma. The goddess had apparently possessed the old wart. She would go on and on like this, her hair let loose, her entire body shaking, and soon, she would start jumping around crying. Thondaka beat the drum as if it was his enemy and the cook kept jingling the bell, totally off key to his haphazard rhythm. The smoke of incense and camphor from the courtyard snuck into the kitchen.

The fat boy looked out through the window bars. Now the entire congregation had started jumping up and down, clapping their hands. The drum and the bell competed with each other in creating absolute cacophony.

'Are they crazy?' the boy asked.

Sivagami burst out laughing again. 'No, they are just being godly,' she replied.

'What is your name?'

'Gundu Ramu,' he said, a bit bashful.

'Gundu Ramu?' she asked.

'Gundu Ramu,' he repeated.

'Sivagami,' she said.

'No, no, Gundu Ramu,' he replied.

She stared at him in disbelief before bursting out laughing again.

'Gundu…' she said, sputtering between her laughs.

'Ramu,' he said, as if Sivagami was finding it difficult to pronounce the second part of his name.

Sivagami fell on the floor, clutching her belly and laughing. 'I said my name, idiot,' she said.

'No, it is my own,' he said. Sivagami stood up and gave him a playful punch on his belly. 'I said my name is Sivagami.'

'And mine is…'

'Gundu Ramu. Yeah, yeah, you've mentioned it a hundred times already. What a funny name! Suits you but—' she said.

'That is the only one I have,' he said, and they laughed together.

Outside, the devotional frenzy was reaching its peak. Now the goddess had possessed the cook too and a few girls in the front row had already fainted.

'Where are you from and how did you reach here?' Sivagami asked. The smile had not left her lips. It felt good to laugh after such a long time.

'Can I finish eating? I am hungry,' he said.

'If they see you eating, that witch will strip you of the hide on your back,' she said, and his face fell. She could see the terror in his eyes; clearly the boy remembered his beating. He looked at the food wistfully and gulped. Sivagami took a plate from the kitchen and started putting all the savouries on it. She then piled it up with sweets meant for Revamma and placed it on the floor.

'Here, eat your fill,' she said.

'But you said... Won't they?' he demurred, pointing at the crowd hopping up and down in the name of god.

In reply, she picked up another plate and started piling up food on it. She sat across from him on the floor, cross-legged. He turned around to ascertain whether anyone might be creeping up on them.

'Will she beat me again?'

'Of course. Every day, for everything and for nothing.'

'My father never beat me,' the boy said and looked down. Sivagami saw his eyes brimming with tears.

'Oh, where is he now?' She knew it was a stupid question as soon as she voiced it. No one with a living father or mother would come to this place, but she had already spoken without thinking and there was no way of taking it back. Gundu Ramu's shoulders started shaking and tears fell from his eyes. It was funny to see a ten-year-old boy cry. She had stopped crying long back. Nothing would make her cry.

'Eat your food, Gundu, before they come,' she said.

Gundu did not stop crying, but he started shoving food down his throat anyway.

'I am from Tamliya village. It is famous for its bards and singers. World-famous bards. Have you heard about my village?' he asked, as he attacked another mound of rice. Sivagami moved the bucket of sambhar towards him and her eyes widened as he started pouring ladles upon ladles of it on his pile of rice. He looked at her expectantly. She had no clue about the village or its world-famous bards. But she did not want to disappoint him.

'Yes, I…I have heard of it. World-famous. Tamliya…'

Gundu's face lit up and Sivagami felt guilty for lying.

'And of course you must have heard the name of Madanappa.'

'Ah, Madanappa. Of course, of course. Great singer. World-famous,' she said. 'Is he your father?'

'Madanappa!' Gundu was horrified. 'No, he is an idiot. He brays like an ass. He was my father's greatest enemy. He never allowed my father to be famous.'

'Oh…'

'Sivagami, you are making fun of me,' Gundu said uncertainly.

'No…I…' Sivagami faltered.

'Of course you know that Madanappa is our village chief.'

'Is it? I mean, of course. Would you care for some more rice?' she said, trying to change the topic.

'No, it will kill my appetite if I eat any more. It will spoil my dinner,' he said, but helped himself to more rice anyway.

Sivagami knew there was not going to be any dinner. Not for the next three days, once Revamma had discovered what they had done. But she did not want to let him know that. The fool was thinking this was some kind of tavern and he could eat his fill. Today, many in the orphanage were going to go hungry. She thought of it as their punishment for bullying the boy and quite relished the idea. Though even she was terrified to think what Revamma's reaction would be. The goddess would soon leave her body and the devil would be back. She felt pity for Gundu, for what was in store for him. She placed a sweet on his plate.

'No, no, sweet is fattening,' he said and kept it aside on the plate. 'What was I saying?' he asked as he mixed sambhar and crushed pappad over it.

'About the world-famous Madanappa,' Sivagami said, suppressing a giggle.

'No, Madanappa is not world-famous. He is just a stupid village chief who never recognized talent. My father was world-famous. Rather, he was not yet, but he would have been, had he not died in the war,' Gundu said, lips quivering. 'He would have made our village world-famous.'

Sivagami fell silent for a moment. 'But Gundu, how could a singer die in a war?' she asked.

'The local senanayaka had commissioned him to write his story. He made my father write all sorts of lies. He made my father sing that the senanayaka was the descendant of Lord Rama. My father's job was to record the great deeds of the senanayaka and compose songs for posterity. Oh, what wonderful songs my father made.'

'I am sure you loved them.'

'No, I hated them. They were all lies,' he said as he crushed another pappad. The final aarti was going on in the courtyard. Sivagami knew that, any moment now, the others would come in. The bucket of rice was almost half empty.

'All stories and songs are lies. There are no honest storytellers. Those who pay will make you write what they want,' she said. She spoke from experience. She remembered the songs they had made up about her father's supposed treason. She hated all poets, bards and writers.

'My father hated to lie. He was a very honest man. But he wanted to be world-famous and it sort of killed him. On the one hand was his ambition,' Gundu parted the rice to one side, 'and on the other was his honesty. Honesty, ambition—ambition, honesty. He was torn in between.'

Gundu took the sweet he had kept in the corner and gulped it down. She wanted to remind him that it was fattening, but stopped herself. The final cries of 'Ammaaaa, Ammaaaaaaaaaa' came from outside. The goddess was leaving Revamma. They would now come to take the prasad and make an offering to the goddess.

Sivagami thought about how their faces would look when they saw that she and Gundu had eaten what was meant for the goddess. She felt wicked and happy. She would pay the price, but it was going to be worth it just to see the expression on Revamma's face. Poor Gundu, though, the boy did not know what he was going to face.

'Could you please give me one more sweet?' he asked.

'Why not? Take three.'

'No, one will do. I am on a diet,' he said and took all three. 'So, I was saying, my father was torn between his profession and his conscience. He used to say that he should've become a politician or a government servant, since he had to lie so much. But we were poor and had nothing much to eat. After my mother's death, he had to take care of me. He said, he was doing all this so that I could have a morsel of food.' Gundu wiped tears with the back of his hand.

'A *morsel* of food! Hmm, then?'

'So he made the songs that the senanayaka wanted. But his honesty rebelled. So he found a middle path. He mixed facts with fiction.' Gundu mixed the two mounds of rice and looked at her hopefully. She emptied the bucket of sambhar, scraping the bottom with the ladle. There goes Revamma's feast, she thought.

'He started ending every line of the song with the phrase, 'Can you believe it?' The common folks loved it, but I don't know why,' Gundu licked his fingers, 'the senanayaka hated it.'

Sivagami laughed. He appeared hurt, so she served him four more ladles of rice. Gundu grabbed the empty sambhar bucket and shook it over his plate.

'It was like…' Gundu cleared his throat and sang:

'Mahanayaka, senanayaka, braver than Lord Indra—can you believe it?

Lokanayaka, Veeranayaka, more handsome than Lord Chandra—can you believe it?

Bhoomipalaka, Shooranayaka, stronger than Hanumanta—can you believe it?

Rajyarakshaka, Shatrunashaka, more fearsome than Srikanta—can you believe it?'

Gundu wiped snot with the back of his hand and sniffled. 'The soldiers in the senanayaka's army loved the song. After every line, when my father asked, 'Can you believe it,' they roared back with a 'Yes, we do,' and laughed. I think it was their laughter that got to the senanayaka. He ordered my father to lead the patrol on the western border. My father could handle a stencil better than any poet and he used to say a poet's stencil is more powerful than a sword. He was… he was killed in the raid of Kiratas. I…I became an orphan. The villagers did not want to feed me. They said, I eat a lot. Someone was spreading rumours against me. Maybe it was all Madanappa's doing. He hated my father's talent. He hated our family and wanted me gone. He said I brought misfortune to the village. When I found out that my father had been slain and I had become an orphan, I cried for a whole day. For one day, I even went without food. Then, I begged for food from door to door. A few women gave me something to eat, but never enough. Most laughed at me when I cried about hunger. So when they came to bring me to this orphanage and promised me a lot of food, I did not think twice. They said they will honour me here because my father is a martyr for the cause of Mahishmathi. And here…and here…that witch caned me. Everyone here is evil,' Gundu sobbed.

He looked at Sivagami and quickly added, 'Not everyone. You are good. I do not think you are evil. Are you evil like the others?'

Sivagami laughed, but tears filled her eyes. 'I hope I am not, Gundu.'

'Of course you are not. You gave me snacks,' he smiled.

'Snacks! Those were not snacks, Gundu. That was a full meal for many.'

'Meal? Oh…' His face fell. 'You mean to say they won't serve me dinner now?'

'No, not now,' she said, feeling sorry for the boy. They might get to eat after three days, if they were lucky. Hopefully, Revamma would beat them unconscious and they would only wake up after three days.

'Okay, I understand what you mean. Here they serve dinner late. I hope they won't delay it too much,' he said, licking the plate clean. Sivagami sighed. She started eating. They would come any moment now.

'You know what, Sivagami Akka? I can call you Sivagami Akka, no? We are friends, right? You are not a high-born noble or something like that, I hope. I am scared of big people. No, you can't be. You are just like me. A girl of the common folk,' Gundu said, looking at her faded dress. Sivagami smiled.

'You can call me Sivagami Akka. And I am just like you.'

'What happened to your parents? Your father must have been a soldier, right?' Gundu asked.

Sivagami's eyes unwittingly welled up. The image of her father hanging from the scaffold flashed before her eyes. 'He died,' she said, her voice hoarse.

'Oh, in some battle?'

Her lips trembled and her fingers crushed the rice. She did not want to talk about it, did not want anyone to remind her of that day. She would talk about her father only when she had destroyed the Mahishmathi royal family. Unaware of the intense emotion he had set off in his new friend, Gundu blabbered on.

'It is always the common folk who die. Some lord or bhoomipathi would have ordered your father to fight for him, I have heard lots of tales like this. My father taught me many songs. Some were in languages that no one speaks now. He tried teaching me the language of the old folks who ruled our lands thousands of years ago. The old tongue has the largest number of songs. Songs that were composed before even Lord Indra was born. Tales of adventures before even Lord Rama and Krishna had descended on earth as avatars. There is a book in that old tongue which has the biggest collection of tales in the world. Tales about dragons, tigers, other animals, princes, bhuta, preta, pisacha, yaksha, kinnara, gandhara, deva, asura, rakshasa, Vaithalika, apsara—you name it, the book has it. The book…err…I forgot its name. Wait, I got it, I got it. It is called *Brihat Katha*. Longer than the *Ramayana*, more vast than the *Mahabharata* or the southern epics and ballads. My father knew many tales from that book of songs. But the old tongue had a strange script. Not like Devabhasha, not like the language of our folks either, but a forgotten language. Akka, why are you looking at me like that? What happened?' Gundu Ramu stared at Sivagami.

'What did you say?' she gripped his hands.

'Did I say something offensive, Akka?'

'No, you fool, what language?' she asked, shaking him.

'Language? I forgot the name of the language. Oh Lord Ganesha, I will give you a hundred modakas, please remind me what the name of that language was. Ah, I remember at last. Lord Ganesha is great. It's called Paisachi.'

Paisachi? Sivagami stared at the boy in disbelief. She stood up, shaking the sticky rice off her fingers and rushed to the storeroom. She shook the bundle and the book fell down. She picked it up and rushed to Gundu Ramu.

'Can you tell me what it says?' she said, thrusting it at him. The boy was taken aback.

'Is it a storybook or a songbook?' he asked, confused. He took it in his hands and started browsing through it.

'Quick, read it, before they come,' she said as she shook him by his shoulders.

'Who will come?'

'Revamma and the others.'

'To serve dinner?' he asked hopefully.

'Read it, you idiot. Read it, read it, read it.'

Gundu flipped through the pages and stared at the picture of a triangle. 'Sivagami Akka…'

'What?' Her heart was beating like a caged parrot. She gripped his wrist.

'Is this a hill?' he enquired.

'That is a triangle, you fool. Read what is beneath it.'

'But…'

'But what? Read it,' she screamed. She could hear footsteps. They were coming.

'I don't know how to read at all,' Gundu said with a bewildered face.

Sivagami let out a loud scream. She wanted to tear him apart. She fell on him and the boy toppled on his back. She slapped him across his face again and again.

'What do we have here? Playing bride and groom on their first full moon night?'

Sivagami heard the shrill laughter of Thondaka. Before she could get up the cane cut across her back. As beatings rained down on her, she stood up, determined not to cry.

'The devils have eaten all the prasad and were into something unspeakable. Apacharam, apacharam. All our prayers have gone to waste, Moodevi.' Revamma started beating Sivagami with renewed vigour. Sivagami stood like a rock, her fists curled into balls. When she saw Bakula rushing to beat Gundu Ramu with the poker used for stirring embers in the stove, her determination broke.

'Please…' she pleaded, only to be rewarded by a cut across her cheeks.

Before the first blow landed on his body, Gundu Ramu started screaming at the top of his voice, 'Please, please don't beat me. I am the son of a poet, please…ahh…ayyo…ayooo… please. My father is a world-famous poet…please…please ayooo.'

Despite her determination to not show emotion, tears sprang to Sivagami's eyes. 'Sorry, I am sorry,' she mumbled.

'Sorry…who wants your sorry?' Revamma hit her again.

She wanted to scream that her apologies were not for Revamma, they were for the boy, but decided that would make matters worse.

Suddenly Thondaka cried in surprise, 'My, my! What is this?' Sivagami felt her head swimming. Thondaka picked up the book from the floor and sniffed it. He was perplexed by the strange script. Revamma snatched it from him, looked at its cover and stared at Sivagami.

'I think I know what this is,' Keki said with a cruel smile as she took it from Revamma's hands.

Sivagami felt her knees going weak.

TWENTY

Kattappa

It had been more than three months since Shivappa had gone missing. Kattappa's injuries from his ordeal with the Vaithalikas were yet to heal. He limped around in his hut, his arm in a sling, foraging for something to eat. As usual, there was nothing he could even munch on. Rains had set in and the work of slaves had increased manifold. His father was too busy serving the king. He had decided to drown the sorrow of losing his youngest son by indulging in more and more work. He did not even take the mandatory rest days for slaves during ekadashi every fortnight. Though Malayappa never put in words the loathing he had for Kattappa, with every word and action he let it be known that his eldest son was responsible for the death of his younger son.

That was the lie Kattappa had told everyone. He and Shivappa had accompanied Bijjala to the forest for hunting. Near Patalaganga falls, Shivappa had slipped and fallen into the swirling waters of the river. The prince and Kattappa tried their best to save him. The prince had jumped in first to help Shivappa. Kattappa had no choice other than to follow his master. All three were caught in the swift current and fell down the waterfall. It was a miracle that Bijjala and Kattappa escaped. But when they climbed ashore, they were attacked by Vaithalikas. Bijjala had fought bravely and killed all of them. Kattappa's life was saved by Bijjala.

Kattappa was surprised at how easily he could lie. It troubled him. More than anything, it showed that he did not have the courage to face the truth. He told himself that he lied to save his master, and saving one's master was the supreme dharma for a slave, but he knew he lied more for the sake of his brother's safety.

A few divers were sent to recover Shivappa's body from the gorge, but they returned empty-handed. After a few reluctant dives, they declared that the body might have been carried away. It was not worth risking their lives for a dead slave boy. Kattappa spent days crying and calling out his brother's name. Convinced by his act, none other than the mahapradhana had come to him to console him. Kattappa was upset with himself; confused and hurt at his own ability for deception.

It hurt him to see the face of his father standing like a pillar behind the king. He could see that grief had aged him overnight. He knew how much his father loved his younger brother. He wished he could at least tell *him* the truth. But it was dangerous. If anyone found out that Shivappa had run away, they would set the best Mudhol hounds on his trail. A dead slave boy was worth less than the carcass of a horse. You could not make footwear with the skin of a slave.

Kattappa had agonized over his lie but justified it to his conscience that it was the only way to prevent the king from knowing where Bijjala had been that eventful night.

With nothing to do for the past few months, he brooded and worried in the thatched hut, blaming himself for his failings. He rarely saw his father and, surprisingly, he even missed Bijjala. He was willing to serve his master even in this condition, but he had orders to not be seen in the palace until he had healed. The prince also was recovering from his injuries.

The queen had been devastated on seeing her injured and unconscious son, and had screamed at Kattappa for not ensuring his safety. She lamented that a prince had risked his life to save a worthless slave. She got Bijjala moved to her chamber and declared she would not leave her son's bed until he healed.

Bards now had a new topic. Songs were sung in every nook and corner of the country about the compassionate prince who was so brave that he jumped into the roaring waters of Patalaganga, fought crocodiles with his bare hands, all to save his slave boys. He had swum against the current holding one boy in each hand. One slave was lost for he was a sinner and the other was saved only because of the compassion of the prince who prayed to the river gods to spare at least one so that he would have a slave to serve him.

Kattappa's mouth filled up with bile every time he thought about the night when he had to flee with Bijjala on his shoulder. He limped outside to clear his throat. The sky was brooding over the wet earth. Trees dripped with mossy green. A crow, its feathers shuffled and wet, tilted its head to see whether he had maybe brought some food. It hopped for some time before perching on a tree and cawing in protest. Far away Gauriparvat was dissolving into the monsoon sky. Was Shivappa hiding in its jungles? Kattappa sighed and, for the umpteenth time, he promised himself that he would go in search of his little brother. What could Shivappa be doing with the Vaithalikas? How much poison had the evil Vaithalikas injected in his innocent brother's mind?

'Kattappa.'

Kattappa winced when he heard the voice. Skandadasa. He had been expecting this visit. Skandadasa had been sent on a forced pilgrimage by the maharaja as a part of his punishment. It was meant to reform his immoral activities. The queen wanted him to be dismissed, but Parameswara had prevailed upon her. Every moment, Kattappa had dreaded the return of Skandadasa. He knew the upapradhana had not bought his lie.

'Son, I will get straight to the point. Tell me, were you telling the truth?'

The bluntness of the question took the wind out of Kattappa. He stood quiet for a moment. Tears streamed down his cheeks. He slowly fell on his knees and touched Skandadasa's feet.

'Swami, I cannot bear the burden of my lie anymore. We had not gone hunting. But I cannot say where we had gone. It is against my dharma, swami. I cannot betray my master,' Kattappa said in a broken voice.

'Just tell me how you got out. I do not want other details. I know who all were there in Kalika's den.'

Kattappa remained silent.

Skandadasa said, 'This country is in great danger. The royal family may be in great danger. Your words will help me do something about the threat. '

After a moment's hesitation, Kattappa said, 'We went in a palanquin brought by Keki.'

'Hmm, but was there anyone else?'

'No one else, swami.'

'Why was the prince wearing a merchant's dress when I found you?' Skandadasa asked. This was one question that had nagged him since that eventful night when Bijjala claimed to have fought the Vaithalikas and saved Kattappa. He knew Kattappa was lying, but he wanted to know who had procured the clothes for the prince.

Kattappa looked down without answering.

'Where did you procure merchant's clothes for the prince?'

'I did not procure it, swami. It was supplied by the palace eunuch Brihannala,' Kattappa said without looking up.

Suddenly everything fell into place for Skandadasa. He had been worrying about the extra drummer and where he had come from. Now he understood that Brihannala had persuaded a merchant to lend his clothes to Bijjala and then smuggled the merchant out as a drummer later.

Skandadasa had always included Brihannala in the group of suspects. Brihannala might have been doing this in collusion with Keki to trap the prince and take him to gamble in Kalika's den. But something told Skandadasa that this was not a straightforward case of greed. He knew some criminal activity was going on, but could not figure out what it was. He wondered whether it could just be a case of raging hormones. The princes were supposed to be celibate till they turned twenty-one, as per tradition. But Bijjala would not be the first prince in the three-hundred-year-old history of the kingdom to break this rule. Something was not adding up, though. Why should so many people be involved in arranging a meeting between Bijjala and Kalika? A woman could have easily been found in the harem of the king. Many women would have happily bedded the future king of Mahishmathi. No, there had to be more to it.

He had to find out who the merchant was, and where he'd gone. Whether he was just a petty merchant who was paid by Brihannala for his clothes, or whether he was someone who had played a more sinister part. How did the Vaithalikas know Bijjala would come down that road, at that time? He could sense Pattaraya's hand somewhere, but there was no proof. Going to Devadasi Street to find witnesses was ruled out.

'Did your master bed any devadasi?' Skandadasa asked the slave.

Kattappa shook his head. Skandadasa was frustrated. This was leading nowhere.

'Did he really save you or did you save him? When I found you, you were grievously injured and on the verge of death, whereas the prince had no injuries except a bloody nose. I found it strange,' Skandadasa decided to play his ace.

The slave's lips trembled. He prostrated before Skandadasa and cried, 'Don't tell anyone, swami. No one should know. If someone knows my master was drunk and had to depend on a slave to save his life, it would be a great insult to him. Please do not tell anyone…'

Skandadasa was touched by the slave's words. He had prided himself for having suffered a great deal of ignominy for the sake of his country, and here was a slave who had almost died saving his master, who did not care whether he lived or died. The slave's sincerity pricked the bubble of Skandadasa's pride. Work without expecting any reward—Nishkama karmi—the word had a new meaning for Skandadasa.

When he spoke next, he struggled to hide the choking he felt in his throat. 'Son, your secret will remain with me till death. I wish we had more men like you.'

He helped Kattappa get up and walk inside. As Kattappa hobbled along, Skandadasa accidentally tripped on his dhoti and tugged it loose. The slave caught it before it slipped to the ground and retied it. Skandadasa averted his eyes. He would remember this incident later, when it would be too late.

He asked suddenly, throwing the slave off balance, 'Who injured Bijjala?'

Kattappa did not reply.

'Did it happen in Kalika's inn?'

Kattappa remained silent.

Skandadasa was frustrated. 'Did it happen during the fight with the Vaithalikas. I know that could not be. Bijjala was holding a spear. No one could've come and punched his nose without being killed. The punch was given much before the fight. Am I right?'

Skandadasa thought he discerned a slight nod from the slave. He was not going to get much more. He decided to cut short the visit.

He helped Kattappa to his bed and said goodbye. At the door frame, he paused and threw the bait he had saved for the end. 'Your brother is roaming around with the Vaithalikas.'

'Where?' Kattappa asked and bit his tongue.

Kattappa covered his face with his palm. He had realized his mistake a tad too late. He had given away his brother. By biting Skandadasa's bait, he had declared that his brother was still alive. That he had lied so far.

Kattappa was terrified of what the upapradhana would do now. He could hear the barks of the Mudhol hounds in his head. He sat, unable to face Skandadasa, scared if he looked at him again, he would suck all his secrets out. He sensed that the upapradhana had gone, yet he sat in his cot, afraid even to breath. He was still sitting in the same position when his neighbour, an old slave woman, brought him some gruel. He continued to sit without moving until the gruel turned tepid and flies buzzed around it. Birds in the rushes by the river called out as the day bled to death. Night sneaked out from his hut and spread everywhere.

It took the cry of the mottled wood owl to shock him out of his reverie. He shivered when the bird cried again. The harbinger of death. Despite the cold wet breeze from without, he was sweating. He had to find his brother before it was too late. He stood up, leaning on his stick, and limped towards the door. He paused at the threshold.

It would be the first time he would be leaving the hut after that night and he felt uneasy. He chided himself for being paranoid. He touched his waistband where he had tied the stone Pattaraya had given him. He slammed the door shut and stepped into ankle-deep slush.

He limped past the rows of slave huts. He wished he had his sword with him but his father had taken it away. He would get it back only if Bijjala took him back into service. It was dark and humid, with rain falling like the sky was melting. He had no idea where he should search for Shivappa. His leg was throbbing with pain and he was out of breath by the time he reached the river. He stood at the banks, watching the inky blackness of the sliding river for some time. Over the spatter of rain, he could hear the dull roar of the Patalaganga falls. It would be suicidal to swim across. With a heavy heart, he was about to turn back when he heard a cough. His first instinct was to go for his sword, but he was not carrying one.

His stick fell from his hands and splashed into the river. Before he could catch it, the current carried it away. Again, he heard the sound of someone coughing. As he stared into the darkness, he could discern the silhouette of a thatched boathouse to his left. He limped over and stood panting, holding the bamboo pillar of the boathouse.

'Can you take me across?' Kattappa asked an old man who was sitting huddled inside. The man suddenly jumped towards Kattappa and came very close to the slave's face.

'Want to go across? Want to go across? Everyone wants to go somewhere. Why can't people be happy where they are? One day, when Yama comes to take them to the only place they belong, they cry and scream and struggle. Why? Answer me!'

A madman. Kattappa flinched from the smell of the man's unwashed body and clothes.

'Where…where is the boatman?' he managed to ask.

'Gone. Gone down to the bottom of the river. Gone up to the heaven. How should I know? Why should I care? When I came here, this place was empty. When I am gone from here, this place will be empty again. Or will it be? Is there any empty place? Answer me! Answer me!'

Kattappa turned away to go, but a firm hand grasped his shoulders. 'Brother, want to go across?'

'Yes.'

'Good, why don't you swim?'

Kattappa tried to shrug off the old man's grip.

'Afraid of dying?' Though Kattappa could not see his face clearly in the darkness, he could sense the mockery in his tone.

'No,' Kattappa said.

'Liar.'

Before he could answer, the old man had untied a coracle from the roof. He laughed again and grabbed Kattappa's wrist. Kattappa found himself being dragged to the river. Pain exploded through his nerves as his injured leg hit the stone steps many times. The old man threw the reed basket into the current, yelled, 'Shambo Mahadeva,' and jumped into water, his head disappearing into the eddies of the swift current. Kattappa hesitated at the edge of the river, not knowing what to do. The very next moment, a hand shot out and pulled Kattappa into the water. His head hit the stones and his scream was cut short by the rush of water. Everything went blank.

When he opened his eyes, he was in the swirling reed boat, hurtling through the darkness. The old man was sitting at the other edge, both his hands out of the basket. His head was thrown back and disappeared behind his arching body. The world swam around Kattappa as he vomited water, gagged and coughed, clutching his belly. He steadied himself, holding on to the edge of the coracle.

They were in the middle of the river, and rain fell in sheets, drenching them. The old man was singing in some unknown tongue. He peppered his song with laughter and howls. Kattappa cursed his luck. He wondered how he could escape the clutches of this madman.

'Why do you want to go to the other side?' the old man asked suddenly. The boat swayed and tilted as he crawled towards Kattappa.

'None of your business,' Kattappa said curtly.

The old man laughed aloud and gave a spin to the basket. Kattappa held the sides so firmly that his palms bled.

'Afraid of death?'

Kattappa did not say anything.

'Good, at least your silence doesn't lie. How about some truth? What is the purpose of this foolish journey?'

'I am in search of my brother.'

The old man laughed again. 'No one is anyone's brother, son. The world is a jungle and each of us is alone. Each of us is the hunter and every one is the hunted. Kill or be killed. In this jungle, only the smartest will survive. Your brother is smart, you are not. You are a fool, filled with stupid notions of duty. Unless you cure yourself of this disease, you are doomed.'

'Who are you?' Kattappa asked.

'I am everyone. I am no one. I am Yama, I am Shiva, I am Vishnu and I am Brahma. In this mad, mad world, I am the only one who is sane. I am known by the name Bhairava, the insane.'

Kattappa had heard about the mad Bhairava from his father. The slave who had served the king of Mahishmathi, faithful as a dog, for many years. The slave whose family was killed at the orders of the king for a crime which no one remembered now. The tragedy that had made him mad. The madness that made him attack the king. The madness that saved his life but left him to rot in his insanity. Kattappa had assumed he was dead. It was terrifying to be alone with him, in a rickety reed boat in the middle of a stormy night, in the roaring Mahishmathi. No one would even know where he had gone.

'Jump,' the mad Bhairava said.

'What?'

Before he knew what was happening, the boat tilted and Kattappa splashed into the water. Panic gripped him as he tried to swim. The current was swift but his hands got hold of some reeds. Reeds! His legs sank into the soft mud of the riverbed. Water came up only to his chest. He could hear the laughter of the madman fading away. He waddled to the shore, dragging his leg behind him. When he reached, he collapsed, catching his breath.

The next moment, ropes made of vines fell on his body, and before he could even cry out, tightened around him. He was lifted up, screaming and struggling, and before he could blink his eye, he was being carried away through the canopy of the jungle. The smell of Vaithalikas assaulted his nose and rough hands gripped him. The world around him turned and tossed—sometimes the sky was below and the jungle above, sometimes he plunged head down and was lifted up at the last moment. The Vaithalikas carried him from tree to tree, across the roaring mountain streams and above cascading falls.

Just as it had started, it stopped. The ropes uncoiled and he landed on his buttocks. He tried to stand up. Pain shot through his injured leg and ribs. His scream of pain was drowned out by the vibrating ululations and drumbeats in the forest. Then everything became silent.

Meanwhile, in the chamber of Skandadasa, the upapradhana was poring over ancient books taken from the palace library. There was so much to do and three months' absence had made work pile up on his table. Someone knocked at the door. Rubbing his tired eyes, Skandadasa went to answer it. A man stood in the shadows, avoiding the light from the lamp Skandadasa was holding in his hand.

'The slave has crossed the river,' he said crisply and vanished into the darkness. *Good*, Skandadasa thought. Kattappa had taken the bait. This was the first piece in the elaborate trap he had laid for the Vaithalikas.

He returned to his books and was flipping the leaves of the manuscript when something made his heart jump to his throat. *Fool, fool, fool!* He slammed his fist on the table, scattering the books everywhere. The lamp went off and the acrid smell of the burnt wick pierced his nose. Skandadasa felt like banging his head on the pillar. He had not done his homework, he had not studied enough. He was not worth the chair he was sitting in.

With trembling hands he rubbed the flint to light the lamp again. He fished out the manuscript he had last read. He brought it near the lamp. There was no mistaking it. In the three-hundred-year-old manuscript there was a picture of the crude Gaurikanta stone. He had seen it sometime back, tied like a charm, in the waist-band of the slave Kattappa. One of the missing stones. He had sent the slave across the river instead of apprehending him and questioning him about how he acquired it. The slave was not as simple as he had thought. Skandadasa felt betrayed. He gritted his teeth and swallowed the bitter truth. With renewed vigour, he started working. By Amma Gauri, he would unravel the sinister conspiracy against his motherland and make sure every culprit was hanged.

TWENTY-ONE

Jeemotha

The merchant ship cruised downstream towards the city of Mahishmathi. On either side of the river Gomukha the jungle peered into the water, as if the river held some secret. When the ship slipped past, things slithered into the river or scampered away into bushes. Except for the creak of the planks and gentle rhythm of the paddles, the wooden ship on which Jeemotha was standing was silent. But even that noise irritated Captain Jeemotha. Silence was the biggest ally in his profession. They should have no knowledge that he was coming. He hoped the creaky sounds of the ships would not carry far—perhaps the drone of the crickets would drown it.

Jeemotha was standing at the prow of the leading ship, looking at the silhouette of the Gauriparvat peak. It was twilight, and darkness had swept over the banks of the river. He could have reached the city in five days if he had used rowers to speed up, but he was letting the ship drift. He had received an owl from Pattaraya about Skandadasa's spies and decided to postpone his arrival at Mahishmathi. The forced delay came as a respite to Jeemotha. He was yet to collect all the merchandise he needed to trade. When the ships reached the spot where the river Gomukha met the river Mahishi, he ordered them to enter the smaller river. Gomukha split into many rivulets upstream, and his oracle Nanjunda had promised to guide them to a few villages from where they could collect their items.

The villages belonged to various tribes that lay beyond the borders of Mahishmathi. It was surprising that Mahishmathi had not bothered to conquer them and make them a part of the empire. Over the past three hundred years, most of the known kingdoms in the land between the Snow Mountains and the three seas had come under Mahishmathi's suzerainty. Yet, this cluster of more than seven hundred independent villages, spread over the hills and jungles between the Gomukha river and table land, had been spared. It suited Jeemotha. Otherwise, it would have been difficult to source the merchandise. Jeemotha suspected that the villages had been left alone for strategic reasons. If they came under Mahishmathi, Jeemotha would not have been able to do his trade, and without the trade Jeemotha was in, the economy of Mahishmathi would have collapsed. *All for a few stones—and they called* him *the pirate,* Jeemotha thought wryly

The air was humid and warm, just like it was before it rained. He was perspiring from every pore of his body, but he had chosen this night after consulting the oracle. Nanjunda might be a drunkard, and even half-crazy, but he was seldom wrong about the weather. With distaste, Jeemotha eyed the old man lying drunk out of his senses on the deck, holding an empty pot of toddy to his chest. *The kind of company an honest businessman had to keep to make a living!* he sighed.

Jeemotha had not given a rat's ass for oracles and holy men for the better part of his life, but now he was slowly becoming aware of his own mortality. He was in his mid-thirties, too old for a pirate and damn lucky to have kept his head on his shoulders for so long. Most of those who had started business at the same time as him were either resting in the muck two hundred feet deep, or had hung ten feet from the ground until crows cleaned the flesh off their bones. He had been lucky so far, but he was smart enough to know that luck wouldn't last forever.

Signs that the tide was turning for him had been evident from the previous month. It had forced him to abandon his disdain for religion and depend on the likes of Nanjunda. True, the oracle's tongue was liquored up, and half of what he said did not make any sense, yet it soothed Jeemotha's heart. The oracle had promised him success in this mission and blessed his ship. Well, not *his* ship exactly, for he had stolen it after murdering its crew, but oracles weren't fussy about such details. A few extra pots of toddy had helped. Jeemotha dismissed the thought—he was trying not to be cynical. He should have faith, is what the oracle said. Faith can move mountains, the oracle said. So be it. He would try to have more faith when he wanted some mountain to be moved.

Getting old forced one to be spiritual, he thought. After he had made sufficient money, maybe he would think of settling down somewhere. He would build temples and have many devadasis. That was the path to respectability. He would bring sculptors from the east coast and get them to build beautiful, ornate temples, of which he would be known as the patron. Future generations would praise him as a man of piety. Maybe they would even call him a saint. He had no objection to that. He was as saintly as the next man. It all depended on today's mission.

As a rule, he never got involved in politics. Politics was a game that was more dangerous than piracy. You needed to be truly evil to survive in politics, Jeemotha used to tell his friends. If the last voyage had not ended in disaster, he would not have agreed to what he was doing now. He had been forced to burn down his own cargo when the royal ships of Mahishmathi surrounded his fleet under the command of Senapathi Hiranya. He was carrying illegal gold water hidden in caskets that were supposed to contain oil. He had no choice other than to sink the ships and escape. In the sulphur powder that made the ships go up in a puff, his dreams too had exploded. He was lucky to have escaped with his life.

He was sitting in a tavern, drowning his sorrow in toddy and cursing Skandadasa—after whose appointment as upapradhana his business had suffered terribly—when a man had approached him. A former sailor who called himself Keera, the man had spoken about a fantastic plan to get fabulously rich. Jeemotha had dismissed the man's talk as a drunkard's banter, until he mentioned the name Bhoomipathi Pattaraya.

Many weeks later, he had found himself sitting across the powerful bhoomipathi in one of the nondescript taverns bordering Kadarimandalam. Pattaraya was disguised as a cattle merchant with Keera acting as his servant. Pattaraya did not touch liquor while he talked, and this had filled Jeemotha with misgivings. An evil man without vices was the most dangerous of all.

The offer Pattaraya made was too good to be true. But when he heard what he was supposed to smuggle in and out of Mahishmathi, Jeemotha had sprung up, toppling the pots of toddy from the table. He had screamed at Pattaraya that the whole plan was too audacious and fraught with danger. He didn't want anything to do with it. Pattaraya upped the offer and they haggled like good merchants until the rooster crowed dawn. By the time they parted, Jeemotha's greed had won over his good sense, and here he was, scouting for his goods.

So far, he had managed to grab three hundred black slave children from an Arab slave galley, and almost as many women from raiding more than thirteen villages—a labour of more than two months. His captives were now in the lower decks of his ship, chained like animals. The upper two decks contained silk cloth from China, barrels of flavoured oils from Rome, horses from Arabia, and pearl ornaments from the silver islands—all purchased with the advance money paid by Pattaraya.

With him was a copper plate token, the licence to trade in the empire of Mahishmathi, a licence issued by the minister of treasury and taxes, Bhoomipathi Pattaraya himself. That was the cover for Jeemotha. There was always a demand for slaves from the nobles of Mahishmathi, but of course it was never in the open. The profit from selling slaves would be his, which—even after bribing various major and minor officials—was substantial. This year was Mahamakam, and Pattaraya had promised that his friend Khanipathi Hidumba would take all the boys for a huge price. The women would be purchased by Devadasis, a majority of them would be snapped up by Kalika. This had been the process many times before. He could understand Devadasis like Kalika paying him money. Her business yielded a lot of wealth; but from where did Khanipathi Hidumba get his money from? He was almost sure that it was the Mahishmathi treasury that was paying for the boy slaves. Either way, it made it possible for corrupt people like Kalika and other bhoomipathis to trade in slaves. If he was caught, they would hang him like a common pirate.

There were other minor pirates like Kathavan but Pattaraya had choosen to give the token to trade only to Jeemotha. There was a major condition attached to it. He would have to smuggle a slave ironsmith and some stones to Kadarimandalam and hand them over to the bastard Princess Chitraveni. From the elaborate scheme Pattaraya had laid out, Jeemotha was sure it had to be Gaurikanta stones. He suspected that the slave carpenter would be one of the experts who knew what to do with the stones. Dark rumours had always floated about the secret group of slave carpenters who created magic with the stones, who could summon djinns that protected Mahishmathi.

When Pattaraya had elaborated on his plan, the first thought in Jeemotha's mind was to escape with the stones and the slave carpenter to some other country once they had boarded his ship. Any king would give a fortune to know the secret of Mahishmathi. It would have been much more than the slave trade could bring him in a lifetime. As if reading his thoughts, Pattaraya had casually remarked that the course of the river Mahishi flowed southeast through the Mahishmathi kingdom, down to Kadarimandalam. Jeemotha got the hint. Any misadventure from the pirate and Pattaraya would revoke his token to trade and send the Mahishmathi navy after him. He was sure to be captured as the entire course of the river, after the Patalaganga Falls to the sea, ran through the Mahishmathi empire or its vassal states. Jeemotha tried to negotiate for payment in gold coins, but Pattaraya had refused to part with even a copper of his own.

An official would never risk losing his money, and would never pay a businessman. It was always a one-way street. It was such a tough country to do business, Jeemotha thought bitterly. The risk was entirely Jeemotha's, but if he was not ready to accept the offer, there were others who would. Jeemotha had no choice but to agree to Pattaraya's terms.

The sky was now a sheet of black clouds above him, and lightning cracked ominously in the distance. It was going to rain, and he had to be out of the bloody village with his catch before it started. A breeze made the sail flutter.

'Idiots, I told you to tighten it,' he hissed. Two sailors quickly clambered up the main sail mast to secure it. A patch of sail snapped and flew away like a huge bat over him. An ill omen. He cursed. This mission had to be successful. Had he not bribed the oracle's god with a sacrificial goat before they ventured out? He hoped the oracle's god would keep her word. Time was running out for Jeemotha. And, it would be a waste of good meat.

Jeemotha hated the river Gomukha and its winding, shallow course. He was more at ease in the wide open sea. The river was treacherous, with hidden rocks and shifting sands. If he had a choice, he would not have ventured out on a new moon night in this river. It was sheer madness, but between madness and ruin, Jeemotha would any day choose the former. This was his last hope. But where was the village the oracle had promised? Soon, it would be dawn. And it would be difficult to hide his ships.

He shook the oracle, calling out, 'Ayya, ayya.'

Nanjunda blabbered some expletives and turned to the other side. Jeemotha lost his temper. He kicked the oracle between his ribs and Nanjunda sat up with a cry.

'Whore son, where is your bloody village?' Jeemotha said, slapping Nanjunda across his face with the back of his hand.

'Shantam, papam! Kali Mahakali...Heaayaaa...' The oracle stood up, grabbing his ritual sword and shaking the trinkets on it.

'The time has come, the time has come.' He jumped up and down on the deck and threw saffron powder on Jeemotha's face. The pirate's next kick was aimed between Nanjunda's legs, and this time the oracle's shriek was more heartfelt. The sword fell from his hands and he sat down on his haunches, clutching his groin.

'If you don't shut your stinking mouth, your time will come soon. Where is the village?' Jeemotha grabbed Nanjunda by his hair.

Fear was writ all over the oracle's face. He made a whimpering noise, and when Jeemotha picked up the ornamental ritual sword, Nanjunda blurted, 'You have to walk from here.'

'You said it was by the river.'

'It used to be. The river changed course a few years ago. It...it is only as far on foot as the time it would take to chew a betel nut.'

Jeemotha considered that. Leaving the ship was risky. But there was no point going back without achieving what he had come for. He let go of Nanjunda's hair and stood up. He turned to Keera, 'Anchor this somewhere safe. We are going to the village.'

Keera wanted to say something, but thought better of it, considering the mood of his superior. Soon a party of six warriors, armed with axes and swords, jumped into the marshy riverbank. Keera was holding the oracle by his neck as they waddled through shallow waters and climbed to dry land. Nanjunda was carrying a rooster in his hand and his ceremonial sword, wrapped in a red cloth so that it wouldn't jingle, on his shoulder.

Something scurried away as the men started walking towards the village. It took some time for their eyes to be acclimated to the darkness. Bushes clustered as inky blots and the trees appeared to have all their leaves fused together. They were nervous that even the sound of leaves being crushed underfoot was too noisy, and every time a twig snapped, they froze. Jeemotha felt uneasy. Vicious remarks about the ancestry of the oracle rose in his throat, but he suppressed them.

'Is a betel nut and a coconut the same in your village, old fool?' Keera asked the oracle, and the warriors chuckled.

Jeemotha hissed, 'Quiet.'

They could see the village in the distance now. It was nestled at the foot of a hill. A country dog barked and soon its pack took up the call. Jeemotha cursed under his breath. They halted under a tree at the edge of the clearing. It was a fairly large village, and Jeemotha counted up to sixty-three houses before the main street forked and the curvature of the hill hid what was beyond. Under the banyan tree at the junction, a lamp was still burning and someone lay huddled near it. Other than that, the entire village was shrouded in darkness, and the huts looked like lumps of coal fallen from a giant's sack.

Jeemotha turned when he heard the jingle of bells from the oracle's sword. Nanjunda was sitting cross-legged and his warriors were standing in a half-circle around him. The oracle's eyes were closed as he mumbled some mantras in a hushed drone. The rooster in his hand tried to flap its wings when the oracle lifted it above his head. A good rooster wasted, thought Jeemotha, but such rituals were important for his men. It was supposed to bring luck. *Fat luck I've had so far*, thought Jeemotha, and waited impatiently for Nanjunda to finish his ritual.

'Can I light a fire for the puja?' the oracle asked.

'Why not? We should have brought some drummers and dancers too and invited the villagers for the party. Bloody fool,' Jeemotha hissed. The oracle put back the arana wood hurriedly. He would have to go without fire.

'Without fire, the blessings of Chudala Kali will be half,' said Keera.

Jeemotha was getting restless. 'You will get all the fire in the world once we are done with our work,' he said. He could sense the uneasiness in his superstitious men but this was not negotiable. Fire was too risky. Someone might wake up, someone might see the light.

'Hurry,' Jeemotha said, and the oracle started muttering his mantras at a vigorous pace. His men also started mumbling mantras and, despite himself, Jeemotha closed his eyes and said a silent prayer. He needed all the help he could get from the gods tonight.

The dogs' barking had become increasingly frenzied, and Jeemotha could sense that the pack was approaching them. The oracle was clearly in no mood to bring things to a close though, and kept on muttering his mantras. Jeemotha was tempted to take the rooster from his hand and cut its head. He was sweating from all pores and the humidity was unbearable. Mosquitoes buzzed around him and made a feast of his legs.

Finally, it was over, and with a shriek that shook the birds out of the nearby trees, Nanjunda cut the head of the rooster. *Even the king of Kadarimandalam must have woken up from his sleep,* Jeemotha cursed. He did not wait for the oracle to apply the blood on their foreheads. He could see someone in the village had already woken up and emerged from his hut. Drawing his sword from its sheath, Jeemotha ran, jumping over the twitching, headless body of the rooster. He could hear the heavy feet of his men following him.

The dogs had found them and were now giving chase. The first dog that attacked found itself headless in a trice as Jeemotha ran, swinging his sword, towards the village. The rest of the dogs scattered, running in circles, keeping a safe distance from the attacking men. His men were screaming at the top of their voices now, intending to frighten the villagers. The village guard who was sleeping under a banyan tree did not even have time to see who killed him. Jeemotha grabbed the lamp that was burning in front of a stone serpent under the tree and flung it on the nearest roof. He then threw the stone idol into a nearby hut and someone screamed. The hut where he had flung the lamp burst into flames.

Before the villagers could understand what was happening, Jeemotha and his men had started their work. Fire spread over thatched roofs, leaping into the sky and arcing over trees. Men and women screamed and ran out of their huts. Jeemotha shouted his orders, 'Surround, attack, and do not spare any of the men.'

Smoke billowed from the huts. Some men came out with sticks, sickles and axes, desperate to defend their village. Jeemotha's men had done this a hundred times before, though. They knew how to use the shadows to their advantage, how to play with fire, how to trip men and hack their heads and limbs before they could blink. The oracle had let loose the animals from the stables. It was a practised act to create pandemonium. He bit the tails of the bulls and buffaloes he could find, enraging them. Panic-stricken due to the smell of smoke and the rising heat, the animals ran helter-skelter. They crashed into mud houses, smashed the carts parked on the streets, and stomped on anyone that came in their way.

By dawn, the village had ceased to exist. Fire had licked away almost the entire hamlet and only a few huts remained, partially collapsed and smouldering. More than two hundred lay dead and Jeemotha had managed to tie up all the women and children. They were too scared to cry. Some whimpered in fear, some were in too much shock for even that. When a baby bawled, its mother hurriedly clasped its mouth. Corpses littered the alleys and streets.

The young women and girls were separated from the boys and old women. Jeemotha's men rubbed their hands in glee, eyeing the young women with lust. Wails rose from hundreds of throats and the old women started pleading with and cursing them in turn. The boys were separated from their mothers and cried for them.

Jeemotha shouted, 'Silence!', and except for the chirping of the morning birds and a few crows that were cawing near the dead bodies, everyone went still.

'I do not want any rapes; anyone touching a woman inappropriately will have his hand cut off,' Jeemotha said from where he was sitting under the banyan tree. Keera tried to protest, but Jeemotha ignored him. The women watched him with no abatement in their hatred and fear.

'Strip them,' he said, and a huge cry arose from the women. Some started running, but his men caught all of them. A few tried to resist, some bit, some scratched, but soon his men had stripped the women of all their clothes. The women desperately tried to hide their nudity. Some of the grown boys tried to run to their mothers, but a sword or two thrust through a few daring hearts made both the boys and the women quiet.

Jeemotha's men tied the women together, their hands fastened behind their back. They were made to stand in a line. Jeemotha inspected them as he walked from one end of the line to another. He was not interested in their bodily charms. They hung their heads in shame as he weighed their breasts or the firmness of their stomach or buttocks. Some spat on him, some cried. Jeemotha was unconcerned. For him, they were like cattle. He felt no stirrings between his legs; his mind was busy calculating how much each would fetch. Not bad for a night's work, he concluded, when he finished his inspection.

Once he was done assessing the women and girls, he walked up to the boys. They were sturdy, most of them at least. He asked the few weak ones to stand in a separate line, and ordered the rest to be stripped and tied together. The boys who had been excluded looked at him with some hope.

Jeemotha ordered the chained women, girls and boys to start walking. One of his men started herding them towards the ship. A few of his men had piled up the clothes of the women and boys in a corner. He asked the remaining, weaker boys to pull all the bodies of their slain kin to one place. The old women started wailing as their grandsons began dragging their sons' inert bodies.

When the bodies were piled up and the clothes spread over them, Jeemotha pulled a burning ember from a hut and threw it into the mound.

'What to do with the old hags?' Keera asked with a grin.

In answer, Jeemotha pulled out his sword and cleanly cut the first boy near him into two. Kicking away the twitching half near him, he said, 'Is this your first bloody raid, motherfucker?'

He wiped the blood on Keera's shoulders and put the sword back in its sheath. He started walking as the cries of women and boys rose behind him. The rooster had been worth it. The gods had started smiling down on him again. He would try to treat the oracle with more respect henceforth.

In the light of the torches, he could see the naked backs of women glistening with sweat as they were led towards his ship. It was such a beautiful sight. He was going to be rich again. First, though, he would have to find good clothes for them. He had sneaked into a vassal kingdom of Mahishmathi, and had kidnapped the inhabitants. Nothing must give away their origin when he went to make a sale.

Not that anyone would bother once he was able to smuggle them inside Mahishmathi after greasing a few palms. But there were some officials who were yet to wisen up, who thought honesty would feed them when they got old. Most of them understood how things had to work before their hair turned grey, but there were always a few… Such people either got killed or 'promoted' to positions where they would not have to deal with intelligent men like Jeemotha.

Jeemotha chuckled at the thought. A few more such operations, and he would be ready to settle down. Maybe he would buy some recognition from a king. Maybe the post of a bhoomipathi or nanaka, in Mahishmathi or somewhere else. There was no honour in doing that, his father would have said, but he had killed that nincompoop long ago.

His father had been a good-for-nothing soldier for Mahishmathi, and had lost both his hands and a leg in some bloody war when Jeemotha was barely five. Until his mother died, his father used to crawl around in the house. The petty compensation the government had given him had run out long before Jeemotha was six. He did not want to think about his home. What had his father gained by serving the country?

Jeemotha was also serving his country, albeit in a different manner. *And see who has been more successful, useless old man*, he thought.

The bitch in Mahishmathi would haggle for the women, but ultimately she would have to pay a good price. And the dwarf too. The boys seemed healthy. They should fetch enough to make him rich.

When the last of the captives had boarded, he walked into the swaying ship. The eastern sky was a palette of colours. Gauriparvat turned blue-black from blue, then to grey and soon to red. Nanjunda was tinkling a bell and chanting some mantras loudly. Behind him the captives were sobbing. The 'hey-ho' shouts of his people shoving the ship with huge poles towards the centre of the river was music to his ears. The sun poured blood over the holy peak. A lark screeched above him.

The oracle was right. Faith *could* work miracles. He turned towards Gauriparvat and folded his hands in prayer. Next time, instead of a rooster, he would sacrifice a boy for the oracle's god. He bit his tongue—it was his god too. It felt good to be pious. The sail unfurled and the rowers pulled harder at the oars to speed up the ship.

Just then, he thought he heard something from the bank on the starboard side. As the ship picked up speed, he stared into the bushes. Was someone watching him? Then he chuckled. No arrow could reach his ship. He was too far from the shore. It might be some boy or girl who had escaped the raid. Jeemotha laughed. What harm could they do? No one could touch Jeemotha now. His luck had changed.

A cuckoo's call came from the starboard side and, after a moment's silence, another cuckoo answered from the port side. As the ship moved on, the calls kept following them.

'Swami, that sounds unnatural,' Keera said.

Jeemotha listened. Another cuckoo call.

'The birds are in heat,' Jeemotha shrugged, and Keera smiled, showing his brown teeth.

'I am too. If you permit, I can…' He eyed the naked women and wet his lips with his tongue.

'Keera,' Jeemotha smiled, and Keera smiled back.

'Yes, swami?'

'I love fishing.'

'I know, swami.'

'Do you know the best bait that can tempt the biggest of fish?' Jeemotha said, and slowly pulled out his dagger from his waistband. He ran a finger over its sharp edge. Keera was silent. The crew was looking at them. In a flash, Jeemotha grabbed Keera by his neck and pulled his sailor's face inches away from his own. He enjoyed the look of terror in Keera's eyes. Jeemotha lifted his arm, and then swung his dagger down at Keera's belly. Keera screamed. Jeemotha smiled.

Keera looked down. Jeemotha's dagger tip was a hair's breadth away from his manhood. Keera's eyes bulged in terror and he gulped. The pirate pressed the dagger above Keera's crotch.

'This is the best bait for fish, Keera. Should I fish today?'

'N…no.'

'Why not?'

'B…because…'

'Because…' Jeemotha pressed the tip of the dagger on Keera's skin and twisted it. A drop of blood stained Keera's dirty dhoti. Gripped by fear, Keera passed water and Jeemotha could feel the warm liquid touching his feet. He crinkled his nose at the pungent smell of urine.

'Time you carry a pot between your legs, whoreson. Now tell me, because…?'

'B…because…a good merchant…'

'Hmm, a good merchant?' Jeemotha pulled Keera closer.

'A g…good merchant never eats from his ware.'

'You are a fast learner. Maybe I will not fish today.' Jeemotha pushed Keera away and he fell on his back on the deck. Jeemotha's men laughed until he stared at them. They looked down and got busy with whatever they had been doing. After a moment, Jeemotha burst out laughing, slapping his palm on the casks tied on the deck. Soon, except for the sobbing women and children, everyone was laughing. Even Keera. The cuckoo calls continued to come from both banks.

'Fuck the cuckoos,' Jeemotha said, and everyone howled with laughter again. Two of his crew rolled a casket of palm toddy onto the deck. Jeemotha slapped Keera's back and the assistant grinned like a monkey. Pots of toddy were passed from hand to hand and Jeemotha lost count of how many swigs he had taken. His crew sang raunchy songs about the old maid of the clove island, who went to the forest in search of her buffalo and got caught by the king of bears. The bear wanted to marry the girl, but so did all the other bears in the forest. Each line was more bawdy than the other, and howls of laughter followed when Keera started enacting the lyrics with lewd gestures.

Jeemotha spotted the oracle and saw that he was not taking part in the celebrations. 'What is wrong with you, holy man? Did Yama take your father?' he asked.

'Laugh not, for she is coming.'

'Who? Your mother?' Jeemotha said and laughed, spitting up some toddy in the process. 'You shrunken coconut, you make me laugh so much.' He hit his head with his palm as he coughed and spluttered.

'I can see her. I can see the future. Laugh not,' the oracle said as another cuckoo call was answered.

'Oh, the great oracle Nanjunda is scared of a few cuckoos. Come on, take a mouthful of this toddy and you will be dancing with the rest of us,' Jeemotha said, offering his pot to the holy man.

The oracle turned to the drunken pirate and said, 'Fool, don't you even know that it is not spring, and cuckoos do not mate now? It is her.'

The pot fell from Jeemotha's hands and shattered on the deck. Another cuckoo call was answered followed by yet another. He could not believe his own stupidity.

'Get back to work!' he screamed at his crew, and his men hurried away. From either bank, the cuckoo calls went on relentlessly. *It is her, it is her,* they seemed to say.

For some strange reason, his captives had stopped crying.

They knew.

TWENTY-TWO

Kattappa

The rain had petered off to a drizzle. Kattappa stood in the clearing where they had dumped him. It was pitch-dark and the ground was wet under his feet. He tried to make sense of where he was. Lightning split the sky then and he saw he was standing before a fierce-looking stone statue of Amma Kali. Like many tribal worship places, there was an iron trident with withered lemons on its tips, stuck into the ground infront of the idol. A stone pedestal for sacrifices was placed near it. As darkness descended again, Kattappa's heart skipped a beat—a ritualistic sacrifice place.

'Kattappa.'

A voice boomed around him. Kattappa turned on his heels. He could not place where the voice had come from.

'Kattappa.'

This time the voice seemed to come from the other side of the jungle.

'Who are you, coward? Come out in the open and fight,' Kattappa screamed.

The forest shook with laughter. 'Fight?' the voice asked, this time from behind the Kali statue. Kattappa ran to the rear of the statue, wincing in pain as his injured heels touched the ground. There was no one. Lightning cracked again. Laughter echoed around him.

'You are going to die, Kattappa.' This time the voice came from the opposite side.

'You could have killed me when you caught me and carried me through the forest,' Kattappa yelled as he inched towards the trident. He was trying to keep his opponent talking.

'We are going to kill you the way we kill wild boar,' the voice said, this time from his left.

'But why? What have I done to you?' Kattappa was only a few feet from the trident now.

'You stopped us from killing that dog Bijjala. You killed our people, Kattappa. For that, you have to die.'

A streak of lightning traced its path through the horizon and this time Kattappa saw a figure to his right, a score feet away. He dove, pulled the trident from the ground, and threw it at the figure in one swift motion. The trident pierced its chest and it fell down. Kattappa limped over quickly to the fallen figure. Lightning cracked open the sky again and he saw the mud-pot head of a scarecrow grinning at him from the ground. The trident had cut through its straw body and buried itself into the ground.

The forest shook with laughter, mocking him. Kattappa pulled the trident out and screamed, 'Cowards, come out and fight if you are men.' The forest went silent. It was pitch-dark again. *When eyes fail to see, ears have to become eyes*—Kattappa remembered his father's words during his training.

'Kattappa, this is how we hunt wild boar,' the voice said, and Kattappa swirled on his feet. He shifted the trident from one hand to the other and stood ready. How do they hunt boar? His mind raced, trying to estimate the direction of the impending attack. A stake came whooshing towards him from the jungle. He smacked it with his trident in mid-air, just inches from his neck. The wooden stake splintered. He had not been fast enough, he thought; he had been lucky this time. He stood still, listening for the slightest movement of air.

'Impressive,' the voice said, from another direction now. 'But that was close, much too close…ha ha…to your neck. Now try this.'

Kattappa blocked the next stake that came at him and the two that followed in quick succession. He leaned on the trident and panted. They gave him no time to catch his breath. The air filled with the sounds of stakes hurtling towards him from all directions. He twisted and turned, smacking, splintering and breaking whatever came to him. Every nerve of his body was alert, every part became his eyes. The trident swirled like the wheels of a racing chariot, forming a shield in motion around Kattappa.

He turned around, yelling at the top of his voice, but he knew it was a losing battle. His injured legs were making him slow, and he was panting for breath. A slight dip in concentration or in the speed of his hands would result in one or more stakes piercing his chest. A few had already grazed his legs and shoulders, making him bleed. He could hold the attack off no more; what strength he had remaining was seeping out of him. He spun, wheezing for breath, waving his trident at invisible enemies, his mouth frozen mid-scream, and then collapsed. He heard the thud of his face hitting the ground. His right ear filled with sticky clay and his face felt warm with the prickle of wet grass. 'Wet, it smells wet, death smells wet,' he mumbled incoherently before his eyes closed.

When he woke up, the first thing he saw were faces. Dark faces with strange tattoos on them were staring down at him. The forest was alive with the chirping of birds, and light streamed in through the gaps in the canopies, drawing curious patterns on the faces around him. He tried to get up and cried out. The pain was back in his legs. It felt good to be alive, though. He looked down and saw that he was lying on a crude bamboo cot.

'When your brother told us what a great warrior you were, we thought it was an empty boast. When you fought so many of our best warriors single-handedly to save your master, I knew you were as good as me.'

The voice was calm and measured and Kattappa turned his head towards the source. A powerfully built man with a flowing salt-and-pepper beard on his coal-black face was smiling at him. Kattappa tried to get up again, but the giant gently pushed him back down. He came around to face Kattappa.

'But when your brother said you could fight in the dark, with your ears becoming your eyes, the speed of your arms your only shield, we laughed at his words. We said such warriors belonged to the tales of yore, like a Karna, like an Arjuna or an Aswathamma. Or they were gods, like Rama or Krishna, or asuras like Ravana. No mortal from these days could do that. Had we not seen you fighting, we would have seen your brother's words as nothing more than a misplaced idea of his big brother's abilities. But I have to admit, Shivappa was right.'

Kattappa looked away. Traitors, a bunch of criminals. It broke his heart to know that his brother was one of them.

'It seems you are angry with us, son,' the man said. Kattappa felt the middle-aged man's rough hand on his shoulder. He pressed his lips together. He would have no dealings with such criminals.

'Is it because of the welcome we gave you? How else could we welcome a great warrior? If only you cared enough to be a patriot…' the man smiled.

That got to Kattappa and he snapped. 'How dare you talk to me like that? Thugs, bandits, rapists, looters, traitors…' he shouted.

The big man chuckled, 'Hmm, then why did you come to join us?'

'Join you?' Kattappa yelled. 'I came to take my brother back!'

'Then take him. No one has tied him down. We are free men here.' The big man sat on a stool which creaked under his weight. He was built like an ox, with powerful shoulders and long limbs.

'Where is he?' Kattappa asked.

'How should I know?' The big man smiled again. His smile was really beginning to bother Kattappa. He tried to get up and immediately let out a scream. His leg throbbed with pain.

'I am here, Anna.'

Kattappa turned towards the voice and Shivappa stepped out from the shadows of a huge tree. He came and stood near his brother. Kattappa had rehearsed many angry lines to chide his brother with; he had often thought about how he would make his brother feel ashamed of his actions, make him feel guilty; but instead he found his eyes filling up. He reached out to feel his brother's arms, shoulders, face and head. 'You are all right, Shivappa?' Kattappa asked.

His brother knelt by him, holding his hands with both of his own and said, 'Now that I have my anna, I am all right. I knew you would come. I waited for you every day.'

Kattappa caressed his brother's cheeks.

'Nanna?' Shivappa asked.

'He…he thinks you are dead, Shivappa. The poor man is broken from within. Kanna, let us go back.'

'Dead? You told him that I was dead?' Shivappa stood up, letting go of his brother's hands.

'What choice did I have, Shivappa?'

'You had the choice of speaking the truth, brother. I never thought you would lie.'

That hurt. He had lied for the first time in his life, and he had done it for his brother's sake, to shield him.

'What are you blabbering about, Shivappa? You wanted the dandakaras to pursue you with their hounds?'

The big man chuckled. 'I told your brother that this is what would happen. He was so sure that you would tell the truth and—'

'Who the hell are you, sir?' Kattappa snapped at the big man. 'What business do you have to interfere in our family matter?'

Kattappa heard the clang of a hundred spears on shields. The big man threw his hand out to stop his agitated followers.

'Brother, you do not know who you are talking to,' Shivappa cried. 'I apologize on my brother's behalf, Your Highness.'

'Highness?' Kattappa stared as his brother bowed before the big man.

'His Highness is the real king of Mahishmathi,' Shivappa said. The Vaithalikas around clanged their spears on their shields and cried, 'Jai jai Mahishmathi Maharaja.'

The man raised his hand after the third cry and quiet descended on the forest once again.

'Don't worry. I am not Maharaja Somadeva in disguise. These boys call me the king. But I am destitute like them. I am Bhutaraya, the leader of the Vaithalikas. It is true that, hundreds of years ago, my ancestors ruled the forests. Where the city of Mahishmathi stands now was also our forest, our domain. We consider the forest to be the holy locks of Amma Gauri. My ancestors ruled all the lands from the borders of Kadarimandalam to the valley of the Snow Mountains. All the tribes and kingdoms, like the Kiratas of the swamplands, the cattle traders in the grasslands, the Chempadavas of the river lands, the Nishadas, Jambukas and Surakarnas in the forest lands that stretch northward of Gauriparvat, all of them used to bow to the Vaithalika king. All except the Kalakeya tribes and the Kuntala kingdom ruled by women.'

Kattappa stared at him with wide eyes. The man was not making any sense. He had not heard of any tribes ruling the forests. The forest lands were under Bhoomipathi Akkundaraya, the pastoral lands under Bhoomipathi Guha, the swamplands under Bhoomipathi Heheya, and the Gauriparvat under Khanipathi Hidumba. Not even the bards sang make-believe songs about Vaithalika kings. In all their songs, Vaithalikas were evil rakshasas, dacoits and looters. They were the epitome of cruelty. That was what the bards sang. That was how the plays and ballads depicted them. That was the truth, for it had been repeated time and time again.

Bhutaraya saw the confusion on Kattappa's face and leaned forward. 'I understand, this is difficult for you to comprehend. The victor's stories tend to be powerful. They have the capability to erase everything that does not suit their narrative. We are the losers of history.'

'Not for long. We will win soon,' cried Shivappa, and the forest shook with the shouts of 'Jai, Jai Vaithalikas', scattering the birds from the trees around.

'That has been the dream of every Vaithalika king for the last three hundred or more years. It is said that no Vaithalika king has ever died in his bed. The usurpers of the Mahishmathi throne have ensured that.' Bhutaraya smiled at Kattappa.

'A deserving end,' Kattappa muttered, eyes aflame. 'No traitor should be spared. As long as there is life in the bodies of slaves…'

'Slaves? How did you become slaves? Have you ever thought about that?' Bhutaraya leaned forward and ran his fingers through his beard. Kattappa had not seen anything more repulsive than the black man's smile.

'It is our fate.' The reply sounded unconvincing even to Kattappa's own ears.

'Yes, indeed. The fate you chose yourself,' Bhutaraya said.

'Leave me, sir. I have no intention of talking to traitors.'

'Some would call your father a traitor.'

'How dare you talk ill of my father?' Kattappa sat up.

'That is the truth, though it seems you don't take to the truth too well. You belong to a family of traitors, young man.'

'My father has served Mahishmathi all his life. He has lived for and he would die for Mahishmathi, just like our ancestors have done for the last eighteen generations,' Kattappa panted with exertion and anger.

Bhutaraya chuckled. 'That just makes him the nineteenth traitor in the family.'

Kattappa stared at the big man. Was he insane? Or was there some truth in what he was saying?

Bhutaraya kept his hand on Kattappa's and said, 'Son, you belong with us. These are your brothers. This is your forest.'

Kattappa stared at him, not wanting to believe what he was hearing. He belonged to the despicable tribe of the Vaithalikas? How was that possible? He had taken pride in the fact that Mahishmathi kings had always been dependent on his family for their protection. And now this Bhutaraya was calling his father a traitor.

'You are lying,' Kattappa said, shaking his head. Angry murmurs rose from all sides.

'Ever heard of Mahamakam, son?'

'The day every twelve years, when the blessings of Amma Gauri reach Mahishmathi,' Kattappa said.

'Listen, you young fool,' Bhutaraya began, and then gestured with his hands. Kattappa saw warriors on either side move away and fall on their knees as a man walked in, carrying something on a leaf. When he reached Bhutaraya, the king of the Vaithalikas bowed down and took the leaf from him reverentially. He turned to Kattappa and showed it to him. 'Do you know what this is?'

Kattappa stared at the lacklustre stones placed in the middle of the leaf with shock. They looked like the stone he had been carrying in his waist-band. The one Pattaraya had given him at Kalika's den. Only these were slightly bigger. He was tempted to check his waistband but he controlled the urge. They should not know that he had something similar with him. 'River stones?' he asked nonchalantly, and extended his arm to touch them, but Bhutaraya pulled the leaf back.

'Fool, these are no river stones. This is Gaurikanta,' Bhutaraya said, peering into Kattappa's eyes. 'These are the holiest relics of our tribe. Being a Vaithalika yourself, it is a shame that you do not know what this is. For many generations, Vaithalikas have bowed before this prasada of Amma Gauri. The gift given to Vaithalikas since time immemorial. The right of the Vaithalikas over Gauriparvat is as old as the hills, as ancient as the seas.'

'I...I don't understand...' Kattappa said.

'There are many things you don't understand. Or you do not want to understand. Why is Mahishmathi the biggest empire?' Bhutaraya asked as he handed back the stone. Kattappa watched it being taken away. All the Vaithalikas remained on their knees with their heads bent till the man vanished behind the undergrowth. Even Shivappa.

'I asked you a question, Kattappa,' Bhutaraya said.

'Because Mahishmathi is blessed by the gods. Because Mahishmathi has the best warriors who are ready to live and die for it.'

'Ha, ha! Do add, because Mahishmathi is willing to kill and maim, rape and loot to keep their power and hold over all others. Don't look so shocked. Every king throughout history has done just that. And about the blessings of gods, ha, that can be bought by sacrificing a buffalo or goat and filling the belly of some priests. There are enough people to live and die for any number of things. All of that does not matter. What matters is the unique advantage they have. And that advantage is the Gaurikanta.'

'How could a stone—'

'I am not finished,' Bhutaraya said, eyes flashing. 'This is no ordinary stone. The swords, the spears, the chain mails, the shields, all have a secret metal extracted from the Gaurikanta in them. It is made by a secret process. The final alloy is called Gauridhooli, worth many thousand times its weight in gold. There are only a few smiths who can forge a Gaurikhadga—the swords made from Gauridhooli—or Gauriastra, the arrows with Gauridhooli tips. They can pierce any armour.'

Kattappa tried to say something, but Bhutaraya gestured for him to listen.

'Three hundred years ago, one of my ancestors was foolish enough to give asylum to a petty vassal of the Kadarimandalam emperor. The vassal's name was Uthama Mahadeva. He was Uthama the noble, but only in name. My forefather, as per our ancient dharma, gave him and his family a place to stay. He was running away from the wrath of the emperor of Kadarimandalam, and he was desperate to keep his worthless head on his neck. My ancestor, Katyayana Vaithalika, took pity on him and his family. He treated that bastard, Uthama Mahadeva, like a brother. And how did he repay him? By taking away Gauriparvat from us. By making us destitute.'

'How can a fugitive take over Gauriparvat and the Vaithalika kingdom? Your story is incredible.'

'Because Uthama Mahadeva was helped by a traitor among the Vaithalikas—Ugranagappa, the commander of the Vaithalikas. He betrayed the secret of Gauriparvat and Gaurikanta to Uthama Mahadeva,' Bhutaraya said. A thick silence followed.

Kattappa understood the import of what the strange king was saying. He looked away from Bhutaraya. He could see Shivappa standing stonefaced. Bhutaraya finally said the words that Kattappa had been dreading.

'Ugranagappa was your ancestor, Kattappa. His daughter was raped by one of the Vaithalika queen's brothers, but that did not give him the right to betray a whole country. And what did he get in return—slavery. Your ancestor was a fool. He signed away his freedom for vengeance. But he also signed away the future of his people and his country.'

'I do not believe this heresy, sir,' Kattappa cried. 'If you possessed Gaurikanta, the so-called invincible stone that can make the deadliest swords, spears and weapons, why did you lose to a fugitive?'

Bhutaraya's nerves became taut with anger. A vein in his neck throbbed. Gritting his teeth, he said, 'We lost because the Gauriparvat was and still is divine for us. The mountain is our mother, our devi. We do not, cannot, exploit her resources. We had only a few weapons, while Uthama Mahadeva had been secretly hoarding them. In the most cowardly fashion, he betrayed us with the help of your ancestor and drove us away. We lost our mother and our home. Since then we have been fighting for her. And we could not reclaim it because we never mastered the art of making Gauridhooli.'

'Gauriparvat is divine for the people of Mahishmathi too,' Kattappa said defiantly.

'Divine?' Bhutaraya stood up and repeated Kattappa's words to his followers. 'He says Gauriparvat is holy for Mahishmathi. Did you hear him?'

The warriors clanged their spears and shields angrily.

'They are destroying what is holy in the foulest fashion. It is a shame on humanity, it is a shame on everything that is right, and you call that divine?' Bhutaraya said to Kattappa.

'Yes, I do,' Kattappa cried, his rising anger finally exploding. 'You had a mountain and you lost it to someone more clever.

And it happened hundreds of years ago. So many kingdoms have been lost and won. You owned Gauriparvat and the Gaurikanta for many generations and now Mahishmathi owns it.'

'Enough!' Bhutaraya shouted over Kattappa. 'Don't talk about that which you know nothing of. We never extracted Gaurikanta from the belly of our mother. We took what she gave. She gave her treasures voluntarily when she bled. Sometimes she bled once in a hundred years, sometimes once in a thousand. The stones flowed in her blood of fire. She is a jwalamukhi, a volcano, and she gives her blessings when she is pleased. We would never have drilled our mother's womb.'

'You mean to say that *we* drill Gauriparvat? You dare say we defile our holy mother, to whom each citizen of Mahishmathi prays? I challenge you to a duel right now. I will avenge this insult to our religion, our beliefs, our people.'

'You are a bigger fool than I imagined. Hear this. Your king and noblemen, who you are so keen to fight for, are fooling you. They have been fooling your people for many generations. The evil they perpetuate is beyond words.'

'You are lying,' Kattappa snarled.

'You want proof? Do you have the guts to face the truth?'

Kattappa was shaken by the emotion in Bhutaraya's voice. But he pulled himself up and said defiantly, 'I don't need proof. My king would never do that.'

'Fool, there are people who do it for him.'

'A few people may be bad. Which country does not have bad people? But my country is great,' Kattappa finished with emotion.

'A few people may be good, but their cowardice makes them worse than useless. There are merchants who would do anything for profits. Heard about Jeemotha? Heard about many others who are struggling to establish this business? Your king and the evil empire he rules over has unleashed the devil in each man. Greedy men, shameless women, corrupt officials—your country is full of them. And, of course, it is full of fools like you who thump their chests and think their country is the best. You have nothing to eat, no roof over your head, nothing to wear, nothing to drink, no land to till—still you fools cry the loudest and shrillest about your country.'

'If you do not like my country, go elsewhere,' Kattappa cried in rage.

'Elsewhere? Your king steals my land, destroys my earth, eats away my forest, mines my mountains, and drives away my people, and his slave tells me to go elsewhere! Bah! Wait and watch. How long can your rulers fool the people? If it goes on like this, your country will collapse. We won't have to do anything at all. You will destroy it all by yourselves before the next Mahamakam.'

Kattappa did not want to hear any more. Despite his outward steadfastness, his notions of right and wrong, duty and patriotism, were all turning topsy-turvy. He wanted to leave. He wanted to be far away from this place, from these people. Everything he held dear would crumble if he stayed here any longer. He got up from the cot and tried to stand on his feet.

'I will not stay a moment longer in this hub of traitors.'

He heard the slap first before his cheeks burned. He collapsed onto the cot. Bhutaraya hissed, 'You think we will let you go now? Do I look like a fool? You are not going anywhere till your king dies. Don't worry, he won't last beyond Mahamakam.'

'Mahamakam is months away…' Kattappa trailed off, ashamed that he was thinking more about his period of captivity than the safety of his king.

'Don't worry, your king will not last till Mahamakam. This year we will not allow it to happen. We are prepared. We will not allow for the carnage that follows the festivities. We have had enough for the last three hundred years. And you are joining us in this great fight for the freedom of your people.'

'I…I cannot break my oath.'

'Fool, our girls are getting kidnapped by Jeemotha and other merchants like Kathavaraya. They end up in brothels. Little boys end up in places worse than that. You expect us to sing praises of your kingdom? I will destroy Mahishmathi.'

'You will fail…' Kattappa said, but the conviction had gone out of his tone. 'And you are lying. Or you are just parroting someone who wants to spread rumours about my country. You are all traitors. This is an ancient land…'

'Enough,' Bhutaraya said, raising his palm. 'I have heard these arguments of patriots a hundred times. Let me fill you in, slave.'

Bhutaraya turned to his men and started imitating what he thought was the accent of a city-bred gentleman. 'I hate anyone who talks ill about our country. Our culture is the best.' Bhutaraya's followers laughed. The leader of the Vaithalikas continued, 'There is no place like this in the world.'

Another round of laughter. Bhutaraya moved his staff from his right to his left hand and continued in his mock accent, 'Ohhhh, there are problems in this country? Why—is this the only country with problems? You always say bad things about our country. Traitors, all are traitors except me and those who agree with me. Why don't you talk about the barbarians? What about the chink-eyed Cheenadesis? What about those who eat horses or those who eat pigs or those who eat sparrows or those who eat snakes? Why don't we talk about them? What about the tribes who eat humans? Why don't you talk about the Kalakeyas? Why are you silent about the Kuntala kingdom? Do you know how bad the situation is in Kadarimandalam?'

The Vaithalikas were now laughing uproariously. Even Shivappa was smiling. Kattappa fumed, largely because he found some truth in the biting mockery of Bhutaraya. He tried to say something, but the Vaithalika king leaned towards him. The smile was gone and his eyes flashed.

Jabbing Kattappa's chest with his index finger, Bhutaraya said, 'Blah, blah, blah. Chatter, chatter and more chatter. Shut your eyes and live in a fool's paradise. Close your nose so that the stench does not trouble you. Close your mouth, so that you don't gag. Open it only to praise your ruler. And call all those who are not blind traitors.'

Bhutaraya stared at him till Kattappa looked away. The Vaithalika king clapped his hands and four men came to stand at the four corners of Kattappa's cot. They lifted the cot on their shoulders and started running. Kattappa screamed, but his voice was drowned by the yells and shouts of the Vaithalikas.

After almost an hour, they stopped at the edge of a clearing. Above them, Gauriparvat towered as a sheer cliff. The air was humid and the breeze carried droplets of water. There was an unbearable stink. They had disturbed a few foxes that ran away with something in their mouths. Kattappa had to shout above the roar of the Patalaganga falls to Bhutaraya who stood beside him with his arms crossed across his broad chest.

'Where have you brought me?' he said, wrinkling his nose. The stink was awful.

'To a place that will open your eyes. Look around.'

'What?' Kattappa asked, scanning the grim faces of the Vaithalika warriors, who were standing with their noses covered with their palms. Kattappa saw only creepers thick as a man's arm winding over towering, fern-covered trees. The smell became unbearable as they reached the clearing.

'Those are rejected assets, Kattappa. They have served their use and have now been disposed of. But this is nothing compared to what happens after Mahamakam.' Bhutaraya pointed at a pile a few hundred feet away. Crows were fighting over the carcasses. Some tiger kills? Kattappa squinted to have a clear view in the slanting sunlight. Rats scampered over the carrions. He looked carefully. Till the far end of the clearing, until the shore of the roaring river, some rotten things were strewn. Dead animals? He tried not to throw up.

Kattappa did not understand. He was about to snap at Bhutaraya, when something fell from the cliff and crashed through the trees. It landed a few feet away from Kattappa's cot. Before he could scream, another one fell and soon another with a dull thud. A group of jackals darted from the bush to fight for them. The scream died in Kattappa's throat when he stared at the mutilated bodies of three young boys.

TWENTY-THREE

Sivagami

Revamma dragged Sivagami and Gundu Ramu to the central courtyard. The boys Sivagami had beaten up pushed and shoved them. Thondaka ran ahead of them, waving her book for everyone to see. He cried, 'The black magic book of the witch. Witchcraft manual. This is how she got the strength to beat even men. Witch, witch, rakshasi.'

Keki followed as Revamma dragged Sivagami by her wrist. The eunuch tapped Sivagami's shoulder and whispered, 'You cooperate with me and I shall get your book returned.' Sivagami's face was impassive. She would not show her panic, she would not let the eunuch know how much the book meant to her. *Let them think it was a book of witchcraft*, Sivagami thought.

Revamma called for the cane. Thondaka ran to get it. He handed it over and sat on the veranda, surrounded by his cronies, to watch the fun. Keki stood in a corner, silently watching them. Sivagami avoided looking at her.

Sivagami debated whether to resist or fight against the punishment, and finally decided that it would be better not to exacerbate the matter. Revamma circled them with the cane in hand. Sivagami was scared about what would happen to the book. If Thondaka did something to her father's book she decided she would kill him. She was startled from her thoughts by the loud howl of Gundu Ramu. He had started screaming his head off before Revamma had even touched him with her cane. She swished the cane and Gundu Ramu ran, sobbing loudly.

Much to the laughter and merriment of the inmates, Gundu Ramu made Revamma run around the entire courtyard. Finally, when Revamma could not run any more because of her huge bulk, Thondaka caught Gundu Ramu and handed him over to her.

Revamma started venting her anger on Gundu Ramu. Sivagami's heart broke on seeing the boy getting caned. She should not have dragged Gundu Ramu into the matter. She had to save him from further punishment. 'Enough of punishing the child, you mad woman,' Sivagami cried. It was intended to provoke, and it succeeded. Revamma came to her, raging like a wild bull.

She beat Sivagami until the cane broke, but it was Gundu Ramu who cried seeing his akka getting punished. She wished he would keep quiet and not draw Revamma's attention to him, but the boy kept howling loudly. He cursed Revamma, saying an elephant would stomp her to death and a bull would gore her for her sins. The other inmates laughed at each of his comments until Thondaka came and slapped Gundu Ramu across his face. The boy cowered with fear and stopped his tirade, but continued to sob quietly as he watched

Sivagami take her punishment stoically. Finally, Revamma left after instructing Thondaka to tie both of them to a pillar and took the book with her. Thondaka quickly set about doing her bidding.

'How about giving this book to me?' Keki asked, stopping Revamma.

'Why would I?' Revamma asked her suspiciously. Sivagami willed herself to look away. Her heart was beating uncontrollably.

'Maybe you could get a good price from me,' Keki said.

'Maybe I could take it to some official and get an even better price, or perhaps a reward, for exposing a witch,' Revamma said.

'Suit yourself,' Keki smiled. Revamma walked away with the book. Sivagami sighed with relief. She did not know whether the eunuch knew the importance of the book, but it would have been difficult to get the book back from her.

Keki approached them and stood before Sivagami. 'Girl, what is in that book? Your face betrays its importance for you.'

So she does not know, Sivagami thought with relief. The eunuch was just trying her luck. 'Witchcraft. I am a witch,' Sivagami threw her head back and laughed at Keki. The eunuch scowled at her.

'Tell me the truth and I can save you. Is it about some hidden treasure?' Keki asked.

'It is about making a man out of a eunuch,' Sivagami laughed. The eunuch's lips curved into a grimace, but her eyes did not smile.

Keki ran her index finger along the contours of Sivagami's face. 'Such a sweet face and such sharp words.' Sivagami flinched at the contact. Keki grabbed Sivagami's chin and hissed, 'Laugh all you want, girl. You'll never see your precious book again. It will be seized by the officials tomorrow and you will be thrown in jail. When the guards rape you, you will be remembering Keki akka's offer of help.'

Sivagami thought of retorting but restrained herself. She should not act too concerned and make the eunuch suspect more. She stood looking into the distance, ignoring the eunuch. Finally, Keki left them.

When it was just the two of them, tied to the pillar for the night, Gundu Ramu started weeping again. Sivagami snapped at him to keep his mouth shut and the boy replied that, if he kept his mouth closed, how would he cry aloud, making Sivagami laugh.

Sivagami laughed so much there were tears in her eyes. It was only when she felt a burning sensation searing into her thighs that she understood Revamma had sneaked up from behind with a hot iron. The pain shut her mouth and blocked the tears. Gundu Ramu, meanwhile, continued to howl in pain until he slipped into a whimpering half-sleep. Hunger pangs kept Sivagami awake till the moon had disappeared behind the slants of the roof. She wished Kamakshi would sneak in with some food, but she was sure they must have locked her in their room.

She woke up dripping wet. With great difficulty, she opened her eyes. Thondaka was standing in front of her with a pail of water. She was still tied to the pillar and her limbs ached. Thondaka moved to Gundu Ramu and splashed the rest of the water on his face. Gundu Ramu woke up whimpering. As Thondaka untied them, Sivagami stood watching the water pooling around her toes. The faded blue of her skirt had spots of the pale rust colour of her blood. A shaft of sunlight fell on her face. The sun had risen over the roofs and was peeping into the courtyard. A crow cawed outside. From the kitchen came the sounds of vessels clattering against each other.

Revamma came up and sat in the courtyard chair. Her mouth was full of betel leaves. She spat a stream of red that splashed near Sivagami's feet. Sivagami raised her head and glared at her.

'Ammamamama, see her eyes. Kali.' Revamma gargled to clear her throat and spat again. A speck of chewed betel leaf fell on Sivagami's toes and she cringed. Revamma stood up from the chair and waddled towards her. Sivagami saw her father's book in her hand.

'What sort of book is this?' she asked, waving it in front of Sivagami. 'What is this language? What is written in this? I am sure it has something to do with your father's treason.'

Sivagami did not reply.

'It might be some sort of black magic,' suggested Thondaka.

Revamma eyed the book suspiciously.

'She is a witch,' Thondaka said. 'Strange incidents are happening these days. Last night she was howling like a wolf. Some say she actually turned herself into a wolf. I think she can become whatever she wishes.'

'Howling? How come I did not hear that?' Revamma asked.

'You were drunk,' Thondaka said and was slapped by Revamma for his impertinence. He retreated, covering his cheek with his hand. Sivagami snorted and he glared back at her over his shoulders. She let her derisive smile stay on her lips. Let him get mad.

'Girl, look here,' Revamma said. 'Either you tell me what this is or I am taking it to the officials. One last time, what is this?'

Sivagami refused to answer her or look at her face. She watched the clouds racing against each other in the rectangular slice of sky wedged between the roofs of the courtyard. She looked at the patterns of the tiles sloping inwards. She gazed at a dragonfly that was buzzing near the tulsi plant. She tried to count the number of beads in the garland around the idol's neck.

'Fine, I have had enough of your arrogance. Change your rags fast. I am going to report this. Ayyo, what sort of devil is this girl? Why are you standing like a cow? Hurry up.'

Sivagami walked into the kitchen where she kept her spare clothes. Her head was in a whirl. How could she get the book out of the woman's hands? Just then she heard Gundu Ramu screaming and looked back.

Revamma was beating him with both her hands on his plump back. 'How dare you ask for food again? Shani! Bakasur! You ate all the food yesterday.'

Gundu Ramu came running to Sivagami. 'That lady is a witch,' he said, gasping for breath.

Sivagami took his hands in hers. 'No, she is not the witch. I am,' she said, and laughed on seeing Gundu Ramu's eyes widen.

It was past noon by the time Revamma dragged Sivagami and Gundu Ramu to the palace. Sivagami was feeling hungry and she could not even imagine what Gundu Ramu must have been going through. At the palace, a few soldiers tried to make fun of Revamma and were shut up promptly by her acid tongue. She stopped to complain to every maid, every servant, about the wards she had to take care of. Sivagami seethed with humiliation. She felt like an animal being led to the cattle market.

They were denied entry into Mahapradhana Parameswara's office, and when they tried to meet Roopaka, a clerk came out to send them away. Revamma's mood grew grimmer. She was sweating profusely, and every time she lifted her arms to wipe sweat off her face, she gave off a smell like a pig sty. The palace of Mahishmathi was not designed for the likes of her. She sat down on the granite steps, cursing her bad luck, panting and puffing. If this continued for some more time, Sivagami was afraid she would start feeling pity for the fat woman. Revamma had kept Sivagami's book inside her blouse, close to her bosom, and every time she took it out, Sivagami's heart sank. The book with her father's handwriting was stained with the woman's sweat.

Gundu Ramu made faces behind Revamma's back, and if he caught Sivagami's eyes, he caressed his tummy and made a pleading face. When they passed by the royal kitchen, the smell of frying fish and spices made even Sivagami's mouth water, and she couldn't bring herself to look at Gundu Ramu. A cat sat by the waste pit, crunching fish bones in its mouth. Gundu Ramu paused to look at it enviously and moved on only when Revamma yelled at him.

Sivagami saw that they were making their way to an office by the southern rampart, before which a crowd was waiting patiently. Revamma puffed and panted her way down the garden path towards the office. Sivagami and Gundu Ramu followed. The granite steps had grown hot in the sun, but when Sivagami tried to step on the sand, she found it even hotter. Revamma cursed the sun, cursed her life, cursed a mynah that hopped across her path, and ambled forward like an elephant.

When they reached the office, Sivagami read the carved sign-stone—Upapradhana Skandadasa. For the deputy prime minister of Mahishmathi, his office was modest. A single-storey building with a sloping stone roof. The only things that looked royal were the carved pillars that ran round the veranda. There was an earthen pot placed on a stool by the steps and a mug balanced over the rim of its narrow mouth. Peasants were standing or sitting near the banyan tree in the courtyard. A few scribes sat cross-legged under the tree with pots of inks and stencils arranged around their writing tables. Heaps of palm leaves lay scattered around them. Some were waiting for clients, while a few scribbled petitions for the illiterate peasants sitting on their haunches before them. Two guards stood at the entrance, with expressions that proclaimed their boredom with life. A horsecart stood in the shade by the wall.

Revamma was allowed inside by the guards when she said she was a government servant in charge of the royal orphanage. She took the book out from inside her blouse and started climbing the steps, clutching her knees and thighs after every step she took.

They waited by the door as the upapradhana instructed a clerk to reduce the taxes of a peasant. The clerk was arguing with him, and Sivagami was taken aback by how boldly a subordinate was talking to the deputy prime minister. A few moments passed, and finally they were ushered in. The peasant was touching an embarrassed Skandadasa's feet, while the clerk looked on with a scornful smile. The peasant left with many bows, and Sivagami could hear his excited voice breaking the happy news to his fellow-villagers outside. The call of 'Upapradhana Skandadasa—jai, jai!' could be heard, and Skandadasa sent the clerk out to calm them down.

The upapradhana asked them to sit. Sivagami could see that Revamma had not expected such courtesies and was rather shocked. No one had even allowed them in, and here was the deputy prime minister of the country asking them to sit.

'No, swami, I shall stand,' she said, folding her hands together.

'Amma, you are elder to me. Please sit; otherwise I will be forced to stand and talk,' he said, pointing to a chair across from his.

'Swami, I am a petty official. I cannot sit before the upapradhana,' she insisted, and suddenly shouted, 'Get up, you idiot.'

Sivagami was horrified and the upapradhana was taken aback. He stood up from his seat—and then he started laughing. Sivagami saw that Gundu Ramu had settled himself comfortably in a chair. Revamma lifted Gundu Ramu by his ears.

'Easy, easy, amma. He is but a small boy.'

'Ayyo, swami. Does he look small to you? Fat swine.'

'How old are you, boy?' Skandadasa asked Gundu Ramu.

'Old enough for mischief, swami,' Revamma interjected. 'Maybe ten or even twelve... Who knows and who cares. Does he act like a boy? He is a devil. Satan. And so is she,' she said, pointing to Sivagami.

'What is their crime?'Skandadasa asked, gesturing for Revamma to sit. She squeezed herself in a chair, ignoring its squeaky protest, and started narrating their crimes, counting them off on her stubby fingers. Going by the invented and exaggerated crimes, she was sure to run out of fingers soon.

Sivagami liked Skandadasa's easy smile. Would he have known her father? She wondered how he would react if she told him she was the daughter of Devaraya.

As Revamma blabbered on, Sivagami's gaze roamed around the room. There was a shelf with manuscripts. A partially open door hid a private room where she could spot a cot. An arched window with a few broken shutters opened onto a narrow path. Beyond the path, the fort wall towered. A banana grove stood near the window, the green leaves gently swaying in the breeze. A bust of Maharaja Somadeva stood on a desk behind the upapradhana. Sivagami could see the tail of a lizard twitching near the bust. There was a pile of palm leaves neatly arranged on the desk, and the royal seal lay near it. A lamp burnt near a container of red lac. Sivagami was tempted to take the seal, dip it in lac, and stamp it on something. The seal held power.

Her gaze wandered to the half-open door as it swayed open and a man walked out with a copper plate covered with a banana leaf and a tumbler of flavoured buttermilk. Skandadasa lifted the plantain leaf cover and the smell of spices spread in the room. Sivagami felt sorry for Gundu Ramu.

'Excuse me, Amma. Would you care to share some food?' Skandadasa asked. Revamma shook her head and continued her barrage of complaints.

Skandadasa said, 'All right, all right. I hope you don't mind if I eat while talking to you. I rarely find time to eat, and the vaidya has said the only way to treat the burning in my stomach is to eat regularly.' The upapradhana spread the little vessels containing curries around his plate and then his gaze fell on Gundu Ramu.

'Hungry?' he asked the boy. Gundu Ramu looked fearfully at Revamma and then down at his feet. The upapradhana offered his guests a share of the food again. Revamma and Sivagami declined. Gundu Ramu gulped and gave a reluctant shake of his head. Skandadasa smiled and tore the banana leaf in half and started serving out a portion of his meal.

'Swami, what are you doing? I have come here with a complaint about them and you are sharing your meal with this lout.'

'Amma, he is just a boy—and a boy who is hungry, aren't you?'

'Swami, he eats like rakshasa—'

Skandadasa raised his hands. 'Amma, I know hunger. I was born into it.'

'Swami, please do not misunderstand if I ask you something.' Revamma scratched her head. Skandadasa nodded as he served Gundu Ramu food from his plate.

'They say you are a shudra,' Revamma said, and Sivagami bit her lip angrily.

'They lied,' Skandadasa's smile did not fade.

'Oh, I knew it. Sorry, swami, I was afraid…' Revamma babbled.

'I am something lower than that. I have no caste. I was raised in an orphanage. But my father was no martyr. He was a thief. An incompetent thief who was caught and lynched by those who were blinded by their righteousness. My mother married again and they did not want me. I ran away from my village and came to Mahishmathi city. For the first few months, I fought with street dogs and beggars for leftovers. Sometimes I won; most of the time they won.

'I learned how to read and write when I got the job of a cleaner in a gurukulam. The monks did not teach me, but that did not prevent me from learning. Later, I did all sorts of jobs—shoemaker, farmer, guard, petty merchant, assistant to a street magician… The mahapradhana met me at one of these jobs, and offered me a post as a scribe. That gave me more time to continue my studies, and I am still learning,' Skandadasa finished and pointed to the bookshelf. Revamma blinked.

Sivagami's eyes filled up. She could see herself in him. No, she was luckier. At least for the first few years of her life she had had Thimma. She'd had a sister in Thimma's daughter. A mother and brothers. She had had a family. But she lost it all for no fault of hers.

Skandadasa turned to Sivagami and Gundu Ramu and said, 'Do you see that folded cloth near the maharaja's bust? That is the first cloth I bought myself. I got it made by a poor weaver who had fed me one night. I spent my first salary on it. It is two decades old. So it will have more holes in it than a fishing net!'

Gundu Ramu laughed.

'Do you know why I keep it? It is a reminder of my humble beginnings. It reminds me of everyone who helped me on my journey. And it reminds me to be grateful to this country and city. For it may have tested me, but this is the only place in the world where a boy can arrive in rags and end up as deputy prime minister, irrespective of his caste, creed and religion. If a son of a thief, an orphan, can do that, imagine what you two, the son and daughter of noblemen, can achieve.'

'I…I …' Sivagami struggled to find words. Skandadasa waited patiently. 'I am the daughter of Devaraya.'

Sivagami waited for the shock to show on Skandadasa's face. Instead, he placed his hand on her head and said, 'I know. You are like a daughter to me.'

Revamma coughed, and when Skandadasa looked up, she grimaced. She pushed Sivagami's book towards Skandadasa and said, 'Swami, see the book she was hiding from us. The girl is not as innocent as you think. I am sure this contains some treason against our country. It was that traitor's book.'

Sivagami tensed as Skandadasa took the manuscript and untied the thread around it. Her fist tightened. She did not know what it contained, nor was she sure whether the deputy prime minister could read Paisachi. She observed him keenly as he flipped through the pages. Did his face express confusion or was it recognition that twitched in the corners of his lips for the blink of an eye? She was frustrated that she could not make out what he was thinking. She gripped the armrest of the chair.

'This seems to be some shlokas in praise of Mother Gauri,' Skandadasa announced.

'Swami, you can read it?'

'No, not much. A few alphabets here and there. It is in old Paisachi, which no one speaks now. It is the tongue of the Asuras of yore. A few Siddhas in the southern forests may be able to read it, perhaps, provided we can find them and persuade them to leave their hermitage and come to this city of sin. It would hardly be worth it. It is just a devotional book of some old Shakta.'

'Nothing treacherous in it?' Revamma was clearly disappointed.

'Nothing that I could decipher,' Skandadasa said, and was about to give the book to Sivagami when the door burst open and a guard announced, 'Bhoomipathi Pattaraya demands an audience with you, sir.'

Before the upapradhana could react, Pattaraya came in with his hands folded in namaste.

'Well, well, I didn't know you had company, Skandadasa.'

'Yes, Pattaraya, but I am honoured by this unexpected visit. What can I do for you?' Skandadasa said, and Sivagami saw with dismay that he was placing her book in the drawer of his table in an absentminded fashion. She tried to catch his attention, but Skandadasa was not looking at them any more. Though he was civil with Pattaraya, Sivagami could feel the tension between the two men.

'I am here because you ordered me to come. Is it your birthday or something? You are feeding orphans?' Pattaraya softened the edge of his words with a smile.

Sivagami shifted her gaze to see Skandadasa's reaction but his face remained impassive. Revamma was sitting at the edge of her seat, not sure whether to get up out of respect for Pattaraya, or remain seated as Skandadasa had directed her to. Gundu Ramu had no such worries. He was wolfing down the food on his leaf.

Sivagami stood up, wondering how she could recover her book. She felt helpless.

'There is no hurry. Please sit,' Skandadasa said, and Revamma, who had made to stand up as well, sat back down on her seat.

'Please be seated, sir, let the boy finish his food,' Skandadasa said.

'Of course, of course. Annadanam Mahadanam. Nothing is greater than feeding the hungry. Have your fill, son,' Pattaraya said. They waited until Gundu Ramu belched and licked his fingers.

'Amma, I will enquire about what you said and let you know,' Skandadasa said then, and gestured to his help to clear the table. Sivagami understood they were being dismissed. Pattaraya occupied the seat Revamma had just vacated.

'One day, we should have food together, daughter,' Skandadasa said as Sivagami began walking towards the door. She wanted to ask for her book, but he had already turned and begun conversing with Pattaraya. There was some bitterness between these two, she could tell, though the tone and words remained civil. She was not too bothered by it, though. She just wanted her book. Should she interrupt them and ask for it? Before she could summon up the courage, Revamma, who was by the door now, called out to her.

She walked away, mortally scared of what Skandadasa would find in the book. She guessed that he was just diffusing the situation by claiming it was a devotional book. She knew he would call for her one day, and she dreaded that call.

TWENTY-FOUR

Jeemotha

Jeemotha stood nervously at the prow of the ship as it floated through the swamps of the upper Gomukha. He was sure the ship was being watched. Was there some movement behind the reeds that bordered the riverbanks? Why were his captives silent? Why had they stopped crying? Since the previous night, things had become ominously quiet. He had whipped a few slaves, just to hear their screams. The strange birdcalls that followed them made him edgy. He was contemplating anchoring the ship somewhere to investigate the shore, when Keera—who was standing near him, blabbering something—collapsed on Jeemotha. For a moment, Jeemotha did not understand what was happening. Then he saw an arrow quivering in Keera's neck. Terrified, Jeemotha pushed him away. Keera was already dead.

Jeemotha scanned the shores on either side. Where had the arrow come from? The captives remained silent. Blood from Keera's body spread on the deck like ink from an overturned bottle. The oracle Nanjunda started crying out of fear and mumbling some mantras. Jeemotha snapped at him to be quiet, but his order was cut short by an arrow that grazed past his nose and hit the sail mast. When the shock subsided, Jeemotha saw something dangling from the tail of the arrow. A message.

It was ominous in its brevity—surrender or die.

Like hell he was surrendering. This was his last chance. If it was Skandadasa's men, he was not going to abandon his wares like the last time. He would fight till the end. He spat for good luck and shouted for all his men to be armed. He could hear his men unsheathing their swords, arrows being notched, spears being picked up. He waited for the enemy to attack. Nothing happened. Not a thing stirred. A few clouds in the sky, some birds hopping around in the swamp bushes, the distant call of larks and his ship gently floating on the water—it would have made a perfect painting.

After they had cruised along for a few hours, the tension abated and the vigil eased. His men started cracking jokes and debating how much each woman would get once they reached the shore. On Jeemotha's orders, his men flung Keera's dead body into the river. They were passing through the cow's mouth now, the gorge where the river was at its narrowest. Hills loomed over them on either side, marking the end of the swamps. Thrushes gave way to jungle.

They were so relaxed that, when the attack came, they were thoroughly unprepared. It started with the ship lurching. The men fell and the slaves in chains tumbled around like ninepins. When he had regained his balance, Jeemotha rushed to the starboard to see what had rammed into his ship. A huge log had floated across, blocking the path of the ship and slowing it down. The crew was engrossed in finding the best way around the log when it started raining arrows. They came down from everywhere: from the tops of trees and from the hills. Jeemotha ducked to the floor of the deck and lay flat on his stomach. He was screaming orders for his men to do the same when he saw a figure jump onto the deck from a hill, soon followed by several others. The log had completely blocked the path of the ship, jamming it in the gorge.

Before Jeemotha could recover, the deck was swarming with the enemy. *Gandhaka—he needed gandhaka*, Jeemotha told himself, as he tried to crawl down to the lower deck undetected. His men were being butchered. If he could reach the deck where barrels of the sulphur powder were kept, he could start a fire and sink the ship. He was not going to allow these bastards to get away with his hard-earned goods.

'Srimant,' a voice called out. He stopped short a few feet away from the ladder that spiralled towards the lower decks and turned back in surprise. There was something odd about the voice. He could see a figure standing on the deck, hunched, leaning on a stick and holding a trident in its hand. Dressed in black from top to bottom, their faces covered with masks, half a dozen warriors stood behind the figure, arrows held ready in their hands. Jeemotha tried to draw his sword, but an arrow pierced his fist. He had half a mind to jump into the river. Who the hell were these people?

'Tie him up,' the figure said. Now he understood what was odd about the voice. It sounded feminine. And old. Fear started creeping up on him from the tips of his toes. The hunchbacked figure was being helped by the archers to climb down the ladder. A wind uncovered its veil for a moment. And Jeemotha saw who it was. Cheers from the captives rose around him. He cursed. He would rather have died in the storm at sea, instead of having to face Achi Nagamma.

They had tied him to the mast of the ship, near the crow's nest, his legs dangling forty feet above the deck. It was a miracle that he was even alive.

The ship was cruising slowly up the river. The breeze was mild and the sails billowed a little, catching the wind. The log that had blocked their way had been freed and he could see it floating behind, secured to the rear of the ship by a rope. *The woman was a curse for mankind,* Jeemotha thought. She and her blasted army of women! Who would have thought he would be defeated by a bunch of peasant women, led by an invalid old wench? The story would spread all around Mahishmathi and beyond. Even in the pearl islands where he traded slaves. Men would laugh at the once-feared sea pirate.

They had questioned him till evening, asking him who he was selling his wares to. He had tried to bluff his way out, but the old woman saw through each of his lies. When night fell, she ordered her women to tie him up. It had not been this scary then, as he could not see how high up he was. Now, with the river swelling with an impending storm and the western skies darkening with swirling, inky clouds, it was terrifying to be up there with both hands tied.

A crow came and sat at the rim of its nest. *It is your bloody nest, so do feel free,* Jeemotha inwardly cursed. The crow hopped and settled near his nose. Its beak glistened in the sunshine. It tilted its head and peered at Jeemotha's face. Before Jeemotha could react, the crow pecked his cheeks.

He was too astonished to scream until the sharp iron smell of his own blood hit his nose, and his lips tasted salty. When he finally yelled out, the crow flapped its wings, flew in a circle above him, and landed back on the handrail. Jeemotha screamed again. The crow cawed in reply. Shrill laughter arose from the deck.

'Should have hung him upside down. It would have been more fun,' one woman said, and the others laughed.

Jeemotha wondered how long he would have to hang like this. He could see dark clouds over the distant Gauriparvat. Lightning streaked across and thunder rumbled towards them. The river's waters had turned grey, with white crusts riding over the waves. A brisk wind started blowing, stopped for a moment, and picked up with double the force. It lifted the ship up and tilted it to one side. He was thrown to the side, his ankles twisting sharply, only to be tossed again to the other side as the boat straightened. He felt giddy as the boat moved wildly with the waves. The crow returned to perch near him.

The women on the deck laughed. Another swell and roll of the boat made Jeemotha vomit on his chest. Trying to gain control over his nausea, he looked down and spotted the oracle Nanjunda's grey hair. The oracle was sitting on his haunches, surrounded by women with their palms extended, eager to know their future. Bloody bugger, Nanjunda—he was the one who had given him the auspicious time to raid the village. Pretty auspicious it had turned out to be. You will reach a very high position within a few days, he had predicted. The pirate had not imagined that those words would come true so literally.

'Bring him down,' Jeemotha heard someone say. There were a few whistles, some comment which he could not hear clearly in the howl of the wind across his ears, followed by uproarious laughter. His head banged against the mast pole, causing him to black out for a moment, and when he opened his eyes, he was being hauled down. He swayed from one side to another, the rope around his wrists cutting into them. The wind had picked up even more and he swung wildly. He felt his arms would tear away from his shoulders and he would fall, armless, head first, onto the deck. A swell rolled the prow and the rope started uncoiling as the boat dipped. Everything went blank for Jeemotha. He was not sure whether it was he who was screaming or the wind blowing past him. The world was a blur of green as the rope uncoiled rapidly and he rotated in the air as he was brought down fast. He braced for the impact but was jerked up at the last moment. He was once again forty feet above ground, hanging from his wrists and swinging wildly. Thunder clapped in the sky and the first drop of rain splashed on his cheeks. The creaking sound of the pulley kept rhythm with the hum of the oarswomen. Another hushed comment and raucous laughter followed from the deck. *They are playing with me, the bitches. If I don't get back at you for this, I am not Jeemotha*, the pirate gritted his teeth.

The wind was turning into a gale. His dhoti loosened at his waist and flapped around him, drawing giggles from the women. For a moment he wished the rope would break and he would fall down and die. Then the rope started loosening again, gently. Suddenly, the rope became taut and tangled around his legs. The wind carried his dhoti away and he dangled there in a contorted position, butt naked in front of the screaming, howling women. Even the rowers stopped rowing and came to watch the spectacle. Slowly, like a sack of bananas, he was lowered down and cruelly dumped on the deck. Another howl of laughter followed.

They jerked him up and untangled the ropes. Only his hands were tied now and it was difficult for him to keep balance. He tried desperately to cover his shame, but every time the boat tilted, it took all his effort to remain standing. Each time he had to uncover himself to regain balance, he was greeted by laughter and screams. Of course, he had done worse to the many women that he had kidnapped when he was riding the high seas. Merchants' wives made the best captives. He would tie them on the prow, naked, as he inspected and graded them for the price each would fetch. Now when the tables were reversed, he felt rage bubbling inside.

I will get back at you, you bitches. You can't treat a man like this. Women have no right to treat any man like this, let alone a fearsome pirate like me, he thought to himself.

Fearsome! Thup! he spat. He looked more like the drunk village idiot. When bad luck comes, it never comes alone. It brings its bloody uncles, cousins, and their whores. His own men, tied near the mast, were grinning at him. After this, even if he survived this ordeal, no one would fear him. Jeemotha's shoulders sank in despair. The news would spread. The next time he walked into a village, they would not run away in fear. Instead, they would laugh. Vidhushakas would mimic how he had squealed in every nobleman's house during the Diwali or Dashami festivals. They might make a fucking play out of this. They would enact how he stood naked in front of a bunch of black, ugly, low-caste women. Bloody peasants. And the legend of Achi Nagamma would grow at his expense.

A girl had fished out his dhoti from the water and she brought it to him hanging from the edge of her fishing rod.

She held it above his head and when he tried to grab it, she raised it higher, out of his reach. Everytime he jumped to try and get hold of it, he had to expose himself, and each attempt was greeted with cries of laughter. Another girl threw a rotten fish that slapped against his back, and soon they were using him for target practice. The oracle Nanjunda sat grinning like a monkey, enjoying the spectacle. *Wait till I get you alone,* Jeemotha thought as a fish hit his nose. He stood without moving, covering his privates with his tied hands. He would not give them the pleasure of jumping around like a monkey for his dhoti anymore. He debated jumping from the deck, but judging from the swiftness of the current and the gale screaming around the boat, he decided it was better to be naked than dead.

'What is going on here?' a voice rose above the din and silence fell. The girl who was teasing Jeemotha with his dhoti, dropped it over his shoulders and ran to join the rest of the women, who were now standing erect. Jeemotha stared at her, trying to look fearsome, trying to imprint her face in his mind.

'Srimant, please cover yourself. There are young women around,' Achi Nagamma said in a soft voice that could have belonged to any grandmother.

Jeemotha glared at her. More than anything, he hated her sarcasm. She was addressing him as 'srimant', as if he was some frigging highborn, as if he was just a soft-fleshed, dumb boy from some noble family. A sly smile came to his lips. 'Devi, kindly untie my hands so that I can knot my dhoti.'

'Why, srimant, you think my girls are incapable of even such a small favour? Hey girls, help the srimant tie his dhoti.'

The girl who had teased him came forward. She removed the dhoti from his shoulders. As she was tying it around his waist, he hissed, 'Wench, you don't know what you have done.' She raised her head and smiled at him. She tugged at the knot of the dhoti to undo it. Jeemotha tried to stop the dhoti from falling down, but to no avail. It coiled around his feet. The deck shook with laughter.

Achi Nagamma thumped her stick and the laughter ceased.

'Ally?' Nagamma asked in a stern voice.

'Pardon, Achi,' the girl said. She picked up the dhoti and tied it around his waist again. Her fingers brushed his skin as she did so, and he cursed himself for the effect it had on him. This was so demeaning. She moved away with a sly smile playing on her lips. The ship heaved and creaked in the gale, but the storm was easing. The old woman stood with her feet firm on the moving deck, gazing at him. While he, who had been a captain of his ship for more than a dozen years, was finding it difficult to keep balance.

The waterfalls that streaked their way through the dense jungles of Gauriparvat had started appearing bigger and clearer. They were moving upstream.

'So?' Achi asked.

'So what?' Jeemotha raised his chin.

'I am too old to play games, srimant. And going by what we all saw, you too are no longer a boy. Tell me who you are working for and I may think of sparing your wretched life.'

'Do I look like a bloody servant?' Jeemotha hissed.

'Tut, tut. Mind your language, sir. There are young women around us.'

'Oh devi, I am sorry. I know they are demure and bashful. My apologies,' Jeemotha said, bowing to the women. They giggled. Achi raised her hand and again a taut silence ensued. Thunder clapped, rattling the ship.

'It seems Indra is angry, devi. The god of thunder is roaring. Your treatment of an honest man has displeased him.' Jeemotha smiled.

'Honest? Of course... Srimant, answer one question honestly and I can persuade the girls to abandon their plans to throw you overboard to appease Varna.'

'Oh no, water scares me. It always has, except...hmm... the time when I swam the entire night when my ship was wrecked near the black waters of Andhakara Bay, or the time when I was alone on a plank for two months after my boat was destroyed in the high seas.'

'You have a talent for wrecking boats and ships, it would appear,' Achi said with smile.

'Oh it happens all the time. I am one unlucky man. Would you please ask your girls to go ahead and throw me overboard? I am scared, but maybe I can persuade myself to swim.'

'Srimant, of course. I just hope you can outswim the crocodiles.'

Jeemotha cursed under his breath.

'Son, enough chatter. Tell me, for whom do you do your noble work?' Achi Nagamma took a few steps towards him, tapping her staff on the deck. He eyed her warily. Was it possible to lunge at her and knock her down? If he could grab her throat, even with his hands tied, he could easily keep her pinned and negotiate his freedom.

The warrior women were standing with their bows lowered. They had become lax, stopped considering him dangerous. He couldn't blame them. It was difficult to be afraid of a man they had seen struggling to cover his shame with tied hands. Let them grow more complacent. Jeemotha shifted his weight from one leg to the other and looked down.

'I am a merchant. I work for myself,' he said.

'Of course you are a merchant—and I am the queen of Mahishmathi.' Achi circled him. A cold breeze hit his face. The boat swayed.

'What do you want?' Jeemotha tried to turn and face her, but she poked his head with her stick. He was tempted to grab the stick, but before he could attempt it, she had pulled it back. She came and stood in front of him, only three feet away. This was his chance.

He lunged at her and she swiftly moved to the side. Jeemotha fell flat on his face. Laughter shook the deck again. He tried to get up, but the tip of her stick pressed down on the back of his neck.

'Srimant, when I was small, my grandfather told me about the sushmana naadi, the nerve that is inside your spine. He used to say that one good tap at the right spot is all that is required. Even a seven-decade-old woman like me can give a good tap. Srimant, would you answer or would you prefer to crawl for the rest of your life like a worm?'

Jeemotha had no intention to check the veracity of her grandfather's knowledge of anatomy. Achi Nagamma pressed the stick a tad more and he felt dizzy.

'Please,' he croaked. 'I will…t…talk.'

He felt the pressure ease and he slowly got up. The boat was taking a turn and the rowers were moving it closer to the shore to avoid a large protruding rock in the middle of the river. Water frothed at the base of the rock, while it flowed swift and deep in the rest of the narrow gorge. It required tremendous skill to row upstream through it. Devil's Gorge, it was called. The graveyard of many ships, one of the toughest stretches in the river Mahishmathi. The water was deceptively quiet, but he knew it had strong undercurrents.

'I acquire my merchandise—'

'You mean, you raid villages, murder the men and take the women and children as slaves...'

'Times are bad and business is poor,' he said. The boat was passing the narrow gorge, its prow cutting across swiftly. A fine spray of water covered the deck. He had to time it properly. He could hear the sound of cascading water.

'The poor is your business. You enslave them, peddle them like wares, kill, and rape, and maim without any mercy. But what we want to know is—who pays you?' Achi Nagamma was now behind him. He wiped water from his face with his upper arm, quickly calculating his chances. He let her talk.

'Men like you are a curse to humanity. How many families you have destroyed, how many kids you have orphaned, how many people you have kidnapped. Srimant, I have been trying to put an end to this business from the day I lost my family to a raider like you. My two sons were killed, my daughters-in-law taken, and my grandchildren went missing. For four years I roamed from one end of Mahishmathi to the other, raving mad, searching for my grandsons and my little granddaughter. Four years, till I met Hatayogi Sidheshwara, who cured me of my madness.'

Achi Nagamma was facing him now.

'Obviously he did a bad job,' Jeemotha said. There was a collective gasp. He heard a few swords being unsheathed.

A cruel smile played on the wrinkled face of Achi Nagamma. 'Yes, srimant. You are right. And unless you are going to sing like a parrot about who buys the slaves, who pays you, where they are taken, you are going to find out just how mad I am. When the government does nothing to save its people, it takes a mad woman like me to do the job. This is my service to the king and my country.'

'Maybe the king himself profits from our trade,' he said. That was calculated to provoke. There was a murmur among the girls and the villagers.

'I will cut off the stinking tongue that talks ill about our king,' Ally said, coming forward. She had drawn out her dagger, but Nagamma stopped her by raising her stick.

'Patriotic rebels? That is amusing. Your devotion to the king is touching. Oh, how I love patriots, especially when they roam around troubling honest businessmen,' Jeemotha laughed.

'Save your dirty tongue for the taverns, srimant. This is Achi's durbar. Only truth will prevail here.'

'Truth is what I spoke. I raid on the king's orders.'

Jeemotha enjoyed the agitation he was causing. The girls were consulting Achi Nagamma. The little fall would be after the bend, and the Yamakanda Fall, ten ship lengths away. It would be too risky to wait till then.

The sun had burned holes in the dark clouds, and shafts of sunshine stretched from the skies to the wavy waters. Silver crests decorated the dark waves. *What a great day to die*, he thought. A few more steps and he could jump over the deck, but that would be too close to the rocky shore. If he could run towards the stern, he could hope to catch the deeper part of the gorge. It was going to be a tough thing, to swim in this current with his hands tied. Hopefully the current would carry him away from the gorge. But it was a choice between dying in some damp cell at the bottom of this stinking boat and a watery grave, befitting a sailor. To hell with it. He should not be thinking morbid thoughts. He had survived much worse.

'Old wench, without people like me, Mahishmathi's treasury would be as poor as yours if you took to whoring.'

This time many swords were drawn out. Ally screamed, 'I want to see what his wretched intestines look like! Achi, let me at him.'

'Back, stand back I say, Ally,' Nagamma tried to control her agitated followers. They were waving their swords at him and screaming murder. Jeemotha inched closer to the edge. He counted the number of steps that would be required to reach the stern. Fifteen feet. Maybe he could make it. He took off. Nagamma had been facing her followers but she heard him moving; she turned towards him and froze.

'Ally,' she roared, and the younger woman took her sword from her scabbard. Without breaking his stride, Jeemotha turned on his heels and kicked a keg that was rolling on the deck. It flew and caught Ally on her face. She fell on her back. Two women rushed towards him from the captain's cabin side, yelling in a shrill voice, their swords raised over their shoulders, but he caught hold of the shrouds and swung himself up. He somersaulted over the swinging swords and landed astern. An arrow struck the captain's cabin and quivered a finger's breadth away from his neck. He could hear the women warriors running towards him. A spear whistled past his ears. A wooden keg whisked past his shoulders and exploded in front of him, spilling wine. He slipped and fell, scrambled up and ran. A sword shaved off the heel of his shoes. A lasso caught his left leg, but he shook it off before it could be tightened. He could hear the old woman shouting, 'We want him alive. Ally, get him, get him alive.'

He swung on the sail rope and jumped atop the captain's cabin. A heartbeat later, he heard the thud of someone else landing on the cabin roof. He could see the water roaring past the stern, twenty feet below. It looked scary and no sane person would dare to jump into Devil's Gorge. He stole a glance and saw Ally lunging towards him. For half a beat, he hesitated. She caught him by his waist, trying to pin him down on the deck. He took hold of her hands, lifted her up and, dragging her with him, leapt into the screaming, howling, frothing black waters of Devil's Gorge.

TWENTY-FIVE

Sivagami

Sivagami had almost finished washing the huge pile of clothes when the messenger came to summon her to Upapradhana Skandadasa's office. It had been a few days since Revamma had taken her there, and she had been dreading the call since then. Had Skandadasa found something that would implicate her in some unknown crime? Or worse, did the book contain something that would taint her father?

Thondaka taunted her from the first-floor veranda as she walked with bowed head behind the messenger. Revamma was excited about the whole situation and wanted to go with her, but the messenger refused to take anyone else with him. The upapradhana had specifically asked that only the girl be brought in.

Sivagami entered the office of Skandadasa with a quivering heart. When the door closed behind her, it startled her. She saw Skandadasa immersed in his work. There were many manuscripts scattered on the table.

'Sit down,' he said, without raising his head. She walked to the table and stood near the chair meant for visitors, but did not sit. She saw he was reading her father's book and her heartbeat increased.

He raised his head and indicated with his eyes that she should take her seat. Finally, she sat down, but stayed on the edge of the chair.

'Where did you get this book from?' he asked.

She wracked her brain to come up with a plausible explanation. Nothing came to mind.

'It is just a devotional book,' she said in a low voice.

'Oh, looking at you, it is quite difficult to imagine that you are devotional. Do not throw at me what I said to mislead your orphanage chief,' Skandadasa said, leaning forward.

'It is my father's,' she said, looking down at her toes.

'Bhoomipathi Devaraya's, eh? Traitor Devaraya's?'

'My father was no traitor,' Sivagami looked up, her nostrils flaring.

'I am not so sure, now,' Skandadasa said.

She did not reply. He was watching her reaction. She did not flinch.

'How did you get it, and from where?'

'I took it from my home.'

'Bhoomipathi Thimma's house?' Skandadasa asked, his eyebrows furrowed.

'No, I said *my* home,' Sivagami said.

'But that is closed. Sealed by royal decree.'

'I broke it open, went inside the mansion and retrieved it. An old servant told me about its existence before I was sent to the orphanage. That servant is dead, so don't bother going after her,' she said. Sivagami leaned back to sit firmly in her chair. Now that she had told the truth, she braced herself for whatever consquences would follow. She crossed her arms, threw back her head, and looked at Skandadasa confidently.

'You are a spirited girl.' A trace of a smile appeared on Skandadasa's stern lips, but it vanished in a flash. His voice became grave, 'Sivagami—that is your name, right? Yes, Sivagami, I want you to listen to what I say carefully.'

Sivagami nodded, but she was becoming increasingly tense on seeing the expression on Skandadasa's face.

'This book does not belong to your father. Your father stole it.'

Sivagami slammed both her fists on the table and stood up. Her chair fell backward on the floor behind her. 'How dare you say that!' she said.

'There is no need to get worked up, girl. I have sufficient proof, or rather most of it. This book belongs to the Royal Library of Mahishmathi. I have been diligently working on creating records of everything about this kingdom. There was a fire in one wing of the Royal Library twelve years back, a few days before Mahamakam. Many books were destroyed in the fire. And this book was supposed to have been one of them.'

He put a bundle of palm leaves before her. 'This book was part of the royal archives. Easy to identify as it was the only book in the Paisachi language. The rest are in Sanskrit or the tongues of the south, Arabic, Greek, Chinese and various other languages. It was marked as missing. The slave who guarded the library was arrested but was finally let off since he had become insane. You might have seen him. He goes by the name of Bhairava and sometimes rows a boat for a living. I was a junior official at that time and I remember it.'

Sivagami remained quiet.

'Now, the question arises—how did the book come into your father's hands? And how did Bhairava suddenly go insane? Was the fire an accident or was it a ruse to steal this book? Bhairava used to be a close friend of the maharaja's slave Malayappa. Was he driven insane in order to save his life? The slaves have medicines that can drive a man crazy, so I would not rule that out. Or is he just acting insane now? I have many questions.'

'Why are you telling me all this?' Sivagami asked. 'My father is dead, killed by the king. He has been branded a traitor by people like you. How does it matter if he was a thief too?' Sivagami's voice cracked.

'It won't make a difference to him, girl. But it would make a great difference to you. The difference between life and death,' Skandadasa said in a low voice.

'What do you mean? The bloodthirst of the Mahishmathi royals has not been appeased yet?' Sivagami asked derisively.

'Listen. Your father was considered a man gone astray. He disobeyed the king and did something detrimental to the interests of the nation. But the maharaja acted leniently with him, for he believed Devaraya was a good man.'

'He showed his lenience by making my father crow-feed,' Sivagami's eyes glowed with unshed tears.

'You are too young to understand, Sivagami.'

'Not as young as I was when I saw him killed.'

'Until now, Devaraya was considered a man who acted as he thought was right; he did not think about what was right for the country. A misguided man, perhaps. So the maharaja ordered only his execution, for the damage he did was immeasurable. But he spared his family and his servants,' Skandadasa said, staring at her.

'How kind of him. I am touched.'

'Can't you understand, girl?' Skandadasa's voice acquired a dangerous edge. 'With this book found in his home, everything changes. It proves he acted with an intention to destroy Mahishmathi. He was a traitor and a thief in every sense. No, don't interrupt me when I speak, and no theatrics again. He set afire, or got someone to set afire, the library with the intention of stealing this book. He then went on to act in a way that would have jeopardized the future of Mahishmathi. He conspired against the king. He was planning to act in such a way that his actions might have resulted in wiping Mahishmathi from the face of the earth.'

'Let the king hang him again if he can. Or let him hang me,' Sivagami snapped back. Her lips trembled with rage. 'You are concocting stories and blaming a dead man who cannot defend himself. Shame on you, sir.'

Skandadasa shook his head in dismay. 'How can I make you understand? I am almost sure of what I am saying.'

'Ah, *almost*—'

Skandadasa raised his hand to stop Sivagami from talking further. 'Yes, almost. If I had all the proof, you would have been arrested by now.'

'Arrested for what? For what my father may or may not have done twelve years back? I was five then, swami.'

'Rules are rules, girl. I am telling you this because I want to give you one chance to escape. Had I got all the proof, I would not have bothered to give you this advice. If your father's guilt is proved, the maharaja would be forced to act as per the ancient code. And don't act brave and foolish and say "let him hang me." Hang you they will, but all those servants who served Devaraya would also be hanged with you. Their homes would be razed to dust. Before that happens, run away from this country and never come back. You will not only be saving yourself, but many other lives. Without you, Maharaja will be forced to spare their lives. The servants cannot be punished before the family member. Run far away so that they can never find you.'

Sivagami was stunned. She did not know how to reply. 'There can be nothing more evil than the government of Mahishmathi,' she said finally, her eyes filling up.

'Rules are often cruel but necessary, daughter. As a person I can never support killing so many innocents for no fault of theirs. But no country would survive if it did not make an example of traitors. I wanted to give you this chance as I too find it unfair to go after you considering you were only five when your father decided to sell this country. That is why I called you—to warn you. Run away and everyone shall be spared.'

Sivagami threw back her head and said defiantly, 'No. You have nothing that can prove my father's guilt. You are lying.'

'You will regret this.'

'I will not run away. Do you want to know why? I will destroy this evil empire that has killed so many innocents like my father,' Sivagami said.

'You may leave,' Skandadasa said in a flat tone.

Sivagami walked towards the door without looking back. At the door, she paused. She had to ask this question.

'I thought you were a good man when I saw you last time, swami. How can you be so cruel?'

Skandadasa walked towards her and stood close to her. The slanting rays of the sun fell on his cragged face, making him look tired and old.

'You think I relish what I am doing? This is my duty, my offering, my prayer. In this job, I have to do many things I hate. But that is my way of repaying this country for making me who I am. I was not born privileged like your father. Neither destiny nor this country gave me anything on a silver plate. But I am still grateful for what I have. There are more instances than I can count when I have hated my job, yet I continue to work like a draught animal. I could have lived a miserable life, criticizing everything about the system. It has done worse things than what it did to your father. It has robbed the diginity of people like me. The illiterate, oppressed and broken people. The entire system has crushed us for many thousands of years. Yet, when the opportunity arrived, I grabbed it and decided to put my heart and soul into the betterment of all citizens. I vowed to myself that I would never discriminate, never be unfair and never do what others have done to us. It is easy to take revenge, to kill and to die. It is tough to be part of the system and change it, inch by inch. I have been fair to you in warning you about the impending danger. But if my country asks me to kill you, I shall do it without blinking an eye. I may not sleep for days after that, yet I will do it for my country.'

'You boast about your sense of duty and yet you ask me to run from mine, swami. Is it not the dharma of the daughter to avenge her father's death? Should I not fight back in whatever way I can?' Sivagami said.

'Fight all you want, but you will never win. You can change a system only by being part of that system, by being part of thc change. You are filled with fury and have lost the ability to think straight. You have only thoughts of revenge in your mind. By staying here, you are risking the chance life is offering you. You can fight or change things only if you are alive.'

'Good day to you, swami. If you find sufficient proof, you know where I live.' Sivagami bowed and walked away from Skandadasa.

Her mind was in turmoil. For a moment, she was assailed by doubts that he could be right. His words rang with sincerity, and it was difficult to ignore his warning. Yet she did not want to run away. *Never run away from a problem*—she remembered Thimma's words. As she walked back to the orphanage, she thought about how she could diffuse the threat. The inspiration struck suddenly. She would steal the book from Skandadasa.

TWENTY-SIX

Kattappa

Kattappa was sitting under a sprawling fig tree, watching the Vaithalika warriors practise in a clearing.

For a few days after reaching the Vaithalikas, he had been sure the slave-catchers would trace him with their hounds. He was relieved and saddened at the same time when no one came for him. He was relieved that his brother remained safe; and he was sad that even the absence of a priced slave like him was of no consequence to his masters. He did not want to think about their indifference—he did not matter; he had always known that—but it still hurt. He was yet to achieve his father's wisdom. He did not want to think about a lot of things. Like the disturbing sight Bhutaraya had shown him.

Even after almost three weeks, the shock of seeing the pile of children's skeletons had not worn off. Kattappa wondered what sort of men would treat children in that way. His sense of righteousness had been shaken. His job did not seem so sacred anymore. His ire against the Vaithalikas and their methods of terror felt hollow. What terrible secrets did each of the nobles of his kingdom hold?

He was surprised at how good a warrior Shivappa was turning out to be. Watching his younger brother, his heart filled with love and pride. It was difficult to believe the young man fighting like an angry cock was the toddler he had once carried in his arms to see the antics of a street jester or mahouts bathing elephants in the temple ponds. He had been just a boy a little while back, following him everywhere. Does a younger brother ever grow up? To him, he would always remain a child.

The forest was silent except for the clang of swords and the twang of bows. Warriors yelled, slapped each other's backs, taunted those who missed their targets and clapped for perfect shots. The sun rose steadily over their heads. Kattappa's hands itched to hold a sword, to swing it above his head, crouch like a tiger with his chest feeling the dew of the grass, to leap up, twist and spin in the air, and land on his feet while swinging his weapon in a graceful arc. He wanted to cross his spear with a warrior, to feel a throbbing horse between his legs, the caress of a breeze on his balding head.

From afar, faint tunes and the hum of crowds could be heard across the river. It would be Mahamakam in another nine days, and he missed his Mahishmathi. Yet, he could no longer think about his beloved city without seeing the images of mutilated little bodies falling from the top of Gauriparvat, without feeling the smell of rotting corpses, without hearing the sounds of foxes and crows feeding on decaying little hands and half-gnawed faces.

The more he thought about the atrocities that the Vaithalikas claimed were being perpetuated by the Mahishmathi empire, the more helpless he felt. He had ceased to think of Bijjala as the epitome of evil. If what the Vaithalikas said was true, Bijjala was just a misguided fool. And if his father, being the bodyguard of the maharaja, knew what was going on…what did that make him?

Kattappa fervently wished it wasn't true, but somewhere inside him, he knew that it was impossible that his father could have remained ignorant. But that meant his father was serving the regime even after knowing what it was doing, which in turn meant that Shivappa was right about him. But his father could do no wrong. His maharaja could do no wrong. Maybe it was the doing of some evil and corrupt officials…but that did not absolve the king. Rather, it made the king an inept ruler. Kattappa bit his tongue. How could he think like that about the king? It was treason.

The word 'treason' sent a shockwave down his spine. His brother was planning something big for Mahamakam. It was not that he had forgotten it, but the fact that the day was approaching soon, and he was still with the Vaithalikas, made him realize that even his commitment to the oath of his forefathers was wavering and his own loyalty was suspect to his mind. Again, Kattappa wondered why no slave-catchers had come in search of him.

He had to escape today, if at all. He had to persuade his brother to give up his foolish dream. They needed to talk to their father and clarify things. Maybe everything would be cleared if they could just do that. His father would be overjoyed to see Shivappa. And they could reach Mahishmathi in time to warn his father about the impending coup.

Kattappa had been wanting to talk to Shivappa, somehow dissuade him from this suicidal mission. But Bhutaraya kept his guards near Kattappa constantly. They stuck to him like leeches, following him even when he went to answer nature's call.

He watched as Shivappa took on four warriors with his bare hands. His brother flipped the first attacker over his shoulder while cracking the next one's chin with his leg. The next two attacked together, yelling and swinging their swords from either side. Kattappa's heart was in his throat when he saw the flash of metal, but his brother jumped, twisted and rolled, evading the cuts, thrusts and blows from the swords. In a whirlwind attack, all four fell on Shivappa together. Kattappa watched, gripping the edge of his cot until the four warriors went spinning to either side. He cheered with the other Vaithalikas while Shivappa thumped his chest and gave a bloodcurdling yell. *Now*, Kattappa thought.

In a swift moment, he drew the sword from the scabbard of the guard to his left, turned on his heels, and before the first guard knew what had happened, Kattappa had taken the second sword from the guard to his right. He ran towards Shivappa, surprising everyone. He threw a sword at Shivappa who caught it in mid-air.

'Show your skills to your brother,' he yelled.

Kattappa saw Bhutaraya stopping the guards who were rushing towards them. Shivappa smiled and said, 'Anna, you are still weak.'

'The king's guards are not a bunch of milk babies like this bunch,' Kattappa said, gesturing with a sweeping hand at the Vaithalika warriors. He was greeted with a roar of disapproval.

'They will make mincemeat of you before you can even sneeze,' Kattappa said, eyeing Bhutaraya.

'Shivappa, get back,' Bhutaraya said, scowling and drawing his sword. Kattappa's heart sank. He had wanted his brother to bite the bait, not Bhutaraya. That was the only way he could get a chance to talk to him.

'Swami, he is my brother. Let me handle him,' Kattappa heard his brother say. Bhutaraya grunted and put back his sword in its sheath.

The Vaithalikas stood in a circle as the two brothers bowed to each other and touched the ground with their right hands in respect. They stepped back and then rushed forward, their swords clanging. They stood pressing their chests against the blunt edge of their swords.

'Enough of this foolishness. Let us go home,' Kattappa hissed.

'Coming there soon,' his brother said and drew his sword back, making sparks fly. 'This Mahamakam, to kill your king.'

Kattappa warded off his brother's strike, twisted and pressed his brother's sword to the ground. They were shoulder to shoulder. 'Don't get yourself killed.'

His brother shoved him, danced back and leaped high, evading Kattappa's thrust and, arcing his sword, landed on the ground. 'Stay here and save yourself. Anna, you are too weak to even walk.'

Kattappa answered with a flurry of thrusts, cuts and strikes. Each one was parried with dexterity and answered back with ferocity. Kattappa felt alive after many days. He was careful not to hurt his brother, yet Shivappa showed no such consideration. *It does not matter,* Kattappa thought. *He is still my younger brother, a little boy.* But he made sure to block his brother's attacks. Every thrust was evaded or returned. Step for step, strike for strike, the two slaves fought as Vaithalikas cheered from all sides. The brothers were soon covered in sweat and out of breath from talking. Grunts were answered with grunts, yells with screams, curses with swear words. A few cuts here and there would not hurt, Kattappa thought, and it was needed to provoke his brother. He feigned weakness and then struck like a cobra when his brother attacked. He drew first blood, which made Shivappa blind with rage. *He is still my competitive little brother*, Kattappa smiled, as the next strike sent sparks flying near his face.

'You are still a boy, Shivappa,' he said and was answered with a kick to his ribs. Kattappa fell down and rolled away just when his brother's sword came down close to his neck. For a moment, Kattappa felt angry. He should not have done that. That was against the rules of combat.

'You are playing unfairly,' Kattappa said as he rolled again.

'When has life been fair to us? Time to pay back in the same way,' Shivappa retorted.

'That is not what our father taught us,' Kattappa said, as he landed back on his feet and nicked Shivappa's shoulder.

'He taught us many wrong things,' Shivappa said as his movements became more aggressive. He attacked Kattappa with a flurry of swings and thrusts. Kattappa backtracked and the circle of onlookers split to give the warriors room. They continued to spar with each other. A few more feet and they would clear the open space. Kattappa eyed the Vaithalikas. They were engrossed in the fight. His brother no longer seemed to be fighting for practice. A chill ran down his back as Kattappa realized that his brother was fighting to kill. Bhutaraya had converted him into a weapon. If he had to save his brother, he had to take him back. He let his brother's sword nick him in his shoulder. As expected, the edge pierced his right shoulder; he threw down his sword and held his wound with his left hand. He could feel the warmth of the blood spurting through his fingers. He feigned fainting.

His brother dropped his sword and rushed to him to catch Kattappa before he could fall down. In a swift move, Kattappa grabbed Shivappa, turned him, and thrust his index finger in his brother's neck. Shivappa collapsed, paralyzed.

Looking at his brother's bulging eyes, Kattappa said, 'There are a few right things our father taught us. Marmavidya, the art of paralyzing people, is one of them.' His brother tried to say something, but only gurgling sounds emerged from his mouth. Kattappa had to act fast—his brother would be paralyzed only for a little while. The Vaithalikas were running towards them now. Kattappa lifted his brother onto his shoulders and crashed into the thick undergrowth. He could hear the Vaithalikas behind them. An arrow swished past his ears. He continued to run, weaving his way through the bushes, zigzagging through the jungle. He could hear the trees coming alive. His brother lay limp on his shoulders. His leg had started paining, yet there was no time to stop. A spear splintered a tree ahead of him. He looked back, running, and crashed into a tree ahead and fell down. His brother rolled down on the ground. He scampered to his feet and was about to pick his brother up again, when a warrior crashed through the bushes. Kattappa caught him by his neck, heaved him up and slammed him to the ground. He picked up his brother, turned left and ran blindly into a thorny bush. The earth disappeared below his legs.

He fell, crashing through the trees, bouncing on branches, cracking them, remaining suspended for the fraction of an eye blink, and then continuing to freefall again. His shoulders hit the ground first and pain shot through his ribs. Everything went blank, the sky was down, the earth was up and there was grass in his mouth as he rolled down the hill. He slammed into a rock and blacked out. When he opened his eyes, he saw that he was at the edge of a cliff. Down below, the river roared its way to the distant sea. *Shivappa, where was Shivappa?* He panicked. For a moment, he thought his brother had fallen down and the river had swallowed him. The hill sloped dangerously towards the cliff edge, dropping a good three hundred feet down to the raging river. He turned on his back, screaming with pain and fear and an impending sense of doom. He screamed his brother's name to the river. All he heard was the echo of his own desperate voice. The river laughed back, taunting him. He slammed his fist down beside him again and again. He was about to slither down the slippery slope to check for signs of his brother, when he thought he heard a noise from above.

There, Kattappa told himself, that could be him! There he was. Or was it just the sound of a rock falling? 'Oh god, let it be my brother, oh gods, oh gods, oh gods,' he chanted as he ran up the slope. He fell down on his knees and slipped back, his fingers desperately grappling for a hold in the ground. The earth gave up the grass without any fight, and he slipped further down. In the slanting rays of the sun, he could barely make out a coiled figure that was somehow being prevented from falling by a protruding rock. He managed to get up again and run up the hill, holding on to shrubs and clefts in the meadow. Loose stones raced down the slope like children, bouncing through the grass, and vanishing into the abyss to the roaring river below. Kattappa reached the rock and pulled himself up. His brother was lying on his back, his eyes staring at the swirling clouds above.

'Shivappa, Shivappa,' Kattappa cried, patting his brother's cheeks. He shook his brother's shoulders and cried, 'Ayyo,

ayyo, Shivappa, wake up, wake up, brother. What have I done to you? NO, NO.'

Kattappa stared at his brother's body and sat back in shock. Then realization sank in and he hit his head with both his hands, 'Oh, I have killed you, ayyo, I have killed you, brother. Oh gods, punish me. I am worthless. I killed my brother.'

An eagle screeched above and circled in the sky. Wind raced through the meadow, making the army of grass bend in submission. Was it the wind that made Shivappa's eyelashes move, or was the setting sun playing tricks with his grief? The slave stopped crying and moved towards his brother's limp body. Kattappa kneeled down and shook his brother again. He dropped his head onto his brother's chest, hoping against hope.

Kattappa felt a powerful hand grip his neck and press his face down. Shocked, he tried to wriggle away, and saw that he was staring into Shivappa's eyes.

The pain started as a pinprick in his back and then exploded in a trice, spreading through every nerve of his body. Kattappa understood what it was. He had been stabbed. Stabbed by his brother.

His brother pulled himself out from under Kattappa and stood over him. His head covered the blood-red sun. Blood trickled down Kattappa's chest, spreading warmth through his body. The smell of his blood made him giddy. The earth swam around him. His brother had tricked him, stabbed him in his back. *Why, my little brother, why,* he wanted to ask.

'Our father taught us more than marmavidya, Anna,' his brother's voice sounded as if it were coming from afar. 'He taught us to consider our duty above everything, even above blood relationships.'

Kattappa wanted to say something, but he was swimming in and out of consciousness.

'My duty is to my race. My mission is to free the slaves. For that I will do anything.'

Kattappa tried to focus on the words, but his brother's voice seemed to be merging with the roar of the river far below, and with the rustle of grass near him. He was slipping down. He was rolling now, and sometimes he smelled the wetness of grass, sometimes the expanse of the sky. Kattappa stopped at the edge of the cliff. A rainbow had arced across the river. *What a beautiful dusk to die in,* Kattappa thought, as his brother stood looming above him.

'I will go to any extent to achieve my dream,' Shivappa said. His brother's voice. Kattappa was so proud of his little brother. He wanted to hold Shivappa's hands once more.

'No one can stop me because my cause is bigger than any individual.' Shivappa's words were so inspiring. *My brother is a hero*, Kattappa thought. They were little now, running through the meadow, laughing, yelling. They were chasing hares through the grasslands. They were playing with wooden swords as their father watched.

Images, memories, useless, precious. The river laughed from below. The rainbow throbbed.

He felt his brother's arms lifting him up. He stared into his brother's eyes with all the love he could muster. His brother was crying. *Shivappa, son, don't cry,* he wanted to say. He wanted to lift his hands to wipe those tears. But he was too tired.

'Anna, forgive me.'

Kattappa heard his brother's words, and before he could reply, he was flying through the air. His brother, standing at the edge of the cliff, watching him falling down, became smaller and smaller. The rainbow parted as the slave fell, as if afraid of touching his black body. The river had no qualms about the colour of his skin. She would embrace anyone who came to her and keep them in her heart. She waited for him below, laughing with her countless hands beating over as many rocks. The river with a heart of stone.

TWENTY-SEVEN

Parameswara

It was a damp day when Thimma entered the room of Mahapradhana Parameswara. The mahapradhana was busy with his assistant Roopaka, and he gestured for Thimma to take a seat. Thimma sat on the edge of his chair, nervously clasping the table in front of him. Behind Parameswara's seat, there was a huge window through which Thimma could see rain falling like thread from the roof. The rains depressed Thimma. *Rain is the sorrow of gods,* he thought as he watched the palace gardens dissolve in a haze of mist and drizzle. As a child, rain meant endless amusement; in youth it meant romance; in middle-age, nothing mattered except the struggle of everyday living; but it was in the last leg of one's life when the rains assumed their sinister avatar.

Thimma knew this day would come; he had dreaded it every moment since the death of his friend Devaraya. Now he could understand Devaraya better. He had come to beg for one last time so he would not be forced to do something that revolted against everything he stood for.

The room was bare except for piles of books and an easy chair in a corner where the old man took his afternoon siesta. Thimma's eyes locked onto something by the side of the chair. He stood up and walked to it. It was a toy elephant, crudely made, as if by the hands of a child. It looked so incongruous in the room of the prime minister of Mahishmathi. Thimma picked it up. The marks of the little fingers that had shaped the mud were still on it. It had such an endearing quality of domesticity, of the innocence of childhood, that he was reminded for a moment of Akhila. He felt a lump in his throat.

'My grandson's, Thimma,' Parameswara said. Roopaka was walking away with a bundle of palm leaves that bore the mahapradhana's official seal. Parameswara stood up, fumbled for his walking stick, and headed to Thimma's side. A smile lit up the old man's face as he took the elephant from Thimma's hands. For the next few minutes, Parameswara talked about his grandchildren. Thimma stood, listening to tales that made his heart heavier. Outside, the rain continued to fall unceasingly. When Parameswara finally enquired after the reason of his visit, Thimma hesitated. But he knew he had to get this over with soon, or he would lose courage.

Thimma said softly, 'Swami, I am resigning. I cannot do this.'

Parameswara stared at Thimma and shook his head, 'If only it were so easy…'

'You are so proud of your grandchildren, swami. Why can't you understand the pain of others? There are many grandfathers who have lost their grandchildren, there are mothers who have gone insane after losing their children.'

'All for the sake of our country, Thimma. If you do not do it, someone else will. Only you can do it with compassion,' Parameswara said sympathetically.

'No, I cannot.'

'The Gaurikanta stones will reach Guha Bhoomi anytime now, Thimma. There are only a few days till Mahamakam. It is your duty to bring them across the river and get them to the workshop safely. The security and safety of Mahishmathi and its people depend on it. Our civilization owes its prosperity and progress to Gaurikanta. You have to do it for the country, friend.' Parameswara tried to place his hand on Thimma's shoulder but Thimma shrugged it away.

'Why can't this be the last time? Why can't we let the boys go? They have toiled enough for us. Why do we have to kill them all and then get a new set of boys every twelve years?'

'It is not killing, Thimma. It is a sacrifice for Amma Gauri, for Mahishmathi, for—'

'Swami, do you believe in what you are saying?' Thimma's eyes flashed with anger.

'For the greater good, a few have to be sacrificed. Aren't the soldiers sacrificing their lives for the country, Thimma?'

'Swami, forgive my impertinence,' Thimma said and took the toy elephant from Parameswara. 'Would you have the little hands that fashioned this to dig Gaurikanta in the mines?'

Parameswara trembled with rage. For a moment, his voice choked. He grabbed the elephant back from Thimma and pointed to the door with his walking stick. 'Out, out of this room, this moment!' he shouted.

'Sacrifices are meant to be made by others, swami? Like the children of the poor, of the helpless, of the destitute, of the lower castes—'

'I won't have this conversation. I will have you arrested,' Parameswara's lips trembled with rage.

'And hang me like you did Devaraya? For standing up against injustice? I will happily hang for it, but I will not commit this sin.' Thimma glared at the old man.

'You think it is so easy? Eh? You think you can become the hero and sacrifice yourself? Last time, when the king hanged Devaraya, it was me who saved his girl by pleading her case with him. The rule is that the entire family hangs for treason, Thimma. Remember that. If the maharaja decides to hang you and your family, I will not lift my little finger to save you.'

Thimma's shoulders slouched in defeat. He bowed stiffly to Parameswara and left without a word.

Parameswara stood in the cavernous room, alone and crushed. His fingers carressed the toy elephant. Outside, the rain had gathered strength and an unhinged window banged against its frame. He pulled himself to his chair and collapsed into it. Thimma's words weighed heavily on Parameswara. The questions Thimma had asked were his own questions. He knew the answers. They were buried deep inside his heart. He had fooled himself by forcing his mind to believe that he was doing this for his country. So far he had suppressed the voice of his conscience with the idea that he was only doing his duty.

But Thimma's question to him about why he was not letting his grandson work in Gauriparvat had forced open the door to his conscience with the strength of a crowbar. From any other man, he would have taken it as an insult. He would have ensured that such a man was ruined forever. But coming from a scrupulously honest man like Thimma, it was as if a mirror had been held to his face, and a stranger had stared back at him. He did not like what he saw. Fifty years ago, when he had joined the service of Mahishmathi, this was not what he had aimed for. He'd had lofty goals; he was proud of his compassion and intelligence. Over time, though, he had fought political battles, he had done the right things as well as many wrong things to advance his career, and finally he had managed to fulfil his ambition: to become the mahapradhana of Mahishmathi. That was the tragedy of his life. Looking back, he wished that, at least once, he'd had the courage of Devaraya. He wished at least once he'd had the courage of conviction to stand up against the maharaja, like Thimma had done against him, and say he would not do something so heartless.

He was a coward, Parameswara told himself. It was a sad realization, after a career spanning half a century. His wife was right. It was time to leave everything and retire. He looked at the toy elephant with fondness. He would spend more time playing with his grandchildren, he thought as he placed it back down near the chair. Thimma's words about the grandchildren of the poor came rushing from the depths of his heart, and with an iron will he pushed them down. There would not be any peace if he kept thinking like that. *I am not only a coward, but a selfish man too,* he thought sadly. He extended his arm to ring the bell to call Roopaka. His sleeve caught the toy elephant and it fell down, shattering into shapeless pieces.

When Roopaka came, he was staring down at the broken pieces. The room was unlit and cold.

'Swami?' Roopaka asked softly.

Parameswara willed himself to turn towards his assistant. He was thankful that there was no light. He would have been embarrassed had Roopaka seen the tears in his eyes.

'Arrange for an appointment with the maharaja now. Also, call for Skandadasa.'

'Yes, swami.' Roopaka turned to go. He paused at the door and asked, 'And if they ask, what should I say…'

In answer Parameswara walked out of the room. He passed Roopaka, walked down the steps and stood in the rain. He waited for the rain to wash away the weight in his heart. Roopaka stood patiently at the edge of the veranda. Far away, the peak of Gauriparvat was hidden in the clouds.

No rain or even all the waters of the Ganga could wash away my sins. There is the blood of so many innocents on my hands. Amma Gauri, do not judge me harshly, for I was a fool, Parameswara thought.

'Swami?' Roopaka called again, as if to remind him of the question.

Parameswara turned around slowly, a bitter smile on his face, and said to his assistant, 'To the maharaja, don't say anything; I shall tell him myself. To Skandadasa, tell him that Parameswara has resigned. And do not forget to congratulate him, for he is going to be the next mahapradhana of Mahishmathi.'

TWENTY-EIGHT

Thimma

Thimma stood by the river as its waters gushed past him, frothing like black, boiling ink. Rain fell like pellets. Thimma was in no state to go home. He had promised his wife that he would not do his duty on Mahamakam. He thought of jumping into the river and ending it all. But that was a coward's way out. He would not do it. He would find a solution, but he had no idea how.

It was not the transport of the stones he dreaded—it was the mass murder of boys. They would be younger than Akhila… *Mahishmathi is living a lie. The empire will crumble, for it is built upon the tears and blood of innocents,* he told himself. Then he felt like laughing. For three centuries the empire had flourished, going from strength to strength, conquering most of the kingdoms from the Snow Mountains to the three seas. The blessing of Amma Gauri, the bards sang.

He thought back to how it had all started. The mining of stones had gone on unabated for centuries. But there was a limit to the benevolence of Gauriparvat. As the years progressed, mines had to be dug deeper into the bowels of the mountain. The mountain became unstable, often caving in. Many miners perished. And soon there was a dearth of slaves to work in the mines. They became expensive to trade, and most of them died very quickly. It was almost a century back that an ingenious and cruel solution was found. It was discovered that smaller tunnels held better than bigger ones. And to crawl through the narrower tunnels, they could use little boys. Initially, on being told that the tunnels were safe, parents sent their sons voluntarily. But while the smaller tunnels were less risky than the larger ones, they were by no means totally safe. As the number of boys dying in the mines increased, people stopped sending their children. No amount of force or money could induce them to send their sons to their deaths. When the maharaja tried to take the boys forcefully, a bloody rebellion broke out. The maharaja was finally forced to declare that he was closing down the mines to end the rebellion.

It was then that the slave trade in boys had started. Merchants and pirates hunted down boys in remote villages in vassal kingdoms. The state acted as if it was trying to control the menace, but often turned a blind eye to it. The responsibility was divided between many officials. Dwarves were recruited to supervise the boys and ensure that they did not escape. Life in the mines made the dwarves extremely cruel, but the officials felt that this was required to get the maximum output from the boys.

The mines began to run deeper and deeper as the years progressed. The Vaithalikas continued to wage their war to regain their holy mountain, but a powerful state like Mahishmathi was never going to let go of its holy cow.

Instead, the propaganda machinery of the state borrowed from the myths of the Vaithalikas.

The bards sang that, once in twelve years, Amma Gauri spat out the stones from her belly. There was some truth to this legend. Vaithalikas used to collect such stones many centuries ago and used them as idols to worship. It was conveniently forgotten that this discharging of stones from the volcanic mountain used to happen perhaps once in many centuries. The priests said that, since Mahishmathi was a blessed country, Amma Gauri gave her blessing every twelve years. It was a lie that was convenient for the citizens of Mahishmathi city to believe. Their children were rarely kidnapped to work in the mines—such atrocities only happened in remote villages where the destitute and lower castes lived.

And such people did not matter to the city folks. They lived in their own bubble, pumped up with patriotism and pride in their assumed cultural superiority. For them, Mahishmathi represented the best of humanity, the pinnacle of glory and human achievement. They celebrated their blessings once in twelve years in a grand fashion when all of Mahishmathi would assemble in the palace grounds. The magical light would glow three times from the top of Gauriparvat to mark the beginning of celebrations. The commonfolk believed the light was lit by gods. Those who mattered, like Thimma, knew it was lit by the dwarves of the mines. It was so easy to sell anything to the common people, if one could add an element of magic and some religion into it.

The more Thimma thought about it, the angrier he became. If only they had given Devaraya enough time.

'Swami, are you planning to jump?'

Thimma was startled by the voice. His hand went to the hilt of his sword.

'Don't kill me, swami. It is me, Brihannala.'

The last thing Thimma wanted was to talk to the eunuch. He nodded curtly and started walking to his chariot.

'Swami, the mahapradhana did not relent, isn't it?'

Thimma froze. 'How do you know?'

Brihannala laughed, 'Knowing is my job, swami.'

Thimma did not want to continue the conversation—he had a gnawing suspicion that the eunuch was leading him into a trap. He climbed into his chariot but Brihannala held the reins of the horse and said, 'I can help, swami. In fact we can help each other.'

'What are you talking about?' Thimma asked.

Brihannala leaned forward and whispered something in his ears. Thimma was shocked.

'No, I won't do that,' he said emphatically.

'Your wish,' Brihannala shruggedand started to walk away.

'Stop,' Thimma said. He had no other choice. He would have to take the chance. Brihannala climbed into the chariot.

'Let us talk as we travel, swami. There are ears everywhere.'

The chariot shot forward and Brihannala and Thimma huddled together to plan.

TWENTY-NINE

Ally

Ally sat roasting a rat on a crude tripod made of twigs. The rat was hung from its tail with a string and it turned slowly as the fire below cooked it. Ally closed her eyes and savoured the delicious aroma of the meat. She wished she had some spices to garnish it; some salt would have helped as well. But this in itself was a luxury. They had been eating either the raw fish or fowl that Jeemotha caught. There had been no way they could light a fire. They had no flint and their attempt to light one by striking stones had yielded no results. The grass was damp and the island they had somehow crawled onto was squishy with mud that oozed a foul smell.

Then the rains had come, and with it, thunder. Jeemotha had been making love to her at the time. When the thunder struck and a tree burst into flame, she had pushed him away and run towards it. He had struck her for that, but later they had made love near a blazing fire.

She hated him then and she hated him now, but Achi Nagamma had taught her well. Achi used to say that, for a woman, sex was her greatest strength. Morality was nothing but a chain invented by man to enslave women. So, for Ally, sex was a tool by which she could control Jeemotha. He might be a fearsome pirate, but he was a man too. Ally knew she was beautiful and she used her beauty and sensuality the way she used her sword. She needed information, and if making love to Jeemotha would give her that, she would do it without any guilt or qualms. The pirate had grown friendly, but so far, he had been frustratingly clever. He would taunt her with bits of information, use her, and then hold crucial information back. There wasn't much she could do about it though. She wanted to get out of the island, but the swamps were treacherous and the river merged with backwaters and hills in the distant horizon. No civilization was in sight as far as their eyes could see.

'It smells awful,' Jeemotha said, crinkling up his nose. He was sitting on a rock a few feet away, fishing.

'For you, perhaps. For me it brings back lots of childhood memories. When famine struck our village, as it would happen often, rats were the only thing we had to eat. I used to hunt them in the sewers or the dry fields with my brother, and for many days, my family survived on my hunting skills,' Ally said, turning the rat to cook its other side.

'No wonder you stink so much,' Jeemotha said and howled with laughter. She did not reply. Memories of her long-lost brother had overwhelmed her. They had been hunting rats in an abandoned palace some distance from their village. Her brother was harassing her with questions and she had snapped at him to keep quiet. He was a curious boy, but in her experience, rats tended to hide unless they were as silent as death. When she had spiked a big fat one, she had turned to show it to him and found he was gone. Vanished. She had no clue what had happened to him. There was no blood, nothing to indicate that he had been caught by a leopard or a tiger.

'What are you thinking?' Jeemotha asked.

'About my brother,' she said and told him the story.

'Hard luck,' he said, but she observed that he was not looking at her.

'Did you do it?' she asked, trying to catch him off guard.

He laughed. 'Wench, I have done worse things, but I am not the only thug around. Your king's men pay anyone who brings them a boy. If you ask me why the king's men need boys, I do not know. Maybe they are as fond of boys as I am of pretty girls like you. Who knows? Who cares a rat's arse for that?'

She hated him from the bottom of her heart. He was sickeningly handsome and gloriously evil. Maybe she should think of killing him. She was about to retort when she observed a huge tree trunk floating by on the river. Perhaps it had fallen in yesterday's rain. But what caught her eye was the figure on it.

'It's a man,' she screamed, pointing at it.

'Yes, looks like it,' Jeemotha said, and turned back to his fishing.

'What the hell are you doing? Go and save him, jump!' she screamed. He looked at her in amusement. The log was flowing by rapidly with the current. Ally ran to the river and dove into it. She gasped for breath as the current pulled her down. The water was muddy and swift and the river frothed and foamed around her. When she surfaced, she started swimming towards the log and the current carried her to it swiftly.

A dark, well-built man was lying on his stomach, unconscious. She tried to get hold of one of the branches of the tree, but she was nervous that it would roll and topple the man over. *Was he dead,* she wondered as she struggled to keep up with the fast-flowing tree. There was a festering wound on his back and flies were buzzing around it. Dead—she felt a wave of disappointment wash over her. It was a corpse she was chasing. She was about to leave and swim back when the man's fingers twitched.

'He is alive!' she cried. She saw Jeemotha diving into the water. He swam with long strokes, confident and easy.

'Hurry, hurry, rapids ahead,' she cried. She could hear the river bashing against rocks a few hundred meters ahead. The water was turning choppy and white crests started appearing over the waves.

Jeemotha caught hold of the log and shook it.

'What the hell are you doing?' she cried in panic. The man was sure to fall.

'Shut up, wench,' he cried over the roar of the river.

The tree rolled, and when it rolled back, the man had vanished.

'Bastard, you killed him—oh god, oh god, oh god,' she cried. There was no trace of the man.

'Jeemotha—' she called, turning to look around. The pirate was not to be seen either. Only the tree was entering the rapids, rolling and pitching in the swirling currents. She struggled to keep herself afloat and swim against it, but inch by inch she was being dragged back.

'Jeemotha…' she cried, scared that she had lost the pirate along with the man she had hoped to save. Then she saw him. He was struggling to drag the man to the shore. She swam towards them. She saw Jeemotha losing his grip on the man and the man vanishing into the raging water. She took a deep breath and went down. Under the surface, the water was calm, and she saw a dark figure slowly settling to the bottom. She was running out of breath, but she knew the man would be lost if she gave up on him now. She swam to him and tried to lift him. She was unable to budge him an inch. Her lungs were screaming for air. She was tempted to leave him and go up for a breath, when she saw his foot was caught in the crack of a rock. Using the last drop of her determination, she swam down. She freed his foot and, holding the man by his armpits, she kicked herself up. Jeemotha was climbing up onto the shore when she came up, gasping for air.

She sucked in air, but the current was carrying her again towards the rapids. The man was slipping from her hands.

'You look like a water nymph, temptress,' Jeemotha said, watching her and biting a blade of grass.

'Shut your foul mouth and come and help me. This man is as heavy as an elephant,' she cried.

Jeemotha laughed and said, 'I am no fool to get into the river again. Let me see how much strength you have in your lovely legs.'

Enraged by his words, Ally's determination doubled and she managed to fight the current and swim to the shore. She climbed up, panting and puffing as she struggled to drag the man up onto the riverbank.

'Give me a hand instead of gawking at my body, bastard,' Ally said to Jeemotha, slightly out of breath, and he helped her pull the man up. She started pressing his stomach.

'The bastard is dead. Throw him back. At least the fish will have a feast,' Jeemotha said.

Ally ignored the pirate and pressed her lips to the man's mouth, blowing air into his lungs.

'Whoa, you are an expert at this. Maybe we should try this tonight,' Jeemotha said, kneeling beside her.

'You drown, and maybe I will do this for you. Or maybe I won't,' Ally said between breaths as she continued pressing the man's stomach.

Jeemotha laughed and muttered, 'Bitch.'

'He is breathing, he is breathing,' Ally cried suddenly, as the man coughed and spat water and slowly opened his eyes.

'Who are you?' Ally asked him.

'The maharaja of Mahishmathi, he is. Woman, can't you understand he is a bloody slave?' Jeemotha said, shaking water from his long hair. The rescued man was whispering something. Ally ignored the pirate and put her ears near his lips.

'Kattappa is his name, he says,' Ally said.

'Who cares about a fucking slave's name? If he lives, he will fetch a good price. That is all that matters,' Jeemotha said, laughing at the look of hatred on Ally's face.

THIRTY

Skandadasa

Even after a week, Skandadasa could not believe that he had achieved his dream. The promise he had made to himself many years ago had been fulfilled. He ran his fingers over the contours of the new chair. It was a gift from his mentor Parameswara. It was an honour and Skandadasa was moved by Parameswara's gesture. The chair was a wooden one, with a high back but the seat was small for him. It was uncomfortable to sit in. That was the whole purpose of it, Paramesawara had told him with a wicked smile when he had made Skandadasa sit on it for the first time. The new mahapradhana chuckled at the thought. He remembered his mentor fondly. By the time, men reached the post of mahapradhana, they were normaly shrunken with old age and were not bulky like a bear, Parameswara had joked. That comment from anyone else would have made Skandadasa seeth with anger, but when Parameswara said it, he had laughed with him. He was the youngest mahapradhana in the history of Mahishmathi. His hard work had paid off.

He owed everything to Parameswara. And to the maharaja, who had overruled objections from the noblemen when he had announced that Skandadasa was to be the mahapradhana. They had brought up his alleged lack of morality,citing the episode near Kalika's inn to stress their point. Maharaja Somadeva had laughed it off, and asked the priest Rudra Bhatta whether the penance Skandadasa had undergone was not sufficient to wash away his sin. Of course the priest could not say the pilgrimage had been worthless. Reluctantly, the nobles had to agree to his appointment.

Skandadasa was aware that the noblemen were still fuming within. He had no lineage to speak of, no formal education, and he belonged to the lowest of low castes, yet the maharaja had chosen him over others. The responsibility was huge and he was sure to get only reluctant cooperation from his subordinates. Parameswara had warned him about the open hostility that his elevation would bring about in many powerful men. He would try to win them over. He would do only what was right and just. He would work harder than anyone. He was determined to prove that he could be the best mahapradhana ever.

But before any other task, he had to pay back someone a small favour. He called for Roopaka. The assistant came in with a morose face and gave him a reluctant bow. He knew Roopaka resented working under him. He passed on a written order to Roopaka and watched his face closely.

'Swami!' Roopaka exclaimed.

Skandadasa had expected this reaction. 'If you think I am closing down Devadasi Street because they insulted me, you are mistaken. Such places of sin destroy the moral fabric of the country and instil criminal tendencies in the minds of our youth. It is our duty—'

'Swami, Kalika is powerful and influential—'

'Not anymore. She will get a small pension and she should learn to live with it.'

'The noblemen will be up in arms,' Roopaka cried.

'The same noblemen who were accusing me of moral turpitude a few months ago? I don't think so. They are all noblemen, as you said. Why should they care about a woman who sells her body for a living?' Skandadasa said with a smile.

'There will be riots in Devadasi Street.'

'Ask Dandanayaka Pratapa to send sufficient dandakaras to ensure that there is no trouble.'

'Many women will be out of a job, swami,' Roopaka said.

'They can work as sweepers or maids if they are illiterate. Or, we can find suitable positions for them.'

'Swami, the Devadasi system has thousands of years' tradition behind it. You cannot tamper with it.'

'I did not call you to give me a lecture on ancient systems. Please execute my orders. Any discussion will be done at the durbar in front of the maharaja,' Skandadasa said in a tone that brooked no argument.

Roopaka bowed stiffly and turned on his heels.

'I did not give you permission to leave, Roopaka,' Skandadasa said.

'But—'

'Send those orders across to Pratapa, but you are coming with me.' Skandadasa stood up from his chair.

'Where?'

'To the workshop where Gauridhooli is made. Lead me there. As mahapradhana, I want to see how the work is done.' Skandadasa did not give Roopaka any time to argue. He started walking out and his assistant had no choice other than to follow him.

Skandadasa had decided that he would record everything for posterity. So much esoteric knowledge had been lost because it was passed on orally. He did not want the same thing to happen to the technology of extracting Gauridhooli. He had almost completed his project of mapping the fort. If possible, he wanted to learn the technique of extraction. He was no ironsmith, but he believed there was nothing he could not learn, provided he worked hard. He had taught himself so many things and reached the top; he could learn the technology of Gauridhooli too.

They reached the underground labyrinth in the afternoon. Roopaka led Skandadasa through a complicated maze of underground tunnels under the palace. As they neared the workshop, the air grew thin and hot. Skandadasa could smell acrid fumes. The cobwebs on the roof were black with soot. He wondered how the slave ironsmiths lived in this cramped space for the better part of their lives. Why were they not tempted to escape or rebel? He had read the reports about a worker escaping from the cellar with a few stones. He wondered how he might have escaped. And who had helped him? Who communicated with him? There were only a few people in the upper echleons of the government who knew about the existence of the workshop. And there were fewer people still who knew where it was. The only people who had access to this workshop were the mahapradhana, Senapathi Hiranya and the king. So how did the man know how to escape?

The huge stone door creaked open and the din of hammers meeting metal assaulted his ears. The heat was unbearable inside the workshop. Fires blazed from the furnace and a pale blue colour stuck to everything. The acrid smell, the hiss of metal being cooled in water, the clang of metal on metal, the heat, and the dark, sooty underground room made Skandadasa claustrophobic. He was finding it difficult to breathe in the smoke.

Dhamaka, the head ironsmith, bowed to the new mahapradhana. Skandadasa started talking to him, and asked for each of the ironsmiths' names. This was new for the slaves. No mahapradhana had ever asked for their names before. Roopaka walked around with a frown on his face as Skandadasa stopped by each worker and discussed the process in detail. Dhamaka began to feel uneasy and tried to distract the new mahapradhana, but Skandadasa continued his interaction with the slaves. One young man grabbed Skandadasa's hand and a collective gasp went round.

Dhamaka screamed, 'Move away, you scoundrel. How dare you touch the mahapradhana?'

Skandadasa asked Dhamaka to be quiet and smiled at the young man. With renewed confidence, the young man led Skandadasa deep inside the cavern. They weaved their way past vaults in which molten metal was cooling and furnaces blazed. Roopaka and Dhamaka followed behind, sulking.

The young slave stopped where there was a patch of water on the floor. He pointed to the roof. Skandadasa looked up and a drop of water fell on his nose. The roof had a slight leak.

'Why has no one seen to this?' he asked Dhamaka. The head ironsmith and Roopaka looked at each other.

'It was seen by Mahapradhana Parameswara and he had asked someone to repair it, swami,' the young slave interjected.

'It was repaired,' Dhamaka said, 'but during high tide the river tries to get in.'

'We will all drown one day, swami. We are scared,' the young slave folded his hands in plea.

'I want it to be sealed. Use lead, use iron, I don't care what you do, but I do not want a drop of water to seep in,' Skandadasa insisted.

'I am afraid we cannot do that, swami,' Dhamaka said defiantly.

Skandadasa's face became black with rage. How dare a slave defy his orders?

Roopaka intervened. 'That is a safety feature. In case Mahishmathi is attacked and conquered by the enemy, they should never learn the secret of Gaurikanta. In a situation like that, the head slave has been told to open the door with one blow of his hammer—'

'And the river will flood in, destroying the secret forever,' completed Dhamaka.

'We will all die, swami,' the young slave cried. 'If water breaks in by accident. And the secret will be lost forever.'

Dhamaka snapped at the slave, 'Hush, you idiot. If that door has held for three hundred years, it will hold for another three hundred. Do not scare the mahapradhana and make him do something rash.'

Skandadasa asked a slave to bring a table. He climbed up on it and started inspecting the ceiling door. He could hear the faint sound of water flowing on the other side. It must be high tide, he thought. He shuddered at the image of River Mahishi rushing into the underground workshop and flooding it. He could not understand why no one had bothered to seal it. If it was meant to destroy the workshop and the secret with it, it served no purpose when it was low tide. The river had changed course, leaving a slushy marshland. The slave who escaped with the stones had probably used this route.

'When did it start leaking?' Skandadasa asked.

Dhamaka shifted uneasily on his legs. Skandadasa noticed that he was avoiding his eyes. 'I don't know,' he said finally.

'It happened after that slave Nagayya escaped,' the young slave said.

Skandadasa had guessed as much. He knew the slave had had outside help. The needle of suspicion pointed at Roopaka. From the beginning, he had not liked the man, and with the suspicion growing in his mind, Skandadasa started hating the officious assistant.

He said, 'If someone could open the door from outside when the tide was low, someone can open it when the river is in full spate too. It only requires a diver with a strong pair of lungs. This is the biggest security risk. I want this closed now,' Skandadasa said, and again his assistant protested.

Ignoring him, Skandadasa snapped at the young slave, 'Hurry, call your friends. Fix the door so that it can never be opened.' The slaves hurried to do the mahapradhana's bidding.

'I want to see the Gauridhooli,' Skandadasa said. The entire workshop fell silent.

Skandadasa repeated what he'd said, and Dhamaka finally replied, 'I am afraid it is not possible without an official order.'

'All right, this is my order,' Skandadasa whipped out a palm leaf, scribbled an order with his stencil, put his official seal on it, and slapped it down on the table. Roopaka tried to object, but Skandadasa asked him to keep quiet. Stung by the insult, Roopaka picked up the palm leaf.

Skandadasa snatched it back and said, 'You are just an assistant. Do not forget your place.'

Roopaka's face flushed red. He said in a cold voice, 'Swami, no mahapradhana has ever treated me like this.'

'Get used to it,' Skandadasa glared at him and then turned to Dhamaka. The head slave hurriedly walked to a wall and opened a secret door. He entered and closed the door behind him. Skandadasa was at the edge of his patience.

Dhamaka came back with a small, closed iron pot. Skandadasa waited impatiently as he opened it. The room filled with an iridescent blue. Skandadasa extended his hand to take the powder in his fingers but Dhamaka moved the pot away. 'Highly poisonous. It will burn your hand to your bones, swami. It should not see sunlight. Hence it is kept underground. It will be mixed while we forge the swords and that is what makes Gaurikhadga, the famous Mahishmathi sword, so strong and flexible.'

'What goes into making it? Have we checked its other uses? Have we experimented with it?' Skandadasa asked with enthusiasm.

'No, my lord, we have not, and we should not. We do not know what disaster it would bring, what ill luck it would—'

'Bah, superstitions. If you are not ready to tell me, I shall find out. This needs to be studied and meticulously recorded for posterity. This discovery should not die here. It has to be bettered; we should find other ways to use it. Give me the pot. I shall do the experiments myself. I am sure some old books will have references to Gauridhooli,' Skandadasa said, reaching out.

Roopaka intervened. 'Swami, this is highly irregular. You do not have the authority. This is against national security. You are dealing with state secrets.'

Skandadasa smiled as he took the pot from Dhamaka's hand. He closed the lid tight and said, 'I am the state now, friend, and this is my secret too.'

He said goodbye to all the slaves, and congratulated the young workers for closing the ceiling door with a huge metal sheet. He walked out with the pot of Gauridhooli. Roopaka walked behind him with a scowl. The slaves looked worried and a few of them closed their eyes in prayer. Superstitious, like most slaves, they believed Gauridhooli always brought ill fortune to the possessor.

THIRTY-ONE

Bijjala

Bijjala was in a foul mood. The ceremonies to mark his twenty-first birthday had started much before sunrise. Now it was almost evening and still Rudra Bhatta continued to drone mantras, and showed no signs of slowing down. There were more than two score priests chanting with the chief priest and adding twigs and ghee into the sacred fire. His mother sat cross-legged near the priest, piously repeating the mantras silently. His father sat with a grave face, but Bijjala could see that the king was bored. When he became king, he would stop all this nonsense, Bijjala decided.

Various dignitaries and noblemen sat in the durbar, dressed in their finest clothes and ornaments. Bijjala was hungry and impatient. The aroma of delicious food from the royal kitchen was driving him mad. Using mango leaves, the priest sprinkled everyone with holy water from a pot between his legs. Bijjala wanted to empty the water into the holy altar and bang the priest's shaven head with the pot. Mahadeva sat patiently, his face serene and smiling near his mother. That irritated Bijjala more.

From the crowd, Keki was trying to catch his attention. After many unsuccessful attempts, Keki took a flower from her hair and threw it at Bijjala. The prince turned and Keki gestured that they should go. That made Bijjala more edgy. He had been under house arrest for the last few months. He had been waiting for his coming-of-age birthday like a hornbill waits for rains in the forest. Now Skandadasa would not be able to control him. He was free to go anywhere he wanted. He hated Skandadasa from the bottom of his heart. Impudent rascal, a good-for-nothing low caste who had pretentions of being a nobleman. When he became king, he vowed to throw out the arrogant swine. He did not know what his father saw in the man. If someone had asked for his opinion, he would have said Skandadasa was fit only to wash the floor of some tavern.

Unfortunately, the king never asked him anything. He consulted more with Mahadeva. His brother was a coward; an effeminate fool. He was able to win everyone over with his words. Bijjala did not find any need to use sweet talk. His sword was enough for him to make people obey him. He would rule over everyone with an iron fist. People should shiver when they heard the name Bijjala.

If his father had had any sense, Bijjala thought, he should have made Pattaraya the prime minister, instead of that nincompoop Skandadasa. That was one gentleman. They did not make people like him anymore. Despite Bijjala losing heavily to him in Kalika's den, Bhoomipathi Pattaraya was grace personified. He was polite to a fault and never even mentioned the debt he was owed. Though the last time he had met Pattaraya, the fat man had blabbered something about some stone. Bijjala had laughed it off. He had asked Pattaraya why he would steal a stone from him. Pattaraya mentioned that he had given it to his slave. As if it was the bloody duty of the princes to know where their slaves went. Kattappa had been missing after he had saved the slave from the Vaithalikas. Good riddance. Bijjala thought it would be a good thing to have a female slave instead of an ugly black one following him around.

Finally the rituals were over and the guests retired, praising the sumptuous meal. Bijjala hurried outside and rushed to his stables. The finest Arabian horse, black as midnight, was waiting for him. A gift from his father, a gift befitting the next ruler of Mahishmathi. Bijjala caressed the silky mane of the horse for a moment and then pulled himself onto its saddle. He kicked the horse with his pointed shoes and the beast shot forward.

He raced through the garden, jumped over the fountain, splashing water and landing gracefully on the other side, and galloped towards the fort gate,jumping neatly over every single hedge. He frightened the geese and trampled over finely laid beds of flowers. An old gardener, who was tottering around with a pail of water, was brutally kicked out of the way, and the prince laughed as he saw the man hitting the ground hard. Bijjala was now standing on the stirrups, urging the horse for more speed. People ran away like frightened chickens as the huge war horse thundered past.

Two soldiers came running and stood at the gate with their spears crossed, blocking his path. Bijjala did not even bother to pull on the reins. They dove to either side as the horse blasted through their puny blockade. *Fools, did they think they could stop Prince Bijjala?* A determined guard ran behind Bijjala and managed to catch hold of the reins. The horse reared to a stop, and it took all his skills for Bijjala to stop himself from being thrown off. He was trembling with rage when the head of the guards at the fort gate came running and bowed deep in front of him.

'Your Highness, you are not supposed to go outside because of the security threat,'the senior man said respectfully. Bijjala beckoned to him, and the man bowed a bit more as he stepped closer to the horse.

'Says who, son of a bitch?' Bijjala said. The man looked shocked. Bijjala knew the maharaja always called him by his name, talked to him with affection and respect. He was an old faithful, having served Mahishmathi for more than four decades. *No wonder these bastards are spoilt and dare to stop a prince.*

'Eh...Mahapradhana Skandadasa's orders, Your Highness.' The man had tears in his eyes. His men were watching how he was being treated. *Good medicine for your arrogance,* thought Bijjala. He decided to teach the old man a lesson he would never forget. The man was wearing a few medals as pendants. *Some frigging tokens of appreciation rendered by the maharaja.* He did not know what deeds of valour the old man might have performed in the wars before he was born. Nor did he care. He grabbed the medals and pulled the old soldier to him, enjoying the look of terror on the craggy old face. What an ugly face to look at, full of scars from sword fights. The old man had only one ear, and that too only half of it. How could his father employ such disgusting men in his service?

Bijjala slapped the soldier across his face. 'That is for stopping me,' he said. He slapped him again, this time with the back of his palm. 'That is for taking the name of that bloody low caste Skandadasa.' Another slap drew blood from the soldier's nose. 'That is to teach you to be more respectful to your superiors.' A final punch from the prince knocked the old man unconscious.

Bijjala screamed at the terrified guards, 'Bloody morons! Know this. I am twenty-one today. I am not bound by the orders of some Shudra. I will be ruling over all of you soon. I go where I please.' He glared at the guards and one by one they fell on their knees around him.

'Water,' he growled. He had polluted himself by touching the ugly old soldier, even if it was to slap him. A guard came running with water and poured it so Bijjala could wash off his sin; he stood a few feet away, careful not to touch the prince even by accident. Bijjala shook off the excessive water from his hands on the face of the guard. He then spurred his horse and galloped past the still-kneeling guards.

The wind whistled in his ears as Bijjala rode past the river towards Kalika's inn. He had been a caged bird for so long. Today, he was free. It was an exhilarating feeling. No one was going to stop him from getting what he wanted now. Images of Kalika sitting naked kept popping up in his mind, and he felt feverish and excited. The horse felt very slow, and the road too long.

By the time he reached Devadasi Street, his horse was frothing at the mouth. He touched the pouch of gold coins he had on him, a present from his mother, and then the three-rowed diamond necklace, a gift from the women of Antapura. Mahadeva had given him a portrait. A worthless gift. And Bijjala would have preferred for Mahadeva to have drawn him sitting astride a horse. Instead, his brother had drawn him sitting by the river, with Gauriparvat in the background. Only a fishing rod was missing to make him look like a fisherman. Bijjala had only contempt for his brother.

As he walked his horse through the street, he realized that there was something odd about the place. There were no whores calling out to him and the pimps were sitting around with morose faces, staring at him with hostility. Many women were sitting in the street. Was someone dead? Why were they so angry?

Last time, he had been taken through a shortcut so Bijjala now asked someone for the way to Kalika's inn. A few men with sticks surrounded him.

'What the hell! Move away,' Bijjala shouted. Instead, the men closed in. Bijjala's hand went to his sword. A guard in employment of the Devadasi guild appeared with a bow, an arrow in it pulled taut, pointed at Bijjala's heart. The women behind them started screaming, 'Kill him, kill him, kill him.' Bijjala was terrified. He tried to pull out his sword and heard the bowstring twang. A blink of an eye later his horse neighed, thrashed its front legs, fell down and started twitching. His father's present, the prized horse, shot dead. The arrow was aimed at him, yet his reflexes had saved him. Even without thinking, he had moved away and the arrow had found its target in the horse.

Bijjala barely had enough time to draw his sword and swing it before the mob closed in on him. He fought like a man possessed, drawing blood, hacking limbs and heads. He kept them at bay, but more and more people came running. He wished he had his bodyguards with him. For a fleeting moment he thought about his faithful slave and wished he was by his side. He was not going to last long for sure.

'Kill him, kill him, kill him'—the crowd chanted. 'I am your prince, Prince Bijjala, the firstborn,' he cried in a shrill voice. The mob laughed at the tremor in his cry. They could sense his fear. 'Death to the prince,' they now began to chant.

Bijjala swung his sword wildly, keeping the mob at bay, but they kept pressing forward. He cut a spear that came flying at him into two. His was a Gaurikhadga, but even that would not be enough to fight a mob of a hundred people and swelling by the minute. He was losing all hope when Bijjala saw a familiar face in the crowd.

'Keki!' he cried over the din of the mob as he parried the thrust of a sword and ducked a dagger thrown at him. 'Keki…help me.'

He saw the eunuch fighting her way through the crowd, screaming at people, pushing, shoving, jostling, punching, dragging and kicking as she tried to reach him. Everything was a blur and he was injured in many places. *I am going to die on my birthday,* thought Bijjala.

Keki reached him somehow and spread her arms wide. Bijjala hid behind the eunuch, ashamed and relieved at the same time.

'Hold on, hold on,' Keki pushed away a few men who tried to reach Bijjala. 'Have you gone crazy? This is our friend. He is not Skandadasa's man. He is our man, our prince. He will help us.'

The mob growled like a beast. Someone cried from behind, 'They have closed our inns, they have rendered us homeless, moneyless and jobless. And the prince comes to gawk at our misery in his finest clothes. We want blood. We know we will hang for this, but we have nothing left to live for anymore.'

'What happened?' Bijjala cried from behind the eunuch.

'He asks what happened as if he does not know,' an angry voice said, and the chant of 'Death to Prince Bijjala' picked up again.

Keki cried, 'Peace. Hold on. This prince is innocent. He is not like the others. He is our man. He is our client. He is sympathetic to our problems.' Keki took hold of Bijjala's hand and raised it high. 'He is our friend. My friend.'

Bijjala blinked. Keki hissed in his ears, 'Say you are their friend and that you will correct any wrongs done to them.'

'What wrong did I do?' Bijjala asked, confused.

Ignoring him, Keki continued. 'As a token of our friendship, the prince has come all the way from his palace to compensate you for your loss. He knows you have been wronged.'

Keki plucked the pouch of gold coins from the prince, drew loose its strings, and threw the gold coins into the air. The mob paused for a moment, watching the gold coins shower down on them in disbelief. And then there was a mad scramble. They began to fight with each other for the coins, and in the melee, Keki grabbed Bijjala's hand and ran.

When they had left the street and entered the jungle, Bijjala pulled Keki to a stop and asked, 'Would you tell me what that was about? I was almost killed—and I have lost all the gold coins I got as a present for my birthday.'

'Thank your stars that you did not come out hacked like mutton chops.'

'But why are they so angry?'

'You would also be angry if someone threw you out of your home and made you a beggar.'

'Mind your words, eunuch. You are talking to the crown prince of Mahishmathi.'

'Go to that mob and declare it, if you dare. Dandakaras came with a huge force and closed down Devadasi Street. They have made our business illegal.'

'Oh no,' Bijjala cried. 'Kalika…?'

'Ran away with what she could grab. Let the devil eat her. Let Yakshi possess her. Bitch. She did not leave anything for this poor eunuch. But I know my darling prince will not forget this poor servant,' Keki said grabbing Bijjala's necklace.

'What are you doing?' Bijjala cried. Keki tugged at the necklace, breaking it. With a swift movement, it disappeared into her breast-cloth. 'A small present for this poor eunuch who saved your life, my prince. Thank you, thank you. You are so generous. Jai Mahishmathi, jai Bijjala deva.'

Bijjala seethed with anger. He had come with lust, desperate to get Kalika, desperate to win back all that he had lost,but he had ended up losing even more.'Who sent the dandakaras?' he asked.

'Who else, but that bastard Skandadasa,' Keki said with a sigh.

Bijjala had heard enough. He vowed that he would put a stop to the arrogance of the bloody low-caste pretender.

'Are you going back to the palace, Prince?' Keki asked. Bijjala grunted in reply.

Keki said with a smile.'Wait, I will arrange for a palanquin, bull cart or chariot. Princes should not walk. On second thoughts, I feel it would be better if I too came with you.'

On the way back, Keki filled him in on the atrocities committed by the dandakaras on Skandadasa's orders. Bijjala decided that he would demand that his father remove the upstart mahapradhana from his post. He was now twenty-one. His father could no longer dismiss him casually. As per protocol, he was equivalent in rank to a bhoomipathi. The mahapradhana was above him in rank until the official declaration making him the crown prince came, but rarely would any salaried official dare to disobey a future king. Bijjala was convinced his father was a fool. He had to drive some sense into the old man's thick head.

Keki excused herself at the entrance of the durbar and Bijjala entered it with determined steps. He paused when he saw the old guard he had hit standing before the king. Bijjala's gaze fell on Skandadasa, who was glaring at him. Something was not right.

'Ah, Bijjala, come in.' His father's voice was calm. Bijjala hated it when his father talked like that. He knew trouble was coming. He decided to go on the offensive.

'Father—' Bijjala began.

'Your Majesty—address us as Your Majesty, Bijjala. We are sitting on our throne and not in our bedroom,' the king said.

This was not going right at all. Bijjala gritted his teeth and said, 'Your Majesty, someone ordered that Devadasi Street be closed—'

'We ordered it,' the king said, leaning back on his throne and running his fingers through his beard.

'Father…I mean, Your Majesty, you ordered it?' Bijjala was confused. 'I thought this basta—I mean this…I mean this Skandadasa—'

'The Honourable Mahapradhana Skandadasa—address him so. He is your prime minister, not your personal slave to address without an honorific. This is the sabha of Mahishmathi, Prince, and not a house of pleasure or a tavern. Decorum has to be maintained, and respect has to be given as well as taken. Talking about respect, did you hit the veteran Mayan?'

'Veteran who? This old beggar?'

'Yes, Prince. This "old beggar", if you care to know, saved the life of the maharaja of Mahishmathi not once or twice, but thrice. If you look at the old beggar's left ear—ah, the one you hit—he lost half of it when he came between us and the sword that was meant to cut off our head. If you see the scar on his left cheek, the one you slapped,he got it while saving us by crawling under a chariot that had splintered in the battlefield. The third time he saved our life it was in much more difficult circumstances, but we will not bother you with that. You have something to say?'

'He tried to stop me,' Bijjala cried.

'From going to a house of pleasure on your name day, if we are right?'

'I am twenty-one, I can go where I please,' Bijjala said.

'You act as if you are twelve. Now you will apologize to him by touching his feet.'

Bijjala was shocked. Mayan folded his hands and cried, 'Your Majesty, no, no, it will be a sin. I am a mere soldier. The Honourable Mahapradhana insisted that I should come with him to see Your Majesty. I am sorry. I am sorry. Please...He is the scion of Mahishmathi. Please...'

'Mayan,' Maharaja Somadeva's voice was soft and respectful, 'we are disappointed in you. We thought you considered your king as just. We thought you considered your maharaja as a human with emotions like gratitude, respect and love. The words you spoke hurt our pride, for that proves we are a tyrant who cares nothing for our people. Are we such a ruler, dear Mayan? Or do you wish we should be known as such a king for posterity?'

Mayan looked down at his toes. Bijjala stood fuming. He looked pleadingly at his mother. The maharani intervened, 'Your Majesty, it is wrong to make the prince of Mahishmathi touch a lowly soldier's feet. I belong to a great family, we trace our lineage to Suryavamsha and if my son—'

'Brihannala,' the maharaja called out,cutting his wife off in middle. 'The maharani is suffering from a headache. Kindly accompany her to the Antapura.'

The maharani stood up. Her face was flushed red with anger and shame. 'I know the way,Your Majesty. But you have lost yours.' She bowed stiffly and stormed out of the sabha.

Maharaja stared at Bijjala and gestured for him to do his bidding. The entire sabha was watching him. Bijjala burnt with shame.The news would spread. He looked at Skandadasa. There was a smile of victory on that black face. He had come to get Skandadasa dismissed, and instead he was being forced to touch the feet of a lowly soldier. He gritted his teeth.

'Prince, we do not have the whole year. We have better things to do,' the maharaja said.

Trying to control his tears of anger and frustration, Bijjala stiffly bowed to touch the feet of Mayan who stood sobbing. Then Bijjala turned on his heel and walked away from the sabha. The maharaja continued his business as if nothing extraordinary had happened.

When Bijjala walked out of the durbar, darkness was spreading in Mahismathi. Keki, who was waiting outside, stood up.

'That was shameful,' Keki said. Bijjala clenched his fist.

Keki placed her hand on Bijjala's shoulder and said, 'All the doings of that low-caste mahapradhana. Worry not, when Bhoomipathi Pattaraya is your friend. We have a plan.'

THIRTY-TWO

Sivagami

Sivagami threw a pebble at Gundu Ramu through the bars of the kitchen window. Gundu Ramu was sitting on the floor, cutting vegetables with a curved knife. The pebble missed him and hit a copper vessel instead. The noise attracted the cook's attention and he hit Gundu Ramu on his head with his ladle. The boy gave a yelp and the cook shouted at him, 'Swine, playing when you are supposed to work? Next time you try such tricks, I will pour boiling sambhar on your head.'

Gundu Ramu crouched like a chastised dog, trying to shrink his huge body as much as possible, and resumed his work. The cook went back to blowing the fire in the stove. Gundu Ramu was wiping his eyes with the back of his handwhen the next pebble hit the mark. He looked at the window in surprise and immediately suppressed a yelp. He shook his head when Sivagami asked him to come out. He looked fearfully at the cook. Sivagami gesticulated wildly, indicating it was urgent.

Gundu Ramu stood up and the cook shouted at him. The boy raised his little finger, indicating he had to use the toilet.

'Don't take the whole day. Go,' the cook said, without looking back. Gundu Ramu ran out and met Sivagami. She grabbed his handand they ran behind the kitchen, where taro plants grew as tall as Sivagami's chin. It covered Ramu entirely. Kamakshi was waiting for them there.

I have thought about it thoroughly,' Sivagami said. 'The only day it will be possible for us to enter the palace premises is on Mahamakam. Everyone in the city will be invited into the palace grounds, and we will get no better opportunity to sneak into Skandadasa's home.'

'I heard he is the mahapradhana now. Won't he have changed his home? He always stays in the office,' Kamakshi said.

'I heard he has not and I hope he has not. We will break in, get the book and escape,' Sivagami said. She felt a pang of worry, but hid it well. Kamakshi was not in favour of breaking in—she was afraid Sivagami would be caught. But nothing was going to stop Sivagami. After her last conversation with Skandadasa, she could not just leave it there. She had been racking her brain, trying to devise a plan to recover it. After she was called to Skandadasa's office, Revamma had made sure that Sivagami was kept away from her friends. That morning she had gone out somewhere, and Sivagami had seized the chance to meet them.

'Even if you get the book, how will you leave with it?' Kamakshi asked. 'They check everyone coming in and going out.'

'For that we have Gundu Ramu,' Sivagami said.

'I am getting scared,' Gundu Ramu said.

'Nothing to be scared of, Gundu,' Sivagami ruffled his hair. 'You will not even be going inside the fort.'

'Not go inside the fort? I will miss all the performances and concerts,' Gundu Ramu said.

'Won't you do even this much for your akka?' Sivagami asked. She felt bad about manipulating the boy, but she had no other choice. She pressed on, 'The road for untouchables and slaves goes by the river, along the west fort wall. Skandadasa's home is near that wall. I will grab the book and give a signal. Then I will throw the book over the fort wall. You pick it up and run back to the orphanage. You can then come back and enter the fort to see all the dances you want.'

Gundu Ramu nodded reluctantly, and Sivagami gave him a confident smile though she knew it was going to be tough. She did not want to mention that the road would not have any light, and that he might have to wait alone for quite a long time.

Kamakshi said, 'I don't like this plan at all, Sivagami. Please, let us not do this.'

'Either you are with me or you are against me,' Sivagami snapped. 'I don't want anything from you, Kamakshi. You are not taking any risk. You just have to watch whether Revamma is looking the other way when I sneak away. I will be back before you know it. And you have to manage any curious souls who are interested in my whereabouts while I am gone.'

'No, Sivagami. Do you think the mahapradhana's home will be left open for you to walk into? There will be guards,' Kamakshi said.

'Of course there will be guards. Don't worry. I will not knock on the front door and say I have come to steal something from the mahapradhana's home, please let me in.

For god's sake, I am going to break in.' Sivagami felt her anger rising.

'You are stealing,' Kamakshi said.

'Taking back my father's book is not stealing. *He* stole the book from *me*. I am recovering it. Will you please stop being so irritating, Kamakshi? If you do not want to help, just stay away. Don't dampen everything and scare the boy too.'

Kamakshi's eyes brimmed with tears and she walked away. There was no point talking to Sivagami when she was angry. In any case, she had a huge pile of clothes to wash. She hurried to take the bundle of clothes and ran to the river with it. Sivagami was not the only one Kamakshi was worried about. She had not heard from Shivappa for a while, and was getting anxious.

It was midday by the time she finished washing the clothes. She bundled them together and lifted it on her back, staggering under the weight. She had begun climbing the steps of the ghat when a mad man jumped in front of her. She screamed and the bundle fell down. It was Bhairava, the crazy man who roamed around the riverbank. A few boys who were coming to bathe laughed at Kamakshi's predicament as the madman danced around her. After a few moments the boys lost interest and went away. The madman left, singing and dancing. Kamakshi sat down on the steps to pick up the soiled clothes. She was startled when she heard a whisper near her ears. Bhairava had come back.

He put his index finger on her lips and said, 'Silence. Listen.' Kamakshi looked fearfully towards the boys who were swimming in the river. Bhairava turned her chin towards him and said, 'On Mahamakam day, he will come for you. Wait for him. He will come after finishing his job and will take you away to the cottage by the sea as you had dreamed. This is Shiva's message. Told by Bhairava.'

Her heart was pounding in her ribcage. She gathered courage and asked, 'Where will he come?'

'Where the king rules, where kings are born, where kings die.'

'In the palace grounds?'

Without answering, the madman went away. She grabbed the clothes and hurriedly tied them into a bundle. She was in no mood to wash them again. Revamma would scream, but that did not matter. Shivappa was coming. *Oh Amma Gauri, you have heard my prayers,* she thought as she ran, wiping away her tears of joy. She threw the bundle into a corner and rushed to Sivagami. Sivagami looked at her and walked away.

Kamakshi ran up to her and hugged her. 'I will come with you on Mahamakam to the palace grounds,' she said.

Sivagami looked at her in surprise. Then her lips curved in a derisive smile. 'Why the sudden change of mind? Is he coming?' Kamakshi looked away and Sivagami quickly continued, 'It doesn't matter. And never mind what you said. I will be with you.'

Kamakshi started crying. 'I…I was scared for you. It was not that I was being selfish.'

Sivagami said, 'I know you, Kama,'and hugged her. 'Everything will be all right. You will have a wonderful life together. See how you blush,' Sivagami teased her as Kamakshi's lovely face turned red.

'See how spoilt you are for choices. You are lucky, Prince,'a voice came from behind them, and Kamakshi and Sivagami stepped apart. They were shocked to see that it was Keki. And behind Keki was Prince Bijjala.

'This one is a virgin,' Keki said, pointing to Kamakshi. 'I am not sure of this boy-girl,' she said, indicating Sivagami.

Sivagami moved Kamakshi behind her back and glared at the duo, 'Who allowed you here?'

'Aha, aha, this is the crown prince, girl. And he rules this country. Besides, he has paid Revamma. Now be good girls and go with him. You will not regret it. But don't forget this poor eunuch,' Keki simpered.

Sivagami looked at the prince and said, 'I was brought up by Thimma, and he checks here every week. If he finds I am missing, he will know whom to complain to. When he visited last, I told him about the business this eunuch and Revamma are carrying on. He will go to the maharaja.'

'Prince, she is bluffing—' Keki started, and then as the prince turned away said, 'Hey, hey, where are you going, wait, wait!' But Bijjala was on his way out, and Keki ran behind him.

Sivagami turned to a sobbing Kamakshi and said, 'Never show you are afraid. Nothing will happen to you. It is only a few days till Mahamakam. They will not dare to touch you or me before that. I know how to take care of myself, and you will join him soon, and then—' she started teasing Kamakshi again, and the girl laughed shyly.

Despite her own brave words, Sivagami had a nagging sense that something dreadful was going to happen. *No, I should not have such silly thoughts,* she chided herself, but the feeling refused to go.

THIRTY-THREE

Ally

Ally aimed her arrow at Jeemotha. His back was turned to her. She was tempted to let it fly. She imagined him falling face down into the river, and his blood spreading like red ink on the water. One day she was sure she would do it—but today was not that day. She was yet to extract anything worthwhile from him. She had given herself to him many times, but had barely anything to show for her efforts.

She watched as the pirate held the slave like one would a dog. Ally had grown fond of Kattappa. It had been a few days since they had rescued him from the river. She thought he would die, but the slave had recovered quickly. Despite her objections, Jeemotha had tied the slave with hemp ropes when he was weak and at the brink of death. It was quite unnecessary, Kattappa had said—it was an ancient code of his tribe to be the slave of the people who saved one's life. Until the master freed the slave, the slave would continue to serve the master. Jeemotha had laughed when he heard this. Despite Ally's best efforts, he refused to believe Kattappa's words. *Everyone judges others by their own standard,* thought Ally. Jeemotha would never understand the meaning of the word honour, just like Kattappa would never know what slyness was.

Ally often wondered whether she should let the slave go. She had only to utter the words, 'Slave,you are free as the wind', three times and he would be a free man as per the ancient rule. She knew that Jeemotha feared she would do this, which was why he had tied the slave and was making him work like a dog. But even if she freed Kattappa, there was no place he could go. They were trapped on this island. She had to wait for the right moment, but she felt miserable seeing the way Jeemotha was treating him.

Kattappa dove into the water at Jeemotha's urging. Ally stood up, her brows furrowed. The pirate was making the slave do a dangerous job. He had discovered that the river abounded with fresh water pearls and he was making the slave dive into the water to fish for them. While he held one end of the rope and stood in the shallow part of the river, the other end was tied to the slave's neck. It was not meant for Kattappa's safety. It was meant to give Jeemotha leverage. If the slave tried to escape, he just had to give a tug and choke him to death.

'He will die one of these days,' Ally cried out.

'The pearls are more valuable than he is,' Jeemotha answered. In her anger, she let loose the arrow. He ducked at the last moment and it fell harmlessly near him. The pirate laughed, 'Better luck next time, whore.'

Ally's face flushed with shame and anger. He called her 'whore' or 'slut' or many other unspeakable words. Not even once did he call her by her name. Not that she cared. She was doing her job. Yet, when she thought that he was utilizing her whenever he fancied, she felt anger and frustration corroding her from within. He shamelessly used her many times even when the slave was looking. Not that the slave looked at them when they made love. He pretended to be asleep. When she protested once, Jeemotha asked if they would have cared if animals and birds saw them when they were having sex. The slave was no better than an animal, he said. Every time Jeemotha said that, she felt like wringing his neck and killing him. Jeemotha knew the effect his words were having on her and would sometimes say things just to rile her.

'Next time I will not miss,' she said, notching another arrow in the string and drawing it. Jeemotha laughed, irritating her further. At that moment, Kattappa burst out of the water, his palm full of fresh water pearls. He wheezed for breath as he handed the pearls to Jeemotha. Ally's eyes brimmed with tears.

'Don't gawk, slave. Jump in again,' Jeemotha said, pushing Kattappa into the water, and the slave vanished. Ally lost her temper. She ran towards Jeemotha, ready to fight him. Jeemotha laughed aloud. She screamed at him as she ran up, and was about to punch him, when a horn blared loudly, shocking both of them.

Ships, hundreds of them, their sails fluttering in the wind. They were coming towards them at great speed.

'Run,' Jeemotha screamed as he pulled the rope.

Ally started running towards the ships, waving her hands wildly. She stood at the edge of the river. The ships were travelling through the deep blue part of it. She howled and screamed, jumping up and down, 'Help us, help us.'

Jeemotha ran towards her, grabbed her, and tried to shut her mouth. 'Bitch, bitch, you will get us killed,' he screamed, but she ignored him and continued to wave and scream at the ships. Finally, one of the ships turned towards them. Jeemotha grabbed her hand and started to run.

'Leave me, leave me. Help, help,' she cried. Out of the corner of her eye, she could see Kattappa trying to crawl onto the shore.

The ship anchored and coracles were lowered. Soon six coracles were travelling towards them. Jeemotha pulled her again and she shoved him. She put her leg between his and tripped him. He fell on his back in the shallow water. She ran towards the coracles. Fierce-looking warriors with body paint were jumping into the water now. They ran towards her and she knew something was wrong from the way they were approaching her. Her mouth gaped open. Before she knew it, they had surrounded her. She kicked down the first man who reached her. She could hear Jeemotha splashing towards them, cursing and shouting. Men were descending from the other coracles and heading towards them.

'Happy?' Jeemotha hissed at her as he struggled to free himself from the six warriors who were holding him tight. Some warriors dragged Kattappa towards them by the rope on his neck. Ally was held by four of them as she screamed and kicked. Some tried to grope her breasts. A man kissed her full on her mouth. She spat in disgust, and he slapped her across her face. He kissed her again.

'Well, well, well,' she heard a peculiar accent. An unusually tall man, almost a giant, had joined the warriors.

'Who would have thought Devil's Island would have people living on it,' he said, looking at them with curiosity.

'We are farmers,' Ally said.

'Oh, I can see the farm, the bullocks, granary, chickens,

sheep and cows. Wonderful. And who is that noble man?'

'My husband,' Ally said, and added as an afterthought, 'And that is our slave.'

'Interesting.' The giant walked towards Jeemotha who had not lifted his head. He kicked Jeemotha between his legs and Jeemotha doubled over.

'When did you get married, pirate Jeemotha?' he asked.

'Bhoomipathi Akkunda, I…I will pay my debts,' Jeemotha said, clutching his groins.

'In cash or kind? It seems you are very rich. How gigantic your palace looks,' he said and his men laughed. Suddenly, Akkunda's demeanour changed. He grabbed Jeemotha's chin and screamed, 'Bloody bastard. Son of a bitch. I was waiting to lay a hand on you. You were warned not to enter my villages, yet you did not spare my people. If someone higher up knows you hunted inside the Mahishmathi kingdom, I will hang with you.'

'Mistake, an honest mistake, Bhoomipathi Akkunda. I will compensate.'

'With what? By asking your wife to bed me? Or with swamp fish? I heard how Achi Nagamma destroyed you.'

'Let me go and I will show you. Please,' Jeemotha pleaded. Akkunda looked at him for a moment and then gestured for his men to free him. The pirate ran to fetch the pearls they had collected so far. He gave it to Akkunda and bowed. 'Accept this and give us a ride to civilization. To sweeten the deal, I shall give you another gift.'

Ally knew what he was going to offer. She watched helplessly as Jeemotha pulled Kattappa and handed him to Akkunda. She was tempted for a moment to free the slave by uttering the words of freedom, but that might only get the poor man killed. The bhoomipathi assessed the slave and grunted. His men dragged Ally, Kattappa and Jeemotha to the coracles and then onto the ships. Once they boarded the ship, Kattappa was taken to the lower deck to pull the oars.

Surprisingly, Ally and Jeemotha were treated better once they were on the ship.

Later, as night fell and countless stars lit the sky above them, Ally approached Jeemotha. Lanterns swayed in the breeze, making their light dance on the deck. Jeemotha was lying on his back, staring at the sky. She sat near him, put her palm on his broad chest, and asked, 'Why are they treating us so well?'

She could see his lips curve in derision. 'Because they know we are not going to get out of this alive.'

Ally withdrew her hand as if she had been burned. 'What do you mean? Why should they kill us? We have paid them.'

'Do you think they will leave anyone who has set eyes on the greatest secret of Mahishmathi?' he asked.

'What do you mean?'

'Do you have any idea what the cargo in these ships is?' Jeemotha sat up and looked at her face.

Ally felt excited and terrified at the same time. 'Gaurikanta?' she asked.

Jeemotha nodded. 'They are going for Mahamakam. After a day's travel, the river enters Gomukha Gorge and the rapids start. The Guha bhoomi also starts from there. These ships will land in Guha bhoomi and the stones will be stored there. It is the duty of one bhoomipathi to transport the stones across the rapids in coracles to Mahishmathi city. Akkunda is the master of the upper river and swamplands. No one who has set eyes on the secret of the Gaurikanta stones has gone free.'

'They will kill us?'

'Worse. They will sell us as slaves to Guha.'

'What is Guha like?'

'Compared to Guha, Akkunda is a saint,' Jeemotha said, as he lay back on the deck.

For the first time, Ally felt she had learnt something. The ships with their bellies full of precious stones continued to cut across the waters of the River Mahishi. Sails fluttered in the wind above them and the ship creaked and groaned. A night bird fluttered its wings and flew above them. Ally leaned on Jeemotha's chest and started kissing him. He had earned it. She wanted him too, for she was celebrating. She was on the verge of striking at the root of Mahishmathi's evil system. Achi Nagamma would be proud of her, she thought as she untied the knots of her breast-cloth.

THIRTY-FOUR

Mahamakam

Pattaraya drummed his fingers on the table as Rudra Bhatta fanned himself with his angavastra and Pratapa paced up and down the room. They were inside Pattaraya's chamber and the nine days of Mahamakam festivities were about to start. The sounds of horns blaring and the excited crowds came in through the window that was cracked open. The room was stuffy and hot, and only the dim light from one lamp on the table illuminated it. Outside, it was growing dark. When they heard a soft knock, Pattaraya stood up. Pratapa rushed to open the door and Keki stepped in.

'Prince?' Pratapa asked anxiously. Keki moved aside and Prince Bijjala walked in. Keki closed the door and latched it. The three men in the room bowed to the prince. Bijjala appeared nervous.

'Your Highness, thank you for coming,' Pattaraya folded his hands and bowed again.

'Are you going to embarrass me by asking for the money I owe?' Bijjala scowled.

'No, Your Highness,' Pattaraya said with a horrified expression. 'Why do you suspect your poor servants? We are ready to wait until you become the crown prince. Have I even asked you once before?'

Bijjala walked to the chair Pattaraya had been sitting on and sat on it himself. He lifted his legs and rested them on the table, and leaned back on the chair. Pattaraya knew the prince was trying to assert his superiority. If that was what the prince wanted, he could play that game. Pattaraya and his friends stood slightly bent at their waist, in a posture of abject subjugation.

Pattaraya said, 'We heard that the mahapradhana is creating problems for Your Highness. Shall we talk to him?'

Bijjala looked at each of the men's faces. Keki was watching him intently, but when Bijjala's eyes met hers, she smiled.

'That man is a pain in the neck, but my father trusts him. He is so frustratingly honest,' Bijjala said.

'Hmm…do you think so, Your Highness? What if I say we can pull away his mask of honesty and prove him to be a traitor?' Pattaraya asked, stealing a glance at his friends. They nodded their heads in agreement.

Bijjala pulled away his legs from the table and sat up straight. 'How?'

'Your Highness need not bother with the details. We do not want to drag Your Highness's name into it if anything goes wrong.'

Bijjala stared at them for a moment. Pattaraya moved near him and whispered, 'He is our enemy too. He is the enemy of all right-thinking people in Mahishmathi. This low-caste pretender…'

'What am I supposed to do?'

'Be with us. Just get him to go to his chamber. And when the time comes, say that you ordered whatever we are going to do. Just leave everything to us.'

'If getting him to his chamber is the only thing you want me to do, why can't you do that yourself?' Bijjala frowned.

'Ah, Your Highness. I am a mere bhoomipathi. I cannot ask him to be in his chamber on the night of Mahamakam. Ha ha, I cannot ask him even on a normal day. I am his subordinate, Prince. But you are his superior. If you order it, he has to come.'

'I will be his superior only when my father declares me the crown prince,' Bijjala said, rubbing his chin.

'Ah, but which mahapradhana would disobey the future maharaja's orders, Your Highness,' Pattaraya said and observed that the prince was pleased. He decided to push his luck.

'Your Highness, on second thoughts, I feel you are right. I appreciate your insight. This low-caste pretender, the son of a bear dancer, he is so arrogant that he may disobey your order. And that would be embarrassing.'

'I will pluck his tongue out if he dares to be impertinent to me.'

'Of course, of course. But the maharaja would not be pleased. Leave such things to your humble servants, Your Highness. Just go to him and whisper that you have to talk to him regarding Gauridhooli.'

'Gauri what—' Bijjala's eyebrows knitted in suspicion. 'Do you mean Gaurikanta stones, the gift of Amma Gauri?'

'Sort of. Don't bother about the details. Just tell him the word, say you need to discuss it, and he will follow you like a dog,' Pattaraya said.

'And once he comes, what am I supposed to discuss? What is this gauri—'

'Leave the discussion to us, Your Highness. Don't get involved. Once you bring him to the chamber, leave him there. We will take the risk. We assure you, you will come out of this a hero.'

'I am already a hero. People fear my prowess with the sword. They shiver when they see me. There is no warrior greater than me,' Bijjala said.

'Of course, Your Highness. The world knows your greatness, but not your father. Tonight, we will let him know,' Pattaraya said.

Bijjala sat scratching his chin, deep in thought.

Pattaraya gestured to Keki and the eunuch came forward and sat on the floor near Bijjala. She started massaging his legs.

'My prince,' Keki said in a husky voice, 'I am readying a gift for you. The one I showed you a few days before.'

Bijjala became alert. 'That one—'

'The very same, Your Highness. Your gift will be waiting for you in your room once you bring Skandadasa to his chamber. A humble present from a poor eunuch, Your Highness.'

Rudra Bhatta, who had been silent all this time, said, 'For the past one week I have been studying your birth chart, Your Highness. I see a glorious future. Your stars are changing from this day of Mahamakam. Glory awaits you. You are going to shine like Indra in heaven.'

'With many apsaras as concubines,' Keki simpered.

Pattaraya bowed low, 'We are always at your service, Your Highness. Just allow us to keep serving you.'

Bijjala looked pleased. He said, 'Should I do it now?'

'No, not now, Your Highness. Keki will let you know when you have to approach Skandadasa.'

'Yes, Your Highness,' Keki said. 'I need time to arrange for your gift to be in your chamber, isn't it? I will indicate the correct time.'

Pattaraya fell on his knees and his friends followed him, 'Jai Bijjala Deva, jai Mahishmathi. Hail the future emperor of Mahishmathi!' he cried and prostrated himself at Bijjala's feet. The others did the same. Bijjala blessed them and walked out with a pleased smile on his face. Keki hurried to join him and Pratapa went to close the door.

From the antechamber, a man stepped out.

'I did not think it would be that easy,' he said.

Pattaraya turned to him. 'It is never easy, Roopaka. Grandmasters make it appear easy. In this game of chaturanga, I am the grandmaster,'he laughed.

'And we are just pawns,' Roopaka smiled.

'And here is the reward for your information,' Pattaraya gestured to Pratapa and the dandanayaka put a cloth bag on the table. Roopaka picked it up and shook it. The coins in it jingled.

'This is so little.'

'More after you finish your task,' Pattaraya said and waved his hand towards the door.

Roopaka took it and tied it to his waist. He covered it with his waist-band and walked out. At the door, he paused, 'Hey, I am not doing this only for money,' he said.

'Money is just the add-on, friend. Keep doing the good work,' Pattaraya said. 'Tomorrow you will have more work to do and more to earn.

When Roopaka had left, Pratapa said, 'Frankly, I do not know what you are planning to do. Are you going to—'

'I will explain everything in its time,' Pattaraya said raising his palm. 'Is the dwarf waiting where I told him to?'

'I hope so,' Pratapa said. 'I have closed the path of the untouchables so that no one comes there even by chance. It was difficult to convince Hidumba to stand there for the whole night. He says he has no faith in your stupid plans.'

Pattaraya laughed. 'Ouch, that hurt. Criticism from a half-sized half-wit. Am I supposed to weep?' His demeanour changed then, and in a grave tone he said, 'This is our only chance to kill many birds with a single stone. I hope the fool doesn't goof it up. For today, everyone will do as I bid. No questions, no doubts, no one-upmanship.'

'As per astrology, our good times start from today,' Rudra Bhatta said.

'That is the only thing that scares me,' Pattaraya hissed. 'Keep your petty tricks to fools like Bijjala. I create my own destiny—not some blasted stars in the sky.'

THIRTY-FIVE

Ally

As far as Ally could see, grasslands stretched over rolling hills. In the distance, Gauriparvat rose, her peak reaching towards heaven. Dusk was creeping up from the hills. On the other side of the river, towards the north, like a faded painting, the city of Mahishmathi could be seen.

Forests and swamps separated the grasslands of Chempadava from Gauriparvat, and thousands of cows, buffalo and sheep grazed on the grasslands. The overlord's mansion was just a glorified hut. It was massive as huts went, but still a hut—made of unpolished planks and with a roof of dried grass. But it was rumoured that the mansion was filled with exotic crystals, stuffed animals and gold lamps. Exquisite carpets were laid on the mud floor and diamonds were used to multiply light in the chandeliers. His concubines wore the thinnest of muslin, his wives the smoothest of silk with gold embroidery. Yet the best of Arabian perfumes mixed with the smell of cow dung and sheep droppings. Bhoomipathi Chandrahasa Guha, the overlord of Chempadava bhoomi, never discriminated among his people, his wives, his concubines, his children, his cows, sheep, hunting dogs or servants. They all stayed under his massive roof, sleeping, eating, drinking and copulating together.

Ally watched Jeemotha drinking palm toddy with Bhoomipathi Chandrahasa Guha and Bhoomipathi Akkunda in the front courtyard of Guha's mansion. It was amazing how the pirate had managed to change the term of slavery to one of servitude. It still rattled Ally that he had offered her up sexually to Chandrahasa and Akkunda. But that had not bought them complete freedom. They were not allowed anywhere beyond the confines of the mansion.

They were not chained now, and were just like any servants in Guha's mansion. Jeemotha said the good times would not last for ever. Guha was waiting for Mahamakam to get over and then he would do as he pleased with them. Guha liked to be unpredictable. She should not try anything foolish, Jeemotha told her. As if he cared.

Ally often wondered what would happen with the stones. She would have given her right arm to know the details and pass it on to Achi Nagamma. If only she could destroy the cache of stones, she may perhaps achieve what no rebel had achieved in the past three generations. That would bring the corrupt Mahishmathi empire to its knees. That would result in the destruction of an inhuman system that used children as fodder for its progress. As Achi Nagamma used to say, their war was against the system and not the country.

Since Ally had been holed up in Chempadava with Jeemotha, she had not seen Kattappa. She often wondered what had happened to the slave. She did not know whether it was pity, respect or love, but she missed the calming presence of Kattappa sorely. She had tried to look for him, but was stopped by guards. There were rumours that the Vaithalikas were preparing for something big, and Guha had placed more guards to secure the armoury where the stones were kept.

Every Mahamakam, the Mahishmathi government somehow brought the stones to the city, or so it was rumoured. Ally wondered how this was done secretly, as almost the entire population of Mahishmathi would be thronging the city. If they just came in the ships, why couldn't Bhoomipathi Akkunda transport them without coming to Guha Bhoomi? And if the stones were being taken to the city, why had no one seen it being transported? What did they do with the stones? No commoner talked about them. It was just whispers among the elite, a hushed rumour, with all the sinister air of a dreaded secret. Yet, Jeemotha hinted it was the duty of a bhoomipathi to take it across. Something did not add up.

The three men were getting drunk and Jeemotha was singing some bawdy song. The pirate sat on the floor while the two bhoomipathis had chairs. This was the time to slip out and see whether she could find out something more. She walked as if bored, kicking a stone out of her way and smiling at the guards, as though merely going for a stroll. They knew her as the woman who pleasured the bhoomipathis and that gave her some respect. She sat by the river, throwing stones, waiting for the guards to stop watching her. It was getting darker by the minute.

The river breeze was cool, yet that did not soothe her tension. She was feeling nervous. Capture meant sure death, but this could be the most important breakthrough if she pulled it off. Ally was desperate to do something for Achi

Nagamma. Achi had been her father and mother, her guru and god. Ally always yearned for Achi's words of praise, which were rarely given.

Ally slipped into the tall grass and started weaving her way through it. She was terrified of snakes, and every step she took, she thought she would tread on the head of a cobra or a viper and it would bite her. She would die here, without doing anything worthwhile in life. Blades of grass scratched her face and drew white lines over her black skin, making her itch everywhere. She willed herself to make her way through the swaying grass. The breeze picked up pace, bending the blades as it howled past her ears. A pale moon was rising in the sky. She wished it was darker and less windy. Whenever the grass moved, she could see the swaying lantern that hung in front of Bhoomipathi Guha's mansion. The three men were still drinking as the women of Guha's household milled around, serving eatables.

Ally only had an idea of where the armoury lay. She had to go northeast of the mansion. Once she was sure she had moved past hearing distance of the bhoomipathis, she started running. The grassland gave way to woods and there was a crude path leading up a small hillock. From somewhere ahead, a pack of dogs barked. A bat flew close to her head. She tried to push down a growing sense of trepidation. *This is madness,* she thought as she ran up the path. *This could get you killed,* a voice whispered inside her. She gulped down her fear and ran up the hill. The dogs' barks were becoming louder.

Ally stopped when she heard a low growl. She looked around, her heart thudding in her chest. The bushes around her exploded then, and she screamed. The attack came from behind. Before she knew it, pain shot up from her ankles. A huge dog had sunk its teeth into her flesh. She tried to kick it with her other leg, when another dog jumped from the bushes on her left, its teeth bared, gunning for her throat. She caught its neck. It struggled, twisting its body to get free. She could feel its foul breath on her face. With a scream she slammed it down. It twisted, yelped and jumped up again. She lost her balance and fell down. Soon more dogs were attacking her. She was being bitten everywhere. She finally managed to roll away, freeing herself from the dogs. She was bleeding all over, but thankfully she was on her feet again. She kicked the next dog that attacked, sending it scampering through the bushes. The other dogs were wary now, and they circled her, growling low all the time. She kicked a stone at a dog's snout, and the animal rolled down onto the ground, yelping. Blood sprang from its wound, and the other dogs ran to lick it. She dove away from the pack and took off. She was aiming for a huge banyan tree ahead. The dogs started chasing her. *Their barks will have warned Guha's men,* she thought with desperation. She could hear their panting. Any moment now one of them would jump on her back and rip open her neck.

When she reached the tree, she froze. There was a chasm separating her from the tree. It was almost fifteen feet wide. She did not know how deep it was, but she could hear the gurgle of water over rocks. The dogs had reached, but they were fanning out. They knew she was trapped. Ally was not sure she would be able to jump across. The pack of dogs started closing in. She moved to the edge of the gap. Her foot dislodged a pebble which fell down the crevice. It hit the water after an uncomfortably long interval. The pack leader of the dogs growled. She knew what that meant. She said a silent prayer to Amma Gauri, and leapt.

For a moment, she saw herself being pulverized on the rocks below. Her fingers touched the swaying arms of the banyan and she gripped it for dear life. The pack stood at the edge, barking loudly, angry at the loss of their prey. She swayed from side to side as she pulled herself up the tree. She sat on a branch, her legs dangling on either side and wept. Her hands were sticky with blood and her body hurt everywhere. She knew they would come in search of her soon, but she didn't have the will to move. The moon had gone behind the clouds, and she was thankful for the darkness.

A dull thud made her start. She looked around. Again that sound. Chisel on wood. It was coming from the other side of the sprawling banyan tree. Gingerly, she started climbing up, making her way using the dangling roots of the banyan. When she reached the other side, she saw that there were lamps under the tree and the idols of snakes. This might be the holy tree of Guha's people, thought Ally. She heard the sound again. And a low murmur. When her eyes adjusted to the darkness, she could see a huge wooden wall reaching almost to the tree.

Ally moved to the far end of a branch and leaned forward. The branch swayed in the wind and bent with her weight. It was a good twenty feet to the ground. It was a huge clearing, fenced off by the massive wall made of logs. She could see something in the distance. A gigantic figure towering over everything. It had eight arms. She blinked at the sight. The sound of pebbles falling on something wooden came to her.

The moon came out of the clutches of the clouds, spreading a dull ivory light on the clearing. Slowly, the distant figure became clearer. Amma Gauri! A gigantic statue of goddess Kali was staring back at her. Ally folded her hands and bowed her head. She had cracked the secret of how the stones reached Mahishmathi.

The wind made the branch sway again at that moment, and with a sickening crack that did not even give her time to yell, the branch gave way, and Ally fell headlong inside the encampment.

THIRTY-SIX

Gundu Ramu

The orphanage was eerily silent. Apart from Gundu Ramu and Uthanga, there was no one else there. Gundu Ramu was scared to look at Uthanga. His vacant eyes stared up at the ceiling and, if not for the slight movement of his chest, he could be mistaken for dead. The only light in the dilapidated building was the one by Uthanga's head. There was a brisk breeze outside; it made the lamp dance, and with it, the shadow of Uthanga moved on the wall. Gundu Ramu wished Revamma had lit lamps in all the rooms before she had left, but she was saving oil.

Sivagami had asked him to come to the untouchables' lane behind the fort after the sixth toll of the bell after sunset. He had counted up to three. He had to leave now if he was to reach by the time the bell tolled six times. He shuddered at the thought of walking alone on the road, but he had to do it for his akka.

Something scurried past in the kitchen and his heart leapt out of his ribcage. He was sweating. Rats, it can only be rats, he told himself. A cat meowed somewhere outside. A window had come loose at its hinges and rattled in the wind. He had to leave. He looked out of the window. It was inky dark. *I will go when the moon shows itself*, he told himself. An owl hooted in the woods. As if in answer, another hooted near the orphanage. It went on and on, driving the boy mad. Near him, the lamp flickered in the breeze. *Was Uthanga moving? Would he turn his head and ask him something?* Gundu Ramu's imagination was running wild. Something crashed in the kitchen and Gundu Ramu let out a cry.

'Who is that?' he said, his voice trembling. There was no answer. After a pause, a cat hissed. The lamp went off and the room filled with acrid smoke. Gundu Ramu did not know how to use a flint, so he could not re-light the lamp. The moon emerged from behind the clouds. Gundu Ramu ran out and did not slow down until he had reached the path by the river. Faint sounds of music came from the palace grounds in the distance. He paused when he heard the sound of oars. Who could be travelling at this time of the night? He ducked behind a bush and watched. Boats were crossing the river and coming to his shore. He watched with bated breath.

The first boat stopped a few feet away from him and a man jumped out. He splashed water when he did so and someone hissed at him not to make noise. The man treaded carefully through the slushy shore and moored the boat to a tree. Other men were climbing out. Gundu Ramu counted up to twenty men. They seemed to be waiting for someone. One of the men brought out something from his waist-band. It shimmered in the moonlight. An urumi, a twenty-foot long whip sword that could be worn around the waist like a rope. Gundu Ramu had only heard about it in stories. The man began to carefully coil it into a smaller circle, almost fist-sized. Others handed over their urumis to him and he wound them too and handed them back.

Time went by and the men began to show signs of impatience. The bell tolled for the fourth time from the palace. Gundu Ramu was getting anxious. He did not dare to go past these men but he did not want to be late either. Soon the sound of oars could be heard again. Another boat was approaching from the opposite side. When it came nearer, the leader of the group hurried to it.

'Nala, you are late,' he said.

'It was not easy getting past the naval sentries. And getting so many kinds of drums was a task,' the newcomer said.

The leader turned to one of his men and said, 'Quick, Shivappa.'

The drums were passed on from one hand to another. Gundu Ramu watched as the man called Shivappa quickly untied a drum, removing the leather straps and the drum head. He inserted an urumi into it and put the drum back together. He repeated the process for each drum. The men then quickly changed into the clothes of performing artistes, which Nala had brought.

'Who can drum well?' asked the leader.

'We can, Bhutaraya,' two men said, stepping forward.

'Then what are you waiting for. We are the tribal artists from the hill of Marutha. We are going to have a great party in the maharaja's palace,' Bhutaraya said.

Everyone laughed. The men who had volunteered to drum rolled their fingers on the drum heads and they boomed. In answer, the others beat their drums. It sounded unusually loud and frightened the birds in the trees. Those who could not drum started dancing. They began walking towards the palace. Nala waited till they had disappeared and then returned to his boat.

When Gundu Ramu was sure that he was alone on the road, he got out from behind the bush and began following the men. He was sure these men pretending to be artistes were up to no good, yet it was comforting to know that there was someone else on the road with him. He was careful to keep a safe distance from them and the drumming sounds they made helped him follow them.

The bell tolled five and he hurried down the road. In the pale moonlight, the shadows of the trees took ominous shapes, yet he found solace in the fact that there were people ahead of him. No spirit or ghoul, yakshi, preta, pisacha or bhuta was going to come with so much noise. They were the creatures of silence and darkness. He wished the night would be over soon. He wished he were travelling down the royal highway, brightly lit, full of festivities and thousands of people milling around. There would be toys to see, savouries to eat. No, he had no money, so he would not have been able to buy anything, but it was nice to think about good food. When his father was alive, he used to bring him tasty laddus whenever he came back from his travels. Tears sprang to his eyes when he thought of his father. He was so immersed in his thoughts that he did not observe that the drumming had stopped till he almost ran into trouble.

Gundu Ramu quickly hid behind a tree when he saw that two sentries had stopped the drummers. He had not expected sentries. He saw some money changing hands and the sentries waved the musicians past. They were tribal and they could use the lane. He did not have any excuse to be on the untouchables' lane at this time of the night. How would he reach where Sivagami wanted him to be?

The boy scratched his head and racked his brain. He thought of dashing past when the sentries were not looking. He thought of jumping into the river and swimming up to the point, and then remembered that he did not know how to swim. He had to go. He had to take the chance. He walked through the bushes and reached near the sentry post. He was about to step out when he heard the sound of an approaching chariot.

Gundu Ramu ducked again and peered out. A chariot was heading towards the palace at great speed. As it neared, he saw two men sitting on the driver's seat. The sentries stood in the middle of the road and crossed their spears, barring the way. The chariot did not slow down. Gundu Ramu was sure it was going to run over the two sentries and he closed his eyes in fear. Then he heard the whinnying sound of the horse and the screech and rattle of wheels as the chariot stopped a finger's length away from the sentries. Dust swirled around.

'Halt!' one of the sentries cried out.

'Can't a nobleman travel to the palace?' a voice cried from within, and the head of a dwarf popped out.

'Noblemen should use the royal highway. This road is for slaves and untouchables and they have been barred, swami,' the sentry said.

'Oh, no one likes to touch my Ranga and Thunga,' the dwarf laughed. 'They are untouchables and slaves.'

'Swami, please, we are only doing our duty,' the sentry said.

'Ranga and Thunga, just show the officers how dangerous it is to touch you,' the dwarf said.

Two giants jumped down from the chariot. The sentries held up their spears, but before they could thrust them, the giants had turned, jumped and, in one swift, synchronized motion, swirled and chopped off their heads with their swords. Gundu Ramu let out a cry and then quickly closed his mouth with his hands.

'What was that?' the dwarf asked.

The giants looked around. 'Must be some wild cat,' one of the giants said.

'Fine, don't waste time. I do not know what kind of stupidity Pattaraya has planned, but he should not say that it failed because of us. Hurry.'

Ranga and Thunga kicked the heads of the sentries into the water and walked towards the chariot.

'Will your father come to dispose of their bodies, sons of whores?' the dwarf said, and added, 'Idiots.' He spat on the road. The giants carried the bodies one by one and plunged them into the river.

'Are you going to come only after doing their death rites, bastards? Get in fast,' the dwarf said. The giants jumped into the chariot and it sped away.

Gundu Ramu let out an animal cry. He had pissed in his dhoti in fear. He started sobbing. He looked back at the forlorn road he had walked. Far away, Gauriparvat could be seen. He looked at the road where the musicians and the dwarf's chariot had gone. He gulped in fear. There was no choice between either direction. He bit his fingers, trying to control his sobs. He sat on his haunches in the middle of the road and saw blood shining in the moonlight. He screamed and ran a few steps. He sat down again and cried. A sense of helplessness washed over him. Even at ten, he was such a coward. *Good-for-nothing, fat, craven boy,* his own voice mocked him from inside.

Then he remembered that he had given his word to Sivagami. He could not disappoint his akka. He might be a coward, but he was a boy of his word. *If someone gives his word, he should keep it, even if it costs him his life*—his father's words came back to him. He stood up and wiped the tears off his plump cheeks with the back of his hands. Arjuna, Phalguna, Partha—he started reciting the ten names of the ancient warrior Arjuna. That was the mantra his father had taught him to keep away his fears. He started walking, constantly reciting the mantra, but his fear refused to die. *Such a coward, such a fool; but he would keep his word,* he said to himself, and started the mantra again as he dragged his fat body on his trembling legs through the deserted street.

THIRTY-SEVEN

Sivagami

Sivagami sat in the crowd, watching the performances of the artistes from a distance. She could feel the nervousness of Kamakshi, who was sitting near her on the sprawling palace lawns amid thousands of others. The classical performances were over and it was time for the folksongs and dances.

The Pulavars and Kurumas came in. They were storytellers. The Kurumas told tales of the ancients. There was a play on the epic Palnati war and also *Kattamaraju Kathalu* by the Komelu singers. Sivagami shifted in her seat and glanced at Revamma, who was watching the show gleefully. She appeared drunk. Sivagami hoped this was the case—it would help her slip by unnoticed.

Next was the puppet show. Leather puppets came alive as characters of the *Ramayana*. Hanuman burning Lanka made the crowds laugh, and the ten-headed puppet of the demon Ravana—majestic and grotesque—made little children in the front squeal in fear.

Then came the Hasya Geyu artistes, who sang humorous songs, some lewd, some philosophical. Sivagami saw that her friend was eagerly scanning the crowd. When Kamakshi caught Sivagami looking at her, she made a comment about how profound the songs were. It was clear to Sivagami that Kamakshi was trying to hide her nervousness. 'What is wrong with you?' she asked, looking straight ahead. 'Why are you so nervous about seeing him?'

'I am scared,' Kamakshi said, after a moment's silence. The voice of the singer soared, making conversation difficult.

'Oh, don't worry. Everyone is so involved with the performances. No one will notice you two if he is able to get inside the fort.'

'It is not only that—' Kamakshi hesitated.

Sivagami turned to her. Kamakshi said, 'They…they are planning something. I am scared.'

Drums rolled like thunder and horns blared in unison from the performance stage. Sivagami mulled over her friend's words. So, there was going to be an attack on the king tonight. That was the reason Shivappa was coming. She looked around and saw the number of guards and soldiers protecting the king. There was no way the Vaithalikas would be able to reach the maharaja. And how would they smuggle in their weapons? The mahapradhana himself was ensuring that every person entering was thoroughly checked. As much as she wished that the attack would happen tonight, she knew it was futile. Besides, she wanted to kill the maharaja herself. It would be a great disappointment if the king was killed by someone else.

'They won't even be able to get in. They will be stopped at the gate, Kamakshi. Just wait here. I will retrieve my book from Mahapradhana Skandadasa's home, throw it over the wall to Gundu Ramu, and be back before you know it. We will go out and then you can meet him outside,' Sivagami said.

Kamakshi nodded, half-convinced. 'I am scared for you too, Sivagami,' she said, grabbing her hand, 'shall I come with you?'

Sivagami did not want to take Kamakshi with her. She would only be an impediment. She laughed. 'But what if Shivappa manages to come in when we are away? Stay here, Kamakshi. I will be back in a trice.'

'Are you leaving now?' Kamakshi asked nervously.

Sivagami shook her head. She had to choose the right moment to slip away. Impatiently, she watched the performance on stage.

An elderly Hasya Geyu and his son were dancing around, drumming their udukkus. The son would ask a question, and the father would answer it.

Nanna, Nanna, why is the soldier so fat? So fat? So fat? Does he eat a pig every day?

No, son, no. Know that he has some special food and drink every day.

Nanna, Nanna, why is the nayaka so fat? So fat? So fat? Does he fry his mutton in ghee?

No, son, no. Know that he has some special food and drink every day.

Nanna, Nanna, why is the adhikari so big? So big? So big? Does he drink the Soma of gods?

No, son, no. Know that he has some special food and drink every day.

Nanna, Nanna, why is the karyakarta so rich? So rich? So rich? Does he eat sweets dipped in honey?

No, son, no. Know that he has some special food and drink every day.
Nanna, Nanna, why is the bhoomipathi so strong? So strong? So strong? Is it because he eats gold?
No, son, no. Know that he has some special food and drink every day.
Oh, Nanna, Nanna, why is the pradhana so wise, so wise, so wise? And why is the maharaja so great, so great, so great? Is it because he too eats some special food?

There was a stunned silence. Everyone looked at the maharaja of Mahishmathi. The queen arched her eyebrow and, with a smile of disdain, turned to the king. Her eyes challenged him to punish the impudent singer, but there was no telling how her husband would react. Her father would have cut off the head of anyone who dared to criticize him. But her husband was unpredictable, and that exasperated her to no end. She watched him intently. Prince Mahadeva, who was sitting near his father, looked at the singers with interest. Behind the royals sat the retired mahapradhana, Parameswara. The king stared at the father-and-son duo and they cowered in fear. The maharaja grunted, signalling for them to continue.

The entire assemblage waited for the answer from the old man. The old man's voice was meek. He muttered something, but drowned out his own answer in a flurry of drumbeats. He bowed and started to leave, but the maharaja gestured for him to put his drum down. With shivering hands the singer did so. His son was sweating.

'Sing clearly,' the maharaja said.

The old man gulped and stood staring at his toes. Suddenly, a voice rose from the crowd, 'Because the maharaja eats a special food like all those in the government.'

Maharaja Somadeva stood up, angry.

The son sang in a soft voice, *'Nanna, Nanna, what is that special food you talk so much about? What is it that all the government eats?'*

The soldiers rushed from all sides to arrest them. The old man continued, looking down at his toes, *'Son, son, it is the blood of the peasant, the sweat of the weaver, the flesh of the artisan, the words of the poet, the trade of the trader. It is us they all eat and become fat, strong, rich, wise and noble.'*

For some time, the only sound that could be heard was the rustling of feet. A baby cried despite its mother's best attempts to quiet it down. Sivagami stood up with bated breath, pulling Kamakshi up with her.

Shocking the entire assemblage, the maharaja began to roar with laughter. 'Mad man trying to talk wise things,' Maharaja Somadeva said, and the soldiers who had come to arrest the father-and-son duo stopped in their tracks.

Maharaja Somadeva slapped his thighs and laughed again. Soon, taking his cue, the entire crowd was laughing. A few repeated the lines of the Hasya Geyus, and people started throwing coins at the father-son duo. The maharaja called them to the dais and they bowed deep to the monarch. He unloosened his diamond-studded anklet and dropped it into the open palms of the elder singer.

'Sing courageously. Sing without fear,' the maharaja said and the singer duo bowed again and again. The air reverberated with deafening slogans of 'Maharaja Somadeva Vijaya'. Sivagami watched the father-son duo walk down from the dais without showing their backs to the king. Sivagami could see how cleverly the maharaja had deflected the criticism and made it a joke to be laughed at. The enemy was formidable, she could see that. It would not be an easy task to get her revenge against such a sly ruler. He had the crowd eating from his hands.

The loud sounds of drums heralded the arrival of the Kula Purana narrators. They sang about the greatness of the Mahishmathi family. How goddess Gauri had given them the holy Gauriparvat. How the great ancestor of Somadeva had thrown away the yoke of Kadarimandalam's vassalage three hundred years ago, and how Maharaja Somadeva's grandfather, Paramabhattara, had conquered the Nishadas, and how Somadeva had brought the Kuntala to vassalage under Mahishmathi and subdued the Kalachuris. They spoke about the great wars that the ancestors of the Mahishmathi dynasty had fought, and about the valour of the princes. They were compared to Rama of Ayodhya and Arjuna the Pandava. In their generosity, they were compared to Karna; in scholarship, to Ravana. Sivagami could not stand it anymore. The bell tolled five. It was past midnight. Time to move.

When the singers started *Tirpu Kathalu*, the stories of judgement, she whispered to Kamakshi that she was leaving. Revamma was dozing a few feet away. Kamakshi requested her one last time to reconsider her decision, but Sivagami was adamant. She loosened her friend's grip, one finger at a time, from her wrist and slipped into the crowd. She did not notice Prince Mahadeva, who had been watching her, get down from the dais and follow her.

The crowd thinned as she walked away from the grounds. The clutter of offices in the south end appeared farther than they were in the dim light. There were sentries standing here and there, and she knew that someone or the other would question her presence in this part of the palace soon. She had her answer ready. She was going to the Antapura. She was a girl sent by Keki to entertain some officials. She was not sure whether they would buy it, but that was the only plausible lie she could think of.

As she had feared, there were a couple of sentries standing at the gate of the palace gardens, beyond which the buildings of the court officials stood. She walked up boldly, as if she had done this a hundred times. They stopped her and she gave them a dazzling smile.

'Where are you going?' they asked.

'Someone has called me,' she said, coyly. She hoped that, in the dim light, they would not see her hands trembling.

'Who? Who has called you?' they asked. She racked her brain for an answer. Whose name should she take?

'Sivagami?'

Shocked, she turned and found herself facing Prince Mahadeva. The sentries bowed, 'We are sorry, Your Highness. We did not know it was you,' they said, moving their spears to make way.

Mahadeva looked embarrassed. Sivagami walked past the guards into the garden. She could hear him following. She cursed her luck. The last thing she wanted was a chat with this stupid lovestruck prince.

'Sivagami,' Prince Mahadeva called. She shuddered at the tremor in his voice. He ran up beside her and stood facing her. Moonlight cast a glow on his hair and he looked as handsome as a gandharva. The breeze carried the fragrance of parijata. She was getting desperate. She knew what was coming, and, meanwhile, poor Gundu Ramu would be waiting outside. The prince was blabbering something, but she barely listened. Her mind was on retrieving the book. He grabbed her hand and looked intently into her eyes. She tried to wriggle away, but he held on firmly.

'Please, please, Sivagami... I...I...' Prince Mahadeva gulped. 'Will you marry me?' he asked finally, gathering courage. For a moment, she could not believe what she had heard. Then the irony of everything struck her. Here she was, determined to take revenge for her father's killing and the murderer's son wanted to marry her. *He thinks I would want to be a bride in the royal family I have vowed to wipe off the face of the earth.* She started laughing though she knew she was hurting him.

'Sivagami, please...' he pleaded.

But she only laughed more. His hand left hers. Without a word, he turned on his heels and, like a chastised dog, he walked away. She stood watching him with rising pity and contempt. She had no time to waste on such idiots. *One day, I will kill you and your entire family*, she whispered. She walked towards Skandadasa's home. It was fortunate for her that he had decided to stay on in his old house. She had removed the latch of a window in the rear during her last visit. She was planning to get in through there. Surprisingly, there were no sentries around. She skirted the house and went to the rear side. The broken window had still not been fixed. She pulled it open and entered. Now she had to just find the book and run. This was going to be easier than she had thought. She started searching the drawer of the table in which she had seen him put her book.

Then she froze. What was that noise outside?

THIRTY-EIGHT

Ally

Ally regained consciousness when a pail of water was splashed on her face. Pain shot up from her feet first and she cried aloud.

'The bitch has woken up,' she heard someone say. It took her a moment to regain her moorings. Where was she? Images of being chased by a pack of dogs flashed through her mind. Another pail of water hit her face and it traced its path past various wounds on her body.

'They have gone to bring Bhoomipathi Guha,' said someone else. 'They will be here soon.'

Suddenly, everything came back in a rush. She tried to run but was yanked back by the ropes that bound her. She realized that she was tied to a pole. She looked around, trying to take in the scene. A rough hand caught her chin and turned her face. She was looking at a man who was leering at her.

'Did you fall from the sky?' he asked. A few of his companions sniggered. Ally did not reply. She was trying to assess the situation. She gritted her teeth as pain shot up her body again.

The man began to grope her breasts and there was nothing she could do as her hands were tied behind the pole. 'I am the woman of your bhoomipathi. If you still want to lay your hands—' she smiled at him through the locks of hair that fell on her face. He pulled his hand away as if he had touched fire.

'Set me free or you will regret it. My man will not be pleased if he sees you have treated his beloved like this,' Ally said, pushing her luck.

'Ha, the bhoomipathi has more concubines than this island has crows. Let him free you if he wants. It is none of Ketaka's business. But until he comes, bitch, you will remain tied up,' Ketaka said. As he stepped away, he shouted at his men to resume their work.

Ally surveyed the place. There was that gigantic statue of Kali, the fearsome form of Amma Gauri that she had seen before her fall. She was tied near it, in front of a row of huts where perhaps Ketaka and the other slaves lived. The statue towered over everything, rising more than sixty feet high and resting on a gigantic chariot with wooden wheels. *Combined, it must be more like hundred feet,* thought Ally. A zigzag-shaped ramp ran from the bottom of the hillock to the crown of the statue. Hundreds of children were dragging carts up the ramp, as supervisors urged them on with abuse and lashes. The boys looked like ants carrying food up their anthill. When they reached the top, they emptied their carts into the head of the statue and the contents rattled into the wooden idol with a lot of clatter. Hundreds of torches burnt on either side of the ramp.

Ingenious, thought Ally. That was how they were transporting the Gaurikanta into the city. Every Mahamakam, a Kali statue from the forest dwellers reached Mahishmathi city with great fanfare in a raft led by a bhoomipathi. The statue was paraded through the streets in a wooden chariot drawn by thousands of fervent devotees amidst the chanting of mantras. People would throw their meagre savings, some even threw their gold or silver ornaments, as Amma Kali rode through the streets. The famous Gauri Jatra. For nine days Mahishmathi would celebrate the coming of Amma Gauri into their city, and on the evening of the ninth day, the statue would be immersed in the river.

They must have some way to retrieve the stones once the statue was thrown into the river. Perhaps an underground passage from the river bottom that led to a place where they could safely get the stones out. Perhaps they got the stones once the tide changed. It would only be a case of recovering the statue in the night from the marshy shore during low tide. Difficult, but not an impossible task.

However distasteful the thought was, Ally was slowly coming to the realization that the king knew what was happening. Maybe he was not directly involved, but he did have the powers to stop the atrocities if he wanted. He was turning a blind eye. Or was he so naïve that the corrupt officials were able to manipulate him easily? That made him an incompetent ruler.

The ingenuity of the scheme angered her the most. Whether the king was directly involved or not, the government got the people to pay for the entire operation, too. Religion, politics and business—everything was closely interlinked in Mahishmathi. Was there ever any other country like this in the world? Ally felt anger bubbling up. She may perhaps have only a few more moments to live. She would have to do something worthwhile, something her mentor Achi Nagamma would be proud of. She had to give a jolt to this evil system before she died. Her time was running out.

She looked around, trying to devise some plan. The statue stood on the chariot atop the highest point of the hill. The carpenters were giving it their final touches. What could she do? *Amma Gauri, show me the way,* she cried. Her eyes locked on the bottom end of the wooden wheels. Wedges! To stop the chariot from rolling down the hill. She wished she was free. She could have done something if only she had not fallen down and gotten caught. She felt tears coming to her eyes, but she willed them to stop. *This was not the time to panic, or cry, but to think*—the words came to her, as if Achi Nagamma was speaking to her.

It was then that she saw him. Kattappa! He was carrying a massive log on his shoulders, waiting in line with the other slaves. Her heart leapt with joy. To know that this man was alive was itself a good omen, a sign from Amma Gauri.

'Kattappa,' she called out. For a fleeting moment, she thought he had turned his head and seen her. But there was no response. He continued walking, taking the great weight of the log on his shoulders. If only she could talk to him, if only…She pressed her lips to control her sobs. Her last hope was walking away. Ally felt tired suddenly. As the feeling of defeat sank in, her wounds started throbbing. Would she get rabies from the bites? For a shuddering moment, she imagined the kind of death that would bring. No, Ally would not die like a dog. She shook her head and raised her face to Amma Gauri. *You are just a wooden statue, with a heart of stone,* she told her goddess.

'Devi.'

She turned, startled by the voice. Before her was Kattappa, on his knees. A guard was standing a few feet away, watching them. He asked Kattappa to hurry. Kattappa had a cup of water in his hand. He rose and brought the cup to her lips. She drank gratefully.

Though the water was over, she continued to act like she was drinking. She whispered, 'Kattappa, can you do something for me?'

The slave looked fearfully at the guard. The guard cried that he did not have all the time in the world.

'Listen, don't look. Just listen. There are two wedges under the front wheels of that chariot. Can you dislodge them?'

For a moment there was no reply. 'It is all right, if you don't want to do it. It may not move and you will lose your life,' Ally whispered again, suppressing the wave of helplessness that washed over her.

'Devi,' the slave whispered back, 'you saved my life. I shall remain your slave until you die or you free me. My life is nothing. I shall do it if that is what you command.'

Ally took a deep breath. Was she sending the poor slave to his death? Let Amma Gauri judge me, she whispered. 'Do it,' the words were out of her mouth and now there was no going back. She heard a whip lashing the slave's back. The guard was livid because Kattappa was taking too much time. The slave did not even blink. He stared at Ally and nodded his head with a smile. Another lash licked his back. In a swift moment, Kattappa caught the whip that was curling in the air to hit him for the third time. He yanked it, catching the guard off balance. The guard fell on the ground.

Ally watched with bated breath as Kattappa ran towards the statue. When she looked towards the other side of the ground, she gasped in horror. Jeemotha, Akkunda and Guha were entering through the gate. They were rushing towards her, led by Ketaka.

'Kattappa, hurry,' she screamed at the top of her voice.

Kattappa grabbed a massive hammer from the work bench of a carpenter and ran up the hillock. The guards were shouting and screaming, but Ally saw him climbing the ramp, two steps at a time. He still had a limp, but that did not slow him down. He reached the base of the chariot and smashed the wedge that held the wheel in place into smithereens. Arrows were being shot at him by the guards, and spears thrown, but he rolled away and was back on his feet in the blink of an eye. He smashed the second wedge under the other wheel. Ally braced for the chariot to roll down. Nothing happened. Her shoulders slumped. Jeemotha was running towards her, and she could now clearly make out the rage on his face.

'Oh god, oh god,' she prayed. The chariot groaned and creaked, but only tottered at the edge of the slope. Guards were running up to Kattappa now, and the slave stood helpless for a moment. Lost, everything was lost; Ally bit her lips. Her plan had failed.

Then she saw Kattappa putting his massive shoulders to a wheel and pushing it. An arrow lodged in his arm and blood spurted, but the slave continued to put his entire strength into pushing the wheel forward. The wooden ramp began to groan and the boys and men on it started screaming. They hurried to scramble down as the ramp bent and twisted. The chariot was shaking, but had not moved an inch. Even from a distance, she could see Kattappa's veins stretching over his bulging muscles. The guards had reached him now.

Did she hear a noise? Ally blinked and looked again. The chariot swayed at the edge. Then with a mighty, creaking noise, the ramp gave way first. The guards who were running up stopped in their tracks. Their weapons dropped with a clang. The torches on the ramp fell down, flared high and were extinguished. The first thud was dull. The ramp broke into splinters, sending wood pieces spiralling in the air. Then the juggernaut started rolling down the hill, gathering momentum with every second.

The guards jumped to either side as it rolled on, but a few were not so lucky and the wheels ran over them. There was pandemonium everywhere as men scrambled to get out of its bludgeoning path. Kali, the goddess of destruction, was marching down at great speed. Guards desperately tried to stop it, throwing anything they could grab and flinging it under the wheels. The chariot did not even slow down; it shattered whatever came under its wheel and bulldozed its path downhill.

Ally saw Jeemotha diving away from the path of the juggernaut and standing up dazed. His face and expression were priceless. He stood transfixed, staring at Kattappa, as the chariot crushed a trail of destruction behind his back. She could see he regretted not having known the real worth of Kattappa. He would not have sold him so cheap. For Ally, nothing could have made for a better revenge.

Ally let out a cry of celebration as Kattappa ran towards her. 'Kattappa, you are free as the wind. Free as the wind, free as the wind. I free you. Go wherever you want,' she cried at the top of her voice.

The slave bowed before her, and with one strike of his hammer, broke her rope. She was free. He touched her feet for a fleeting moment, but before she could thank him, he had taken off. She watched the chariot carrying Goddess Kali smashing the wooden wall at the far end. The chariot rolled on and she could guess what lay beyond the wall. The chariot was too big to fall into the narrow gorge. Instead, it toppled over, smashing the statue and the chariot into pieces. She could see many stones spinning and landing everywhere. Through the rupture in the wall, a few child workers ran away into the jungle. The stones that landed inside the wall caught the light of torches and started throbbing with a ghostly blue light. Ally saw Kattappa vanish through the breach in the wall.

Ally had destroyed the fruit of months of preparation. It would not be an easy task to get all the stones back and it would take several days to make another statue. She felt proud: for the damage she had caused, but much more so for Kattappa. By freeing him, Ally felt she had done something noble, something divine. Ally laughed through her tears and dried her eyes. She felt happy and alive. She turned to see where Jeemotha was but could not spot him anywhere. Time to escape, she thought.

She turned, and was face-to-face with Jeemotha. For a moment, she was taken aback and her hand flew to her mouth to stifle her scream. Then she started laughing, clapping her hands together.

'You were using Vajrayudha to cut vegetables. Fool, you used him to fish for pearls, and see what he is capable of. I will die laughing,' she said with scorn.

'No, bitch, you will not die laughing,' Jeemotha said, as he unsheathed his dagger.

THIRTY-NINE

Brihannala

Though the bell had tolled five times, people were still flowing into the fort from the royal highway. Inside, performances were going on before the king and the nobles. Brihannala walked to the gate through which lower castes and untouchables were being let in. When she reached the gate, her heart sank. What was Skandadasa doing here? Brihannala waited near the fort gate, nervously biting her nails.

Drums boomed from the palace courtyard. Outside the untouchables' gate, many tribal artistes who were going to perform once the classical artistes had finished were waiting excitedly. Several had already assembled at the fort gate the previous night. Some had come a couple of days ago and slept in the open ground that sloped from the gate to the river. The road for untouchables and slaves had been closed by evening and only those who had reached the venue before that could make it inside.

A performing monkey came near Brihannala and extended its cupped palm for money or food. She shoved it away with her leg and the Kurava who had the monkey on a leash cursed her and walked away.

Brihannala's eyes scanned the crowd waiting to get in. There was no trace of them in the crowd. Skandadasa was still standing at the gate, supervising the security arrangements. Soldiers were checking each of the entrants thoroughly. Any weapon found on anyone was confiscated by the guards. Even kitchen knives, carpenter's tools or small knives used to cut betel nut were taken away, ignoring the protests of people that those were their work tools. Skandadasa was not allowing any exception. Brihannala wiped sweat from her face and looked back. The mahapradhana was supposed to be by the side of the maharaja, enjoying the classical music concert. Why was he standing in the dust and heat, checking the unwashed and unclean? This man was turning out to be a real pain in the neck. At the far end of the sprawling palace grounds, on the elevated dais, she could see the maharaja with his queen. Why were they late? Had something happened to them? Brihannala knotted and unknotted the pallu of her sari.

A man came with a dancing bear but was stopped at the gate. An argument broke out. The man claimed he had been bringing the bear for the last two Mahamakams, and before that his father had brought the bear's father in previous Mahamakams. No one had stopped him or his father or his grandfather before that. The bear sat on its buttocks and scratched behind its ears.

Skandadasa ordered the man to tie the bear by the side of the gate and go in if he wanted. The bear could not be allowed in. The man cried that he would complain to the mahapradhana who belonged to his own caste. Some people in the jostling crowd sniggered. The soldiers suppressed their laughter with difficulty. Brihannala saw the mahapradhana blush a dark red in the light of the burning torches. It was evident that the bear dancer had not recognized Skandadasa. The mahapradhana ordered him to move out of the line or go in after tying the bear outside. Mumbling curses, the bear dancer went to do as he was bidden. He walked a few feet, then came back and sat on his haunches near his bear. He did not want to leave his bear alone. He sat caressing the bear's smooth hair, whispering sweet things to it, and the beast licked his hand. Soon it was sleeping on its paws.

There they were! Brihannala saw them at the back of the crowd. They were drumming hard and a few of them were dancing. She moved towards the gate. Skandadasa was supervising the checking of each and every entrant. The drummers were nearing the gate. Brihannala clasped her hands together to hide her nervousness. She saw that some of the men looked awkward, and their anxiousness could be seen on their faces. She fought her way to go outside and reached the drummers. She started dancing to the beat.

'You are late,' she whispered as she swirled around Bhutaraya.

'As if you have made the path clear. What is that man doing here?' Bhutaraya hissed back.

She swirled round and round like one possessed. Her skirt ballooned and the diamond-shaped mirrors in them caught the light of the flaming torches. The drummers moved near her and started a frenzied beat. The crowd parted to watch the famed court artisan dancing on the streets. Other drummers joined in, beating their instruments to the rhythm.

She danced near Skandadasa, but the mahapradhana stood unfazed. The drummers were about to enter the gate, when the mahapradhana threw out his hand.

'Check their drums,' the mahapradhana said to his guards.

'Swami,' Bhutaraya bowed low, careful not to show his face. He bent down to touch the mahapradhana's feet. 'This is our livelihood, swami. We came thinking we will get gifts from the maharaja. Allow us in, swami. I beg you. Inside of the drum is like inside the head of poor people like us, swami. They would be empty, swami.'

'Open your drums and show us if they're empty. It is just a security check. You can go in if the drum is hollow as you say,' Skandadasa said.

'They are sacred to us. One should never open them except on the auspicious day of Vijayadashmi,' Bhutaraya said in a reverential tone.

Skandadasa clucked his tongue and grabbed Bhutaraya's drum.

'Swami, swami, I am an untouchable, swami. Do not get polluted by touching my hands or drums,' Bhutaraya cried.

'I am also an untouchable. The son of a mere bear dancer who was lucky to become the mahapradhana. There is no pollution for me. Now, open the drums,' he said, snatching the instrument from Bhutaraya.

Brihannala saw Shivappa's hand gripping his drumstick. He would pierce the drum head with it and pull out his urumi if she waited any longer. She moved swiftly to the bear dancer and kicked him. 'Now,' she said. The bear dancer blinked at her and then nodded his head. He untied the bear and gave it a kick. The bear gave out a blood-curdling roar, and everyone froze. The bear dancer pricked the animal with a small knife between its back paws and the bear charged towards the gate. Brihannala dropped a pouch of coins into his extended hand and he quickly slipped it into his waist-band.

People ran screaming as the beast stood on its hind legs to its full height and gave another roar. The bear went past Skandadasa, knocking him down, and the drum rolled away from his hands. The bear entered the fort and started running through the crowd. People panicked; some fell down and were trampled. The bear chased and mauled a few. It ran here and there, starting a stampede. Skandadasa tried to control the crowd. He shouted instructions to calm people down and ordered his soldiers to catch the bear.

The drummers slipped into the fort, taking cover under the pandemonium. Brihannala followed, her eyes sparkling with amusement as she watched the bear running amidst the screaming crowd. She looked at the stage where the maharaja was sitting. It was far off and a huge crowd separated her and the king. The drummers had merged with the crowd. Now it would be impossible to identify them. Brihannala whispered with glee, 'Mother, I have achieved what you could not even dream of.'

FORTY

Kamakshi

Kamakshi was tense after Sivagami left her, but worry about her friend had given way to anticipation of meeting Shivappa. How he would find her, she had no clue. She kept scanning the crowd to catch a glimpse of him.

A group of men were performing magic tricks. A snake charmer came with a basket and a pungi. He opened the basket near the dais and started playing his been. A rope started rising up, dancing, twisting and coiling like a cobra. It went higher and higher as the music increased in frenzy. The snake charmer danced around it, playing the pungi with vigour. It was haunting music and it woke up hidden fears in Kamakshi's mind. It went on and on, driving her mad. The rope had risen more than thirty feet, and yet it danced to the music. The audience was cheering the trick.

The snake charmer called his ten-year-old son. He asked the boy to climb up the rope which, according to him, had stretched up to heaven. Get me the vajra of Indra, the snake charmer demanded of his son. The boy started climbing up as his father resumed playing his been. The rope wriggled as if to shake the boy off, and the audience screamed in delight. The boy held on and clambered up quickly. Soon he vanished into thin air. The snake charmer started shouting at the boy, asking why he was taking so much time, and from up above the boy said he was not going to return, he was going to marry Rambha and live in heaven. This drew laughter from the crowd.

Despite herself, Kamakshi became engrossed in the magic rope trick, but a loud noise at the fort gate broke the spell. A few people craned their necks to see the cause of the disturbance. Some were shouting 'Bear, bear,' but that did not make any sense. The disturbance soon subsided. Kamakshi tried to enjoy the performance, but her thoughts went again to Shivappa. It was already past midnight. He had promised he would come. Should she go and seek him out? She tried to get up but was pulled down by a girl sitting behind her. Reluctantly, she sat back down to watch the trick.

The snake charmer warned Indra to send his son and Indra's laughter from the sky filled the ground. Indra said he was going to adopt his son. It was a great trick of ventriloquism. The man made it appear as if the voice was coming from the sky. The snake charmer pretended to get angry and asked what he would do in his old age, and pat came the reply from heaven—die young. The audience exploded with laughter. The snake charmer danced around, abusing Indra and his son, and said to the audience that he was going to teach them a lesson. He opened his mouth and drew a four-foot sword from his mouth, making the audience applaud with wonder. He started climbing the rope and soon he also vanished into the darkness. Loud sounds of battle came from the sky. Swords clanged; there were screams and yells and shouts; and suddenly limbs and blood started falling everywhere. Severed hands, heads, fingers, ears, noses, legs—the audience screamed in terror. They scattered as severed body parts fell amidst them.

Kamakshi also moved from where she had been sitting. She looked around and a thrill passed through her. Shivappa. She had seen him. He was carrying a drum. She tried to call out to him, but her voice was drowned out in the cheers of the audience. The crowd shifted then, and she could no longer see him. She started weaving her way through the sea of people. Behind her, the snake charmer climbed down the rope, holding a sword dripping with blood. He started picking up limbs, checking each piece to see whether any belonged to his son. He found a few and mumbled a few mantras. He heaped them together, uncoiled his turban, and placed it over the pile. He invoked Yama and Brahma, Vishnu and Shiva, and when he removed the turban, the boy came out smiling. The audience erupted with thunderous applause.

Kamakshi had now moved far from where she had been sitting and had left the crowd behind. She had spotted Shivappa again, moving towards the palace, through the ranks of slaves and untouchables who stood at a distance from the stage. He was skirting the wall, keeping himself in the shadows. Sometimes she got a glimpse of him, sometimes she despaired that he had vanished.

Kamakshi pushed her way through the slaves, ignoring the look of surprise in their eyes. Finally she saw him, leaning against a wall, intently watching the king. She reached him and touched his shoulder. She expected him to sweep her into his arms and blushed thinking about the touch of his lips on hers.

He turned, but there was no love in his eyes. His eyes burned with anger when he saw who it was and he hissed, 'What the hell are you doing here?'

'You…you told—' Kamakshi's eyes filled up. *He hates me,* she thought pressing her lips together, holding back her sobs. With trembling hands she tried to touch him, 'Shiva—'

'Get lost. Don't come near me,' he said. He was not even looking at her. He was watching the king. It was not for this that she had spent every moment pining for him. She turned on her heels, her skirt swirling, and started walking back.

She half expected him to call her back, say it was just a prank. She would have never guessed he could be so heartless, so cruel.

She turned for one last time and their eyes met. His eyes were blank, but she felt they were telling her something. Perhaps there was some explanation for his strange behaviour. But then he looked away.

She ran through the mass of people, uncaring about the tears streaming down her cheeks. She hated her life. She hated Shivappa. She started to head away from the crowds. She wanted to be alone. She wanted to cry her heart out. She wanted to talk to Sivagami, cry on her shoulders. Sivagami! She had forgotten about her. Why had she not come back? It was Amma Gauri's punishment for leaving her friend alone and waiting for a man she thought had loved her. She had to find Sivagami.

Kamakshi walked towards the offices. The crowd thinned as she moved. The sound of dance performances faded and the shadows thickened as she headed away from the main grounds. The torches had died a long time ago. She turned to the garden. A sentry was dozing, leaning on his lance. She tiptoed past him, trying to suppress her apprehension and misgivings. Why should she care anymore what happened to her, she thought.

She continued walking and paused when she heard a soft rustle. It was foggy and dark. Early morning mist was rolling from the river and visibility was shrinking. She resumed walking and heard the rustle again. Taking a deep breath, she turned. Nothing. Only the long shadow of the inner fort wall slanting towards the lawn. A singer was singing his heart out. A song about unrequited love. Kamakshi sighed and turned. An arm shot out from the shadows and grabbed her neck. She wanted to scream, but the hand held her tight. She struggled to see who was holding her. Her scream died in her throat when she saw who it was.

Keki's grinning face looked like a spectre. The eunuch pouted her lips and blew a kiss with her other hand. Slowly, she started squeezing Kamakshi's neck.

FORTY-ONE

Mahadeva

Mahadeva was sitting alone by the river in his usual place. He was thankful the madman Bhairava was not around. He wanted to be alone. Above him, countless stars blinked in unison, as if mocking him. The river Mahishi flowed by and the waves lapping on the ghat steps sounded as if the river too was laughing at his plight. He had rehearsed the words he had said to Sivagami tonight, a hundred times before in his mind. From the day he had seen her for the first time, he had not thought about anything else. He often conducted conversations with Sivagami in his mind. He had imagined her walking beside him, their hands clasped together, and talking sweet nothings.

Every time he visited the orphanage, he had found an excuse to talk to her. With a pang, he realized that, each time, Sivagami had been indifferent to his advances. Yet he had been blind. He was a fool to think that a beautiful girl like Sivagami would love him. Such things happened only in stupid songs and old fables.

She loathed him. Her laughter still rung in his ears. She could have at least been more kind. She could have lied to him that she had another lover. He would have continued to love her of course, but he would have never disturbed her again. She had been cruel to him. No, she had not, he corrected himself. He had asked for something he did not deserve. That is how a strong-willed girl should react to a fool who does not know his place.

The signs of her dislike had always stared him in the face. He had been fooling himself with convenient justifications for her behaviour. He had assumed her reluctance to talk was shyness, and that had made him love her more. He felt like weeping. He was no great warrior. He was a good-for-nothing person, just like his mother always told him. Maybe she had heard the stories about his cowardice; she knew how clumsy he was with arms, how he preferred to sit in the garden and dream. He was no warrior like Bijjala. His brother had a great temper, but was that not the mark of a warrior? In front of him, men trembled with fear. In front of Mahadeva, they feigned respect but he knew they were probably laughing behind his back. No wonder Sivagami had laughed in his face. At least she had been nice enough not to laugh behind his back. He loved her for her frankness. He loved her for everything. Every moment, every breath. He laughed at the thought, and the laughter soon dissolved into sobs. He loathed himself for crying like a girl, but there was no one to watch, no one to see his plight, and no one to care. He let his tears flow freely. Would they even miss him if he vanished into the welcoming bosom of the river Mahishi? Would Sivagami care? Or would she stand at the shore and laugh?

The breeze caressed his body, as if to soothe him. The river invited him with a thousand arms: Come, come and hug me. He took a tentative step and waves rushed to embrace his ankles. Another step and they reached up to his knees, jumping, eager to climb up his body. One step more…

'Swami…'

A voice from the darkness. He froze in fear.

'Who is that?' he called, squinting his eyes at the darkness. A figure moved from the bushes by the river.

'It is me, your brother's slave, Your Highness. Kattappa.'

Kattappa! Was he not dead? A ghost? Mahadeva screamed. He lost his balance and fell into the water. Kattappa pulled him up and fell at Mahadeva's feet, apologizing profusely to the embarrassed prince. Mahadeva felt helpless and angry at the intrusion. He did not want to talk to any slave. He wanted to die. But what the slave said grabbed his attention.

'Your Highness, there is grave danger to the maharaja and Mahishmathi. Vaithalikas may attack any time during Mahamakam. The maharaja has to be warned, but I cannot get past the sentries. They would kill me for I am someone who is thought to have deserted.'

'How do you know about the attack?'

Kattappa quickly narrated to the prince how he had gone in search of his brother, and learnt of the Vaithalikas' plans.

'I am ashamed to say that my own brother is the biggest traitor. Next time I see him, I will kill him,' Kattappa said.

Mahadeva was speechless. He was moved by the dedication of the slave. He had come back, risking his life, to save Mahishmathi. If what the slave said was true, he had to inform his father. The fort had to be secured.

'Come with me,' the prince said, grabbing the slave's wrist.

He started running to the opening of his secret path. He led Kattappa into it, and when they had emerged out of the well and reached inside the fort, Kattappa started towards Bijjala's chambers.

'Where are you going?' Mahadeva asked.

'Let me go to my master,' the slave pleaded.

'Your master?'

'Yes, His Highness Prince Bijjala.'

'You still consider him your master?'

'Until I am freed by him or killed, I shall remain his slave.'

His master, who had treated him no better than a dog. Mahadeva shrugged and hurried to find his father or someone responsible. Someone who could thwart the Vaithalikas' attack.

FORTY-TWO

Keki

Keki carried the present to Bijjala's chambers. The prince had gone to tell Skandadasa to return to his rooms, and she wanted to keep his gift ready for him.

The sleepy guard at the palace wing in which Bijjala's chambers were housed waved her in. She was the eunuch from Kalika's den, and the guards were familiar with her face and her methods. He took the usual bribe and let her pass. She walked through the dimly lit corridor, suppressing her fear. Men never frightened her, and she was confident of her ability to talk her way out of any difficult situation. But an old palace like Mahishmathi scared her, especially when she was alone and in the dark. She loved bright lights, exotic perfumes and all the good things in life. Dark and damp palaces where rats scurried around were not her choice of a night outing. But this was her promise to the prince. In her profession, a promise well kept was an investment well made for the future. And she had given him her word that she would gift him something unsullied, pure and virginal. She had known Kamakshi would come for the celebrations and had racked her brains for a foolproof plan to get the girl into Bijjala's chamber. Fortunately for her, the deer had walked into the lion's den. Catching her so easily was luck beyond her wildest dreams.

As she had advised, the prince had removed his guards who normally stood sentry at the doors to his chambers. She fished out the key Bijjala had given her from her breast-cloth and turned the lock. The faint light from a lamp placed by the huge bed did not do much to diminish the darkness. Keki gently placed Bijjala's present on the soft bed. She stood for a minute, admiring the beauty. The prince was going to love this.

Keki sighed, adjusted the pillow under Kamakshi's head, and arranged her in a sensuous pose. She took out a small pot of perfume from her waist-chain. There would be extra reward for this perfume from Bijjala, Keki smiled, as she smelled its exotic fragrance. She dabbed some perfume all over Kamakshi's body. The girl stirred. She would soon gain consciousness and find a prince in her bed. How fortunate! Keki untied the knot of Kamakshi's breast-cloth but did not expose her breasts completely. She admired her art from various angles. Keki took the whip from the wall and applied perfume on it. She knew what Bijjala liked, and she prided herself on giving the best service to her clients. She placed the whip on the bed near Kamakshi.

Keki paused at the door one last time, appreciating the scene she had laid out for the prince, and then gently closed it behind her. She heard footsteps while she was locking the door. A shiver passed down her spine. Someone was coming. She stared into the darkness. The footsteps paused and then resumed. A spectre floated from the darkness and Keki's mouth gaped open.

That slave who had died—Kattappa.

Keki was terrified. All her fears were coming true. Old palaces were the hunting grounds of ghosts, she knew it. She started running. From behind, she could hear the ghost of the slave calling out to her.

She ran for her life.

FORTY-THREE

Kattappa

Kattappa had reached the wing of the palace where Bijjala's chambers were located after jumping over two inner walls. He waited on the veranda on the ground floor for some time, near the stairs that led to the first floor where the prince had his private chambers, puja room and game room. He was gathering his courage to face the prince. He paced the empty courtyard, wondering why there were no guards. Had the prince shifted his sleeping quarters? Suddenly, he thought he heard a noise from the chamber above. Maybe the prince was in his room, he thought. He ran up. As he approached his master's door, he thought he glimpsed a figure slinking away, around the corner. He ran behind the figure, calling out to it, but when he reached the end of the passage, it had disappeared.

He returned to the door of the chambers. It was locked. His master was probably at the festival. He considered going in search of the prince, but it would be too risky—he might get caught, and would then be in no position to serve his master when he needed him the most. It was already late and Bijjala would come back soon to retire. He would fall at his feet and ask for pardon. He would take whatever punishment his master chose to give him. And he would never leave his side. He would wait outside while his master slept, guarding his precious life. No Vaithalika would ever harm his master.

Kattappa sat on the doormat and waited for his master to return. An uncomfortable memory cropped up. *A good place for a dog.* Shivappa's words. He had no use for such thoughts. He tried to suppress it, but like undigested food it kept coming up. With rising anger, Kattappa realized that the greatest crime Shivappa had committed was not treason. It was shattering Kattappa's innocence. Kattappa vowed he would not think like his wayward brother. He was his father's son, a proud slave of the Mahishmathi royals. He would live and die for them. His father used to say, if it was a choice between one's father and the king, a good slave would choose the king and slay the father. That was his dharma.

Kattappa waited.

FORTY-FOUR

Skandadasa

Skandadasa's throat had grown hoarse from shouting. It had taken some time to calm the bear and bring the mob under control. He was relieved that the disturbance had not spread to the front of the crowd. It would have been embarrassing to face the king had it disturbed his enjoyment of the performances.

Soldiers dragged the bear, tied in ropes, to the mahapradhana. Behind the animal came the bear dancer, struggling to escape the grip of two guards who were holding him.

'Shall I?' One of the guards pressed his sword to the neck of the bear. A slight movement of his fingers would ensure the death of the beast and its owner. Skandadasa looked at the beast. Its eyes did not speak of cruelty to him. He went near it and the bear looked at him with pitiful eyes. His soldiers were watching him. He could hear them whisper to each other. They were expecting him to kill the beast. If he let it live, they would attribute it to his caste. That would become another joke in town. He sat near the gigantic bear and extended his hand. The bear sniffed it for a moment and licked it. He let it do so for a while and then, with his other hand, he patted its back. It was such a mild creature. What had provoked it? He was running his hands through the thick black hair of the bear when his fingers touched something sticky. He rubbed his fingers together and smelled his hand. The smell of blood hit him. The bear had been wounded. Someone had purposefully stabbed it. It struck him like a thunderbolt. Where were the drummers? The bear was a diversion. He had been tricked.

'Hurry. Search the crowd. Apprehend any drummer and bring him to me.'

The guard who had placed his sword at the bear's neck raised it to strike the beast.

'No, don't harm it. Ask the rajavaidya to dress its wounds. It has been hurt,' he said. Let the others laugh at him, he thought as he patted the bear once again, but why should he take the life of a dumb beast because of his insecurities. He had been mocked and laughed at behind his back throughout his life. One more incident was not going to make any difference. He watched the soldier take the bear away. He wished the beast would look back to acknowledge his kindness, but it tamely followed the soldier. He turned to the bear dancer, 'And you, swami, have a lot of questions to answer.'

Someone tapped Skandadasa's shoulder and he turned in irritation. 'Prince Bijjala,' he exclaimed and gave a curt bow as an afterthought.

'I have something important to talk about, Mahapradhana,' the prince said.

Skandadasa frowned. 'Prince, can we talk tomorrow? There is an important issue that I need to sort out.'

Bijjala folded his arms across his chest and stared at the mahapradhana. 'It is about Gauridhooli,' he said.

Skandadasa stared at Bijjala in shock. He looked around, afraid someone would have heard the word Gauridhooli. How did the prince know about it? It was only after being anointed as crown prince that he should have found out.

'Do you want to discuss it here, or should we go to your office?' Bijjala asked, glaring at the mahapradhana.

Skandadasa did not like the prince's tone. Did the prince know about the Gauridhooli he had carried from the workshop? Was the prince aware of the workshop at all? Skandadasa felt angry and frustrated. He was at a loss for words.

'There has been a security breach, Prince Bijjala. Some drummers have got in without the mandatory check at the gates,' Skandadasa said.

'It shows your incompetency. But I think that is the least of your problems. You have much graver things to answer for,' Bijjala said.

Skandadasa glared at Bijjala. He clenched his fist. The prince had insulted him. He had questioned his integrity. Yet, he had to find out how much the prince knew about the workshop. 'Fine, Prince,' he said finally. 'Let us go to your chambers to discuss this. I am sure I can explain everything.'

Bijjala faltered. This was not what he had expected. This was not part of the plan. He was supposed to take Skandadasa to *his* office-cum-residence.

'No, we should go to your office,' Bijjala said.

Something in his tone made Skandadasa alert. 'Why? Your chambers are nearby. If you want to have a talk we can very well do it there,' Skandadasa said, knitting his brows in suspicion.

'No, we cannot go to my room.' Bijjala said.

'Why not, Prince?' the mahapradhana asked.

Bijjala racked his brains for a suitable reason. He felt annoyed that Pattaraya had not told him how to tackle a difficulty like this. To hell with Pattaraya. He would handle it his own way.

Bijjala's eyes flashed with anger. 'It is none of your business. When I order you somewhere, you better come. I am twenty-one now, and you have no right to question my orders. I do not care what the custom says. I care a damn if some old books say a mahapradhana is superior to the prince of Mahishmathi until he is declared crown prince. To hell with your protocol. In a few days I will be anointed crown prince anyway. And then you will have to pimp for me if I order you to do so. You arrogant bear dancer.'

Skandadasa controlled his rising anger. A crowd was gathering around them to watch the prince and the mahapradhana's spat. He was nervous the prince would foolishly talk about Gauridhooli.

'Fine, let us have it your way. We will go to my office,' he said with a sigh. He observed a smile that appeared like a flash on Bijjala's lips. It vanished in a blink, but it put Skandadasa on guard again. As he walked behind the prince, he tried to put the pieces of the puzzle together.

How had the prince found out about what he had done? *But why should I feel guilty anyway? I have done things only in good faith*...Who could have leaked the secret? The answer flashed in his mind. Roopaka! Everything suddenly clicked into place.

Roopaka must have helped the thief Nagayya run away from the workshop with the stones. Apart from the mahapradhana and the king, it was only Roopaka who had access to the slaves in the workshop and the world outside. He could have easily made contact with and tempted a foolish slave. He could have stolen the keys from the former mahapradhana, Parameswara, and used the opening on the roof to let Nagayya outside during low tide. The opening doubled as a flood valve, but only a few knew its actual purpose. That was the trap door through which the Gaurikanta stones were brought in. A few days after every Mahamakam, divers would fetch the Gaurikanta stones hidden inside the immersed Kali idol and bring them into the workshops. Until he had become the mahapradhana, even he was not aware of the existence of the workshop or what it was for.

Skandadasa felt frustrated at how flawed the security of the system was. When the workshop was designed, the river flowed over it during both high tide and low tide. Now the river had changed course, and the trap door was no longer in the middle of the river as it used to be. That was the first security lapse. The second was the fact that there was a key to open it from the outside, from the river bottom, as well as from the inside. He had got this corrected on his last visit to the workshop. He had made the slaves close the door permanently from the inside. Every Mahamakam they could break it open and reseal it. Now, to open the door, one would need a key for the outside, and simultaneously break the metal door from the inside. The only catch was the workshop could not be destroyed in case of an enemy attack. But who was going to attack Mahishmathi and conquer it? Mahishmathi had to fear its corrupt officials more than any external enemies. Skandadasa was willing to take the risk.

As they reached his office, Skandadasa started feeling uneasy. He had posted many dandakaras to guard the office complex, but the corridors looked deserted. Maybe they had sneaked out to see the performances. He vowed to give them a piece of his mind the next morning. But why were none of the torches lit? As he neared his home, he froze. Did he hear a door being shut?

The realization came rushing in—he was walking into a trap. That explained Bijjala's insistence that they should talk only in his chambers. Someone was inside his house. Someone was waiting for him. Someone who knew about his one mistake, that he had breached security protocol and carried the Gauridhooli outside the workshop. Perhaps blackmail was their aim. He had confirmation from his spies that Bijjala owed a lot of money to Kalika's inn, but he had destroyed the den. Maybe some of the pimps were harassing the prince and he was trying for an easy way out. Perhaps the prince and Roopaka were working together.

If they tried to blackmail him, he would trap them. He would pretend that he was scared and agree to their terms. Later, he would inform the maharaja and the two of them would be punished. That would put an end to the dreams of Prince Bijjala of being the crown prince of Mahishmathi. There were many precedents where a king chose a younger son over the elder. Mahadeva was innocent and gullible, but a naïve king with a good heart was better than a stupid king with a cruel mind. Mahadeva could be moulded. Skandadasa thought of being a mentor to the young prince Mahadeva and smiled. It would be like the way Parameswara had been for Maharaja Somadeva. No, he would do better than his predecessor. Unlike Parameswara, he came from a humble background. He would be able to teach Prince Mahadeva to be more empathetic and kind to the common people. With his inherent good nature, Mahadeva would become an ideal king, and history would hail Skandadasa—the humble bear dancer's son who rose to become mahapradhana—as the mentor of a great emperor. He would be Chanakya to a new Chandragupta. He smiled at the thought. He would teach these fools a lesson tonight.

He was a score feet away from the door of his home when the next thing clicked into place. The noise he had heard just moments before—the sound of something being shut—it could only be his drawer. Oh God! That made Skandadasa's blood freeze. Someone was searching for something inside his room. It could only be the Gauridhooli. Roopaka could easily blackmail him without stealing the Gauridhooli from his chamber. He just had to demand that the workshop slaves be called as witnesses. It was someone else in the room. Someone who knew about and wanted the Gauridhooli. It was no stupid hustle by a broken prince and a corrupt official. It was something more sinister than that. How foolish he had been, dreaming dreams of glory even as he was being hoaxed like someone who was still wet behind his ears.

Without a word, he began to backtrack. Bijjala became aware that Skandadasa was not beside him only after a few seconds. When he turned, Skandadasa was hurrying back the way they had come. Bijjala ran after him.

'Hey, hey, where are you going?'

'To the maharaja. Anything you want to discuss, we will discuss it before him.'

Bijjala grabbed Skandadasa's hand. 'You are not going anywhere.'

Skandadasa looked down at Bijjala's hand and calmly prised his fingers open. 'We will talk in the morning, Prince. Now I have a job to do.'

Suddenly, from the shadows, three men moved in front of him. 'We hate procrastinating important things, Skandadasa,' a fat figure said in a low voice.

'Pattaraya,' Skandadasa exclaimed.

'At your service, Mahapradhana.' Pattaraya moved forward and bowed with mock humility. Behind him stood Pratapa and Rudra Bhatta. Skandadasa turned back and saw Bijjala had taken out his sword and was running his index finger along its sharp edge.

Pattaraya put his plump hand on Skandadasa's shoulder and said, 'It would be better if we keep this between ourselves. What do you say Pratapa, Rudra Bhatta? Our mahapradhana is kind enough to invite us in. Swami, please open the door.'

Pattaraya and Pratapa led Skandadasa to the door. As the mahapradhana opened the door with his trembling hands, he wondered who had opened and shut his drawer a few moments back if these people had been waiting outside.

FORTY-FIVE

Shivappa

Shivappa had watched Kamakshi walking away and it had broken his heart. Initially, he was angry at her behaviour. Why couldn't she understand the importance of his mission? His life was in danger and all she cared about was a sweet reunion. But when she had left, guilt started growing and soon it consumed him.

He had not told her anything specific. He had asked her to be ready for the day and she might have come with great dreams. Dreams of living together, dreams of a family, dreams of living a free life and not that of a slave, in some faraway land, dreams of living as man and wife with many children playing around them. Their shared dreams, their wishes, their love for each other. Against their love, thoughts of revolution, the freedom of the Vaithailikas, Gauriparvat—everything looked silly, everything a coloured lie. Nothing was more precious than Kamakshi for Shivappa.

Shivappa began to follow her through the crowd. It was difficult, and many times he lost sight of her. Then he saw her entering the garden path and sneaking past the dozing sentry. At the far end of the garden was the office complex that housed the residences of many high officials, but they would be closed at this time. He stood frozen, worried that he was far away from where he was supposed to be as per Bhutaraya's plan.

Shivappa knew the bell would toll six any moment. That was the time that had been decided for the coup to start. By the next bell, they were supposed to weave their way in stealth towards the king, but Shivappa was moving in the opposite direction. The drum he was carrying felt heavy on his shoulders. The urumi sword lay coiled like a snake under the drum head. He had only to whip it out and wave it and his men would rush from all sides to the dais to cut off the head of Maharaja Somadeva. Instead, he was walking in search of his lover. He felt horrible for betraying his cause. But then, he told himself, he was just another cog in the great wheel of revolution. An insignificant speck. They would manage without him. But his Kamakshi had only him.

He walked up to the garden gate, by which time the dozing sentry had woken up and another had joined him. Shivappa had no plausible excuse to be there. He was supposed to be at the far end, along with the tribals, slaves and untouchables. They eyed him suspiciously and barked at him to return the way he had come. Shivappa was getting desperate—he had to find his Kamakshi. One of the sentries shoved him back and ordered him to go away. His hand went to his drum. At that moment, he saw Prince Mahadeva running towards them.

'Shivappa!'

Prince Mahadeva was as shocked as he was. For a moment they stood facing each other, too startled to move. Shivappa was the first to recover. With a punch he broke the drum head and whipped the urumi from inside.

Mahadeva screamed, 'Arrest him!'

Before the sentries could react, Shivappa's urumi lashed out and coiled around one of the guards' necks. Shivappa gave a pull and the urumi came coiling back to his hand. The guard's head rolled on the ground. Prince Mahadeva screamed in fear and stepped back. He cried out to the other guard, 'Go, soldier, run—tell them the Vaithalikas have got in. The maharaja's life is in danger…'

The soldier ran screaming and Shivappa lashed his whip sword at him. The urumi's sinuous end twisted around the guard's neck and ripped off his head. Mahadeva stood there, shocked, his limbs trembling with fear. He knew he was no match for Shivappa. He had been beaten by the slave several times during practice. He saw Shivappa wind the urumi back into a tight coil. The words of Kattappa came flashing to his mind. His family's life was in danger and his country was in danger.

Mahadeva rushed towards Shivappa and caught him by his waist. Shivappa had expected the prince to flee. The sudden action took him by surprise and together they fell down on the ground. The long ribbon sword was useless as Shivappa did not have enough space to use it. Mahadeva held on to Shivappa and they rolled on the grass. The sword wound around them, cutting into both their skins. Shivappa pushed Mahadeva but the prince clung on, not giving him space to move. Somehow he managed to free his left hand and punched Mahadeva in the face, splitting the prince's lip. Yet his grip did not loosen. Shivappa pounded at Mahadeva's face repeatedly. The prince screamed and cried out in pain, but he held on. Shivappa was growing desperate about Kamakshi.

Mahadeva knew it was a losing battle. He had never been a fighter. He was tackling an opponent bigger than him and more skilful. He wished it was Bijjala instead of him tackling Shivappa. His brother would have overpowered the rebel. Instead, god had willed that a coward like him had to shoulder the responsibility of saving his country. The urumi was cutting into his back, and he had gone numb with the punches he was receiving. He was going to die, he was sure of it. Killed by a slave—even his death would be a blot on the illustrious dynasty of Mahishmathi. A prince who could not even defeat a slave. A sharp pain shot through his stomach and he found himself flying through the air. Shivappa had managed to free his leg and had kicked him. Mahadeva fell on his back, his head slamming hard on the ground. For a moment everything went blank.

Mahadeva lay wheezing on the grass. Tears of defeat made everything hazy. He waited for the slave to cut off his head. He had tried his best to stop Shivappa, but his best had not been enough. He saw Shivappa's face looming above him. He closed his eyes, waiting for the cold steel to coil around his neck.

Then he heard footsteps fading away. With great difficulty he turned his head. And he saw Shivappa stumbling into the garden path, yelling 'Kamakshi'. Mahadeva wondered why Shivappa had not killed him. Maybe the rebel had felt pity for him. Maybe the gods were giving him a second chance. He tried to get up, pressing his palm on the ground for support, but collapsed and vomited. *Amma Gauri, give me strength to reach my father and warn him.* The earth swam before his eyes.

He coughed up blood, and it frightened him. Coward, *coward*, a voice said in his mind. *Amma Gauri, please…give me a few more moments to live,* he prayed, and with a supreme effort pulled himself up onto his feet. He started running towards the dais, to his father.

The palace bell tolled six times.

FORTY-SIX

Bijjala

When Keki reached Skandadasa's house, they were leading the mahapradhana into his room. Keki tapped Bijjala's shoulder and grinned. 'Your Highness, the present is ready. Keki has kept her word.'

Bijjala looked at Pattaraya, who gestured that his presence was no longer necessary. Bijjala caught Keki's hand and, in nervous excitement, asked her, 'Where is she? Take me there.' Though he knew where she would be, it would be nice to hear it from Keki's mouth.

Keki had no intention of going back to a place haunted by ghosts. She pressed the key in Bijjala's palm, gave his hand a squeeze, and said, 'She is waiting in your chambers, Prince. You go to your heaven and drink the elixir. This poor eunuch's place is here.'

Bijjala let go of her hand and hurried to his chamber. Keki watched him go and congratulated herself on a job well done. She considered warning him about the ghost of the slave that was haunting the palace and decided against it. The prince would know how to tackle a ghost. He was a great warrior. She sighed at the closed door of Skandadasa's room and wondered what they were discussing. She felt scared to stand alone in the darkness and drifted towards the garden.

Bijjala rushed to his chamber. He had seen Kamakshi many times and had fantasized about her a lot. He had never thought his wishes would come true so fast. He must remember to reward Keki for her efforts, he thought. And Pattaraya, too, for the services he was rendering to the country. He hoped they would put the upstart Skandadasa in his place.

When he was climbing the stairs to reach his chambers, he had been pleased that none of his guards were present. He had given strict orders, in anticipation of the night. He did not want someone to inform his father. But as he walked through the dark corridor he felt some misgivings. He gripped the hilt of his sword and increased his pace.

His heart skipped a beat. What was the dark shadow that was huddled near his door? He slowed down, cautiously drawing his sword from the scabbard. The figure stood up. Something about it was vaguely familiar. The figure rushed towards him. In the faded moonlight, he saw its face and gasped. The dead slave—Kattappa.

'Swami,' the ghost called.

'Don't come near, you pisacha,' Bijjala screamed, holding out his sword and pointing it at the approaching figure.

'It is me, swami. Your humble slave, Kattappa.'

Kattappa fell to his knees and bowed low, touching his forehead on the floor.

'You...you are not dead?' Bijjala asked.

Kattappa touched his feet with both his hands. Bijjala felt relieved for a moment that it was not a ghost. Then anger came rushing up. The slave had seen his fear. How dare he come here and scare him like this? Bijjala raised his boot and kicked Katttapa across his face. The slave fell down, shocked and hurt. He folded his hands and cried, 'It was a mistake to leave you, swami, I'm very sorry.'

'You son of a bitch, you bastard—' Bijjala rained kicks on Kattappa, who did not even raise his hands to protect himself.

'Swami, swami, there will be time enough for you to punish me. But right now, there is grave danger to the king. I have told His Highness Prince Mahadeva, but the country needs you, swami. Please save your father. Please save His Majesty,' Kattappa cried between kicks.

'Shut up, dirty slave. Giving me advice! *Thuph*,' Bijjala spat on Kattappa. 'Stay here until I come out. Then I will decide how to punish you,' Bijjala said, wagging a finger at Kattappa's face.

Then he paused. No, it would not do if the blasted slave stayed outside while he was enjoying Keki's present. He turned to Kattappa and said, 'Why are you standing here, you oaf? Out, out—go down and wait in the courtyard. Out. I don't want to see your ugly face when I wake up.'

He waited until Kattappa had walked away. When he was sure that Kattappa had reached the ground floor, Bijjala opened the door, entered and slammed the door shut.

Kattappa sat on the first step of the stairs, staring emptily into the dark courtyard. Frustration and anger were raising their ugly heads in his mind. He had come to the palace, sacrificing his freedom for his master, and his master was treating him like this. He did not deserve it. Shivappa was right. *No, no, I should not think like that,* he corrected himself. He slapped his cheeks with his palm. It was a sin to think like that. His father's words rang clear in his mind. 'Your master may behave cruelly and unfairly towards you. You may feel anger towards your master for the way he treats you sometimes. That is human. But when such doubts come, the only thing you have to remember is, it is not the master you serve, but your job. Your dharma is to be true to your job. That is your worship. If you love your duty only when your master treats you well or pleasant things happen to you, you are no better than an animal that seeks pleasure and shuns pain. You are something beyond that. Kattappa, promise me that you will remain true to your dharma, your duty, irrespective of how your master treats you or your life treats you.'

Kattappa stood up and wiped away the white marks that Bijjala's boots had made on his dark skin. He walked with his head high and stood in the courtyard,his arms folded across his broad chest, staring straight ahead at some invisible point far away.

Inside his chambers, Bijjala raised the wick of the lamp and a golden light illuminated the room. His breath stopped for a moment when he saw Kamakshi lying on his bed. He gazed at her, his eyes lingering on her heaving bosom and navel and her curving hips. He lay on the bed beside her and moved away her breast-cloth. He looked at her breasts, and then traced spirals with his index finger on her flesh. Then he saw the whip near her and smiled. Keki knew what he liked. He took the whip in his hand. The smell of musk made him giddy. He looked at Kamakshi and her fair skin. He closed his eyes, smelling the whip and imagining how her skin would be bruised when his whip would lash it. He started sweating and his lips trembled with fervour. His body heated up and his throat went dry. He raised the whip and cracked it across Kamakshi's breast.

Kamakshi woke up screaming in pain. She saw Bijjala grinning like a maniac and winding the whip around his fist. He beckoned her with his fingers. She became aware of her nudity and hurriedly covered her breasts. Bijjala laughed. He lashed at her again, enjoying her pain. She ran towards the door but he got to her before she could reach it. He grabbed her and threw her on the bed, ripping her breast-cloth into two. Grinning, he climbed back on the bed and she tried to shrink away from him. He teased her by laughing like a maniac, shooting his hand out to grab her breasts, and withdrawing it at the last moment. She covered her shame by folding her arms across her chest. She tried to scream but no sound emerged. She wept, her body wracked with heartrending sobs.

Bijjala grabbed her wrists and tried to separate her arms. She turned her face and shut her eyes. He pulled her towards him and tried to kiss her. She kicked out with her knees, catching him between his legs. He howled in pain.

Kattappa heard the noise. He ran up, taking two steps at a time, and banged on Bijjala's door. 'Swami,' he called. Bijjala abused him and asked him to get lost. Confused, Kattappa started walking down the steps. When Bijjala turned, he saw Kamakshi was near the window, trying to jump out of it. He lunged forward and grabbed her by her waist. She held on to the window frame and tried to resist him.

Shivappa was desperately searching for Kamakshi and had reached the courtyard when he heard the struggle. He ran, calling out her name. He saw a glimpse of her at Bijjala's window before part of the frame splintered and Kamakshi was pulled in by Bijjala.

Bijjala threw her back on the bed. He picked up the whip from where it had fallen. When she tried to get up, he lashed her across her face. When she tried to scream, he followed it with a back-handed slap. The girl was struggling too much. He thrust a part of her torn breast-cloth into her mouth, and when she tried to take it out, he tied her hands with the other half. He ripped away her skirt and her underclothes. He wound the whip in his hands and approached her. She jumped up from the bed and ran, but he stood blocking her way to the door. She sat cowering in a corner on her haunches as he moved towards her with the whip.

Shivappa ran up the stairs and came face to face with Kattappa on the landing.

'Anna,' Shivappa gasped. He had thought his brother was dead.

Kattappa's kick caught Shivappa in his chest and he tumbled down the stairs and collapsed on the first floor veranda. Kattappa dove to grab him, but his brother rolled away and fell down to the courtyard. Shivappa was up on his legs in a flash with his urumi uncoiled. He rattled his whip sword and screamed, 'Move away, Anna.'

Kattappa stood facing his brother, with his arms on his hips and said calmly, 'Traitor, this time you die.'

FORTY-SEVEN

Sivagami

Sivagami had been searching for her book for a while. She had heard sounds outside the room and a couple of times she thought someone would walk in. When nothing happened, she became a little more relaxed. She wished she could light a lamp. Without it, she had to carry each manuscript to the window and check it by moonlight to identify whether it was her book or not.

There had been nothing in the table drawer and she had begun going through the huge shelf of manuscripts in the room. Except for two outfits, a gold-tipped stencil, and some copper bracelets given for exceptional service to the state, the mahapradhana had few earthly possessions. She felt guilty about stealing into his chamber. The kind way he had dealt with Gundu Ramu's hunger was still vivid in her memory. Not many officials had the same kindness when dealing with their inferiors.

There were only a few manuscripts left when she heard raised voices outside. In a panic, she dropped the manuscripts she was holding. She waited with bated breath. The manuscripts lay scattered at her feet. The argument continued outside. She knelt down to pick up a manuscript and ran with it to the window. She hit her thigh on the corner of the table, but she did not have the luxury of even crying out. No, this was not the one. She ran back to pick up all the manuscripts that had fallen on the floor. *Hurry, hurry, hurry,* she told herself. She pressed the pile of manuscripts to her chest with her left hand as she picked up the rest from the floor. She would take all the manuscripts she could hold and look for hers at leisure. She promised herself that she would return what was not hers.

The bell tolled six.

The door swung open and a rectangular piece of light fell across the floor. She suppressed a scream with great difficulty. To reach the window, she had to cross the patch of light and risked being seen by whoever was entering the room. She quickly ducked behind the table. Several pairs of legs walked in—from her position that was the first thing she saw. Some of the manuscripts had fallen from her hand again.

She heard the door being shut and someone walk towards the table, straight at her. Her heart pounding in her ribcage, she quickly hid behind the chair of the mahapradhana. A lamp was placed on the table and, fortunately for Sivagami, the chair threw a massive shadow on the floor and on the wall behind it. She was well hidden between the chair and the wall. For now.

She peeped out. Skandadasa was sitting on his chair. A fat man, a priest and a high official in dandakara uniform were sitting across the table. It was then that she saw her father's book. It was lying near the fat man's chair. If he moved his feet an inch, he would step on it. She bit her nails, not knowing how to retrieve it. She calculated her chances of grabbing it and making a dash for the window. She could fling it across the fort wall and, hopefully, Gundu Ramu would catch it and race back to the orphanage.

'What do you want, Bhoomipathi Pattaraya?' Skandadasa said suddenly.

'The thing you are hiding, swami,' Pattaraya said with a smile.

'I have nothing to hide. My life is an open book,' Skandadasa said.

'Let us not waste time, Skandadasa. We know you have taken it. We can understand the temptation. Even a nobleman like…hmm…this Dandanayaka Pratapa, could be tempted by such a golden chance to make money. The temptation for a bear dancer's son who finds himself in such a responsible post is quite understandable,' Pattaraya said and leaned back on his chair.

Skandadasa slammed his fist on the table, 'Out!' he yelled, pointing his finger at the door. 'Get out of this room. Now. Or else I will call the guards.'

'Oh, we are terrified,' Pattaraya laughed. He leaned forward and said, 'Bastard. Enough of your act. You are more corrupt than anyone else. We have a deal. We will share the profit. Four of us. You don't worry about how we will sell it. You hand over the Gauridhooli to us, keep supplying us once in a while, and we can make you rich beyond your imagination.'

Pratapa added, 'Don't worry about Roopaka. We will work out his profit too.'

Sivagami saw that Skandadasa's hand was searching for something in the drawer of his table. His hand stopped foraging when he found what he wanted.

Rudra Bhatta said, 'I will give you a better offer. I will change your caste. I will proclaim you and your family as belonging to Kshatriyas. As per karma, you are doing a Kshatriya's work. Of course, you have to pay a fortune to the temple and feed many Brahmins for the ceremony, give away many gifts, cows—I shall guide you. The money Pattaraya is offering would be more than sufficient for it.'

Skandadasa flashed the dagger he was now holding and pointed it at Pattaraya's neck, 'Get out this moment.'

Pattaraya shook his head in dismay. 'I thought you were an intelligent man. But on second thoughts, why am I surprised by your stupidity? You have displayed an ignorance befitting your lineage.' The line was delivered with great disdain, calculated to provoke.

With a yell of anger, Skandadasa jumped up, brandishing his dagger. The chair hit Sivagami and she put her hand over her mouth to prevent herself from crying out.

Pattaraya and his friends stood up. 'Easy, easy my friend. You are so touchy,' Pattaraya said and walked to the door. Sivagami crawled out and snatched the book.

At that moment, Pattaraya turned and cried, 'What is this—you have a girl here? No wonder you were acting so heroic.'

Sivagami stood up, clutching her book behind her back, and took a few steps back. Skandadasa stared at her. 'You?' he asked in surprise.

Sivagami screamed, but before she could warn him, Pattaraya and Pratapa had grabbed Skandadasa. Pratapa prised away the dagger while Pattaraya held him firm. Pratapa said, 'Bhatta, search everywhere. See where he has kept the Gauridhooli.'

Someone knocked loudly on the door. 'Hurry,' Pratapa cried.

Sivagami walked one step at a time to the window. The priest threw down everything that was on the shelves, pulled down the curtains, and ransacked the table.

'It is not here, it is not to be found, Rama, Rama, Krishna,' the priest cried in a shrill voice.

The knock on the door became a bang. 'Open, open,' a frantic voice cried.

'It is Keki,' Pratapa said, and Pattaraya indicated with his eyes to the priest to open it. He hissed to Skandadasa, 'Stay still, you vermin.'

Rudra Bhatta opened the door and Keki rushed in. 'There is a coup. Vaithalikas are attacking the king. There is a great battle raging. The palace has caught fire.'

Skandadasa struggled to free himself but Pattaraya held him firm. He started laughing, 'That is wonderful news. A god-given opportunity.'

'But we did not get what we have come for,' cried the priest.

'You are a fool, Brahmin. So am I and so is this Pratapa,' Pattaraya said. Through the open door, the orange hue of distant fire danced around in the room, drawing patterns on the wall.

Pattaraya pressed Skandadasa's neck and said, 'This vermin, this low-caste bastard, almost outwitted the great Pattaraya.'

'What do you mean?' said Pratapa.

'If he had the Gauridhooli in this room, do you think he would have left it unguarded? Brahmin, check Skandadasa thoroughly. If I am Pattaraya, I vouch that he is carrying it on his person.'

Sivagami saw Skandadasa's face becoming pale. *A few steps more, a few steps more,* she repeated in her mind as she inched towards the window. Rudra Bhatta hesitated, unable to bring himself to touch an untouchable. Keki stepped in and started searching Skandadasa. The mahapradhana somehow freed his right hand and smashed Pattaraya's chest with his elbow. The bhoomipathi's grip loosened and Skandadasa freed his other hand as well. He hit Pratapa who was thrown back with the impact. The dagger fell from his hand. Skandadasa tried to run but Keki caught hold of his leg, bringing him down on his face.

'Whoa, whoa, where are you going, bear dancer?' Keki cried as she held on to Skandadasa's legs. Pratapa jumped up from the floor and started kicking the fallen mahapradhana.

'Sivagami…' Skandadasa yelled as she was about to jump over the window. She paused. Pratapa had pinned the mahapradhana to the floor and Keki was searching him. Skandadasa managed to take out a small copper pot from his waist-band and threw it to Sivagami. The lemon-sized pot landed near her feet with a thunk and rolled to the wall.

'Take that and run,' he managed to say.

Sivagami took the pot in her hand, unsure of what to do. The room was silent. She looked at the men, and then at the strange-looking pot which was sealed tightly.

'Girl, give us that,' Pattaraya stepped forward, extending his hand.

'No, no, run, Sivagami, run. Never let these villains get hold of it. Please…' Skandadasa cried.

Pratapa slammed his fist down on the mahapradhana's head. 'Quiet, you low-caste scoundrel,' he said as he punched him again.

Sivagami hesitated. She had no love for the country. Why should she get involved?

'This man has stolen the country's secret, girl. We are officials trying to recover it from the thief. Give it to us and we shall let you go. Do not interfere in official matters and get implicated,' Pattaraya said.

'Run to the maharaja or Parameswara. Your country's future depends on it, please,' Skandadasa struggled to speak as Pratapa slammed his head on the floor again. Skandadasa's nose broke and blood squirted out. Sivagami let out a gasp. This was the man who had been kind to her. He was being tortured and she was watching without doing anything. She felt sick.

Pattaraya was observing the effect their violence on Skandadasa was having on Sivagami. She was close to the window, and if she jumped out and ran, it would be difficult to catch her. The girl looked young and sprightly. He knelt before Skandadasa.

'Tell her to hand it over or she will watch you die,' Pattaraya said in a matter-of-fact tone which sent a chill down Sivagami's spine.

Skandadasa mumbled, 'Run, Sivagami, please…'

Pattaraya took the dagger from the floor, pulled back Skandadasa's head by his hair and pressed the tip of the dagger on his exposed neck. He stared at Sivagami but said to Skandadasa, 'Vermin, ask the girl to hand over the Gauridhooli to us or you die.'

'Sivagami, run,' Skandadasa managed to say.

Pattaraya grinned at Sivagami and thrust the dagger into Skandadasa's throat. Blood squirted in an arc and drops of it fell near her feet. She saw Skandadasa's eyes go white and his knees limp. Blood gurgled out of the wound in his throat, through his mouth and nose. Pattaraya let go of Skandadasa, and the first and last mahapradhana of Mahishmathi who had known hunger and starvation, who had fought against discrimination and risen to the highest position in the country by sheer hard work and sincerity, fell dead at the foot of the table where he had toiled for the good of the country for three long decades.

Sivagami rushed to him, forgetting about her own safety. Blood was spreading around his head on the floor. She stood watching him. She had witnessed the most despicable crime. The death of an honourable man, slain by evil men, and she had not been able to do anything. Something in her died that moment. Her belief in good triumphing over evil was shattered by what she had seen. She held her head and wept in agony. Pattaraya smiled. As expected the girl had run back to the centre of the room from the window. She was trapped. Now it was a matter of killing her too and taking the Gauridhooli.

Pratapa cried, 'What have you done?'

'Me?' Pattaraya feigned surprise. 'What did I do? The Vaithalikas killed Skandadasa. The corrupt mahapradhana stole Gauridhooli and invited in the Vaithalikas to kill the king. That is why he was standing at the gate. This traitor let the rebels in to kill the maharaja. They had a tiff about how to share the profits, and the Vaithalikas killed their partner in crime. What has poor Bhoomipathi Pattaraya got to do with such evil men, friend?'

'So you are going to surrender the Gauridhooli?' Rudra Bhatta asked anxiously.

'Ha Ha,' Pattaraya laughed. 'Everything about the plan remains unchanged. I will throw this over the fort wall and Hidumba will take it where we planned. Meanwhile, we will be playing heroes, fighting to save the maharaja from the Vaithalikas. That is the only improvisation. We are patriots, aren't we?' he laughed.

'You are a genius,' Rudra Bhatta said.

'I know,' Pattaraya smiled.

'But what about the girl?' Keki asked.

'This daughter of a traitor?' Pattaraya rubbed his thick lips with his fingers and cocked his head. He smirked at Sivagami who was crying over Skandadasa's inert body. 'Do you need me to spell these things out, Pratapa?' he asked.

Pratapa smiled and took the dagger from Pattaraya's hands. He tiptoed towards Sivagami. His shadow loomed large and filled the room. From the corner of her eyes she sensed him coming. She waited. A second before he had anticipated, she grabbed the lamp and slammed it on Pratapa's face. The lamp went off, plunging the room into darkness. Sivagami ran to the window and dove outside, clutching her book in one hand and the pot of Gauridhooli in the other.

'Catch her,' she heard Pattaraya say. 'Finish her and get the godamn powder.'

She wanted to run but she remembered Gundu Ramu would be waiting alone outside. She threw the book, but it did not clear the wall. It hit the wall a few feet below the top and fell down. She ran to pick it up and saw Pratapa jumping from the window with the dagger in his hand.

Sivagami grabbed the book and threw it again. This time it cleared the wall. She took off. Pratapa screamed behind her, brandishing his dagger as she ran for her life. She had no idea what the pot contained, but if big officials were willing to kill the prime minister of the country for it, it must hold something important. A man like Skandadasa was ready to die for it. She thought she would be able to use such a significant secret and then felt ashamed that she was having such thoughts. The face of Skandadasa as he died came rushing to her mind. His death should not be in vain. She held on to the pot firmly and continued to run.

FORTY-EIGHT

Gundu Ramu

Gundu Ramu had been waiting near the wall for a long time. He was sitting on a stone that had fallen from the fort wall. Across the road, wild grass obstructed his view of the river. He was thankful for it. The river frightened him. He was scared of the darkness. He was terrified to be alone. Yet he was sitting near the river on a deserted road in the night. Every time fear raised its ugly head, he reminded himself was that he was doing this for Sivagami akka. He thanked God that the evil men he had seen earlier were nowhere around. Even the slightest sound made him tremble with fear and he repeated Arjuna's name over and over in his mind. He fell asleep after some time and woke up with a start when the bell tolled six times.

It was dark and eerie. The only sound was the drone of crickets and the occasional frog croaking. Ahead of him, the branches of a tree started shaking. He quickly shut his eyes and his fingers dug into his thighs as he intensified his prayers. He heard a sharp squeal and cried out aloud. When he opened his eyes after a few moments, he saw a bat that had been hanging upside down from the tree branch, flapping its wings and flying across the river. It was only a bat—he smiled and sighed with relief. The bat rose high and for a moment Gundu Ramu saw it frozen like a scary picture, with the moon in the background. All the ghost stories his father had told him came rushing back.

Suddenly, he felt that a pair of eyes was looking at him from the bushes. He could sense it. The eyes were boring into his plump body. The air felt cold. A breeze picked up the dry leaves near his feet and made them dance and cartwheel. He started chanting the mantra again and felt relief. God would save him. He had never harmed anyone in life. His father always said god was there to protect good people from evil ones. But why had God not protected his father? No, he wouldn't doubt God and incur his wrath. He started chanting the mantra again.

When the breeze from the river stopped, a burning smell filled the air. He sniffed the air and heard shouts and screams from a distance. An orange hue started spreading over the shadows, lighting them. Somewhere a massive fire had started. The wind carried luminous flares that spiralled and glided above him. Why was Sivagami akka taking so much time?

Suddenly he heard a noise. He went to the middle of the road to wait for the book to come flying over the wall. He saw something rise high in the air, flying over the fort wall. It caught the light of the raging fire on the other side of the fort for a moment, and shone as it spun in the air. Then it came down faster than he had anticipated. Gundu Ramu tried to catch it but it fell past his hands. He knelt down to pick up the book but, astounding him, a dwarf shot out of a bush. Gundu Ramu screamed in fear, snatched up the manuscript and ran. Did he actually see it or was it his imagination playing on his fears? He heard a sharp whistle. He turned back and found that he was looking at a dwarf and two gigantic men who towered over him. He recognized them as the evil men who had killed the sentries. The dwarf whistled again and pointed at what he was holding.

Gundu Ramu stepped back, suppressing a sob. He wanted to run but his legs had turned wooden with fear. He could feel himself lose control of his bladder, and the water traced a warm path down his legs and puddled around his feet. The pungent smell of urine filled his nostrils. He was ashamed of what he had done.

'Aha, what a surprise,' the dwarf said as he walked around Gundu Ramu. 'I have been watching your idiocy for some time, son. You are so cute. Do you want to come with me? I will ensure you will reach a high position in life.' The two giants laughed.

'In fact, you can live at the top of a mountain where the air is clean, fresh and cool. And there are men—not big men like these two, but men like me—men who do not like girls but who would love to have a soft plump boy like you to cuddle,' Hidumba winked and his two thugs laughed again. Hidumba pinched Gundu Ramu's cheeks and said, 'The men will love you, and if you are lucky, at some point the great Hidumba will love you too. Do you know Hidumba? He is a great man. Have you seen him, sweetheart? Look, he is before you. Tch, tch, why are you crying? Don't you want to be loved, my boy? Don't you want a shove from behind to…err…come up in life? Tell me, tell me?'

Gundu Ramu shrank back from Hidumba's touch. It was very creepy. He tried to run, but one of the giants blocked him. He caught Gundu Ramu by his shoulders and turned the boy to Hidumba. This time, the smile had disappeared from the dwarf's lips and his pig eyes burned with rage. He jumped and slapped the boy's cheeks. Gundu Ramu held his face with his palm and started weeping. His entire body shook when he cried.

'You turn away my offer of love? Wait till you reach my place. I will teach you how to treat great men with respect. Take him, Ranga. He is coming with us to Gauriparvat. We will give him a new job.'

Gundu Ramu took to his heels but the giant tripped him and the boy fell on his face. The giant pressed his knee down on the boy's back, twisted his head towards him, and started punching and slapping Gundu Ramu till he stopped struggling. Soon Gundu Ramu's cries of agony turned to whimpers. The giant tore off Gundu Ramu's dhoti and wrapped him in it. Still, Gundu Ramu held the book to his chest. He lifted the boy up and carried him on his shoulders to the chariot. He threw the boy down near the wheels. Gundu Ramu cried in pain but he would not let go what was Sivagami's. Despite his best efforts, though, he was no match for the giant's strength. Ranga prised open Gundu Ramu's plump hands from his chest and the book fell down.

'What is this? The boy's fucking textbook?' Hidumba took the manuscript and turned it over. He shook it to see whether something would fall from it. Gundu Ramu lay moaning near the wheels.

'Blasted fat man. He made me wait in this ass-soaking humidity for a schoolboy's textbook,' Hidumba cursed.

'That is Sivagami akka's. Please give it back to me,' Gundu Ramu whined.

'Shut up, you devil. Fuck your akka, and fuck you, son of a bitch. Blasted balls of a holy bull, I have been made a buffoon by the fat man.'

'Give me the book, you dwarf,' Gundu Ramu cried, trying to get up.

Hidumba kicked Gundu Ramu on his face repeatedly, taking out his frustration on the boy.

'Some people are coming this way,' Ranga cried. Hidumba turned to see a crowd running towards them. The fire inside the fort had become an inferno, and people were escaping from the palace grounds through whichever way possible.

'No point staying here anymore. The fat man will throw his shit next time and we will be standing with our mouth open to catch it. Bloody Pattaraya. Wait till I get back. Boys, lift me into the chariot. Let's go back home,' Hidumba said.

'How about this fat one?' Ranga asked as he lifted Hidumba into the chariot.

'Bring him. He will be of some entertainment in the frozen heights of Gauriparvat. He is buttery soft,' Hidumba said with a wink. Gundu Ramu, covered in blood and bruises, was lifted and dumped near Hidumba.

'How about this book?' Ranga asked.

'Shove it up you know where. On second thoughts...give it to me. The boy seems to prize it. We can use it to make him dance to our tunes,' Hidumba said. He sat near Gundu Ramu, who shrank back with fear, and started running his pudgy hand over the boy's body. The chariot shot forward with Gundu Ramu tied and bound in it, heading to the mysterious Gauriparvat, to the land of Khanipathi Hidumba the great.

FORTY-NINE

Kattappa

Shivappa collapsed on the floor. He had tried his best to defeat his brother, but Kattappa had fought like a tiger, bare-handed against the deadliest of swords. He ducked, spun, twisted and rolled, every time the urumi shot out, and in the moments it took for the whip sword to wind back, Kattappa attacked using the ancient martial art of marma vidya. Every time he came in contact, he hit Shivappa's muscles, making them numb and useless. He managed to prise away the sword from Shivappa's hands and slammed him to the floor. Shivappa could not even move. When he tried to talk, Kattappa poked his throat with his index finger and after that only gurgling sounds emerged. Kattappa tore Shivappa's dhoti and tied and bound him with it. There was no need. Shivappa was not in a position to move a finger.

'You deserve no mercy,' Kattappa said in a hoarse voice. 'This is not revenge for stabbing me in the back, brother. I am just doing my duty. I will not allow any traitor to live. You will face trial and—' Kattappa turned away; his voice choked, '—and if they decide to hang you, I...I will do it happily.'

Shivappa wanted to tell him that he had not come to fight, he had not come to rebel. The woman he wanted to marry, the girl with whom he had weaved countless dreams, was getting raped inside by his master. He would have gone away with her, leaving this bloody country and its inhuman practices to rot in its own hell. *Why did you stop me, brother? Why? Why?* Tears streamed down Shivappa's eyes, but he could not talk.

Kattappa stood up, bathed in sweat and blood. Though it broke his heart, he had done his duty. He had done his dharma without bothering about the consquences. An ideal slave has to be a karmayogi—those were his father's words, and he had been true to them. Suddenly, he heard a scream from the floor above.

'Swami!' he cried. Was his master in some danger? He jumped to the veranda, ran up the stairs, and reached the door. He could hear sounds of struggle in the room. He hesitated for a moment. Something fell inside. His master had told him not to even come near the door. But as the protector of his master, it was his duty to overrule his master's orders if his life was in danger. Later, the master could punish or reward him, but now, he had to disobey his master to save him.

He kicked the door open and froze. In the corner of the room, a girl cowered, struggling to cover her nakedness with her bound hands. In front of her, Bijjala was standing with a whip. Bijjala was shocked to see Kattappa. His face contorted with rage.

'Out, you dog, out,' Bijjala screamed, snapping the whip.

Kattappa stood transfixed at the door. His first instinct was to obey his master, but the face of the shivering girl, covered in whip welts, made him stop. He removed his dhoti and threw it at the girl. She grabbed it and covered herself. Bijjala roared with anger and approached Kattappa who was standing in his loincloth.

Bijjala cracked his whip on Kattappa, 'Get lost, you dog,' he yelled.

Kattappa walked to the girl and stood between her and Bijjala, his hands folded over his chest. His mind was in turmoil. The girl's eyes were pleading with him to save her. He shivered when he saw her face. Kamakshi—his brother's lover. It broke his heart. Perhaps Shivappa had come to save her, and he had immobilized his brother. The gods were throwing more tests at him.

'Leave her there, bastard, and get out before I kill you,' Bijjala screamed, lashing his whip across Kattappa's shoulders. It seared his flesh. He suppressed a scream and stood with his eyes closed. The slave was in a dilemma. He was supposed to obey his master without any questions. There was no threat to the life of his master. But his conscience rebelled—he could not leave the girl to be tortured. He decided he would stand there between the girl and his master. He would not defy his master but he would not allow him to hurt her. Bijjala brought down the whip again and again on his slave's body. The slave stood without moving, his eyes closed as the whip ripped his skin apart. Kattappa could only hope someone would come and stop Bijjala and save the girl before he died. Frustrated that the slave was not moving, Bijjala threw the whip down and tried to push Kattappa away, but the slave stood like a rock. Bijjala was no match for the ox-like strength of Kattappa.

Bijjala took a flower vase that was in the corner and slammed it on Kattappa's head. It shattered into shards, but

Kattappa stood erect, not moving, not even letting out a cry of pain.

Kamakshi watched what was happening to the slave. She knew Kattappa was dying for her. If her mouth was not gagged, she would have pleaded with Bijjala to leave the slave alone and do whatever he wanted with her. She crawled to the window and scrambled up. Bijjala saw her and rushed towards her, but Kattappa moved to obstruct his way. The slave stood still, bleeding from everywhere, but not allowing his master to reach Kamakshi.

Kamakshi looked down and saw the immobile body of Shivappa. He was lying still. In the pale moonlight, he appeared dead. She looked back and saw Kattappa swaying on his legs. Bijjala was punching the slave, trying to bring him down.

Shivappa could hear the noises, but he was helpless and unable to even move. He saw Kamakshi at the window, and when he saw her face, he wanted to scream NO. He watched helplessly as his love jumped from the window. The dhoti of Kattappa flew away and fell near the wall. Kamakshi landed near him, hitting her head first. Her face only a few feet from Shivappa's. She gave a small smile and extended her fingers to touch him, and then her eyes went lifeless. A trickle of blood crawled from her ears and crept towards her lover.

Shivappa wished he could cry his heart out, but his brother had taken even that faculty from him. His Kamakshi was dead. She was lying so near yet so far, naked and bruised, killed by the man he had always despised. He wished he was dead with her. But he did not have even the freedom to cry. Not even the freedom to die. He saw a glimpse of Bijjala at the window, peering down, and then he saw his brother's face.

Inside the room, Kattappa collapsed to his knees. What had he done, what had he done, he lamented. He buried his face in his palms. He had done his dharma, he had acted as per his conscience, yet he felt no solace in that fact. Bijjala gave him a final kick and left the room. Kattappa could hear the heavy tread of his master's feet. He heard his laughter when he saw Shivappa.

'Ah, who do we have here?'

Kattappa could hear the dull thud of his master kicking his brother. 'Why are you crying, you bastard? Was it your girl? Ha, Ha, I have taken your woman, and she was delicious. Now I will see you hang. Take this and this and this,' he heard Bijjala say as the prince continued to kick his brother.

Kattappa heard the cheers of a few soldiers. He heard the voice of Keki crying out that a coup had been suppressed. He heard Keki exclaim as she found Shivappa. When Kattappa heard Bijjala say about his brother, 'This bastard slave killed the poor girl and I have captured him', he started crying. But his sobs were drowned out by the loud cheers of soldiers who were hailing his master for the great act Bijjala claimed to have performed.

FIFTY

Sivagami

Sivagami ran towards the garden. In an open space, maybe she could put up a fight. She could scream for help and say the man was trying to molest her, get an audience with some high officials and then tell them what had happened. But he was gaining on her. She ran, holding the pot close to her bosom, her eyes darting here and there to find a suitable spot to turn around and fight. As she crossed the garden, she tripped over something and fell. The pot flung away from her. She jumped to get it and saw her pursuer closing in. She quickly bent down to get the pot and froze. She had tripped on a headless body lying by the gate. Pratapa jumped over a hedge and ran towards her, brandishing his dagger.

Sivagami took off again and reached the palace grounds where she saw that hundreds of fire-fighters were trying to suppress the raging fire. Part of the fort wall had collapsed and elephants were being used to ram the remaining stones so they could bring water from the river. Finally, with a loud crash, a large portion of the wall fell down. People tried to rush out to save themselves, but the soldiers pushed them back. They did not want the crowd to block the elephants' path to the water. People ran to the other side, confused about how to escape. Fire was spreading to other parts of the palace and elephants were being used to spray water, aided by men who tried their best to quench the fire. Thick smoke coiled towards the sky and the smell of burning flesh filled the air.

Sivagami tried to merge with the crowd but found herself being pushed back towards Pratapa. She saw that he had stopped a few feet away from the crowd and was talking to a group of dandakaras. They spread out and she was sure they were after her. She ran blindly to the farthermost part of the palace. Women from various blocks were also running around in panic. Screams and shouts filled the air. She ran past the men busy drawing water from the fountain towards a building that loomed in the shadows. She had to find a place to hide until she could figure out how to escape from the palace.

She skirted the buildings, careful to keep herself in the shadows. After some time, she slowed down to catch her breath. The air was acrid with smoke and ash. A door flung open near her and a dandakara carrying a huge sword came out. For a moment, he froze as he came face-to-face with Sivagami. His sword was dripping with blood. In the swaying flames of the torches on the wall, his face, splattered with blood, looked grotesque. He lunged at her, but she ducked and ran past him.

Sivagami was running blind; she took a random turn and dashed through a half-open door. It was eerily quiet inside the building. And dark. She recognized it as the one she had come to with Uncle Thimma. It was the Antapura, the harem of the maharaja. She heard faint noises of swords clanging from somewhere inside and turned to go back the way she came, but saw that there were dandakaras conferring at the door.

Sivagami ran deeper into the Antapura. In the light of the lone torch that was sputtering at the far end of the corridor, the sight that greeted her was straight out of hell. Bodies were lying prostate in various positions, cleaved limbs, torsos without heads, severed heads in pools of blood. Most were women of the harem, some appeared to be those of males. The rusty smell of blood mixed with the smoke from outside. The faint smells of human excretion and urine hung in the air.

She felt sick and dizzy. From without, the sounds of men fighting the fire were subsiding. Perhaps they had brought the fire under control. That ruled out going outside now. The chances of getting caught were very high. She wondered where Pratapa was—had the dandakara told him she had slipped into this building? As if in answer, a long shadow stretched from the door she had entered.

She moved behind a pillar and prayed the man would go away. Instead, he took a hesitant step inside. From somewhere above, the noise of swords clanging continued, followed by feet tramping down wooden steps. As Sivagami stood behind the pillar, shivering in fear, Pratapa walked inside holding a long sword in his hand. He looked around and stopped when he saw the scene before him. He hesitated for a moment, immersed in thought. Then he stared at the floor. Sivagami felt like kicking herself. He had spotted her footprints on the floor. He began to walk towards the pillar behind which she was hiding. A scream rose from one of the floors above, and Pratapa paused for a moment before continuing towards her. The tip of his sword caught the light from the distant torch and sparkled gold. Sivagami had no choice other than to run upstairs.

She dashed towards the flight of spiral steps and started running up. She could hear the man following her. Round and round and round it went. The steps spiralled to the ceiling and vanished into darkness. She could see at least three landings that led to their respective floors. They were plunged in darkness and looked deserted. She did not want to get caught in a place where Pratapa could easily finish her off. She had no clue what she would do when she had climbed right up to the top. But there was someone on the topmost floor for sure. Pratapa would hesitate to kill her in the open. She glanced back and saw that he was gaining on her. The noise from the swordfight was suddenly clear as she reached the second floor. Pratapa too hesitated when he heard the sounds. Sivagami peered into the landing.

Maharaja Somadeva was fighting a man whose face was masked. Another man was taking on a bald-headed slave with his sword. All over the floor lay the bodies of the dead or dying. She looked down the steps and saw Pratapa was only a few feet away. Her safety lay in revealing everything to the maharaja and giving him the pot, as Skandadasa had said.

'Your Majesty,' she yelled, and the man who was fighting the king spun around and swung his sword out at her. It came flashing at her head and she closed her eyes.

'Sivagami!' She heard a voice.

She opened her eyes and saw the sword was a finger's length away from her neck. The masked man's eyes stared into hers. She did not think. With a yell, she grabbed the sword—the edge cutting into her fingers—and yanked the man down. The masked man had not expected it and he lost his balance. Sivagami watched him tumbling down the steps, past Pratapa. She dropped the sword on the floor and shook her palm in pain.

The masked man collapsed on the last landing and soon she heard many footsteps on the ground floor. Seeing that the maharaja was around, Pratapa slithered down, holding the railing of the spiral staircase, and vanished into the first-floor landing. When she saw Pratapa vanish, Sivagami decided to hold her tongue. The fight was raging on with the huge man facing the maharaja and the slave Malayappa. Sivagami wanted to run away, but the fighters were blocking her path. She quickly reconsidered her options. How would she explain her presence in Skandadasa's room? She did not want the king to find out about her father's book. No, much as she wanted the killers of Skandadasa to be punished, she did not want to land in any trouble that would slow down her quest for revenge. She tucked the pot into her kaunchika. This was a golden opportunity—the king was engrossed in the fighting. She tried to pick up the sword from the floor.

The huge man saw what she was doing and, as Sivagami knelt down, he slammed his heel on its hilt. It flew up, and in one swift motion, he caught it with his left hand while fencing off the maharaja's thrusts. He threw it at the slave. Malayappa twisted away, but the sword pierced his shoulder, making him stagger and fall.

The maharaja cried, 'Malayappa!', and ran towards the fallen slave. The huge man with the mask tried to thrust his sword into the maharaja's back, but as if he had anticipated it, Maharaja Somadeva deftly stepped aside. The man lost his balance and leaned forward to prevent himself from falling. With a clean sweep of his sword, the maharaja cut off the head of his opponent.

It rolled down, spinning, spilling blood everywhere.

The maharaja knelt before Malayappa, who was struggling to get up. 'Are you all right? Malayappa?' Sivagami was surprised at the concern in the king's voice. Did he really care for the slave so much? Or was it all just an act—like how he had feigned a spontaneous reaction and run towards Malayappa when he had fallen. Sivagami had not missed it.

Maharaja Somadeva pulled out the sword from Malayappa's shoulder, set it down, and helped the slave sit up. Malayappa's face was crumpled with pain as he cupped his wound with his palm. The sword was a few feet from Sivagami. She quickly picked it up and raised it above her head to kill the king.

Maharaja Somadeva turned quickly and stared at her and the sword in her hand. A door opened from behind the maharaja and Brihannala walked out. She froze when she saw Sivagami. Sivagami saw a glimpse of a dagger in her hand, but it vanished behind the folds of her saree.

'You saved the maharaja's life,' Brihannala exclaimed. She went past the maharaja and hugged Sivagami. The maharaja stared at both of them. As if realizing her mistake, Brihannala bowed deep to the king. 'The coup has been defeated and the fire contained, Your Majesty.'

She moved to the head of the man who had been fighting the maharaja and removed the mask. 'Here lies the Vaithalika leader Bhutaraya, slain by the maharaja of Mahishmathi.

'And the other rebel was slain by this brave young woman. I was hiding in the room and saw everything. I am scared of weapons and fighting. She fought with the other rebel and flung him down the stairs. With one act, she has wiped the stain on her family's reputation. She has proved her loyalty, Your Majesty. The daughter of the traitor Devaraya bravely fought on your side and proved that she is more than equal to any man in your service. Reward her, Maharaja, for it is difficult to find such dedicated men, let alone women.'

The maharaja stared at Sivagami; he saw the blood stains on her hands and on her dress, and a rare smile lit up his face. 'Who would have thought that the traitor Devaraya would give birth to such a brave daughter? You shall be rewarded. Brihannala, get the rajavaidya, for my beloved slave is injured. And take this brave girl to your room and attend to her needs. She shall be suitably rewarded in the sabha.'

Sivagami stood, stunned by the turn of events. Other soldiers came in with the good news and took the maharaja and the injured slave with them. Sivagami heard that the other rebel, the one she had pushed down the stairs, had not died but was grievously injured. The maharaja expressed pleasure at that. It would be very useful to know the conspirators behind the failed coup, she heard him say as he climbed down the steps.

Brihannala took Sivagami's hand. 'I saw what you were attempting to do.'

Sivagami snapped back, 'And I saw your dagger.'

Brihannala laughed and winked, 'Good. Now we both know which side we are on. Know that you have a friend.' Sivagami tried to say something, but she hushed her. 'Girl, do you have a reason for why you came to the Antapura? They are sure to ask you,' Brihannala smiled.

Sivagami debated in her mind whether to tell the eunuch the truth. She did not want Skandadasa's murderers to go unpunished, but revealing that she was inside the mahapradhana's house when he was killed would give rise to more questions. She felt the small pot inside her kaunchika. Pattaraya was ready to kill Skandadasa for it. It was important for Mahishmathi, Skandadasa had said. Maybe it would help her achieve the dream. Maybe this was the key to destroying Mahishmathi. She had to find out more. She decided not to tell anyone about the pot. Pattaraya was sure to come after her for it, but he knew she would make his crime of killing Skandadasa known to the world. He would be as afraid of her as she was of him. He was a dangerous man and she needed allies. She would wait for the right opportunity to strike.'You have to be part of the system you want to change'—Skandadasa's words came back to her. She did not want to change the system but destroy it; and it would be easier to destroy it from within. Remembering Skandadasa filled Sivagami with an inexplicable sadness, and she vowed not to let his death go unavenged. Destiny was handing her an opportunity. If the situation demanded that she align with this sly eunuch, she had to act the part. To survive, she needed all the rewards or positions the king might offer. She realized Brihannala was staring at her.

'I...I was chased by a Vaithalika,' Sivagami lied.

'Good. You panicked and you did not know this was the Antapura. You ran up the stairs chased by some Vaithalika soldiers. You saw the king in danger and acted without thinking about your own safety. You wanted to remove the blot on your family's name. Good story. Stick to it. We will have a detailed talk later,' Brihannala placed her hand on Sivagami's shoulders and smiled.

Sivagami glared back at her. 'That is the truth,' she said.

Brihannala laughed, 'For now, that is your only truth, butknow that the maharaja is not so naïve. He might offer you a reward to make you believe that he trusts you. Beware of the man. And together, we can win one day.'

Brihannala extended her hand as if in truce. The eunuch watched her, waiting to see what she would do. Sivagami smiled and took Brihannala's hand. The eunuch patted her cheeks and said, 'My dear, you will do exactly as I say. Victory will be ours soon, trust me.'

That is the last thing I will do, thought Sivagami, but she matched Brihannala's smile with all the charm she could muster.

As Brihannala took her to her chambers, Sivagami looked down at the sword in her hand. Something about it disturbed her. The sword of the man she had pushed down. That was something she did not want to think about.

FIFTY-ONE

Sivagami

The palace was being rebuilt and Mahamakam festivities had been suspended for a month while priests looked for the next auspicious dates.

Sivagami stood in the durbar of Mahishmathi the day after the rebellion. She had not been allowed to leave the palace since the encounter with the king. Brihannala had made her stay back so the rajavaidya could look at her injuries. She wondered where Kamakshi and Gundu Ramu were—hopefully they had made it back to the orphanage safely. She had to find a way to get out of the palace soon. She prayed they would not search her and find the pot.

The durbar had not suffered much damage but she could hear masons and carpenters working to repair what was destroyed in other parts of the palace. The sabha had lost some of its sheen but there was an air of celebration. She had had a chance to kill the king and she had frittered it away. Why had she hesitated, when all she had to do was plunge the sword down his throat? She was still trying to find the answer.

She feared the affection the king showed to his slave might have softened her attitude towards him. But she had only to remember her father to wipe away any such feelings. Through the night, Brihannala had tried to extract information from her. The eunuch had not bought the story that she had come to the Antapura because she was being chased by Vaithalikas. She was wary of the eunuch. Maybe she was laying a trap for her. Sivagami had been reserved in her replies. Besides, worry about the sword she had in her hand had occupied her, and she had not heard half of what the eunuch said.

The maharaja and maharani arrived with great pomp and regalia, as if to prove a point. The sabha reverberated with chants of 'Maharaja Somadeva Vijaya' and 'Jai Mahishmathi'. Maharaja Somadeva thanked his loyal soldiers for defeating the dastardly coup and said that he would ensure that the guilty would not be spared. A few of the rebels had already been apprehended, he said. He announced that, in place of Skandadasa, Parameswara would resume charge as mahapradhana.

'If not for the timely intervention of Parameswara, things might have ended differently for us,' he said to thunderous applause.

Parameswara stood up and bowed. 'I am happy that everything turned out all right. Mahishmathi is resilient. It is resilient because its people are resilient. We will bounce back to our full glory.' A deafening applause followed, along with chants of his name along with the maharaja's.

'I was sitting with Maharaja Somadeva when I saw a brave prince coming towards me. He was bleeding from everywhere. He was injured, yet he came to inform us that the rebels had entered the fort. I could move the maharaja to relative safety because of the few precious moments I got. Prince Mahadeva,' the mahapradhana called affectionately. Mahadeva limped up and touched the feet of the mahapradhana and his parents. When he turned towards the sabha, a gasp went through the crowd. His face was swollen and shapeless; he had a black eye and puffy lips.

'I request the maharaja to sufficiently honour him for his great act of courage,' the mahapradhana requested.

'Getting beaten to a pulp is no act of courage,' Bijjala said, standing up, and there were lots of sniggers from the crowd.

Mahadeva looked at his brother and smiled. 'Anna, you are right. I am not a great warrior like you. Nor was I born courageous. It was only the love I have for my parents and my country that made me brave.'

Bijjala laughed, 'Yes, for an effeminate prince, even getting beaten up is remarkable. How many women can stay for so long without crying?' Many people joined in the laughter.

'What is courage, Anna?' Mahadeva asked, unfazed.

'Something that you lack, Mahadeva. Courage is to face the enemy without fear, to not even bat an eyelid when your sword cuts off the foe's head, to attack a military formation alone, to slay a tiger bare-handed. One's eyes should have fire in them, not fear like yours often show,' Bijjala said with disdain.

Looking into Bijjala's eyes, Mahadeva recited in his rich voice:

'Courage is neither in the show of power
Nor is it in the absence of fear
Courage may be shown in a war against others
What use is it, if in the war against self it withers?
Enemy is not the one to hate,
But enmity and the cause for it

Courage is not in slaying man or beast
War creates nothing but a vulture's feast
Eyes should neither have fire or fear,
But the sight to see all that God holds dear.'

The entire sabha rose to its feet and gave a standing ovation to the impromptu recital from Mahadeva. Bijjala flushed red with anger.

'When I am king, I shall make you the court poet,' Bijjala said, and a few of his cronies laughed. 'Or perhaps the court jester,' Bijjala added, winking at a few servants who found it extraordinarily witty.

'Enough,' the maharaja said, raising his palm, and the sabha fell silent. 'Mahadeva, come here,' the king called, and the prince limped to his father. The king removed a diamond necklace from his neck and put it on Mahadeva.

Placing his arm around Mahadeva's shoulders, Maharaja Somadeva declared, 'From today onwards, Prince Mahadeva will also be known as Vikramadeva.'

There was a stunned silence in the sabha. Not many princes had been conferred the title of Vikramadeva in the history of Mahishmathi. A title given to the bravest of kings and princes, a title taken by the great monarchs after an important military victory, a title made famous through stories and legends of yore had been bestowed on the shy prince of Mahishmathi. Brihannala was the first to react. She pumped her fist in the air and shouted, 'Rajakumara Vikramadeva,' and with one voice the sabha roared back, 'Vijaya.' Brihannala repeated the call three times.

Bijjala slapped his thigh in despair. He felt insulted and slighted. It was he who deserved the title, he thought, and not his cowardly brother. His eyes glowed with hatred and jealousy as the sabha erupted in loud cheers. His brother stood beaming, his palms joined in pranam. Mahadeva did not deserve it; he had not captured the rebel. It was he, Bijjala, who had captured Shivappa. Perhaps he had got a little help from his slave. But it was *his* slave. The credit rightly belonged to him. His brother was beaten up by the same rebel and now he was being bestowed the coveted title. It was unfair. Bijjala scanned the crowd and his eyes met Pattaraya's. The bhoomipathi put his fist on his chest and nodded his head, indicating that he would take care of things. That pacified Bijjala a bit, but the enthusiasm of the sabha for his good-for-nothing brother was still difficult for him to digest.

'Work harder and you will be all right,' the king whispered and ran his fingers through his son's hair. Mahadeva felt grateful for the honour. He had only been doing his duty, and his father, the people of Mahishmathi, the sabha—all of them were cheering for him. He folded his hands in pranam again and thanked them for their kindness. He was climbing down the steps when he saw Sivagami. He stood still, proud of his achievement. He wanted only a smile from her.

Sivagami looked at the severely injured face of Mahadeva. It was as if the prince had changed into a different man, and she felt a certain respect for him. But if she went by the cheering of the crowd, he was becoming popular. That would one day make him a formidable enemy. She did not relish the thought. Try as she might, she found it difficult to see him as her enemy. Enemies should be evil, not soft-spoken, good-hearted, handsome men who showed admirable inner courage. He had always been awkward with her and that had made it easier to despise him, to ignore that he was handsome, laugh at his clumsy attempts to make her love him. Now he looked at her with confidence, as if he was sure that she would recognize the sincerity of his love. That disturbed her. She did not want to be in love with a prince of Mahishmati. She wanted all of them dead. She hoped he would go back to his old ways once the sheen of the new title wore off. She looked away.

Bijjala was called to the dais and given a bag of gold. As the maharaja ceremoniously hugged his elder son, he said in his ears, 'Life may be a gamble, but never make gambling your life.'

Bijjala stared at his father incredulously. Did the king know about his gambling and the debt he owed? How much did his father know? He was terrified. The king patted his shoulder and gestured for him to return to his seat. Bijjala did not bother to acknowledge the cheers of the sabha. When he passed Mahadeva, the younger prince stood up to congratulate him. Mahadeva hugged his elder brother. Bijjala stood stiff, refusing to return the embrace. He hissed in Mahadeva's ears, 'You think you have become a big hero? Eh? You are just a worthless coward and soon the world will know it.'

Mahadeva shrugged and smiled sadly. 'Anna, have I ever pretended otherwise?'

Bijjala stomped his feet and walked away.

Next was Pattaraya's turn, the bhoomipathi who had led the counter-attack. He had brought the soldiers together and led the attack from the office complex, effectively cutting off the retreat of the rebels. The king gave him land and estates, bungalows and chariots, and Pattaraya made a tearful speech, vowing eternal loyalty to this great country of Mahishmathi and the king. The chief priest and other Brahmins were gifted cows, houses and gold, for without their blessings, Mahishmathi would have fallen into rebel hands. Pratapa was awarded for the exceptional work of his dandakaras. Maharaja announced compensation for the families of the dead soldiers.

No one spoke about Skandadasa. Sivagami waited for someone to mention the slain mahapradhana, but it was as if such a man had never existed.

Finally, it was Sivagami's turn. The king called her to the dais. She walked, suppressing the hatred she felt. As Brihannala had advised, this was the first step. To take revenge, she had to be powerful enough. She knew how vicious Pattaraya and his coterie were. She could feel their eyes boring into her as she walked with her head held high. She would accept what the king gave and use it as a platform. She would play the game. She had powerful friends now, like Brihannala. She was ready for it.

She stood proud and erect before the maharaja, who looked at her with an amused smile. She faltered, for she knew this recognition was something that she neither wished for nor deserved. But destiny was giving her a chance, a stepping stone, and she had to grab it. She looked back with confidence and Maharaja Somadeva beamed at her.

'This woman is amazing. She saved our life,' the maharaja said, and the sabha cheered.

'We had to hang her father twelve years back for treason, yet she fought for my life. That is loyalty. Something we have to reward generously. Or else, we would be called stingy and miserly for posterity. We reward her with the title of Bhoomipathi, the title her father and many of her illustrious ancestors held. And we restore to her her father's land.'

Sivagami could not believe her ears. From the orphanage to a position of power. She had reclaimed her father's lands, and his title. She felt like sobbing with joy. She pressed her lips together and squared her shoulders.

'Do you accept our offer, devi?'

Sivagami's answer came after a few moments as she was overwhelmed by emotion. She bowed stiffly and said, 'Yes, I do.'

'Do you promise to obey our orders without question, show the same spirit of loyalty and patriotism and render justice and law to those under you, on behalf of us?'

'Yes, I do,' Sivagami said, and in her mind, *Until I get a chance to finish you and your accursed dynasty.*

The maharaja raised his hands in blessing and the sabha cheered for Sivagami. She looked at Pattaraya and her lips curved into a smile. She would not let him go free for what he had done to Skandadasa. He looked at her with cold eyes, his face expressionless. Only his fingers fumbling with the gold-covered rudraksha chain around his neck gave away his agitation.

'We are going to assign you a wonderful job,' Maharaja Somadeva smiled at her. She tensed. There was something wrong with the maharaja's smile.

'In fact, you almost completed the task yesterday, but fate willed otherwise. The one you pushed down the stairs is still alive. Your first job would be—'

Sivagami took a deep breath. Memories of her father's execution came rushing back. She did not relish the thought of killing someone who had tried to murder this evil king. But she wanted the title of Bhoomipathi desperately.

'To hang him,' she whispered.

'Yes,' the maharaja said. He turned to his soldiers and said, 'Bring him in.'

The soldiers dragged a hooded man in chains into the sabha. Sivagami tensed.

Maharaja Somadeva gestured to the soldiers to remove his hood.

'Uncle Thimma!' Sivagami cried, and rushed to the man in chains.

She collapsed to her knees in front of him and started crying, covering her face with her palms. Thimma's trembling hands caressed her head, just as they had when she was a little girl.

'My daughter has grown up to be a bhoomipathi. I am so proud of you, child.'

Acknowledgements

This book series is a tribute to the vision of a great director, artist, and human being, Sri S. S. Rajamouli. *Bāhubali* is a landmark film in the history of Indian cinema, and the sheer scale of it is mindboggling. One can only wonder at how much effort would have gone into making such a classic. Taking the responsibility of working on a prequel of such a story was a daunting task. Had it not been for the absolute freedom, encouragement, and kindness shown by S. S. Rajamouli, this book would never have been possible. I am indebted to him for life, for the trust he has shown in me.

Sri K. V. Vijayendra Prasad is one of the greatest living screenplay writers in the Indian film industry. Sri Prasad, who is S. S. Rajamouli's father, has penned many classics, among which *Bahubali* happens to be one. My first meeting with him is still etched in my mind. It was his story I was going to rework and expand, and I was apprehensive about how he was going to take it. He was grace personified and the tips and advice he gave me on writing are more precious to me than anything I have ever achieved. I consider him my mentor and this book is my humble tribute to his art.

Prasad Devineni and Shobu Yerlaggada, the producers of *Bāhubali*, the film, and promoters of Arka Media deserve special mention for their unstinting belief and trust in my skills as an author. *Bāhubali* has gone much beyond a great film. It has become a global brand. I hope I have lived up to their expectations and hopefully added some more sheen to the brand. Having worked with many producers in the past, I can vouch for the fact that people who give complete freedom to the writer are rare to come by. Thank you, gentlemen, for being there to support and encourage me whenever I was assailed with self -doubt.

I had almost finished my fourth book, *Devayani* and was about to submit it to Westland when this amazing project came up. Gautam Padmanabhan, C E O of Westland, is more a friend than my publisher and it was he who advised me to shelve the book I had been working on for the last two years and take up the Bāhubali trilogy. His enthusiasm gave me confidence and if not for his support, I would not have finished the entire book—including plotting, planning, drafting and revising—in 109 days.

I should thank my editors, Sanghamitra Biswas and Deepthi Talwar for the mammoth effort they put in to edit the book at a blistering pace. They deserve special thanks for putting up with a writer who was assailed with insecurities and who kept harassing them every hour with a new rewrite. The stunning cover and the maps were designed by Vishwanath Sundaram, the graphic designer and VFX artist of Arka Media. He was assailed by two perfectionists, S. S. Rajamouli and yours truly for even minute detail and he has done amazing work. Thank you for the great piece of art.

Krishna Kumar and Neha of Westland deserve a special mention for all the public relationship work they have done for me. Arunima arranged for some fascinating interviews.

I am grateful to the press and TV journalists too for the extensive coverage of the book.

Preetam of Arka Media who handled the social media campaigns along with Hemal Majithia and his team in Oktobuzz Media deserve special thanks.

My friends often say, my better half, Aparna deserves a Nobel prize for tolerating me. Thank you for being there, my dear. It may be a great trial to live through my mood swings, but after more than 15 years, I am sure you are used to it. My children Ananya and Abhinav have been my greatest critics and inspiration. They bring me down to earth often from my flights of fantasy. And my pet dog Jackie deserves a special mention, as he was the one who often heard my stories during our long walks together.

My extended family have always stood by me, even when I wrote books that challenged their beliefs and convictions. They have been my source of inspiration from childhood. My siblings Lokanathan, Rajendran and Chandrika, my in-laws, Parameswaran, Meenakshi and Radhika, and my niece and nephews, Divya, Dileep and Rakhi have always made our family get-togethers lively with many debates about the Ramayana and Mahabharata.

My friends for more than three decades, Rajesh Rajan, Santosh Prabhu and Sujith Krishnan; other friends like Sidharth Bharatan, Jayan CA and Venkatesh Satish Lolla and Anubhooti Panda who was my beta reader of various drafts all deserve special thanks for keeping me inspired. My batchmates of EEE 1996, from The Government Engineering college, Trichur , especially Cina, Gayatri, Ganesh, Malathi and Maya who have read some of my works and Mathew, Gopu Keshav, Anjali, Brinda and Habibulla Khan who have never read and are never going to read any of my works but still encourage me to write, all deserve my heartfelt gratitude.

My special thanks to all the readers of my last three books. Your words of criticism, praise and suggestions have been my inspiration and the reason I continue to write.